INSTRUMENTS
OF
Darkness

INSTRUMENTS

OF

Darkness

IMOGEN
ROBERTSON

headline
review

First published in Great Britain in 2009
by HEADLINE REVIEW
An imprint of HEADLINE PUBLISHING GROUP

1

ISBN 978 0 7553 4839 8 (Hardback)
ISBN 978 0 7553 4840 4 (Trade paperback)

Typeset in Poliphilus and Blado by Ellipsis Books Limited, Glasgow

Printed and bound in Great Britain by
Clays Ltd St Ives plc

HEADLINE PUBLISHING GROUP
An Hachette UK Company
338 Euston Road
London NW 1 3BH

www.headline.co.uk
www.hachettelivre.co.uk

For

The Family

ACKNOWLEDGEMENTS

To the following all my thanks: to Ros Taylor and Rachel Halliburton for their crucial advice on early drafts; to the judges of the *Daily Telegraph* 'First Thousand Words of a Novel' competition for their encouragement and lunch; to fellow writers Roddy Lumsden, Ahren Warner, Camellia Stafford, Amy Key, Heather Phillipson and Wayne Smith for teaching me about cadence, amongst other things; to the staff at the superb British Library, where I did much of my research; to Kath, Emma, Neel, Sam, Shona, Nat, David, Stephen, Duncan, Jonathan, Ned and my parents for the necessary emotional support; to Annette Green for liking the book enough to sell it; to Jane Morpeth and Flora Rees for liking it enough to buy it; and particular thanks to Ed Stern and family for kindnesses too numerous to mention.

PART I

I.1

Friday, 2 June 1780, West Sussex, England

Gabriel Crowther opened his eyes.

'Mr Crowther, sir?'

The light in the room was weak. Morning light.

'Whoever it is, send them away,' he said.

He blinked. The maid was still there.

'She won't go, sir. It's Mrs Westerman from Caveley Park. She said she is determined, sir. And she said to give you this.'

The maid held out a piece of paper, staying as far away from the bed as she could, as if she feared her master would bite.

The intrusion was unusual. Crowther had done a good job of ignoring his neighbours since taking up residence in Hartswood, near Pulborough, the previous summer, and their visits had swiftly petered out. He did not need companions with whom to pass his time and had no intention of participating in diversions, picnics and subscription dinners of what passed for society in the county. The rest of the village never expected to have much to do with him, but after a month or two of observation, many of the local women found the easiest way to still a child was to threaten it with Mr Crowther and his big knife. He was a student of Anatomy. He wanted to know how bodies lived, what record a man's life left on

1

his physical remains, and he had the leisure and means to inquire.

His habits soon became known. To the educated, he was a man of science cursed with an appalling lack of manners; to everyone under ten he was a devil doctor who cut the souls from the living bodies of naughty children and ate them.

The maid still held the note out towards him; it trembled a little. He snatched it from her with a low growl and flicked it open. It was written on notepaper – taken from his own desk downstairs, he noticed – in an educated female hand. The writer had not troubled with compliments or excuses about the hour, but confined herself to some dozen words: *I have found a body on my land. His throat has been cut.*

Crowther passed the note back to his maid.

'My compliments to Mrs Westerman, and tell her I shall wait on her as soon as I am dressed. Have my horse got ready and brought round.'

The maid stared at him open-mouthed.

'Do it *now*, if you please, madam.'

The previous evening, Adams Music Shop, Tichfield Street near Soho Square, London

Susan Adams pressed her ear to the floor. On the first of each month her father hosted a little concert in his shop for his neighbours and friends. It was a ritual of his since he had begun, in a small way, to succeed with his business of engraving and printing musical scores and selling them, along with collections of popular songs and airs, to London's musically inclined residents. It was a kind of offering he made in thanks for his seven rooms, workshop and yard. His children built their own rituals around it. Jonathan would come into Susan's room, claiming he wished to hear the music better, then be asleep before the first piece was over in the comfort of his older sister's bed.

'Susan?' he grumbled. 'You're supposed to be in bed too. You can hear the music from here, and it is not so hard as the floor.'

'Shush, Jonathan. I'm listening.' She heard a sigh as her brother gave up and fidgeted the bedclothes around him. The air was still heavy with the heat of the June day passed.

'Well, tell me what is happening then.' He yawned.

She smiled; one of her blond ringlets tickled her ear. She tucked it away and considered.

'Mr Paxton, Mr Whitaker and Miss Harding have all arrived. Mr Paxton has his cello, Mr Whitaker is to play my harpsichord and Miss Harding is to sing. They are all drinking punch in the shop.'

'I helped sweep it this afternoon.'

Susan had watched Jonathan's attempts to help the maid, Jane, while she tidied away the scores and parts with her father. She did not think he had been very helpful at all, but he was still only six, and should therefore be indulged by someone three years his senior such as herself. Though he could be annoying. She ignored the interruption.

'The chairs have been dragged into long rows. Mrs Service is sitting very shy in a corner, because she never buys any music, and her dress is old. Mr and Mrs Chase from Sutton Street are here, because Mr Chase loves a little music when business is done. And Mr Graves is here, of course, frowning and trying to rub inkstains off his fingers because he's only just noticed them.'

There was a sleepy giggle from the bed, followed by: 'Is Miss Chase here?'

'Of course.' Susan leaped up suddenly and stood very straight, pointing one bare and not very clean foot in front of her. 'She is walking in right now, like this.'

The little girl bent her head to one side, adjusted the shawl over her narrow shoulders and put one hand to her waist; the other gathered a pinch of her nightdress like the full skirts of an evening gown and she moved between the imaginary chairs, smiling to left and right. The room seemed to flood with candlelight and conversation.

Jonathan sat up in bed again. 'And Mr Graves is watching her?'

3

'Yes, from his corner.'

She hopped into a high-backed chair by the empty fireplace and became a tangle of limbs, a young man trying hard to look at his ease, and not entirely succeeding. His mouth opens as if he would like to address someone, then he stops himself and returns to examining his fingernails.

Jonathan laughed again. Susan held up her hand. Faintly from the room below came the first low rasp of Mr Paxton's violoncello.

'They are beginning.'

Susan jumped from her chair and crouched again, her ear pressed to the gap between the floorboards. She could feel the music from the room below entering through her hands. She could feel it on her open lips.

Crowther was not afraid of silence, but the morning seemed unnaturally bare of birdsong for early June. His visitor had already remounted when he came out of the house, and was waiting with her groom by his own chestnut bay. She had greeted him with nothing more than a nod of her head and then urged her horse forward out of the yard and into the roadway as soon as he had taken the reins. Crowther's house was the first of any significance in the town, so in moments they were among the fields and hedgerows.

He was surprised, even a little annoyed at her silence. He looked sideways at her profile. A woman in her early thirties perhaps, neatly dressed and at some expense. She could never, even in her first bloom of youth, have been very beautiful. Her face was a little too long, and a little too narrow. Her carriage and neat figure suggested good health and habits, however. Her gloved hands rested easily on the reins and her hair was a dark red, curled under the edge of her riding hat.

'Do you like it?' she asked. 'My maid Dido always rejoices when I agree to have my hair curled. I find it gets in my eyes.'

Crowther started, and faced forward at once. 'My apologies, madam. I did not mean to stare.'

She turned to him, looking at him squarely for a moment or two, then smiled. Crowther noted the dark green of her eyes, was surprised to find himself wondering briefly what she might think of him.

'No, *I* am sorry, Mr Crowther,' she said. 'And I must thank you for riding out so early. I have been wondering what to say to you, and I'm sorry to confess that nothing that seems appropriate has occurred to me. I could ask you what you think the weather will be today and how you are enjoying Hartswood, but it hardly seems fitting, given our expedition. So I waited until I had the opportunity to be rude to you instead.'

He almost smiled. 'Perhaps you can tell me about your discovery and why you have called me rather than the Constable or the magistrate.'

She nodded at the suggestion and tilted her chin up as she chose her words. Her voice was light.

'Well, my footman has gone to the Squire, in fact, but I read your paper last spring in the *Transactions of the Royal Society*; you wrote, if you recall, about the signs murderers can leave on their victims, and when I found the body I thought you might be able to read his death like the gypsies read picture cards.' He looked at her with frank astonishment, and she frowned suddenly and looked out at the road in front of her again. 'Just because I have my hair curled doesn't render me incapable of reading, you know.'

Crowther could not decide whether to be offended at her tone, or to offer his apologies again and so did neither as they turned off the main road to Balcombe and then London and entered a narrower lane that, he guessed, must mark the boundary between the lands belonging to Caveley Park and those of the great estate of Thornleigh Hall.

'The body is in the copse at the top of the hill,' she said. 'The best path to it lies through the woods, so we must continue on foot. My man will see to the horses.'

Susan could tell by her brother's breathing that he was asleep. The music finished in applause, and a low female voice began to introduce the next item. As Susan strained to hear, a floorboard in the passageway outside her door suddenly groaned, making her jump. She could hear people talking.

'I should have gone years ago, when Elizabeth died. She told me I should, that the past must be looked at squarely or it will chase you down. But there was always a reason to delay.'

It was her father's voice. On hearing her mother's name, Susan's heart squeezed a little in her chest, and she was lost briefly in an odd confusion of pain and comfort. Her mother had smelled of lavender, and had had very soft brown hair. She had died a week to the day after Jonathan was born. The little girl had held her hand till her father told her it was time to let go.

Another voice replied. It belonged to Mr Graves, and was nearly as familiar to her as her father's. She had heard it almost every day in the shop or at their table, ever since he had come to London. She had seldom heard it so low or so serious as now, though. She thought of how his face might look, and her own tilted down in unconscious mimicry. His collar was not always neat but his grey eyes were always sympathetic, and though he was slender as a reed he could still pick her up and swing her round the shop till she was half-sick with laughing. Miss Chase had come in once to find them playing in this way. Mr Graves had become very red and set her down a little heavily. Susan did not think Miss Chase had minded what they did, or noticed that his brown hair had got rather ruffled.

'You have spoken so little of your time before London, Alexander,' he said now. 'How can I advise you? Why has losing the ring concerned you so? Was it valuable? I have never seen you wear it.'

'It had no great value to me, or at least I thought not.' There was a pause. 'I am surprised that losing it has caused me such upset. It has been nothing but a plaything of Jonathan's for some years – he likes the lion and dragon on the seal, and I keep it in my bureau and let him play with it whenever I wish to keep him quiet and still – but it was a last connection to my old home, and now it is gone I begin to worry again. Perhaps I owe something to the people I left there, or to the children. I have told myself I did not, but it itches at me.'

Graves spoke again. 'There must be some reason you have held back so long. Think further on the matter. You are happy now and it is a fragile and delicate thing, happiness. Jonathan will not grieve long over a ring. Why so disturb your life over a trifle that he will have forgotten in a week?' He hesitated. 'Do not attract the attention of the gods now, when you still have so much to lose.'

'You are right . . .' Her father stopped again and sighed. Susan knew from his voice that he would be rubbing his chin with his right hand, and shifting the weight off his bad leg. 'Perhaps the ring will turn up somewhere and my mind will be quiet. I'll have Jonathan search the workshop again in the morning. He was quite determined that he hadn't taken it from the bureau without my leave, however, and is rather indignant that I think he may have done so.' Susan could hear the smile in his voice and looked back towards the bed where her brother slept. He had not mentioned the ring since he had cried so on finding it gone from its little box, but she did not think he had forgotten it yet.

Silence, then the lady downstairs started singing. Susan scrambled to her feet and went to open the door. Alexander and Mr Graves jumped like guilty truants as the light spilled from the children's room across her shoulders and onto the landing.

Graves smiled at her. 'Listening to the music, Susan?'

'Yes, but what are you talking about? Is Papa going away?'

Her father looked between his friend and his daughter and knelt down.

'Come here, daughter of mine, and tell me something.' She took the hand he held out towards her. 'Are you happy, Susan? Would you like to have a maid and a carriage and a large house and a hundred pretty dresses?'

She looked at him to see if he were teasing, but his eyes remained

7

steady and serious; his breath smelled a little of punch. She was confused.

'I like this house. And I have seven dresses.' She heard him sigh, but he pulled her to him at the same time, so she supposed the answer had pleased him.

'Well then. If you have dresses enough, I don't think I need go away at all. And I am glad you like this house. I hope we may share it a long while.'

Then he released her and said, 'Now, as you are awake I think you may be allowed to join us downstairs for a while. Mr Paxton is to give us his Concerto.'

For the rest of her life Susan would search out that music, or any that reminded her of it, not only for its elegant passions, but for the memories that it carried of the long parlour by candlelight, the profiles and shoulders of her early friends and neighbours, and the feel of her father's chest rising and falling below her small hand, her cheek pressed against the silver threads of his waistcoat.

I.2

IT WAS A particularly handsome, particularly English summer's day, and the Sussex countryside was full of the pleasing and fruitful colours of the season. The meadow where Harriet and Crowther dismounted was glowing with tall buttercups and purple knapweed, and the morning wind that stirred them was lazy and good-humoured. Any civilised man, or woman, might be expected to pause a moment and consider the landscape and his or her place in it. A good season to be away from the city, its bustle and stink. Here the earth was preparing to offer up its gifts to its lords and their dependants. Crops grew, the animals fattened and the soil served those who had cared for it through the year. Here was England at her best, providing reward to satisfy the body, and beauty to feed the mind and soul.

Mrs Westerman and Crowther, however, were indifferent to the scenery. Neither paused to admire the picturesque swell of the valley's flanks, or philosophise on the greatness of the nation that had borne them. They disappeared into the woods without a backward glance. The groom dismounted and made his arrangements to lead the horses in his charge to their stables, and it was left to the beasts themselves to admire the view and tear up the wild flowers in their satin jaws.

The path ended in a clearing after some thirty yards of roughish rising ground, overhung with the branches of elm and oak. The way was dry – Crowther tried to remember the last time he had heard rain from the confines of his study – and the air was heavy with the scents of the woodland uncurling into its summer wear. Wild garlic, dew. It would be a pleasant place to walk before beginning the duties of the day, he thought; no doubt that was why Mrs Westerman had happened along this path.

Crowther realised he had not noticed the year was already blooming into its height. He would have been able to tell any man who enquired that today's date was 2 June, of course, because he had written the date of the previous day in his notebook as he began work, but he never felt the shift of seasons in his bones, as so many in the country claimed to do. He knew winter because it was the best time to dissect, and summer because servants were more likely to complain then of the smells. From the world outside in its greatness, its bulk, its multitudes, he had turned away to pick apart the smallest vessels of life. He had stayed faithful now for years to the mysteries he could confine to his table-top. It had therefore been some months since he had lifted his eyes. Now he could feel the first prick of his sweat under the cotton of his shirt, felt his heart begin to labour with the climb. The sensations were oddly novel. He put his hand to his face where the sun reached it through the leaves.

Mrs Westerman came to a halt, and pointed with her riding crop.

'There. About ten yards along the track to Thornleigh. My dog noticed it first.' Her eyes dropped to the path. 'I took her back to the house before I came to you.'

Crowther glanced at her. The voice was steady enough; her face was perhaps a little flushed, but that might be only a result of the climb. He walked in the direction she had indicated, and heard almost at once a small sigh, and her own footsteps following him.

The body lay just off the track and one might have thought it a bundle of old clothing but for the arm and its waxy grey hand extended at right angles from the tumble of a dark blue cloak.

'Has the body been moved?' he asked.

'No. That is, I got close enough to see that he was dead and how – I lifted the cloak to do so – then covered him again. That is all.'

A little swarm of flies had gathered, and were walking as daintily as shop girls in Ranelagh Gardens around the edges of the cloak, and into the nooks and crannies it hid for their private business. Crowther knelt down, lifted the fold of cloth away from the corpse's face and looked into the dead eyes. The flies buzzed angrily, and he waved them away without judgement.

He had heard it discussed as a student that in death the retina was imprinted with the last image the eyes had seen. The idea had intrigued him in his younger days, and he had made experiments in his former home with a number of unfortunate dogs and two cats before he had given the idea up as impossible. The signs murder left on the body were at the same time more subtle and more commonplace, but he did believe one could often read the expression of a human corpse. Some looked at peace, others, like this face before him, looked only surprised and a little disappointed. The man was wearing his own hair. Dark blond and thick. Crowther lifted the body a little and felt the ground below the corpse, and the back of his cloak. Both dry. And the body stiff, though perhaps not fully so. The flies settled again as he let the ground take the body's weight once more.

'There was dew on the body when I found it, and the body was not as stiff as it seems to be now,' Harriet said.

Crowther nodded, but did not look up. 'Then I imagine that he died last night.'

'That he was murdered last night,' she corrected him.

Indeed, the wound through the neck was unequivocal. Crowther waved away the flies again and bent towards it: a single, violent blow completely severing the carotid artery, leaving the man with an extra, gaping mouth. He would not have suffered long, Crowther thought. The blow had been delivered with enough force to almost sever the neck, leaving the shocking white of the man's vertebrae visible at the back of the wound. A quantity of dark staining around the collar showed where the heart had continued, briefly, to push blood through the body. Crowther looked along the man's trunk. He was wearing clean-enough looking linen and an embroidered waistcoat that was made of some richer stuff; black stains were dappled across it in ugly dark pools. He could see in his mind's eye the man caught and held from behind, the knife at its work, then the release of blood glutting out onto the soil with vivid and final force. He looked about him. Yes, there were marks on the trunks of the trees directly in front of him, and the last of the lilies of the valley had caught a little of his blood. They looked as if they were fading under the weight of it. This man lay where he had first fallen.

Harriet followed the movement of his eyes with her own.

'There is a legend that takes place not far from here,' she said. 'A saint did battle with a terrible dragon, and wherever the saint's blood touched the ground, lilies of the valley have bloomed from that day to this.' She sighed. 'Though I doubt we can blame a duel with a dragon for this death, don't you agree, Mr Crowther? It was not a fight at all, I think. One stroke, from behind. He was probably dead before he fell.'

Crowther never liked to be hurried as he worked, and he found her enthusiasm a little grating. He punished her by standing silently and looking about him, particularly behind where the body lay, where a killer might have stood. The thornbushes curtsied at him and he reached among their white flowers to pull free a few threads he saw hanging there; he drew out his handkerchief to wrap them in. Only when they were securely in his pocket did he attempt to make any sort of reply.

'And you have concluded this as a result of your extensive reading, I suppose, Mrs Westerman?'

'I have irritated you. Forgive me.' The frankness of her answer rather embarrassed him. He bowed swiftly.

'Not at all, madam. Your conclusions are in tune with what I see here.'

She was quiet a moment, twisting the riding crop between her fingers, then spoke softly.

'It is hard, don't you think, Mr Crowther, to draw conclusions and have no one to discuss them with? One begins to doubt one's own judgement, or trust it too much. I did not mean to hurry you. Perhaps I wish to prove to you I am not a fool, and in trying to prove it — behave like one.' She met his eye briefly and looked away again. 'To answer your question, I do not read as much as I would like. It was by chance I happened on your article. But perhaps my lack of squeamishness offends you. Before we bought Caveley, and my son Stephen was born, I sailed for three years with my husband. I have seen men killed in war and in peace, and served as a nurse, so I have witnessed more than perhaps I should.'

Crowther looked directly at her and Mrs Westerman turned away, a little embarrassed. Well, Crowther thought as he bent down again to the body, it was a universal truth that in the presence of a corpse people often said more than they intended. He felt it was as a result of this phenomenon that some people believed a corpse could condemn its murderer by bleeding again in his presence. No, the truth was simply that people had a nasty tendency to run on and confess before such a vivid *memento mori*.

Crowther began to run his hands over the body. His hand stopped at a bulge in the corpse's waistcoat pocket and he pushed his long white fingers between the silvery folds of cloth to withdraw a ring. It was heavy in his palm, and as he turned it he saw a crest stamped into the gold. He recognised it from the carriage that rolled through the village from time to time, and also from the gates to the great park. He heard his companion draw in her breath and stood up, dropping it into her outstretched hand. She closed her fist round it, and Crowther could have sworn he heard her curse softly.

'The arms of Thornleigh Hall, of course,' he said dryly. She looked at him, then away. He raised an eyebrow. 'I should have asked before, Mrs Westerman: do you know this man? Is he from Hartswood? Is he from the Hall?'

As she replied she tapped her riding crop against her dress. She did not take her eyes from the body, and her tone was that of private contemplation.

'He is a stranger. I think if he were from Thornleigh or the village I would know him, but . . . How old do you think this man, and of what condition in life?'

'I would put him between thirty-five and forty-five. About his condition – I would say he is not poor. He has a coat and cloak, and his hands are clean enough, and unscarred. You can see that yourself. What is it you know, Mrs Westerman, that I do not?'

'Nothing. Merely local history. And the history says the eldest son of Lord Thornleigh left the protection of his family some fifteen years ago, and would be now of this age. His name was Alexander, Viscount Hardew. He is a blond-haired man in the portrait I have seen.'

She took a pace away from the body and turned to look up the path towards the Thornleigh lands. A breeze murmured through the trees and tugged gently at the edge of Crowther's coat, as if trying to take him back to his rooms and his books before any more was spoken, before some line was crossed.

'You see, sir,' she went on, 'I cannot help wondering if this poor man is the heir to the great estates of my neighbours, and if so, why he received so cold a welcome home.'

I.3

A S SUSAN PRACTISED in the shop the morning after the concert, she wondered if she had been a little too quick to turn down the maid and carriage that her father had offered her the night before. The heat was oppressive: she could feel the sweat gathering under her arms and on the back of her neck, and in London heat brought the stench of the city all through the house. It might have been pleasant to drive round the park with a pony and a pretty dress on instead of going through her exercises here in the shop, with the scores and parts of music her father printed and sold piled round her.

Normally the room stayed cool even in the summer, for it was a long and elegant space with nothing to disturb it but her own harpsichord, the counter running along one wall and some small displays of the latest airs and themes arranged on table-tops below the windows, but already this year the air felt hot in her chest. These exercises her body knew almost better than her mind. She could watch her fingers on the keys and hear the pluck and thrum of the instrument as if she watched from outside her own body. It left her free to think while appearing busy, so she let her mind wander through the city outside.

She had seen carriages enough stopping at the shop, and the ladies who tended to get out of them. She had not seen anyone of her own age in them, though. The ladies in carriages tended to have maids with them or more ladies, never young girls. They were all very beautiful, but all seemed to look rather tired as if wearing those heavy dresses was a great deal of work. She remembered a lady who had come in when she was at her instrument once, and who had wanted her to play at a party for her friends. She had called her a little Mozart and had gone into raptures. That is what she had said. 'I'm in raptures!' Her dress made a great deal of noise, and she had red stuff on her mouth. She had put her face right up to Susan's and declared her 'such a pretty thing'.

Susan had not liked it. And her father neither. He had been relatively firm with the lady, and she had not come back. He had told Susan that if she met 'that woman' on the street she was on no account to go anywhere with her. Susan wondered if she was a Cyprian. She knew about such women from the talk in the Square: they let men kiss them and do other things for money, but as she thought it was something her father would not want her to know, she had not questioned him. There were other ladies who smiled at her without coming so close, and her father often asked her to play through some of the music they sold so the ladies could say if they liked it and take it away to learn. They did all seem only half-alive to her, though. She thought how horrible it must be to walk around so slowly all the time. She found her fingers were playing the next variation all by themselves.

'We all need time to think, Susan,' her father said, smiling over his ledger at the counter. 'But I know perfectly well you have not been concentrating at all in the last little while. If you wish to stop, you may. Otherwise, never forget you are in search of the music under the mechanics.'

Susan looked up. Her father was pushing a thread of his yellow hair out of his eyes. She grinned and sheepishly turned back to the keyboard, trying to remember the music, the cut and run of counterpoint growing under her hand. Alexander was a lover of music. The backyard of their house contained the brute force of his enterprise, the place where the copper plates were kept on which he carved other men's notes, the presses that fixed them, and he had passed on the love and the craft to his daughter. Yet, at times when the metal smelled hot and bitter and her hands were reluctant and weak on the keys, music could seem a tyrant and a bully. It mocked her, being always a little beyond what she could do, what she could know. She had seen her papa often enough late and tired sorting through his accounts to suspect he felt the same. Yet music was mother to her now, and her father's beloved. Her nine years had been spent smothered in music, fed by it. She could not imagine any other way of life.

A gentleman came in through the door, bowed slightly to them both, then turned to browse through the open scores on the counter-top. Susan looked at him again. Perhaps not a gentleman, after all. When her father turned back to his books, the man covertly studied him with a narrowed, calculating look. Her fingers tripped, and he noticed and glanced round at her. His skin was rather yellow. He smiled – and she saw that his front teeth were missing. Just then, the bell rang again, and a woman in a skirt wide enough for three ladies swept in with a loud greeting and offered Alexander her hand. The yellow man slipped away before the door had time to close again. Susan shivered. The feeling of oppression the man had brought into the room lasted with her for much of the rest of the morning, and whatever her efforts, her practices were wasted.

I.4

M RS WESTERMAN'S HOME, Caveley Park, was acknowledged to be a well-run, handsome estate, flourishing under the care of its new owners. True, it had none of the pretensions to greatness of its nearest neighbour, Thornleigh Hall, but Commodore Westerman was a talented and, still better, a lucky commander of some seniority, and it showed in the size of the purchase, and the care with which the refitting of the house and investment in the estate had been carried out. His wife had acquired a reputation as a capable manager of his interests, and her arrangements were approved of, and often copied by others in the area.

Harriet Westerman had not intended to remain ashore when the purchase was first discussed, but a number of circumstances had rendered her presence on the estate both practical and necessary while her husband continued abroad, first in the Channel and since the New Year serving his Sovereign by cruising the West Indies. She had therefore given up life aboard ship, or at some far-flung naval base, dining sometimes with potentates and kings, sometimes with fishermen and the threadbare officers of the more uncomfortable postings round her country's growing empire, and taken on instead the more settled life of a country gentlewoman.

The first of these circumstances was the realisation that an estate of this size would need more close attention than the irregular and unreliable communications from a ship of His Majesty's Navy might allow. The second was the birth of her son, Stephen who, though now he seemed to be thriving and strong, had been a weak, sickly sort of baby – reluctant to grow fat in sea air. He had been born afloat on his father's ship as she laboured against unseasonable winds home from a posting in the East Indies. The Westermans had already lost one child in the previous year, and the grief of that little boy's loss was a small burning place between them. He had been born and died on the far side of the world, and lived long enough only to be named. His little body was laid in the ground of the East India Company's church in Calcutta. Harriet still sometimes saw that little patch of foreign soil under her feet even as she walked her paths of English lavender. She spoke of that time rarely even with her sister. The Westermans would do all they could to avoid such another grief. The question of the little boy's remaining on land with some respectable family had been touched upon, but Captain Westerman put the case forcefully for the advantages of a mother's care.

The third consideration, and perhaps this last was sufficient in itself, was that Mrs Westerman's father, an unambitious West Country clergyman already a widower himself for some years, had failed to recover after a riding accident and died, leaving his younger daughter, Rachel, without protection, poor, and at only fourteen, scarcely capable of making her own way in the world.

Mrs Westerman came home then with her child and gave up any intention she might once have had of going to sea again. She made herself manager and guardian of the Commodore's lands and offered her sister a permanent home. Mrs Westerman's and Miss Trench's arrival was celebrated in the neighbourhood, and Harriet became a valued member of local society as soon as her sense, sound principles, and the value of the Commodore's lands were generally know. She could, perhaps, be a little sharp at times, and a little inclined to enthusiasm, even contradicting her older neighbours if she felt they erred in matters domestic or political, but these mis-steps were put down to her strange experiences following her husband around the world, and allowances were made. The sister was generally thought of as a good, refining influence in the household, and was encouraged by the matrons of the county to regard herself as such. However, her own disappointments had been the occasion of some sad reflections in the past, and her future was still uncertain.

Miss Rachel Trench had heard the commotion of voices in the hallway and the yap of her sister's greyhound as she drank her breakfast chocolate, looking out at the view to the woods from the salon, but it was the little suppressed shriek from Dido, their maid, that caused her to stand up and open the door. Mrs Heathcote glanced at her, then shooed Dido away towards the kitchen. William, their footman, nodded to her also, but set out through the main door before she could speak to him, pulling his hat over his ears as he went. Rachel looked at the housekeeper. She seemed very white, and Rachel felt herself pale in preparation for bad news.

'What's happening, Mrs Heathcote? My sister . . .'

'Mrs Westerman is quite well, but there's been a body found in the spinney, Miss Rachel. A man with his throat cut.'

Rachel felt the world shift around her and put out a hand to steady herself against the doorway. In the sudden blank of her mind she heard her brother-in-law's voice. She had once demanded some useful knowledge from him after his years of travel as they dined one afternoon. He had laughed and said, 'If there is an earthquake, my dear sister, stand under the doorframe and wait till it is over.'

Mrs Heathcote took two small steps towards her, shielding her from the view of the retreating maid.

'Miss, be calm. They say it is a stranger.'

The housekeeper laid one hand under the girl's elbow. Rachel nodded, and not daring to look the woman in the face, retreated back into the salon.

'Where is the body to go? Do you have something in mind?' Crowther asked.

'I have sent a note to the younger son of Thornleigh Hall – Hugh. I despatched your man, in fact, while I was waiting for you to dress. If this *is* Alexander, I imagine they will wish him to be taken to the house. If not, we may receive him at Caveley, my home, and wait for the Squire.'

Crowther decided not to offer his thoughts on people who gave orders to other people's servants, merely remarking, 'Mrs Westerman, you know I have made it my business this year to learn as little as possible about my neighbours.'

She smiled sideways at him. 'Other than to observe the types that pass in front of your house, you mean, sir?' He looked at her with a frown as she said almost gaily, 'Your habit of watching your neighbours go by like exhibition specimens from your parlour window has been noted.'

Crowther felt a little exposed, but Mrs Westerman did not wish to tease him. She became serious.

'I expect you would like to know more about the Thornleigh family? Very well. Thornleigh is not the richest estate in the county, but it is one of the largest.' She pointed with her crop to the north. 'Lord Thornleigh is the Earl of Sussex, and the extent of the lands reflect his exalted state. Theirs is the land to the horizon there, and they own some of the farms beyond. The house itself is magnificent, hidden from its neighbours in a great park, and full of treasures ancient and modern. A wonder. I have not been there for some time, though the housekeeper gives tours to the curious, and we are told the last King himself has rested there. I understand they have a pocket-knife that belonged to James the First in a drawer ready to be displayed to anyone who asks to see it.' The crop flicked back over her shoulder up the hill they had just climbed. 'They own all the land to the west of the village, of course. It is a fine estate, though I suspect it to be run these days in a cheese-paring sort of way.'

'Lord Thornleigh is still in residence?'

'Yes, as is his second wife. But he is very ill. He had a seizure of some sort shortly after we arrived at Caveley and has not spoken since. He is very rarely seen and never mentioned. I believe he is cared for by his own staff in the upper part of the building. There are three sons. Alexander – the eldest, and missing heir to the title – and Hugh, whom you will soon meet, are sons of Lord Thornleigh's first wife. His second wife also has a little boy, Eustache.'

'I have seen her with him driving past my house.'

'Yes.' Harriet paused, as if unsure what further to say. 'Hugh served with the Army in the Americas, and was wounded. He returned almost four years ago when his father was taken ill.'

Crowther thought of a gentleman he had noticed in the village; he had been searching for the book that had been his company over dinner one evening and from the front parlour, where he found it, he had seen this gentleman meeting friends outside the Coaching House, some little way along the street from his own front door. Or rather, he had heard a loud greeting and turned to see who it was who had reason to be so demonstrably pleased with themselves. He had seen a young and solid-looking gentleman in profile and Crowther had recognised in himself the typical mix of envy and contempt men of his age commonly feel for the young, and was meditating on the emotion in the gloom of his empty house, when the young man turned to greet another – and Crowther saw that the right side of his face from the middle of the cheek to the hairline was badly scarred, and one eye milky and dead. Even in the darkness of the evening the skin looked freshly torn. It was as if some devil had so envied the young man's looks, he had forced a partial trade.

'A musket misfired,' he said, almost to himself, then catching Harriet's look of surprise: 'I have observed him from my front window,' this with a wry smile, 'and the injury is distinctive.'

Almost at once Crowther heard steps coming up the path from Thornleigh. The gentleman himself was approaching fast.

He should, given his features and form, have been handsome, but the wound was violent, his expression was ugly, and his dress a little slovenly. As the distance between them shortened, Crowther took the chance to study him as he would a subject on a table: broken veins around the nose, a high colour and darkly rimmed eyes. A drinker. Liver disease in all likelihood already advanced. Crowther would not be surprised to smell wine on his breath even this early in the day. It still surprised him how many great houses could turn out sons who failed, in his opinion, to be gentlemen.

The man began to speak in a hoarse baritone before he had quite reached them.

'Mrs Westerman, do you know how many times in the years since I came home I have been asked to look at corpses of men likely to be my brother? Four. Two itinerants who decided to die in Pulborough without leaving any convincing address, one unfortunate drowned in the Tar and dragged up a month later when his own mother wouldn't know him, and one corpse in Ashwell who turned out to be dark-haired and a foot shorter than Alexander was when he left home. And now *you*, ma'am, are scouring the countryside to find me others.'

Crowther glanced across at his companion. For the first time that morning she looked a little shocked, and he thought he saw a tremble in her hand. He stepped forward and bowed – low enough to suggest sarcasm.

'Well, at least, sir, this gentleman had the consideration to be murdered relatively close to your home. So the inconvenience is kept to a minimum.'

The young man started and turned to face him, Crowther realised he had been standing where Mr Thornleigh's damaged vision might have missed him, and wondered if he would have spoken in such a manner to a lady if he had not thought she was alone. He looked strong, powerful still in spite of the drink. Riding probably, though youthful bulk was already beginning to turn to fat. Crowther imagined what his muscular forearm would look like with its skin removed. The younger man cleared his throat, and had the decency at least to look a little embarrassed.

'You are our natural philosopher, Mr Crowther, are you not?'

'I am.'

'I am Hugh Thornleigh.' He bowed and shook his head, and seemed to deflate a little. 'My apologies, Mrs Westerman. I spoke very ill-naturedly. Thank you for your note, and I hope the shock of finding this unfortunate has not been too great.' He paused again, and cleared his throat. 'I hope your family is well.'

Crowther could almost like him now. There was a residual charm under the ill-temper, a pleasing deference to Mrs Westerman. It was as if when he had shaken his head it had dislodged a mask, and he had found his own better self beneath it. He was a bear in a frockcoat. A beast – domesticated. Crowther remembered his own brother.

Mrs Westerman, though, was still angry. Her voice was cold, and she looked through the young man as she spoke rather than at him.

'We are all well, Mr Thornleigh. Here is the body.' She flicked aside the cloak again from the body's face with the tip of her crop. Thornleigh sucked in his breath.

'I had thought perhaps a vagrant. You did say murdered . . .' He stepped nearer. 'Was anything found on him?' Harriet dropped the ring into his outstretched hand then withdrew, pulling on her glove again. Hugh shuddered a little as it hit his palm and caught the sun. Then he looked at them again quickly. 'Nothing else?'

'We have not completed rifling through his pockets, I'm afraid,' Crowther said. 'May I ask, sir, do you know this man?'

Hugh caught his tone and steadied himself.

'I am sure he is not Alexander, though this man is of his age and colouring. Again my apologies, madam. I do not know how he came by the ring, though. That is indeed Alexander's. I wear one very much the same.' He extended his left hand, showing them the twin of the ring they had found, shining on his middle finger.

'Can you be sure?' Harriet asked. 'I think you once said you have not seen Alexander for many years.'

'I saw him last in sixty-five, shortly before I joined my regiment. But I am sure. If Alexander ever lay before me, I would know him, however many years had passed. This man means nothing to me. I believe, therefore, it cannot be my brother.' He turned to Crowther. 'My brother broke his leg badly as a child in a fall. After, he walked always with a slight limp. Would you be able to tell if this man had had such an injury, were you to examine him more fully? But perhaps I ask too much.'

'The injury would show, and I am happy to examine the body further.'

Hugh nodded shortly. 'Well, that may serve as confirmation for the Coroner and his men, and you have my thanks. But I am sure in my own mind that this is not Alexander. And thank God for that.'

Mrs Westerman sighed. 'Well, I am glad to hear it. I believe the body is just in Caveley Park lands, so I will have this poor man taken into my house till the Squire arrives, and we find out what is to be done – unless you have any objection, Thornleigh.'

Hugh looked at her longer than perhaps he should have done before he spoke, and as he looked, Crowther saw an expression of longing and shame that made him think of a whipped dog, pass over his face. Crowther found himself speculating. The young, battle-scarred neighbour, the husband away at sea . . . Then he smiled at himself. He was turning romantic.

'Of course, Mrs Westerman. Can I be of any further assistance?'

'No. The men from the park will be here shortly and we will accompany the body.'

'Very well.' And with no more than a bow to them both, Hugh turned and made his way back down the hill again – as fast, it seemed, as he could manage without running from the place.

'He drinks,' Crowther said, as he watched the blue frockcoat swallowed up again by the woodland. Harriet had leaned against one of the ash trees on the edge of the path.

'Yes, I'm afraid he does. The steward, Wicksteed, runs the place while he keeps company with a bottle.'

'It will kill him in the end – and fast, I think, if he is already at this stage in such relative youth.'

'Good.'

Crowther twisted round to stare at her. An unusual woman certainly, but to say such a thing! He had not realised he could still be shocked by the speeches of a gentleman's daughter. His manners must have remained more nice than he had thought. Mrs Westerman continued merely to look at the ground in front of her, tapping her crop. It was only moments before he heard more footsteps and saw Harriet's groom with another man approaching up the path. She sighed and lifted her eyes.

'My poor peaceful copse. It is as busy as Cheapside this morning.' She straightened and gave the men their orders with calm good sense, then turned back to Crowther. 'Come over to the house with me, Mr Crowther. We shall meet with the Squire and then examine this man a little more closely.'

As her servants made ready to carry the body to Caveley, Crowther noticed her gaze at the path down which Hugh had disappeared. Her anger seemed to have dissipated, and her face was filled now only with regret.

I.5

THE FEAR THAT she was about to hear that Hugh had slit his own throat nearly within sight of her home had left Rachel pale and nervous for some time, but she had recovered enough to greet her sister and Mr Crowther when they arrived and pour tea for them both without any shake in her hand.

She had seen Mr Crowther once or twice in the street, and once through the upper windows of his own house, staring out into the road apparently unaware of anything before him, and naturally she had heard the gossip about him from her maid when he first arrived. A recluse and a mystery. She had not thought of him a great deal, however, over the year he had been in Hartswood, her mind being much engaged with her own concerns, but she was glad of the opportunity to study him more closely now. She guessed him to be in his fifties, he wore his own hair, was very pale and almost painfully thin, but his height and the steady confidence of his deportment gave him a presence she could not help admiring. She had expected the brusqueness she associated with professional men, but his movements were smooth. There must have been a time, she thought, when he was used to company. His features were fine, though the lips were thin and his expression was, if not welcoming, then not outright hostile either. He looked around their salon with polite curiosity and so she decided to like him.

Rachel had often thought her sister was not the most gracious of hostesses, but even she was surprised at the complete lack of any attempt to make conversation with their guest. Harriet was staring out across the room with her chin in one hand, rapping her fingers against her cheek. Rachel felt the duty of the house fall on her shoulders; she was young and therefore keen to supply what deficiencies she sensed in others.

'I am glad to meet you, Mr Crowther. You are a man of mystery in our society.'

Crowther looked at Mrs Westerman's sister and struggled for a minute to remember her name.

'I am not sociable, Miss Trench. I am sure it is my loss.'

Harriet snorted. 'Oh, most definitely, Mr Crowther. My sister is a fiend at backgammon and whist. You have missed any number of stimulating evenings by your refusal to know your neighbours.' There was an unmistakable sneer in her voice, and Rachel felt it directed at herself. She blushed and got up a little quickly.

'You must excuse me,' she said. 'I need to go and speak to Mrs Heathcote about dinner.'

Crowther barely had time to bow before she had left the room, and Harriet watched her go with a frown.

'Damn. I have upset her. I am an unfeeling sort of sister at times. But she is only eighteen, you know, and rather prim for her age.'

Crowther said nothing, but continued to observe Mrs Westerman over the rim of his very elegant tea cup.

'I am trying to decide what is the right thing to be done, Mr Crowther, and poor Rachel's attempts to be polite were an irritant.'

Crowther decided not to comment on her temper, but asked instead, mildly enough, 'And what do you conclude, Mrs Westerman? What *is* the right thing to be done?'

She looked up into the corner of the room.

'I shall start by saying what I think will happen now, and trust you to catch me if my conclusions are faulty.' He nodded. 'Well, then. First the Squire will arrive, and tell us that the Coroner is summoned and will be meeting with his jury in the Bear and Crown tomorrow afternoon. He will ask us for our opinions and agree we should examine the body for any further indications as to who the man might be, and why he has come here, and check that our unknown friend does not have a leg-break such as Alexander must have.' She ticked the points of her narrative off on her fingers. 'We will find nothing conclusive to add to what we already know. Tomorrow the Coroner will listen to us in a gentlemanlike manner, and the jury conclude that this unknown was killed by other unknowns for unknown reasons and ask God to have mercy on his soul. Ideally, someone will have spotted him coming from London and from there, as we know, all vice and evil makes its way. We shall therefore conclude that his destruction followed him from town, and that will be an end to it. Apart from the fact that you will be watched carefully for a day or two after the burial to check that you do not dig up the body to experiment on in your godless manner.'

Crowther smiled. 'And that will be that.'

They were silent for a little while.

'Do you think, Mr Crowther, that he was in those woods by chance?'

The question was asked lightly, but as he replied he looked at Harriet quite steadily.

'No. I think he went there to meet someone, and either that person or another who knew of the meeting, attacked and killed him.'

'And given the meeting place . . . ?'

'And given the meeting place, he expected to meet someone from either Thornleigh or Caveley. I think you believe the same, and yet I doubt you suspect anyone in your own household. But that does not necessarily help us understand what the right course of action might be.'

Mrs Westerman stood and walked over to where the French windows gave out onto the lawns at the side of the house.

'My husband and I were a little naive perhaps, when we bought this estate. It has not been easy to manage a household of this size, and look after its interests while he is away. I did it all at first for my husband and my son.' She turned quickly, smiling at him. 'I have a daughter too – just six months old. Her name is Anne. Born the day before her father sailed for the West Indies.' Her features softened a little when she spoke about her children. Crowther began to ready himself for some fuller discussion of their unique gifts and graces, but she moved on. 'Perhaps if I had my own way, I would abandon it even now, but I can be stubborn, Mr Crowther. This is now my home, the village is my home and Thornleigh seems to sit above it all like a great black crow. There is something wrong in that house. Something wounded and rotten. I am sure of it.'

He set aside his cup and looked up at her a little wearily.

'And have been sure for a while, I dare say,' he replied, 'and now you have all the moral authority a corpse on your lands can give you, so you may have the adventure of exposing it. It will make a change from estate management. Oh, and as you described Thornleigh as nestling in its own valley a little while ago, I don't think I can allow you to have it as a crow towering above the neighbourhood. Perhaps the black dragon in its cave.'

She looked surprised. 'I am glad I called you, Mr Crowther. You are very frank.'

'You summoned me from my bed before noon, have shown a terrible lack of deference to the local lords, and sworn at least once in my presence. You should not expect me to bother with the normal forms of politeness.'

She looked at him, but there was no sign of a smile to lighten his words.

'I prefer it so,' she replied, looking more pleased than he expected.

'And you are probably right about my metaphors. I have always had a fondness for dragons, though I shall not malign them with comparison to Thornleigh. Thornleigh Hall can be a malignant spider's nest when I next feel my rhetoric take hold of me.' He did allow himself to smile a little now. She looked at him directly. 'Are you not curious also? Do you not wish to know why this man died, and by whose hand? Those threads you gathered in the copse . . . I took that action to mean the puzzle interests you?'

He sighed and shifted in his seat.

'This is not a parlour game, madam. You shall not complete a riddle and gain polite applause for it. You must ask impertinent questions, and however just your cause, it is unlikely you will be thanked for it. Many good men and women have refused to go down that path and perhaps you should think about following their example. I confine my work to the dead as a rule because the dead speak a great deal more truth, and are often better company than the living. For many years now I have preferred a dead dog to a hand of cards.' Harriet was surprised into another laugh, as he continued unemotionally: 'Perhaps I will help you drive out your nest of spiders, or dragons or crows, but I do so from a position of strength. I have nothing to lose.'

'And I do? My reputation you mean? It is already known I can be a little outspoken, but yes, possibly I may do further damage to it by pursuing this business. So be it. I must do what I think is right if I am to look my family in the eye. Your assistance would be invaluable. I wonder how I can ask it, though. You may have nothing to lose, but I cannot see any gain for you in this. I do not flatter myself you offer your services for the pleasure of my company.'

'Perhaps you should.' She raised her eyebrows. 'No, madam, I have no intention of flirting with you, but you spoke before about the dangers of being isolated and how one's judgement may become warped as a result.' He looked down sadly at the design of the carpet under his black shoes. 'I fear I am looking in the wrong place in my current work, so you take me from nothing of importance, and you know from my paper that I occasionally indulge an interest in the markers of murder. I have nothing better to do than help you ruin yourself.'

'Whatever your motives, sir, you have my thanks.'

The door opened and the maid stepped into the room.

'Ma'am, the Squire is here.'

'Very good, Dido.'

As the Squire bustled in he beamed at Harriet with such open-hearted pleasure, Crowther's thin frame was almost thrown back by the force of it.

Squire Bridges was a well-built man, perhaps some ten years older than Crowther, and could never have been mistaken for anything in his life other than an English country gentleman of the old school. He had the red complexion and solid girth of a man who enjoyed vigorous exercise and noisy dinners. Indeed, his personality seemed altogether too solid and massive for the gentle confines of the salon – it seemed to strain at the walls, questing amongst the furniture to spread as much goodwill as possible. Crowther felt immediately tired, looking at him.

The Squire flung himself towards them with his hands outstretched.

'Dear Mrs Westerman, what a pleasure to see you! An ornament to the morning! And looking as ever the picture of health! I must take a proper look at you, my dear. For you know, Mrs Bridges will not let me rest till she has extracted every particular of your appearance from me, as well as all the news! And Miss Rachel is three times more beautiful this month than last – we just exchanged our good days in your hallway. We do not meet often enough, my dear. I feel it, and my wife feels it, and tells me so!'

Harriet stepped forward with a laugh and shook the Squire's hand with great friendliness.

'I am very well, as you see, sir. You may deliver good reports of us all. Stephen is blooming, the baby strong, and the latest news of Commodore Westerman full of fine winds and good officers! That is to say, he speaks well of those under his command.'

The Squire's attention sharpened a little. 'He has some doubts over Rodney, perhaps?' Harriet said nothing. 'Well, we shall see, we shall see.' Then he looked enquiringly towards Crowther, who had slunk into whatever thin shadows the room could afford as if he feared the Squire would eat him.

'Squire, this is Mr Crowther who took the Laraby house last summer. Mr Crowther, our local Justice and good friend to all, Squire Bridges.'

They made their bows, the Squire's face lightening still further with the anticipation of a new acquaintance.

'An honour, sir. I have heard of your reputation as a man of science and am glad to know you. Very glad indeed.' He peered eagerly into Crowther's face for a moment. Then, turning back to his hostess he became in a moment all serious concern. 'Now Mrs Westerman, tell me of this sad business. All I know is a body was found in your woods this morning.'

Harriet proceeded to share with him all they knew of how the man had died and Hugh's conviction that it was not his brother. The Squire's face grew gradually more sombre, and as she continued, he could not refrain from exclaiming under his breath, 'Oh, a sad business! How shocking!'

Harriet finished and the Squire was quiet a few moments. Then: 'I am at a loss, Mrs Westerman. We can, of course, enquire in the villages to see if any stranger has been seen over the last two nights, and if anything might have given rise to reasonable suspicion. This is beyond all my experience, I am afraid. Dear madam, we are old friends so I shall not scruple to announce myself deeply uneasy. Enquiries must be made, indeed. The ring is a confusing factor; it darkens matters, darkens them considerably. Did the family have any knowledge of Alexander's whereabouts over these past years?'

'I have heard of none.'

'There have been rumours,' the Squire said, 'mostly centred on London. I have not heard the matter discussed at the Hall. Well, the Coroner and his jury must be summoned. May I borrow one of your lads to show me the spot, and I shall view the body, of course, and dash off a note or two. A sad business indeed.' He turned to Crowther. 'And are you willing, sir, to make the necessary examinations of the body? We would be most grateful.' Crowther bowed.

The Squire beamed. 'Of course, of course. Capital. Good fellow.'

'And who is the Coroner?' Harriet asked.

The Squire spoke as much to the fireplace as to either of his companions, and scratched absently behind his wig as he did so.

'Oh, a mean little man from near Grasserton. He took on the duties to add lustre to his lawyering. He'll hold his session tomorrow afternoon at the Bear and Crown, I imagine. I'll have to ask you to attend, my dear. And no doubt one of the jurors will write it all up for the London papers – they always do, these days. So sorry.'

Harriet put her hand on the Squire's sleeve.

'No matter, sir. Will you be able to dine with us when we have finished examining the body?' If Harriet noticed the flick of the Squire's eyes at the suggestion that she would be examining the body with Crowther, she gave no sign of it. 'I believe Mrs Heathcote intends for us to be at table at four. If Mrs Bridges can spare you, of course.'

The Squire immediately brightened again. 'Why! If I get sufficiently detailed news for her of yourself and your doings, she will gladly spare me most of the evening! I will go to the Coroner and arrange for the jury to be summoned.'

Harriet touched the bell, and Dido appeared to lead him away.

The Squire turned to Crowther. 'Your servant, sir,' he said, and left the room with a bow.

I.6

WHILE THE SQUIRE began to marshal the limited resources of the law – himself, the Coroner and a Constable chosen by the local parishioners as the person least likely to give them any trouble – Harriet led Crowther out of the house and towards the body. They turned in at a collection of outbuildings, and passing by the current generous stables, Harriet took him to a smaller building in the corner of the yard which had housed the horses of Caveley Park in earlier times. It was a large open space, the north and south walls each partitioned into three empty stalls, and with a large unglazed window to the east with the shutters thrown back. The raw beams rose, ghostly, into the shadow of the roof's incline, and the stone flags under their feet were patterned by the heavy sunlight from the window and door. Motes of dust and straw shifted in the air. Odd pieces of tackle still hung from huge iron nails driven between the stalls, and the air tasted of lavender and old leather. In the central space in front of them a long table had been set, used normally in the yard for holiday and harvest feasts, Crowther supposed. Now the body was laid out on it, decently covered in a white linen sheet. It looked like an offering. There were cloths, a wide bowl and ewer on a bench under the window.

Crowther placed a hand to his brow and exhaled. When he opened his eyes again, he found Harriet's gaze on him, her head tilted to one side.

'Forgive me, but you look very tired, Mr Crowther.'

'I am, Mrs Westerman. It is my habit to work at night, and keep to my bed in the morning when not viewing the slaughtered gentry of the neighbourhood.' He weaved his hands together and stretched his fingers, making them crack, then continued in a practical tone: 'Now, this will not be a full dissection. This is not the weather, the

33

body must be viewed by the Coroner's men in the morning, and I think we can be certain as to how this man died. We will confine ourselves to externals and examine his leg for any old injury.' Harriet drew herself very straight and nodded. Crowther suspected she was fighting the impulse to salute.

He had removed his coat and was turning to hang it on a convenient nail when he noticed his own tools, wrapped in their soft leather roll on the bench beside the ewer and bowl.

'How came these here?'

'William picked them up from your people as he came back through the village. Had you not required them, they would have been returned before you had noticed they were gone.'

'Your house is well run.'

'William and David were both at sea with my husband and myself. Mrs Heathcote's husband serves with him still. I could not wish for a better family. The maids still come and go, but in general I believe a woman never had better servants, or more loyal.'

Crowther turned to the corpse again, wondering if Miss Rachel Trench had ever been to sea, and if not, what she thought of the family now gathered round her.

He had been expecting Mrs Westerman to leave him at this point, but she did not. Instead, she folded back her habit from her wrists, and picked up an apron to cover her skirts. Catching his look, she gave him a wary half-smile.

'You did say it would not be a full examination.'

'Indeed.'

'Then I think I shall stomach it.' She moved to the body and folded away the linen cover, then, her attention caught, she bent down to examine the hand.

Crowther had studied with some of the best surgeons and teachers of anatomy in Europe. They were busy practical men, their inquisitiveness their main feature, their niceties blunted by their commerce with the dead and the necessary dealings with the underworld of bodysnatchers and resurrection men. He had seen any number of corpses cut up and manhandled, the floor slippery with blood and air thick with human effluvia while a dozen men in powdered wigs jostled over a body to examine some peculiarity pointed out by their instructors. He thought now that he had never seen a sight as shocking, or as strangely beautiful, as Mrs Harriet Westerman taking the stiff fist of the corpse between her own white hands and stooping to examine the dead flesh. Its grey, waxen emptiness alongside the delicate colouring of her face and intelligence in her eyes, seemed a metaphor of divine spark. If she had breathed on that hand and made it warm again, and alive, Crowther would have accepted the miracle and believed.

'He has a hold of something. Do you have a pair of tweezers?'

'Of course.'

He handed them to her and watched as she pushed them between the man's fingers. She bit her lip when she was concentrating.

'There!'

She passed the tweezers back to him with a flourish; in between their delicate silver tips Crowther saw a scrap of paper. The corner of a sheet, torn off.

'He had something with him. A note or letter to go with the ring and it was taken from him,' she said immediately.

'Perhaps. Or perhaps it was a note from his tailor.'

She narrowed her eyes. 'I doubt anyone goes to meet someone in the woods, in darkness, with a note from their tailor clasped in their hand. Though I understand you. I am too quick.' She reclaimed the scrap of paper, folded it into her handkerchief and put it to one side.

'You are perhaps a little hasty. But your methods are just as I would advise.'

'You forget. I read your article and watched you this morning. I am your student.'

Crowther raised his eyebrows briefly and returned to the body.

The cloak revealed no more than a purse with a few shillings and Crowther wondered where this man's other possessions, if he had any, might be waiting, dumbly, for him to return. His boots were rather dusty, but whole. The clothes he wore were of passable quality, though a little worn in places, but only the material and design of the waistcoat showed any pretensions to fashion. Was its purchase one indulgence in an otherwise sober existence? An attempt at gentility? Crowther rubbed the stuff of the waistcoat between his thumb and forefinger, feeling the quality of the fabric. It might have been his own at one stage of his life.

'How far away are we from Pulborough? And does the stage stop there?' he asked, and Harriet looked up at him with surprise. 'I have not needed to make the journey since my arrival in Hartswood,' he explained.

'It is about four miles. The stage to London passes there on Tuesdays, from London on Thursdays. You are wondering how he reached our village.'

'I am. But it is most likely if he came from London, it was by coach and then on foot. He has the dust of the road on his feet.'

Mrs Westerman merely nodded then took up a cloth, wet it, and began calmly to clean the blood away from around the horrid gash in the neck. Crowther stared for a second, then fetched a cloth of his own and started the same work opposite her. Their silence stretched into minutes, and Crowther slowly became aware of a sense of reverence, of humility in the warm room making its way into his bones. He recognised it from his own workroom; that sense of wonder that came to him as he concentrated on these bodies, these vessels through which life so fleetingly, and often with such cruelty, flew. The sensation was, he had recognised long ago, the nearest he would ever come to religion.

Returning to the window, he dropped his cloth into the basin, watching for a moment as the water bloomed pink around it. He recalled Harvey's words: *All the parts are nourished, cherished, and quickened with blood, which is warm, perfect, vaporous, full of spirit . . .'* This wondrous substance that flowed through the hearts of every man, whatever his condition or nature, this symbol of love and death floating free from his fingertips. He thought again of the dark marks on the tree trunks in the coppice, and wondered how long it would be till the local children made a little shrine of terror about them.

Turning back to the body, he crouched down to examine the wound afresh, and with infinite gentleness placed a finger on the edges of skin.

'Mrs Westerman.' His voice sounded unnaturally loud in the room, after their long silence. 'If you have the stomach for it, come and look at this wound again and tell me what you see.'

Her greenish eyes searched his face for a moment, then she walked slowly round the edge of the table, her bloodied cloth still in her hands, and gave her attention directly to the place he indicated, her face bent to the horror of the wound. Her voice as she spoke was composed.

'The cut is deepest here, on the right side. So if he was surprised from behind . . .' She frowned.

Crowther took a knife from the roll behind him. 'May I?'

'Of course.'

He stood behind her, took the knife in his right hand and said, 'You are looking forward . . .'

'Waiting for whomever I am meeting to appear in the clearing . . .'

'I come up behind you. Take you by the shoulder . . .' He did so, placing his left hand on her shoulder, and with his right brought the knife in front of her body, hovering a few inches from her throat. His own mouth went suddenly dry and as if from a great height he saw himself, the woman, the body.

'I see,' Harriet said. 'The force came on the right side of the wound as the cut was completed. He was murdered by a man who favoured his right.'

37

'And who was of about the same height, since the cut goes straight back to the vertebra.'

Harriet looked at the knife that hovered still in front of her. 'Whereas if *you* were to cut my throat,' she told him, 'the wound would most likely be angled upwards, given your superior height.'

He bowed and moved carefully away.

Mrs Westerman stood a little apart as Crowther looked for evidence of a break in the lower limbs of the corpse. He opened the flesh to expose the bone from knee to ankle. Again he felt the sweat slowly gathering at his neck. The bone in both legs was solid and clean. 'Harriet did not speak as he worked, merely nodding as he showed her that the bones were true. He felt her attention as he folded the flesh back over the leg and with a curved needle of his own design knitted the skin back together with silk. It was neatly done, and some part of him expected to be praised for it, but when he looked up, he saw that her mind was already elsewhere.

'This was a cowardly attack,' she said.

'To cut someone's throat from behind, in the night? Yes, that is cowardice – or desperation. You never believed this was an affair of honour, I think.'

'I did not, but I have been thinking further as you sliced up his shins. The murder was done swiftly, quietly. There is no sign to suggest this was done in the heat of the moment, in a fight or argument.'

'Though words may have been exchanged and the murderer returned.'

'Perhaps. In either case the murder was done, and the note taken . . . the note – but not the ring. It was not hard to find and it indicates a connection to the family at Thornleigh Hall. If the murder was done with an aim to secrecy, as the wound indicates, why not take the ring and conceal the body, at least to some degree?'

Crowther walked to the ewer and found himself briefly confused about how to wash his hands without getting matter on the water jug. Harriet came over and lifted it to pour over his wrists. He worked the blood free from his short nails, then took up a fresh cloth and began to dry his fingers, looking up into the shadowed roofspace above them. Harriet moved away to cover the body again.

'Perhaps the murderer was disturbed,' he said to the empty air above him.

'Someone, other than the murderer, arrived to keep the appointment? That would be interesting,' Harriet mused, then continued with a sigh, 'I wish we knew more about this man, Crowther. Neither rich nor poor, tall nor short. He is a blank.'

'As you say, Mrs Westerman. But the clothes tell us something. It is they that convince me this man is not Alexander Thornleigh—'

'The Honourable Alexander Thornleigh – Viscount Hardew to give him his proper title. One should address an Earl's son properly, even *in absentia*.'

'I stand corrected,' he said, then continued, 'As I was saying, the contrast between cloak and waistcoat convinces me more than the soundness of his leg bones or even his brother's word. This is a man who would spend a large amount of money on a waistcoat, but not his travelling cloak. That speaks of one who wishes to pretend in company that he has more money than his cloak tells us he has, yet Mr Thornleigh, from what you tell me, has abandoned for fifteen years great rank and fortune.'

Harriet looked at Crowther for a long time, considering, then threw up her hands.

'For a man so unwilling to look his fellow creatures in the eye, you are a subtle student of psychology,' she declared, and he bowed.

There was a gentle knock at the door, and Dido put her face around the opening. Seeing the body covered, her expression became less fearful and she came far enough into the room to drop a curtsy to them.

'Excuse me, ma'am. The Squire has returned from the village and Cook is ready to serve dinner.'

'We shall come in at once.' The maid let the door drop behind her. Harriet turned back to Crowther with a half-smile.

'Well, it seems we have had all the private dealings with this poor wretch that we may expect. I suppose we'd better make matters known to the proper authorities.' As she turned towards the door, Crowther held his ground and cleared his throat.

'I have made an examination of the body, ma'am. That is all the true expertise I can offer in this case. I must ask you then, why have you made me an ally in this puzzle-solving of yours?'

She looked at him. 'Because I think you are by nature a clear-headed man, and you are an outsider, sir, who cares little for the politics of society in this place. That makes you very important to me. I am trusting you to keep us honest. You have already been very rude to me on several occasions, so I am more and more convinced of my need of you. There are very few independently-minded, unencumbered and intelligent men in this neighbourhood, particularly when my husband is at sea, so perhaps my hand was forced.'

'And would your husband approve of your actions in this matter, madam?'

She looked at the floor. 'Probably not. He is more of a politician than I am, and he is rich enough already.' Crowther frowned, and she continued, 'But it will be six weeks before he can hear of this, and another six before any scolding he has for me will be able to reach Caveley. He can clear the decks of any embarrassment I cause when he returns. He has done so in the past. Does that concern you?'

'No. Though perhaps it should concern you.'

She smiled at him mildly, then turned and without further comment began to walk towards the door.

I.7

'F ATHER,' SUSAN CALLED, running back into the shop from the family parlour. She came to a sudden stop in the doorway, seeing Alexander by the shop window peering out into the street, and remembering a little too late that now she was nine she was supposed to have stopped dashing about the house like a street urchin. He turned when he heard her, and although he was frowning she thought it was not so much at her as at his own thoughts.

'Is everything well, Papa? Would you like to eat? Jane and I have made a pie!' She became serious. 'Are you still fretting about your ring? I am sorry we could not find it.'

He smiled at her. 'No. I have decided not to miss it and the pie sounds wonderful.' He glanced out into the Square again. 'I think all is well. Lord George Gordon has roused up a mob. They think giving Catholics the right to own their own property is an offence against every English Protestant and wish to stop the Bill allowing it from being passed. Fools. Mr Graves just came by to tell me that Parliament itself is under siege, but the mob should not worry us here. Does Jonathan miss the ring? I think he thought more of it than you or I.'

Some half-memory stirred in the back of Susan's mind. The ring appeared before her, the picture on it, and something Jonathan had told her when he came back from play some days before. He had said something about a waistcoat.

Susan had just opened her mouth to tell her father this when her brother swung into the room.

'No popery! No popery!' he shouted, waving his handkerchief in the air and dashing across to their father. Alexander swung him up into his arms.

'No need to ask if you have been out at play, sir. But watch your

41

words, young man. They cause hurt to your friends and do you no honour.' Jonathan looked a little confused and was about to question when his father shushed him. The serving girl had appeared behind them, looking anxious.

'Sir, they say the crowds are coming back from Westminster, and looking black.'

Jonathan opened his mouth to shout again – then, catching his father's eye, shut it.

'You are worried about your people, Jane?' Alexander looked with a friendly concern at the girl.

'A little, sir. They say the crowd are heading for the fancy houses, but our religion is known, and there's only my mother there. I'm afraid she'll be nervous, sir.'

'Well, you must go to her. And give her our best wishes.'

Jane had begun to untie her apron as soon as the first words were out of his mouth, and spoke again in a rush.

'Thank you, sir! I'll be back as soon as it's quiet. Miss Susan and I have made a pie that will do for dinner, and there is cheese in the crock, and bread for supper.'

'We will manage. Go and see to your family, and come back again when you can.'

Susan looked about her unhappily. She had never seen Jane look so nervous before, and she did not like the tone of her father's voice. Jane disappeared out into the kitchen and away, and Alexander crossed over and put a hand on his daughter's shoulder.

'Don't fret, little woman. Just silly people making a lot of noise and trouble for their entertainment. We're safe enough. Now let's go and try this remarkable pie of yours.'

Crowther and Harriet were walking up to the French windows that gave onto the main lawn, when they heard a sharp slap and a child's cry of surprise. Crowther looked to Harriet, who hurried over the last few steps to the house. He followed. As they stepped into the room, Crowther saw Rachel, her cheeks flushed, holding a boy of about five by the arm and vigorously shaking him. There was already a red mark rising on the little boy's cheek and he was clutching a paintbrush in his free hand. Rachel's voice, as she spoke, was quavering and hot.

'Stephen, you naughty boy! How could you?' The boy caught sight of Harriet in the doorway and, shaking himself free, ran over to her and buried his face in her skirts, crying lustily. Miss Trench saw them both and gave a start. She held out her arms to Harriet in appeal.

'Oh Harry, I am sorry. I did not mean to, but he has painted black marks all over my picture just out of badness – and it was just as I wanted it!'

Harriet knelt to better embrace the boy and, having removed the dangerous brush from his hand, she handed it wordlessly to Crowther and stroked her son's hair. His crying slowed a little. He put his face into her neck and mumbled something between sobs.

'What is it, Stephen? I can't hear you,' Harriet asked him softly, still not looking at her sister.

'Crows. She forgot the crows,' he said, then his voice rising to a bitter wail, 'I was helping!' He tucked his face into Harriet's neck again, his small hands gripping the collar of her riding dress in determined fistfuls.

Rachel looked more stricken than ever. Crowther remained in the shadows of the drapery, as if Harriet's curtains might provide some protection from the emotions flying round the room like the Chinese fireworks at Vauxhall. He looked down at the dirty brush between his fingers.

Harriet waited until the little boy was calmer and spoke to him gently.

'Perhaps Aunt Rachel did not want crows in her picture, Stephen. Have you thought of that? You would not like it if she painted all your soldiers yellow, now would you? Even if she thought they looked better that way.'

The little boy's sobs stopped suddenly, and he pulled away from his mother as he considered this horrid possibility. He shook his head. She took his small face in her hands and smiled at him, then kissed him on his hot smooth forehead.

'Well, you do not seem much hurt, young man. Apologise to your aunt and perhaps she will not paint on your things in revenge.'

Stephen shot a glance towards Rachel, then walked carefully over to her.

'I'm sorry, Aunt. I thought it would look nicer with crows.' He thought for a moment and extended his hand. Rachel knelt down and took it with great seriousness.

'I didn't realise you were helping, Stephen. And I am very sorry to have been so cross. May we be friends again?'

'You won't paint my soldiers yellow, then? Because they should all wear red coats.' She shook her head. Crowther found he was smiling a little, and stepped clear of the curtains. Stephen grinned with relief and pounced forward to kiss his aunt on the cheek, then struggling free from her embrace, turned and started with surprise as he caught sight of Crowther hovering in the doorway behind his mother and twisting the brush between his fingers.

'Who are you, sir?'

'I am Gabriel Crowther.'

The little boy considered for a moment, then his eyes widened considerably.

'Do you eat children, sir?'

Crowther stooped slightly from the waist, till he had brought his thin body to the point where he could look the little boy in the eye.

'Not as often as I would like.'

Stephen looked at him with awe and pleasure, thrusting one small fist to his mouth. He then announced to the world in general that Mrs

Heathcote had made cake and he would be allowed to eat the crumbs from the tin, and raced out of the room. Harriet stood and smiled at Crowther, then, her eyes growing more serious, she turned to her sister.

'I'm so sorry, Harriet. I didn't mean, I—'

Harriet looked irritated, and held up her hand. 'This is not like you, Rachel.'

Miss Trench flushed red. 'I have been more upset than I know. There was a moment when I heard of the body when I thought . . .'

Harriet put the heel of her hand to her forehead for a moment, then moved across the room to take her sister's arm and lead her to a chair.

'Oh Rachel, I'm so sorry. It never occurred to me . . . Then I was unkind to you. You must have wished us all to the devil.'

Rachel shook her head. 'It was stupid, and only for a moment.' She glanced up at where Crowther hung awkwardly in the background. 'I'm sorry you have seen me display such a temper, sir. I am ashamed.'

Her sister laughed. 'Oh, I've said at least seven shocking things to him this morning myself, Rachel. Have I not, Mr Crowther? He could blacken us across the county if he has a mind. But then, as Mr Crowther hardly moves in society at all, he can do no more damage to our reputations than we do ourselves. Please, take a seat, sir.'

Rachel looked across at Crowther as he sat, placing the brush gingerly in a vase on the side-table.

'Still, I am sorry you were witness to my bad behaviour, sir. I trust you will try not to think ill of me, and I rely, as my sister does, on your discretion.'

Crowther felt the warmth of her eyes and voice like a benediction; to the family good looks present in the elder sister was added real feminine grace. The girl's hair was more honey than her sister's, though the sunlight caught the fire in it and made it shine. Her eyes were the same green as Harriet's. Softened a little, and a little wider

45

perhaps, but their close kinship was obvious. She was a little thinner than she should be, but it gave her a delicacy that Crowther had already noted as rather lacking in Mrs Westerman. The younger woman still had the freshly unwrapped softness of youth in her skin. She looked as if she had, as yet, suffered no rough weather. Again, she could not be ranked as a remarkable beauty, but he felt his old character of connoisseur of women stir in his breast.

'Till death, ma'am.'

Harriet raised her eyebrows. 'Well, let's hope that will not be necessary, sir.' Crowther squirmed a little on his chair. 'Now Rachel, could you tell me if you have hidden Squire Bridges somewhere in the house?'

Rachel gave a slight choking laugh under her breath.

'He's in the library finishing his letters. We should dine shortly or we will annoy Cook and Mrs Heathcote. She so loves the Squire, I think the whole of the store room is coming to table, and it will be all the worse for us if it is spoiled.' She turned towards Crowther and continued: 'Will you be joining us, sir? We dine quite informally and you'll be most welcome.'

Crowther felt somehow, and by doing very little, he had made himself a touch ridiculous.

'I fear not, Miss Trench, though I thank you for the invitation. I dine at a later hour and at home.'

Harriet did not turn towards him, but said nevertheless, with a slightly bored tone that suggested she found these society shufflings rather wearying, 'Please let us persuade you, Mr Crowther. The Squire will certainly dine with us, and I would be glad to talk further on your impressions of what has passed.'

Mr Crowther felt Miss Trench's encouraging smile on him and, bowing as best he could from his perch on the edge of one of Harriet's neatly upholstered chairs, he accepted the invitation.

'I will tell Mrs Heathcote,' Rachel said, giving him a slight curtsy as she stood and hurried out of the room. Crowther could hear the rapid scuff of her shoes on the flagstones of the passageway while the door was still closing; she was running as if she were still a girl.

Harriet rose and walked up to an elegant desk at one end of the narrow salon, where she began to glance through some of the correspondence neatly piled upon it. Crowther realised that this room must be her main place of business as well as leisure. It suited her, he thought, being pleasant and practical, but without the profusion of frills and fancies that Crowther had found oppressive in many feminine apartments. The room was long and well-lit from the garden; the furniture was modern and practical but showed taste. The wall behind the desk was lined with volumes bound in brown leather, and the little *objets d'art* collected on the side-tables and above the mantel were interesting and well-chosen for the spaces they occupied. Her husband had obviously collected a deal of prize money as well as household staff on his voyages, and delivered his wealth to a careful manager. Harriet put the papers back down on her desk with a sigh.

'Nothing of importance here, I think. Well then, sir. Shall we dine?'

Normally when the shop bell rang while they were at table, Jane would go into the public room and let them know if the master was required. Since she had now left for her parents' home, Susan leaped to her feet when they heard the bright brass chime in the parlour and dashed into the shop before her father could put down his napkin.

She had forgotten about the yellow-faced man. He closed the shop door carefully behind him and pulled down the blind, then turned towards her with the same unpleasant smile of the morning. She came to a sudden stop in front of him. He took a step forward and bent down to her.

'And what is your name, young lady?' His breath smelled like Shambles Lane where the butchers threw the meat that had spoiled.

'Susan Adams.' This seemed to amuse him.

'Adams, is it? That's charming, charming. And is your father at home, Susan Adams, and your little brother?'

'Can I help you, sir?'

Susan turned to see her father, his coat off and his eyes severe, coming into the room. He came up behind her and gently moved her out of the way. She slunk gratefully behind him a little, glad he kept his hand on her shoulder.

The man looked deep into her father's eyes for what seemed a very long time, before saying, 'I believe you can, sir. I was told to give you a message from the Hall.'

Susan saw the man move, and heard her father grunt as he did sometimes when picking up a bundle of scores. He pressed down suddenly on her shoulder and she stumbled under his weight; they landed heavily on the floor together. She struggled to sit, and looked up in confusion. The man was standing over them, still smiling. He was holding something in his hand she had not noticed before, red and wet. She could hear her father breathing hard, ragged. She turned to him; his hand was pressed to his side where he had been struck, his eyes wide with surprise. She looked up again at the yellow man for explanation. The man looked back.

'Stay easy, child. It'll all be over soon enough.'

She could not move, but her hand found her father's and she felt it grip her own. Jonathan, bored at being left so long, wandered into the doorway.

'May I eat the pie crust if you do not want it, Papa?'

The yellow man looked up quickly and smiled his twisting smile. Susan thought he must be very old. His skin was deeply cracked, like porcelain badly repaired. The hat he wore low over his wig was greasy and shone in places.

'Hello, Puppy! Come over here and see us a moment.' There was an urgency in his voice now. Susan tried to open her mouth, her voice was whispering.

'No, Jonathan.'

'Now, don't you listen to your mean old sister, my boy. Come when your betters tell you to.'

Susan could not see her brother, she could only watch the glint of the man's eyes. Without taking them from the little boy, the yellow man wiped his knife on the inside of his coat. Susan felt her heart throb as if for the last time.

Just then, the brass bell rang again, and Mr Graves walked in with his usual quick step.

'Alexander!' he said excitedly. 'You won't believe the progress of the mob. They are making an attempt on— Good God! What is this?'

The yellow man gave a yell of rage, and spun round towards the door. Susan saw Graves start towards him, blocking his way; the yellow man's arm swung up in a wide arc, and Mr Graves staggered back, falling onto his side. The yellow man ran out into the street; the door rattled behind him. Jonathan began to scream. Graves struggled onto his knees and crawled over to Susan and Alexander.

'Dear God! Dear God! Alexander!'

Susan looked down at her father again, and saw a red alien bloom across his waistcoat, just where their clasped hands lay; even his cravat was stained and that had been clean on this morning. Jane would complain at the extra work.

Mr Graves groaned, then looked up at her. 'Susan? Susan! Listen to me! Are you hurt?'

His face had a long thin slice of red across it, beaded here and there like jewels on a string. He grabbed her shoulders and shook her.

'Are you hurt, girl?'

She looked at him in surprise. He seemed a very long way away.

Jonathan was hysterical. She must keep him quiet or he would wake Mama, and she needed her rest very much now. She shook her head. He held her gaze.

'I'm going to fetch a surgeon. Lock the door behind me, and only open it for me, you understand. For me!' He turned to the crying boy. 'Jonathan, go and fetch water for your papa.' He put his hand on Alexander's shoulder. 'Don't move. No! For God's sake – don't try to speak, man.'

Alexander tried to lift a hand. His stertorous breathing formed into words. The two men looked at each other.

'Care for them, Graves.'

'I swear it. Now . . .' he stood and dragged Susan to her feet, forcing her to let go of her father's hand, which made her yelp in protest like a kicked dog. He held her shoulders again, and looking her straight in the eye, said: 'Come to the Door, Susan. And lock it behind me.' She managed to nod. 'And remember: you *must not* open the door again to anyone till I get back. Will you remember that?'

She nodded again and he pulled her to the door, waiting outside, his eyes wild with impatience till he heard the lock being turned, then set off down the narrow street at a run.

Susan watched him go, almost wondering why he ran so fast, then turned back to her father. She dropped on the floor beside him and gently lifted his head onto her knee. She tried to give him a little of the water Jonathan had brought from the table, weeping whenever he spilled a drop in his hurry. It was difficult, for her hands were all slippery and red, but she thought a little went in between her father's lips. Jonathan burrowed into her side, and Susan shifted a little so he could get close to her. When she moved she was sorry to see the red had become a pool and her own dress, and Jonathan's breeches were steeped in it. She set down the water glass and with great care took her father's hand again. Jonathan took the other. Alexander's breathing became more ragged still, and slower. He forced his eyes open and swallowed.

'Susan . . .'

She did not move. Everything was very far away, as it is just before sleep. The world swam in and out of existence around her. She stroked her father's hair. It had become disarranged when he fell, and he thought it always so important to be neat.

'Susan . . .' His voice was so deep, it hardly sounded like him at all. 'Listen . . . there is a black wooden box under the counter, hidden under the Bononcini scores.' He paused and shut his eyes again. The breaths were single gasps now. Susan continued to stroke his hair. His eyes opened again, and fixed on hers. 'You must take it with you wherever you go . . . Talk about what you find in it with Mr Graves.' Again he closed his eyes, again the sucking gulp on air. Stuff trickled from the corner of his mouth, red and thick. Jonathan began to cry again and hid his eyes. 'Do not blame me, Susan . . .'

She did not speak, but continued to stroke his hair. A memory came back to her of lying ill in bed as a child. She remembered the cool of her mother's hand smoothing her forehead and her singing to her. Her father gasped again, and a tremor ran through him; she felt her hand held almost painfully tight, then his grip suddenly relaxed. Jonathan gulped, and looked up at her.

'Shush, Jonathan. Papa needs to rest.' She wet her lips, and never ceasing to smooth her father's hair, began to sing in a cracked and whispering voice:

> *'Will you sleep now, my little child?*
> *For the sky is growing dark.*
> *Will you sleep now, my lovely child?*
> *For the sky is growing dark.'*

She was careful of her word, and would not let anyone into the shop until Mr Graves returned a quarter of an hour later with a surgeon panting and complaining behind him. When he arrived he had to

51

fight his way through a crowd of the concerned citizenry who had gathered in the doorway, having heard the shouts and seen men running. They were pressed to the plate glass of the window, staring and exclaiming at the sight of the straight back of the little girl, who knelt with her brother in a seemingly shoreless pool of their father's blood, stroking his hair and murmuring lullabies.

I.8

DINNER AT CAVELEY Park was a pleasant enough affair considering Crowther said very little, and all were aware of the body of the stranger lying in the stable block.

The various dishes having been brought to table, the family waited on themselves and each other. The scrape of knife on plate and the comfort of good food well prepared provided all the background and counterpoint necessary to the Squire's news and enquiries, and Harriet's and Rachel's good-humoured responses.

Crowther let much of it pass without interest or remark until he heard Harriet ask, in response to some light remark of the Squire's which touched on Thornleigh Hall: 'My dear sir, I hope you will not mind me asking in the circumstances, but I am curious about your impressions of Lord Thornleigh. We know so little of him. What did you think of him, as a man, before his illness?'

The Squire did not reply at once, and pushed his plate a little way from him. He pursed his lips, and for what seemed to be the first time that afternoon, thought carefully before he spoke – and when he spoke, his tone was serious and considered. Crowther saw a more thoughtful man appear to take the Squire's place, or rather saw the mask he habitually wore put carefully aside. Crowther examined him with renewed interest.

'Well, I struggle to say much that is good of him.'

He drew a long slow breath and let his eyes rest on his half-worked plate, though it was clear he was seeing something else.

'I knew him in the blossom of his life, though we were not closely associated, his rank and fortune being so much greater than my own. He was very proud, and the people he had about him I could not like. They held, it seemed to me, their fellow creatures in contempt. Among the staff in his house, good honest creatures did not seem to thrive, and those in this neighbourhood I had least cause to love, and most reason to doubt, always seemed to do better in his service than their virtues might merit.' He dragged his gaze upward to meet Mrs Westerman's for a moment. Then cleared his throat as if to drive some troublesome taste from it. 'But these are idle prejudices, and I must not speak ill of one brought so low.'

Crowther spoke for the first time since dinner had begun.

'I understand, sir, that Lord Thornleigh fell victim to a seizure some years ago.'

The Squire nodded and gave a slight shrug of his massive shoulders.

'I am not a medical man, Mr Crowther, but yes, that is what I believe. It was within a year of his second marriage. He lost almost all his capacity for movement, and all his abilities of speech. Yet he lives. What sort of existence it can be I cannot say, yet live he does. Perhaps the Almighty in His infinite mercy is giving him time to repent the wrongs of his youth, though the servants say he is to all intents and purposes an idiot now.'

'Has he so much to repent?' Rachel asked lightly.

The Squire did not choose to hear her, but instead lifted his head and stared into the corners of the dining room.

'We assumed he would not long survive the attack, yet still he continues. It speaks well to the care that is taken of him, yet it seems a cruel fate to me, and one I could not wish on any man.'

'You'll forgive me, Squire,' Crowther said, 'but you speak as if you suspect him of some greater sin than pride?'

'Perhaps I do. But that suspicion must remain between me and my God at this moment. I will not slander a man who cannot make a reply, nor share unpleasant stories with the ladies for the time being. I know, Mrs Westerman, you have the stomach of a warrior, but there are things I would not have your sister hear me speak of.'

Rachel looked down at her plate, and Harriet smiled at him, while gently placing her hand over her sister's.

'Shall we have rain tomorrow, do you think?' she asked brightly, and the Squire took up the subject. Nothing more of significance was spoken of until the ladies retired.

When the wine had been poured and the servants released, Crowther introduced the subject of the Squire's suspicions once more. The older man put down the wine in front of him, and slowly shook his head. Crowther looked hard at the soft red profile the Squire presented from under his hooded eyes. He let the silence between them lengthen till it formed a pressure in the room. The Squire was frowning a little, and began to turn Harriet's delicate wine glass distractedly with his sausage-like fingers until Crowther wondered if it were quite safe.

'Mrs Westerman wishes to know the truth of what has happened here,' Crowther stated. 'It is clear she suspects some dark doings at Thornleigh, and the murder took place on her land. She will not be satisfied with a simple "killed by persons unknown" at the inquest. She has requested my help and I have given my word to assist her.'

As Crowther spoke, the Squire let his glass rest, and his profile hardened with deep attention. Crowther had the sense that his companion was listening not merely to the words themselves, but their undertow, what they brought with them. He felt some judgement was being made on him.

'Well, Mr Crowther, I shall tell you then, since you ask in such a manner,' the Squire said heavily. 'I have no reason, however, to believe it pertains at all to the death of this poor wretch. You cannot say you speak for the family here without drawing me to you in some degree – though I sometimes feel they might do better in some other place. For all her experience in the larger world, Mrs Westerman does not yet understand the pull of the little threads that hold us all together and in our place in such a society as ours. Nor do you. Just because the head of Thornleigh is in some ways cut off, it is still a great power. A little King in stone for the county. And she wishes to bang on their gates and cry murder! Her husband has his connections, of course, but not many. I can tell you my story, but I advise you to forget it. Retire to your previous seclusion and persuade Mrs Westerman to confine herself to her proper duties.' He rubbed his chin with his palm. 'Perhaps my story may serve as a parable that in the end we are wise to leave justice in the hands of God.'

He looked up at Crowther's face. Crowther merely blinked slowly at him. Bridges took a swallow of wine and, having settled himself in his chair, he began to speak.

'Well then, when I was a young man – oh, some forty years ago now, long before Mrs Westerman was even born or Lord Thornleigh married for the first time – there was a girl killed on the edge of the village of Harden, some two miles south of here. She was a good child, a general favourite in the area and respectably brought up. Search-parties were organised and in short order her body was found. Her name was Sarah Randle. She was twelve years old.'

The Squire paused and drained his glass, nodding his thanks as Crowther refilled it.

'I found her, I'm sorry to say. I would rather have lived my life free of that image, but the only service I can render her is to remember. I was out riding and came upon one of the search-parties as they neared the woods on the outskirts of Harden. Knowing the girl myself, I dismounted to join them. It was a summer's evening, much this time of year, the air warm and delicate, the paths and fields so alive with the buzz of creation – everything becoming, it seemed, more perfectly itself. Such a pale little thing she was. She had been thrown down, some yards from one of the smaller paths in the wood. So terribly wrong, it seemed, that she lay there all broken and stopped amongst such a profusion, such vigorous life. Her face was quite unmarked, but her clothes were black with blood. Her body had been stabbed about in a frenzy. Thirteen wounds I counted in her breast and stomach. She was in her holiday clothes, and they were so torn and bloodied about her . . . It was sunset when we found her, and the sky was gold and red, with magnificent deep purple clouds draining from the day. The two images are linked in my mind. Her broken body and the glory of the sun sinking in the west. Poor innocent. It could not have been an easy death, or a quick one.'

Crowther did not trust himself to speak. He realised he was held by a narrator of talent; he had felt the late sun on his back, heard the thrum of life in the hedgerow.

The Squire continued, 'Her belly was swollen. There was no doubt she was with child.'

'No one knew who the father could be?'

'There was gossip that damaged several good men over the coming months, but she had been close. Not one of her friends had, I believe, been confided in. Nor had the sister who shared her bed. Some passing pedlar in the village was taken up by the hue and cry, but he was vouched for by two or three of the better people, and the crowd had fixed on him more in sorrow than in anger. He got away unharmed. The whole village turned out for the burial, but Lord Thornleigh did not attend. However, he did ride by with one of his friends, while we were burying the poor sinner. They were laughing at something and I looked up from my prayers and caught his eye. That look I saw on his face is the only reason for the suspicion I have ever had against the man. It chilled my soul then, and the memory of it does so still. It was triumphant, exhilarated. Quite wild.'

One of the household passed along the passage outside the dining room, their shoes skimming carpet and stone. Crowther drank deeply.

'And no one enquired further into his connection with the girl?' he asked.

'I believe I have said enough of his character to suggest why no one had the stomach to enquire more closely,' the Squire said. 'The girl certainly had no Mrs Westerman to champion her, no one so wilfully naive. Or if she did, perhaps he was warned away early and well and has learned his lesson since. Mrs Westerman may have the same path to tread.' The Squire looked a little angry. 'Nor did Randle need a champion, nor does this fellow in the woods. Thornleigh has lost his eldest son to the world, his second to drink and lives an idiot while his third is brought up by a whore.' The Squire's voice had become almost hoarse on his final words.

Crowther did not move, merely continued to watch his tented fingertips, his face without expression.

'Sarah Randle died before Thornleigh's first marriage, you say?'

The Squire looked up again, as if surprised to find he had been speaking aloud, and to another. He shrugged, and his voice returned to something like its usual pitch and phrasing.

'Indeed. He spent much of the next few years in London, then returned to us with a wife. And an unhappy affair that was, though the first Lady Thornleigh bore him two sons, as you know, before her death. Three girls died before they reached four years old.'

'And did she die in childbirth?'

'No, a fall, only three years after Hugh was born. I fear the death of her daughters left her . . . a little nervous. From that point until Thornleigh's second marriage we saw little of him. He lived mostly in town, only coming to hunt with small parties, and always reluctant to stay long. The children were brought up by the servants, then sent away to school. They seemed good enough men in their youth, though.'

He shifted his chair a little.

'I am grateful to you for examining this wretch, but I wish you would trouble yourself no further in the matter. Mrs Westerman, and I mean no disrespect, can be impulsive, a little quick to judge. It is the penalty she pays for her own prodigious energy, so I am glad she is to have your counsel, Commodore Westerman being away, and he acting as he does as her sea-anchor in the general run of things, if I have understood that term correctly.'

Crowther bowed slightly. The Squire nodded, interpreting the gesture according to his own desires.

'The place where you must come to, where damage will be done, you must come to very quick. And if you do not hold her back, you must take a share in the blame for whatever comes to pass. And, of course, your own association with the family, if you intervene or not, may harm them.' The Squire paused, watching Crowther's forehead crease with a slight frown. His voice took on a certain soft sheen. 'I should perhaps tell you, while we are being so open, that I know your name was not Gabriel Crowther at birth.'

The silence in the room was like an act of violence. Crowther held himself absolutely still. The corner of the Squire's fat red mouth twisted a little.

'I am that which I appear to be, Mr Crowther. But there have been other chapters in my career, and some of the habits I learned, I have kept. I make it my business to know a little of the people of note in the area, beyond the usual gossip. But I shall not address you by any other name or rank than that you have chosen for yourself.' He paused. 'I can assure you that my enquiries have been discreet, and my silence on the subject is absolute – for the time being. To my knowledge at least, no one else within the county suspects you to be anything other than who or what you say you are. I will say no more, other than to repeat my request that you attempt to hold Mrs Westerman back, for her own sake.'

Crowther was conscious of little more than the passage of the air into his lungs and out again. He did not trust himself to speak. The

Squire sighed deeply and scratched again at his stubble before continuing in the same low voice.

'I am very fond of the family at Caveley Park, and would like to be assured they have protection and support from a man of intelligence and skill such as yourself.'

When Crowther finally spoke, his voice sounded to him like a thing apart. He had no will in it.

'As you say, there may be no great mystery here, but I will do all I can to support the family.'

The Squire lifted the wine and filled their glasses, smiling expansively as if he thought Crowther an excellent fellow and charming company. His voice lost its serious tone, and he became once again the expansive country gentleman he had at first appeared to be.

'Excellent, excellent. Now tell me, sir, is that your bay I noticed in the new stables as I came round? Do you hunt? She reminds me very much of a filly I had as a boy. Marvellous jumper, she was . . .'

Crowther let him talk and drank his wine, though it tasted to him suddenly bitter and black.

1.9

M R GRAVES HAD promised not to leave the house, and Mr and Mrs Chase and their daughter were happy to let him keep watch within calling distance of the old nursery where the children slept. He had taken them to that family's house, old friends of Alexander's, as soon as it was clear nothing could be done for his friend, and before he would allow anyone to see to his own wound. It stung now, but the pain was nothing next to the horrified throb in his throat. He wondered if Susan would ever recover. She had been white and silent since they found her, apart from the moment when he had pulled her away from her father's body again, and she had let out such a terrible yell that several in the crowd had crossed themselves. The yellow man was searched for, but no one could name him, and with the growing disorder in the town, there was not a man free to look further for him.

Miss Verity Chase stepped into the room, carrying a steaming glass.

'Do drink some of this, Mr Graves. It is my mother's restorative, and mostly brandy, I think. She and some of our neighbours have gone to see to Alexander and fetch clothes for the children. And you should know that their girl, Jane, came back with her mother as soon as news reached them. They will look after the shop. But then what will happen after that, Mr Graves? The children are orphans now. Do you know of any family that might take them? If not, we must hope their inheritance shall pay for some school or other, though if they are poor and without relatives to fight for them, their lives will be hard.'

Mr Graves passed his hand over his face, and Miss Chase felt suddenly like the worst sort of fool. She had spoken the first words that had come into her head, and had offered him worries to heap upon the horrors he was already victim to. She watched him holding the glass. Even his hands seemed suddenly older.

'I have little enough, nothing but what I can earn with my pen. It makes me a poor prospect, but I will always have a place for them. I hope you will also stay their friend.' She nodded. 'As to family . . . that may be difficult, but must be tried.'

He stretched out his long legs, then noticed with a pulse of horror that a little of his friend's blood was still visible, dried and dusty, on his shoes. He pulled himself straight again, and drank for want of anything else to do or say.

The brandy hit his stomach and glowed there briefly before the cold and dark of his body extinguished it again. Her presence was a comfort though. It had been in the past a torment and delight, ranked as he was in the legions of admirers; he had never before felt it as this. He glanced at her profile again then back at the glass in his hand before he continued.

'Alexander told me that he left his family when he married for love, but that his family is at least well to do, I think. He wondered if he had done the right thing, cutting the children off from their inheritance, but he seemed glad to have left the influence of his house. I doubt Adams was ever his name.'

Miss Chase looked shocked and serious. 'What is to be done then?'

Graves shifted awkwardly on his chair and looked around the room as if he might find answers posted on the fire irons or hanging from the bell pull.

'I shall go to the magistrate and the Coroner in the morning, then let us bury him under the name he chose. There is no more family to shift for him and his if we shall not.'

'You have no idea why Alexander was murdered in this way?'

She picked up her sewing from the table at her side as she asked the question and let a few moments pass. She found that her hands were still trembling too much for the fine work she had in front of her, so she let it lie on her lap again, and traced the emerging pattern with a fingertip. Graves frowned, and the wound on his face twisted painfully.

'I have no idea. I do not think it was cards, or women.' He held up his hands in miserable frustration. 'We may know more when Susan decides to speak, if she decides to do so. But I cannot question her.'

His voice struggled under the last words, and he felt more than heard Miss Chase's soft response: 'Of course.'

Her father came into the room and prevented Graves's attempt to stand with one fat hand.

'Don't you even think of getting up, boy. I've set up a truckle bed in the side room of the nursery. Not much comfort, but I thought the nearer you are to those children tonight, the easier you'll rest.'

'What news, Father?' Verity asked. Mr Chase looked worried and bit his nail. 'Don't bite your thumb, dear sir.'

The words were automatic, but she blushed to find herself correcting him this evening. Mr Chase did not seem to resent the comment, however.

'They say Lord Boston was dragged from his coach, but no one was hurt more than ripped clothing and injured pride. Half of the House seem to have lost their wigs though. All the great legislators of the land, struggling about with their fine coats in tatters and mewling like infants.' The thought amused him, and he struggled for a moment to maintain a proper gravity, but as his thoughts moved on his tone evened. 'Troops appeared at the House of Commons to guide them out again, but they cannot act against the crowd till the Riot Act is read and the magistrates are in hiding or besieged. An evil night this is, an evil night.'

Graves stirred himself and looked up into Mr Chase's broad face. 'Who then do we inform of Alexander's death? The proper authorities . . . He must be buried. The children.'

Mr Chase's paw tapped him gently on the shoulder again. 'Do as you can in the morning, Graves. But if I read it right, the law will be no help to you while this disorder lasts. Let us look to our own and bury him decently. There are enough of us to swear to what was done when this is passed and the law can turn to us again.'

Graves settled in his chair. 'Thank you, sir, for allowing me to stay near the children.'

'Dear boy, as if I'd send you away with your face in pieces and all of London, it seems, ready to fall to flames. And I was very glad you came to us. Speaks of a trust, boy, that I value. Your place is not fit for a family, I imagine, and they cannot stay in the shop. No, we must hugger mugger here, keep a watch on the children and an eye on those drunks and warriors staggering about outside.' He saw a look of alarm on his daughter's face. 'Briggs and Freeman have gone to fetch your mother home, my dear, and see poor Alexander is secure. I hear the crowd broke up a wine shop owned by some poor Catholic, so now they are drunk and hungry for whatever they can grab. A dark day it has been, and who knows what the morning will bring us.'

I.10

CROWTHER LEFT THE house after sitting with the ladies awhile, silently, as the Squire entertained them. He was aware that the current situation in America, and Commodore Westerman's part in it – crucial, apparently – had been much discussed, but he had not attempted to pay any close attention. He heard, however, the tone and temperature of the conversation and so learned that Commodore Westerman was loved and missed by his family.

His attention was directed to a portrait to the right of the fireplace. The Commodore looked very young to him, and pressingly vigorous. He wondered why Mrs Westerman kept the picture here in the formal salon, rather than in the room where most of her daily business was conducted. Perhaps she did not wish to be always under his eye. He watched her a little coldly in the candlelight – the flutter of her hands as she talked, the play of red in her hair as she gave enthusiastic agreement to some truism of the Squire's. He wondered how her manner would change if she knew of the conversation the men had just had. Her friendly reception of Bridges in her house looked suddenly like the worst sort of naivety. How could she see into the mess of murder if she thought this man was her friend? But he would not hold her back. The Squire had angered him, and in so doing had bound him tightly to the body in the stables.

Having taken his leave early and pleading a tiredness he no longer felt, Crowther let his horse walk at its own pace through the modest gates of Caveley, and turned the animal's steps back towards the village with the merest pressure of his knee against its flanks. The evening was beginning to darken, reluctantly, as if holding on to the pleasant sun of June as long as it possibly could.

He supposed that to an extent his system was recovering from the sudden shock that another man knew the secret of his identity. The sharp chill that had spread through his bones had faded, but he was left uneasy. The wall he had constructed between himself and his past, that had seemed so solid mere hours ago, had become weak and porous. It was true the Squire had no reason to expose him, not at the current moment at any rate, but if Bridges traded his way through life with information and politics, it might at sometime be worth more to him to expose Crowther, than to keep his knowledge to himself. And as Crowther knew he had no intention of withdrawing, or persuading Mrs Westerman to withdraw, that moment might come suddenly and soon.

Crowther was angry with himself. His secure existence seemed suddenly a sham. He had been building his self-respect on an illusion. And if the truth were generally known in the neighbourhood, what would the world then say? Would they condemn the women of Caveley for having had him in their house? He pulled his cloak up around his face, and let the horse walk on. Probably not, and it was unlikely that Mrs Westerman would care if they did. But her husband might think differently, and worse than that she herself might pity him, and he was not sure if he could stand her pity. He would become again merely a walking freak show. People would point him out on the street to tell his story to their neighbours. He would be shamed, tainted with more horrible stories than any of the Gothic fairy tales that were told of him and his butcher's knife today.

He should never have written that paper, but he had been flattered into it. He was proud, that was his difficulty. He sighed, and ran his hand through the black mane of his horse, testing its coarse texture against his hands. He had taken the identity of Gabriel Crowther more than twenty years ago, travelled with it, studied with it, corresponded and dealt under it, till he felt it become far more his own than that with which he was born. The week after his brother died he had put it on like a new skin and left England to study anatomy in Germany, so turning in his thirtieth year that which had been a casual interest of his youth into the reason and occupation of his waking hours. He had walked the hospital wards in that country and others. He could, and did, pay for the privilege without having to concern himself with examination boards and fighting for a paying position in any hospital. From the beginning his fellow students ignored him. Once they realised he was no threat to their chances of employment he ceased to be of interest. He was glad of it, feeling already too old and worn for their entertainments or friendships. His studies then took him to lecture halls all across Europe, studying the vessels of humanity watching them being opened up, learning to make the same – and further – investigations of flesh. He was not squeamish, nor sentimental. He had done his part for his masters, waiting to collect the bodies of the freshly damned from under the city gallows to dissect and study, and made use of what he had learned in order to develop his own theories and lines of enquiry. His knowledge earned the respect of his teachers even if his manners estranged them.

After ten years he had returned to London to study with John Hunter, a man of talent and energy for whom he had done some of his best work, though at the time he refused to take any credit for it. He remembered now as the summer scents drifted up to him from the hedgerows the strange specimens Hunter would pay a fortune to lay his hand – and then his knife – on: a crocodile brought all the way from the African coast alive in the hold of a merchant ship; a lion that Hunter had bought sagging with old age from a travelling menagerie. Both had shared his home a while. Crowther had flourished under the influence of the man's questing intelligence, his rough disposal of fools or knowledge untested. His grounds were always full of the strangest creatures in God's creation. As were perhaps his lecture halls.

Crowther himself had been drawn back again and again throughout the years to the marks that violent death leaves on a body. He had made observations and documented them, handing out his conclusions to the world in anonymous papers or in conversation and correspondence. Only once had he put the name of Crowther to a paper, that which had fallen into the hands of his neighbour. His remarks had been general, the specifics referring only to experiments conducted on animals, but when his colleagues had encouraged him to work deeper in the area, he had shrunk away. When his work was questioned, he had retreated rather than take his theories into the world. He wondered if Mrs Westerman had read those responses to his work, the ironic enquiries as to why Mr Crowther did not make use of the multiple murder victims London could offer, and the final punishing line that if ever a madman took it into his head to attack the city strays, Crowther would no doubt prove their avenging angel. His move to Hartswood and Laraby House had been an attempt to distance himself from that branch of his studies; to begin afresh on contributing to the growing knowledge of his age, some small but useful discoveries of fine detail. The attempt, it appeared, had failed. His work over the last year had not been good, and now here was another corpse.

Crowther looked about him at the deep silhouettes of shadows in the lane and, like an incantation, mouthed the old syllables of his lost name. They conjured the image of his father, his lands, his brother. He saw the faces and vistas of his youth and early adulthood, and felt them crowd about him. He had told himself they were lost and forgotten, yet he knew in truth, if he were as honest with himself as he claimed to be, that they had never left him for a moment in all these years. So, beyond his talent with eye and knife, this then was all he knew of himself: he was a man who had seen his brother hanged for the murder of their father. He was a man who had angrily, bitterly, pulled free of his brother's hands when the latter had protested his innocence and begged for help. In those deaths, in that action, his whole fate and being was bound. The rest was merely dressing and show.

Very well. Flight had finally proved impossible; he must turn about and look the world in the face again. He sighed and looked down at his hands. He had been twisting a loop of the reins so tightly round his fingers, he had driven the blood away and left them stiff and aching. He released them, and felt the warmth of circulation pricking again under his skin. He must risk living a little more in the world, and see how the world responded.

A shadow suddenly freed itself from the hedgerow some yards in front of him, and stood waiting for him in the road. Crowther felt himself pulled from his thoughts and back into the very present. Should the fellow try to rob and murder him, he would still at least have to thank him for taking him from his own preoccupations.

'Captain Thornleigh?' The voice was a loud whisper, impatient and nervous. Crowther kept his cloak high, felt his fear ease away and his curiosity awake, and rather than respond he brought his horse to a stop.

'You left me waiting, Captain. My servant will become nervous if I am gone all evening. I am sorry indeed that it did not come out right with Brook, but I must know what you will have me say tomorrow. I would not bring anything disagreeable to the Hall for all the world, but my mind is troubled, sir, troubled.'

The man stepped forward, and caught his first glimpse of Crowther's face. His own went white.

'My mistake, sir. I thought you came from the Hall. My apologies for disturbing your ride.' He looked down and stepped clear of the track. Crowther did not move, however, but continued to stare into the man's face. It was broad and pleasant enough. A well-preserved specimen of middle age, and middling means. Crowther felt a dim light of recognition spark in his brain.

'You run the draper's shop in the village.'

The man looked up again with a little reluctance, and a not entirely convincing smile. He continued to glance up and down the lane as he replied.

'I do, sir, I do. I sold the gloves you are wearing now, sir. I remember, as gentlemen normally come to buy their own, but your maid Betsy came in with an old pair, and we endeavoured to find a match in size and quality. I hope we managed to your satisfaction, sir.'

Crowther was aware of a slight reprimand in his tone. Aha, so he had offended this little man by not coming into the shop and discussing leathers and fits with him, had he? Indeed, villages were as complex to negotiate as the courts of Europe. He lifted his hand and looked at his glove in the fading light as if for the first time in his life. The man had good eyes to recognise his merchandise at this hour and distance. The shopkeeper did not like to be kept in suspense.

'I hope you find them a comfortable fit, sir?'

'Very, Mr . . .'

'Cartwright, sir, Joshua Cartwright. It is writ above the door of my shop.'

Crowther folded his hands across the reins, and watched Mr Joshua Cartwright's eyes skip right and left along the path.

'So it is, forgive me. And you are waiting for Mr Hugh Thornleigh?'

'Captain Thornleigh he is to me, sir. Always shall be. As you say, though I think I may have mistook the evening, so I shall head home now, begging your pardon. I do not like to leave the shop long. With the death of that man my maid will be worrying herself over me, and I don't want her coming out to search for me in the dark, sir. Wouldn't be right.'

'Indeed.' Crowther nodded, smiling his chilly smile.

'Good night then, sir.'

The shopkeeper stumbled a little, climbing over the stile under Crowther's suspiciously benign stare, and set off back towards the village with busy officious strides through the uncomplaining grass of the meadow. He turned back every other minute, as if hoping

Crowther might simply disappear, though without apparently slackening his pace, an impressive manoeuvre on uneven ground. Crowther remained mounted and still until the shopkeeper was lost in the gloom of the first cottages, then slid from his horse and led it behind the hedgerow, returning to assume Cartwright's position leaning on the low stile. He hoped he would not have to wait long.

He was lucky; the moon had shifted her position but little in the sky when Crowther heard someone moving down the road towards him. He stepped into the road, just as the man who had surprised him had done. A figure on horseback approached. When he spoke, Crowther knew him at once as Hugh Thornleigh.

'Joshua?' And when Crowther said nothing: 'Well, what will you have of me? Much good your assistance, or that of this Carter Brook, did me. We have nothing to speak on. Send me no more messages, but give your Hannah this coin at least – get her a salve for her sore feet. She must be exhausted, the number of times you've sent her tripping up to the Hall today.' The voice was fat and slurred; a gloved hand reached towards him. 'Well, take it then, Cartwright.'

Crowther stepped closer and lowered his cloak.

'You may keep your coin tonight, Mr Thornleigh. Joshua found it necessary to return to the shop. He seemed rather concerned, however, about what he should say to the Coroner tomorrow.'

Hugh was surprised enough to jerk at his reins, and his horse whinnied and shook her head in protest.

'Mr Crowther! You have a talent for coming up on my blind side. What do you mean, skulking around the bushes?'

'It is a pleasant evening. I have no reason to hurry home.'

'Aye! This is a coincidence, is it? You sent Joshua running away, did you? Damn it, what business is it of yours whom I choose to meet and where!'

Crowther opened his eyes innocently wide, and waited for Hugh to calm his ride before he replied.

'I think it may be a matter of more general interest at the moment, Mr Thornleigh. Who is Carter Brook, and in what way was he to assist you?'

'Again I ask, what business is it of yours? By what right do you, sir, question me?'

'In the cause of the general good, naturally.'

Hugh snorted, and Crowther stepped forward a little. 'And as I spent the better part of the day examining this Mr Brook's body, I would say my curiosity is therefore both right and natural in the circumstances.'

'Reaching, I call it. I have never met Mr Brook,' Thornleigh paused, and his voice became a little lower, 'though I was due to do so last night. I was prevented from keeping to the time of the appointment, but I did intend to meet him in the copse. When I managed to get there, no one was waiting, so I stayed till my coat was getting dew on it, then came home. It may well be *his* throat that was cut – though never having seen the man I could not say for sure. But I still see no reason to answer to you on that.'

'You may have to answer to a higher power than myself.'

'You a religious, Crowther? How does that square with cutting up bodies and leaving them all mangled?'

Crowther raised an eyebrow. 'I meant the Coroner.'

'I have every intention of telling the Coroner,' Hugh said irascibly. 'Cartwright has no reason to fuss at me. But, yes, it is likely that the body is that of Carter Brook.'

'You will also tell the Coroner the manner of your business with the man, I suppose?'

'He was employed to find out the address of my elder brother. I had hoped he had met with some success. The ring would seem to say as much, but whatever else he knew, he can no longer tell.'

Crowther plucked one of the white flowers free of the hedgerow next to him and stared into the darkness.

'Yes, he was very effectively prevented from sharing any secrets.'
Hugh looked down his nose at the elder man.

'You suggest his errand and his death were connected?' He laughed.
Crowther thought the similarity to the noise his horse had made
moments before, uncanny. 'No, Crowther, you are pursuing a false
trail there. I am simply a man cursed with the worst sort of luck in
the world, and any step forward I attempt will always send me sliding
backwards again. I dare say some other business followed him from
London.'

Crowther found he was uninterested in whatever conclusions Hugh
decided to draw.

'And why did you arrange to meet him at night, and away from
your home?'

'Perhaps I had hopes of it being a fine night,' Hugh said with a sneer.

'Could the shopkeeper, Mr Cartwright, identify the body?'

'I believe they knew one another. Joshua met him in London and
engaged him on my behalf. I will ask him to address himself to the
Coroner.'

Crowther nodded, and began to move away towards his horse.
Hugh raised his chin.

'You have been whipped up by the women of Caveley, I presume.'
Crowther could hear the edge in Thornleigh's voice. 'How exciting
for you. Go careful there, sir. A nasty, pushing family. Visit them
more than twice and it will be chanted through the neighbourhood
that you have made a bid for the hand of the little one. And the elder
is a shrew, and a bluestocking, everyone admits it. The Commodore
is likely very happy to have stowed her ashore and gone on his way
himself. Perhaps he finds women who know their place and duties a
little better away from home.'

Crowther turned back slowly towards the speaker, brushing the
remains of the flower he had plucked from his fingertips.

'I have heard that many disappointed men find comfort in wine

71

and slander. You give a thorough example of it. I wonder if your ill-luck caused you to become what I see, or if it was your behaviour that has brought the ill-luck upon you.'

The worst thing about these words, spoken so clearly into the evening air, was their lack of passion. An Earl could not have spoken more coldly of a dog. Crowther continued to watch Hugh as he smarted under them. Even in the relative darkness he could see the unmarred cheek of the young man flush indignantly.

'Do you wish me to ask you to name your friends?'

Crowther felt himself smile. This was what came of leaving the dissecting room, he thought – his secrets discovered, murder, duels, missing sons and dead children. He should have kept his doors locked more tightly.

'If you wish to fight, I shall certainly meet you, Thornleigh. Though I warn you, my hand is always steady at dawn. I doubt if you can say the same.'

They held each other's gaze a moment.

'Damn your eyes, Crowther,' Hugh whispered, jerking hard at his horse's head and he turned away, riding hard back towards Thornleigh.

Crowther led his own horse out into the lane again, and mounted with a grunt of effort. He looked up to see the first of the stars appearing above him. Well, he thought, we must follow where the signs lead us. As we follow the pathways of the body to their sources and springs, so this blood spilled must take us to the heart of the matter. He had already stepped clear of the path advised by the Squire. Now he must see where his steps took him, and if the family at Caveley had to pay for their curiosity, then so be it. They would be wiser for it, and Mrs Westerman seemed eager to be educated. He thought again of Hugh, his scarred face and dead eye, and wondered how much the devil had marked him for his own under that torn skin. The family at Caveley had liked him once, and yet now the Mistress seemed happy to see him killing himself with drink. Crowther urged his horse forward.

7 April 1775, Boston, Massachusetts Bay, America

C APTAIN HUGH THORNLEIGH of the 5th curled awkwardly over his writing desk and stared at the wall of his billet, trying to compose his thoughts.

He understood little of the complexities of the political situation of the colonies and cared less. The legal niceties of taxes and teas did not concern him. The Army had appealed to him as a career, not just because of the possibilities to give further glory to his ancestors' name, and create a comfortable life for himself independent of the family estate, but also because it knew how to use men of action like himself. He hoped he would one day lead armies rather than companies into battle, but he fully expected to leave the rationale for those battles to other men. He cared for those under his command, and was known as a fair commander. Ready with his fists, but as ready to laugh and knock the air from a man's lungs with a slap across the back. He needed only a wife to spoil and a son whom he could teach to shoot, to make himself content. Still, this letter to his father must be written. He began as follows:

My Lord,

I wish I had better news for you since our arrival in America. The situation of Boston is indeed pleasant – good, green, rolling country not unlike our own – so the provisions are plentiful and our men remain healthy and alert, for the most part, to their duty. There are some gentlemen in town with whom one would be happy to dine anywhere in the world, but the manners of the common sort show a strange lack of regard for rank. It is hard to put across. It is not the surliness of the London mob so much, but a rather more insidious habit of behaving as if we were all cut from the same stuff, if you take my meaning. By way of example – if eating outside the

*regiment, a fellow may serve you your food and sit down to conversation
as if you had both just come in from the fields together. This lack of
awareness of station and position in the ordinary sort of people must be
the root, I believe, of the mood of rebellion that approaches like a contagion
both from the countryside around us, and even within the town itself. The
people are arming, and though they are in no way proper soldiers, and any
but the largest force of them must be short work for a small company of
His Majesty's Own, they have begun to gather in great numbers and a
dark mood. We may have to slaughter a fair number of them before they
are willing to slink back to their farms. A sad state indeed, when the King's
subjects find themselves facing each other in such a situation.*

Thornleigh paused, and resumed staring at the wall again with a
worried frown till a voice called from his door.

'Thornleigh, drop your pen. No one can read a word you write
anyway. I am ordered to see how the hospital arrangements are being
managed. Will you come with me?'

Hugh turned towards the voice with a ready smile. It was his friend
Hawkshaw, so light and thin he seemed to have been wound together
out of odd bits of rope. Thornleigh unfolded himself from his round-
shouldered hunch over the letter, and placed on it his pen with the
awkward delicacy of a bear attempting to arrange roses for a drawing
room. Hawkshaw walked quickly across the room and peered over
his shoulder at the page.

'Did you never go to school, Thornleigh? My masters would have
whipped me to shreds for having such a horrible hand.'

Hugh grinned. 'Old Lobster Grimes beat my hands till they bled.
Funnily enough, it never made me write any better. I'll come to the
hospital with you, though I cannot let another packet sail without
reporting to my father. He likes to claim first-hand intelligence in the
House.'

Hawkshaw grimaced. 'Lord! Politics! Well, it may come to nothing

74

as yet. We must be all civility and neatness and keep our powder dry. In the meantime, let us enjoy the air a little and look at all these pretty green hills and roads like travellers till we must watch them like soldiers.'

'I did not come here to admire the country.'

Hawkshaw did not reply, but looked out of the window into the quiet streets of the town. The trees planted at intervals along the wide and pleasant streets gave the whole an air of peace and solidity. A woman, her maid following close behind her, was walking by. She blushed a little to see the officer watching her, then with a smile, she looked back down at the path in front of her.

'Ah, the fair ladies of this city,' he murmured. 'Yet she may slit my throat soon as lie with me, sell my pistols to the Minute Men and call herself a daughter of liberty.' He turned back towards Thornleigh with a crooked grin. 'Which is why I always visit the ladies of this town wearing my sword only, so as not to tempt their revolutionary fervour.' Hugh laughed. 'There are rumours that some of us may see action soon enough, Thornleigh. Talk of a march on Concord to relieve them of the arms we suspect are being collected there.'

Hugh snorted. 'Hardly an action. I have stolen apples from my neighbours' orchards with more risk to life and limb. These rebels are cowards and braggarts. As soon as they see a company of British soldiers drawn up in front of them, they shall hand over whatever we ask for.'

'I wish I had your confidence. They may not look like an army at the moment, but I think I see a determination in their eyes that could make any soldier cautious. Some of them fought in the last wars alongside us, remember. The reports of them were not all bad.'

'What good will determination do them against ball and bayonet and trained men? Determination doesn't render them bulletproof.'

'Nor us our red coats.'

'They are farmers! Hunters! If they can reload more than once in a minute I'll buy them all the tea and stamps they want myself.'

'If they fire straight with every shot,' Hawkshaw said quietly, 'they need not worry if they fire slow.'

Captain Thornleigh was not by nature a reflective personality, but his friend was. Indeed, the friendship that had grown up between the two Captains since Thornleigh had transferred to them had surprised many in the regiment. They were now known among the officers as the Bull and Whippet; if either man knew, they did not seem to mind it.

As they left the room, a breeze knocked the shutters against their frames, catching the curtains between them so the clack was muffled, like gunfire echoing across a body of water.

The building requisitioned for the hospital was a former warehouse situated on the wharf. The surgeon obviously saw their arrival as something of an imposition, and having greeted them briefly, turned to his nurses, both wives of Sergeants in the regiment, to further instruct them on the preparation of bandages, and asking the officers to direct any further questions to his assistant.

The young man he indicated stood up from his desk and approached them. He was well-made, dark in his colouring and moved with a certain grace. Hugh was reminded of the foxes on his estate. The impression was strengthened by the man's high cheekbones, the cautious assessment of them apparent in his dark eyes.

'I am Claver Wicksteed,' he introduced himself. 'You are Captains Thornleigh and Hawkshaw. Did the Colonel send you down to see how we get on?'

'He did.' Thornleigh was a little taken aback by the man's attitude. Wicksteed continued to watch him.

'And how *do* you get on?' Hawkshaw asked pointedly. 'Do you have all you require? You are new to this doctoring line, are you not?'

'Not sure if you could call it doctoring, sir, what I do. The surgeon said he needed more help and here I am. He saws and sews people up, I help hold them steady then write out the requisition for blades and needles. Would you like to see around the place?'

The Captains nodded and Wicksteed bowed. 'Very well. This room we have reserved for surgery. As you see, men can be brought in direct from the wharf, and there is space for seven at a time, we think.'

Hugh could not help feeling the man came a little too close, for comfort. He was as slender as Hawkshaw, but his movements seemed more sinuous. He held his hands together when he spoke, though the right would occasionally swim out to emphasise some point of the preparations made, only to be firmly clasped again by the left, as if it were a wayward animal in need of control. It seemed as though he was stirring the air between them into something more dense and difficult to breathe.

They made their way through a broad corridor into a larger space, hurrying to keep up with Wicksteed's brisk pace.

'In this main area we will keep most of the beds, and we have a store of straw laid in.' Again the right hand flew up to describe in the air a cartload. 'The space is the largest continuous one in the building, and of course we believe the high ceilings may provide a quantity of clean air, it being so beneficial in a sickroom, I am told.'

'It is indeed a large space, Wicksteed. I hope we may have no occasion to fill it,' Hawkshaw said. Wicksteed blinked at him, then shrugged.

'As you say. Though we are at present one of only two proper hospitals on the island, and there are a great many of us soldiers, sir, running about the place. And though we have been lucky to avoid great sickness so far, who knows what the summer may bring.'

'I presume, Wicksteed —' as Hugh began to speak, the man swung his whole body round to face him — 'that prisoners will be treated in Stone Gaol?'

'As you say. Who knows if these rebels are the sort to carry off their wounded with them, or leave them to us to deal with? There are family bonds between many of them, most likely, and shared blood can make a man carry his comrade farther than he should, I believe. The only family that has ever carried me anywhere has been the Army, and I've yet to see if it's taken me anywhere to my advantage. Any they leave behind will likely be beyond our help.'

'You like your work then, Wicksteed?' Hawkshaw asked after a pause.

The man shrugged again, and slouched against the wall. 'For the moment, Captain Hawkshaw. We must take the chances that come to us.'

Hugh was becoming bored. 'All is in good hands here, Hawkshaw. Shall we return and report?'

'I am with you, Thornleigh.'

Wicksteed's comments on blood ties had irritated Hugh out of his usual good humour. They itched as if the man's sharp white teeth had bitten him. Back in his own quarters he found himself thinking of his brother Alexander for the first time in years. They had hardly known each other, sent to separate establishments for young gentlemen soon after their mother had died, but Hugh had always been glad to see him. He was rather more bookish perhaps, than Hugh's chosen friends, but they dealt well enough together.

In the end Alexander had grown up under the protection of a family rather than in the dog eat dog world of thrashings and bad food that served for an education among the upper classes. He had removed himself from his own school before he was ten years old and declared he would live with a Mr Ariston-Grey in Chiswick. The man was a gentleman and musician. Their father had thought the idea ridiculous, but faced with Alexander's calm determination he had in the end relented. Or rather ceased to care about the matter and let his heir do what he would.

In that house Alexander had met his wife. He remained there until his majority, and then moved no further from them than into a neighbouring street, ignoring the fashions and habits of his own class, though his allowance was generous and unconditional. Hugh heard him speak of the lady only once, the last time the brothers were at the Hall together. They had ridden out to the northerly edge of Thornleigh's lands, and as they watched the light play across the expanses that were Alexander's to inherit along with the Earldom and all the pomp great position can bestow, he had told his brother simply that he had met the woman he would love to the end of his days and meant to marry her. Hugh had laughed at first, unused to such soft language spoken between men, but the serene, almost sympathetic smile his brother had given him in return had stopped the sound in his throat and made him serious.

'Is she suitable?' he asked.

'No,' Alexander smiled. 'She is perfect – but not suitable. I will speak to Lord Thornleigh, but I suspect he will cut me off. Very well. Elizabeth has inherited a little money, I have saved more from the allowance my father has made me, and my education has made it more possible for me to earn a living than many men of my class. We will take ourselves into London and see how we shift.'

'You will work?' Hugh asked, rather shocked.

'Yes! Many people do, you know. And I would rather have Elizabeth's love and work for it, than . . .' he lifted his hand and let it sketch out the landscape in front of him '. . . all of this.'

'How romantic!'

His brother reached into his coat pocket, producing a miniature in a silver case which he flipped open to show his brother. It revealed a remarkably pretty woman, smiling at the observer with wide blue eyes.

'I was standing behind the artist as he made his sketches. This is how she looks at me. Now, don't you think she is worth it?'

Hugh turned away from the little picture, saying, 'How could any woman be worth this sacrifice? And what do you mean to do when my father dies? Will you come and reclaim the estate then?'

Alexander frowned. 'I may be tempted to reappear, but I think not. When Lord Thornleigh dies, you may declare me dead and become an Earl yourself, for all I care.'

'Thank you.'

His brother tried to explain. 'I know you must think it odd, Hugh, but I have never found happiness here, except in your company perhaps. With Elizabeth I am happy every single day. That seems a greater gift than all the pomp and gilt my father bathes himself in.'

'I wish you well,' Hugh mumbled.

'Thank you. And Hugh, should you need me in years to come, you will find a way to discover me, I am sure. There are ties that bind us together, bonds of blood beyond titles and land. If you cannot free yourself, call for me, and I shall come to you in some way or other.'

Alexander clicked his tongue, and his horse shook its mane and started down the flank of the hill.

PART II

II.1

Saturday, 3 June 1780

HARRIET WESTERMAN'S DUTIES for the day started early.
Her destination was a narrow room in the upper corridor
at Caveley, where she knew from the moment daylight woke her,
Mrs Belinda Mortimer would be at work. Mrs Mortimer sewed for
several houses in the neighbourhood, spending from time to time two
or three days at each to deal with the linen and dresses of the ladies,
and doing whatever fine-work fashion and utility suggested to the
gentry. Fabrics were not cheap, and nothing that could be used again
or altered would be replaced by any but the most improvident. The
woman was no gossip, however, and Harriet knew she would not
be able to bully her into confessing the deeds and misdeeds of her
other clients. No one liked a servant who was known to talk intimately
of the families she visited, after all. She paused for a moment, reflecting
on this, before pushing open the door to the room reserved for Mrs
Mortimer's use.

She emerged almost an hour later, knowing a great deal more than
she had, despite Belinda's reticence, and having acquired a new stable
boy in the shape of Belinda's nephew. She folded Crowther's
handkerchief with its few threads back into the pocket of her skirt.

Harriet was slow to reach the breakfast room even though she did not pause to visit her son or baby girl that morning. Instead she took time to consider what she had learned, walking round the fruit garden to the east of her house. She was proud of the trees that flourished under her care, and found being among them soothing. The movement of the wind in the leaves reminded her of the sea, and when she closed her eyes she could almost call up the sounds of wind and wave making the timbers of a sailing boat shift and groan, almost catch the tang of salt in the air. But she was now a long way inland.

When she got into the hallway, she was told that Crowther had arrived, and was already at the breakfast table drinking chocolate with her sister. Harriet found them sat close together with Rachel's sketchbook open on the table between them. Rachel looked up as her sister entered.

'Harriet, Mr Crowther has been looking over my sketches of Mrs Heathcote's cat, and he thinks I have talent!'

She looked as smug as the cat in question, an animal Harriet had never warmed to.

'But he says I must understand the webbing of the animal's muscles to get it quite right, like Da Vinci! Next time he has a dead cat to dissect, he has promised I may go and watch. Isn't that good of him?'

Harriet raised her eyebrows. 'Charming, you unnatural beast.'

Rachel looked back down at her sketchbook, riffling through the pages, and gave a little shrug.

'I follow you in everything. And it was you who told me "we must not be afraid to know".'

Harriet took her coffee from the sideboard and sat down.

'I was quoting someone else – "*Aude sapere*" – and I recall he came to an unpleasant end. Still, there are worse words to live by.'

Crowther lifted an eyebrow. 'It was Horace and I believe he retired from more active business to run an estate. Many would consider him lucky.'

Harriet gave no sign of having heard him.

There was a moment of silence. Rachel looked from one to the other and rose with a sigh.

'Well, you have things to discuss, I imagine. So I will leave you. Harry, a note came from the Squire. It is there by your plate.'

'I see it. Details of when the inquest is to be, I suppose.'

She looked up at her sister's soft face. Rachel would make a good manager in a wealthy man's home, and look for no other satisfaction in her life than providing comfort for those she loved. Harriet felt a wave of affection for her sister, but was disturbed to find within that affection a breath of jealousy. She had fallen into the role that her sister was formed for, and felt herself wronged in it. The world gave its gifts, but its pains also often came wrapped in pretty papers.

Rachel let the door close behind her, and Harriet found Crowther observing her over the edge of the newspaper. He caught her eye and turned his attention back to the little items of horror and amusement that made up the *Daily Advertiser* till she was ready to talk to him.

'You seem to have been made a favourite,' Harriet remarked.

Crowther glanced up briefly. 'I'm honoured. But she might think me less her friend when I accuse the man whom she loves of murder.'

Harriet became very still.

'Though,' Crowther continued with the air of a man commenting on the weather, and folding the paper again, 'he is a stupid, brutish, unpleasant sort of man. He almost challenged me to a duel last night.'

Harriet turned swiftly, her lips parted in surprise, and knocked over her cup. Some of the coffee splashed on the tablecloth.

'Oh, damn! I've ruined yet more of the Commodore's linen.' She sprang up and dabbed at the stain with a napkin. It seemed to spread and darken. 'A duel, Crowther? What on earth are you talking about?' She picked up the napkin again, and used it to hide the stain, arranging it carefully as she went on, 'And as to any feelings Thornleigh once encouraged in my sister, I assure you . . .'

He put up his hand. 'Mrs Westerman. Please do not let me frighten you into trying to protect the reputation or conduct of your sister or yourself. I am sure it has been above reproach.'

There was a dryness in his tone that made Harriet uncomfortable. She tried to think what he had seen of them the previous day. A horrid image of herself appeared in front of her; her worst traits blown up and highly coloured, her motivations petty and foul.

'And now you think I wish to attack Thornleigh and the Hall as revenge for his jilting my sister?'

Her voice was crystalline. Crowther looked at her with surprise. Harriet noticed his cravat had been tied very sloppily, and there were crumbs of bread on his sleeve. She was sorry to find it did not make her feel any better.

'No, madam,' he said gently. 'I do not think that, though Hugh may suggest it to your neighbours at some point.' He sighed and shifted in his chair. 'Mrs Westerman, we both know any discussion of the relations between your sister and Mr Hugh Thornleigh between us is irregular, and I am well aware I am neither confidant nor counsellor to you. But not knowing these things leaves me more in the dark than ever. The Squire tried to persuade me last night to convince you to go no further into the concerns of Thornleigh Hall. It irritated me. But he promises matters will become unpleasant, and if you are too nice to speak to me of Hugh Thornleigh without worrying about your reputation, perhaps he is right, and you *had* better keep to household management.'

His voice had risen a little as he spoke. Harriet held up her hand without looking up from her napkin and nodded.

'I do trust you,' she said simply. 'And for some strange reason, I seem to value your good opinion.' Her fingers plucked at the tablecloth. 'I am not sure I behaved well. It is ridiculous, I like to tell myself I do not care what the world thinks of me. But I find it unpleasant to talk about these matters.'

'I very much doubt, Mrs Westerman, if anything you can say will alter the opinion I have of you.'

He said these words almost tenderly, and when Harriet looked up it was with a smile and a faint blush.

'Lord! That almost sounds like a challenge. Oh, very well. I will be as frank as I know how. And I am sorry to be so overly sensible.' She put her elbows on the table, and rested a cheek on one hand. As she talked, the fingers of the other tapped out an irregular rhythm on the stained tablecloth.

'Hugh came back from the war in America with the injury to his face and eye that you see. He had been away since before we purchased Caveley – indeed, it was only two months before, that we had met Lady Thornleigh. The family had not been in evidence at all until Lord Thornleigh's illness. I believe Hugh wished to continue to serve, since the injury did not stop him being a useful soldier, but when he heard of his father's illness, and that Alexander's whereabouts were still unknown, he thought it his duty to return home. It was the first time he met his stepmother, you know. She was a dancer before she became Lady Thornleigh, and only a year or two older than Hugh. They were not friendly. Still, I was glad he had come back, and he became a regular visitor here.'

Harriet looked up into the air to her left, and Crowther waited in silence for her to continue. 'Hugh was not then as he is now. A little prone to bluster perhaps, rather loud – but there was humour there and, I thought, a generosity of spirit that wanted only encouragement. He did not drink much more than other men, and though life at the Hall was not perfect, he seemed very happy to sit here with us, swapping war stories with me or listening to Rachel read.' She smiled briefly. 'She has a talent for it, you know. I should put her on the stage.'

Crowther returned her smile, then, leaning back in his chair with his fingers tented in front of him, he waited once more for her to continue.

'I say he seemed content enough, but he was still a troubled man. Hugh had black moods from time to time, and twice stood up in the middle of conversation with us and left the house without a word. I never did reason out the cause of those strange departures. We were talking the dullest of estate business on both occasions.'

Crowther stretched his fingers in front of him, apparently absorbed in contemplation of his short nails, and spoke to the air in front of his nose.

'You know better than most, I think, Mrs Westerman, that time in battle can do strange things to the spirits of the bravest men.'

She picked up a teaspoon from the tablecloth and spun it between her fingers.

'Just what I thought. So I did not worry over-much, and when I saw an affection growing between Mr Thornleigh and my sister, I thought it would be a help to him.' Her smile twisted a little. 'In fact, I congratulated myself that Rachel would be so soon and so well settled. I thought it was all but decided on, and that he was waiting only for the Commodore's next leave to ask to pay his addresses.'

'And then?'

'Then things began to change. This was about two years ago, so two years after he had returned to Thornleigh. He drank more, his moods became darker. Sometimes he seemed quite wild.' Crowther felt her regret, her sympathy for the man, flow from her. 'Then he arrived here one evening very drunk. Raving even.' Her mouth set in a line. 'I had David and William throw him down the steps. There were bitter words.'

'And your sister?'

'I suspect she tried to speak to him shortly afterwards, and he said . . . unpleasant things to her. She was desperately unhappy for some time.'

She let her forehead drop into her palm, and brought the teaspoon in her other hand down onto the table with a dull crack.

'I was a fool. I should not have let her be so friendly, but society here is so limited, and I truly believed he loved her. My husband calls me naive, and there have been times perhaps when I have not been such an asset to him in his career as I should have been.'

'An alliance with such a great family would have had its advantages.'

'James is a fine Commander. And as for Mr Hugh Thornleigh – yes, there was that, but also . . .' she began to twirl the spoon again, watching it pick up the sun flowing into the room, and throwing it up along the walls '. . . Crowther, I enjoyed his company. I think we both felt ourselves creatures out of their natural sphere.' She looked resigned, letting the reflection of the light hover over an Italianate landscape above the empty fireplace. 'I believe the business did our family's reputation some damage. But then my husband came home for some months in the summer and made us show our faces at every event and gathering within five miles. Rachel is so sweet-natured, anyone who meets her knows she is no schemer, and my husband is every inch the gentleman, and Hugh's behaviour continued so . . . Well, people began to talk of poor Rachel's lucky escape. And I was glad. He had made us very wretched.'

Crowther waited till she looked up and met his eye, and asked her kindly, 'Do you think there is any connection, any link between that change of behaviour and the events of yesterday?'

Harriet tilted her head to one side. 'Rachel is afraid she did something wrong, something that made Hugh cease to love her, and I wish I could make her easy on that point. She has not been happy since.'

'And yourself, perhaps, Mrs Westerman? You too would like to make yourself easy on that point?'

She did not reply, but nodded sadly. Crowther returned his gaze to his fingertips.

'Did anything else of significance occur at about that time?'

'His new steward, Wicksteed, arrived. I will tell you what I can of him.'

Crowther abandoned the study of his nails, and brushed some of the crumbs from his sleeve, having noticed them for the first time.

'Very well. I am content you are not a pair of scheming harridans. Before you tell me of this steward, however, shall I tell *you* about my conversation with the Squire and my meeting with Mr Hugh Thornleigh last night?'

Harriet gave a horrified laugh into what was left of her coffee, and still choking a little, waved her hand to encourage him to continue.

'Very well, I shall. But only on condition you stop playing with that spoon.'

She put it down very smartly and sat straight. The model of an attentive audience.

II.2

ALEXANDER WAS TO be buried in St Anne's churchyard, half a mile or so from his home. There were burial grounds far prettier, but it was here that his wife had been laid to rest, and Mr Graves believed that Alexander would not wish to be separated from her. Graves's first duty though was to reach the magistrate of the parish and find what the law could do to pursue the murderer of his friend. Morning had only just begun to stretch across the city before he was on his way, leaving the children in the care of Miss Chase. Susan was still silent, but more watchful than stunned now, and Jonathan repeatedly found himself caught by sudden waves of grief that seemed to lift and drop his little body at will.

It was not long before Graves came upon the signs of the previous night's work. The destruction of the Catholic Church in Golden Square shocked him. The ground was dotted with pages ripped from the hymn and prayer books, the words singed, wounded, fluttering. The smouldering remains of a bonfire brooded in the centre of the embarrassed-looking square of houses. He could see the bars of pews and other fittings of a church rearing within it like the blackened ribs of an animal caught in a forest fire. He paused for a second and a plain-looking man crossing the Square halted next to him.

'Shocking, isn't it, sir? Don't they know it's the same Bible we use?' He rubbed the stubble on his chin, and settled the linen bag of goods he carried more comfortably on his shoulder. 'How do you call yourself a defender of true religion and then burn down a church? That's what I want to know.'

Graves nodded sadly, then stepped back in slight alarm. Apparently out of the black and clinging ashes of the fire another man reared up, like a devil come to claim them from the ruins of the destroyed church; he staggered towards them, a damp blue cockade hanging from his hat and his back black with the soot of the fire, next to which he had presumably slept. Graves and his companion stood their ground as he weaved across the Square towards them, mistaking them for admirers of the handiwork of his crowd. He looked at them both, then leaning forward into Graves's face said with a leer, and with a broad wink, 'No popery!'

Graves recoiled at the stench of stale alcohol on his breath, and thrust the man away from him. The Protestant hero was still too out of himself to maintain his balance and tottered backwards, tripping over the remains of a burned cross at his feet and landing heavily on his arse.

Graves's companion laughed heartily and pointed at him. The man ignored him but fixed an angry eye on Graves.

'I'll have you for that, you Catholic bastard! I'll know you again, and I'll have you.'

He made no move to rise though, and Graves turned on his heel without bothering to reply and continued on his way. The journey was wasted, however. The Justice's house was besieged, and the mob would not let him through. Some of the rioters of the previous night had been taken up and were to be examined and confined to Newgate for trial. Through the crowd he could see the flash of redcoats. Soldiers on the steps to guard the gate.

'It's a matter of murder!' he protested. 'I must speak to the Justice!'

Some of those nearest to him turned enough to look him up and down.

'Will be murder, if they send those prisoners down. True Protestant heroes, every one.'

Graves tried to step forward, and was shoved back by a vicious-looking man twice his size.

'Get out of here, boy. Your business will wait.'

Graves made one more attempt and the same man twisted his arm hard behind him and whispered in his ear with horrible intimacy, 'Will your business be served better when this crowd has torn you all up to pieces? Get away, I say.'

Graves slunk back, only able to comfort himself with Mr Chase's words of the previous night, and went to make his arrangements with the priest of St Anne's. The man was sorrowful and kind, and confirmed the wisdom of letting Alexander be buried and turn to the Coroner when the city was calm again.

Graves returned briefly to his own lodgings – a room in one of the least disreputable houses in the vicinity of Seven Dials – to change his clothing, on which he at least could still see the marks of his friend's blood. As he changed his clothes, he paused a long moment before the pocked and dusty mirror. He no longer looked, he thought, like such a young man. His own wound was still fresh and livid, of course, but the real change was a heaviness in his eyes he did not recognise.

Owen Graves was only twenty-one. He had come down from the country three years before, from his father's home in the Cotswolds, determined to make a living in London with his pen. It had caused a breach with his family who, struggling to live like gentry on a clergyman's income, had hoped he might find advancement in the law. But Graves had been romantic. He had struggled to feed and clothe himself through those three years with the work of his pen, and though his work was often admired, it had yet to prove profitable.

He wrote best about music, offering his short reports of concerts to the various presses turning out papers to entertain and inform the capital, but the publishers often complained that though he wrote prettily, he had an unfortunate tendency to write more about the music itself and how it struck him, rather than give a list of any fashionable personages in attendance, and describe their manner of dress and behaviour. He often tried to combine the necessary with what he regarded as the essential by claiming that some darling of the *haut ton* was particularly captivated by a certain melody in a certain piece. The trick served him well enough, as those to whom he gifted this great musical sensibility seldom wanted to contradict him, and so he lived. Barely.

He had loved music since childhood. His mother had a beautiful soprano voice, though she had given up her own career as a singer to marry the man she loved and live in uncomfortable poverty. It was family legend that Mr Handel himself had said her leaving the stage was a waste, and a damn shame. His father would tell any new acquaintance the story with pride, but Graves noticed that his mother always seemed to wince when it was mentioned.

So Mr Graves arrived in town, and found Alexander at one of the first concerts he attended in the capital. He had been so engaged by the playing he could not resist sharing his pleasure with the gentleman next to him at the interval. He had chosen to praise a piece that was a favourite of that man's, and his opinion was listened to with appreciation.

Alexander, being a much older man than himself, had taken the place of a parent for him in those early months, encouraging and counselling the young man even while the grief from the loss of his wife Elizabeth was still raw. In return, Graves gave him his love and loyalty, his enthusiasm and quickness. Alexander's house had become a second home to him. The man's children were like the younger siblings he had never had; in their chatter he had found an escape from his own fears and failures, while in Alexander he had found a mentor who rewarded him with his trust and faith. Now he must earn what had been so freely given.

It took Graves a great effort of will to leave the house again. Before he left, he moved the loose pages of his writings around on the table top as a child spins buttercups in a pond, and wondered, without knowing why, when he might come back here, and what sort of man he might have become before he next lifted the latch.

Harriet did not feel any pleasure at the idea of calling on Lady Thornleigh that morning. It would look unusual, and she shrank a little from putting herself in a position where her behaviour could be questioned.

The purpose of the visit was unclear even in her own mind. She knew she wanted Crowther to see Thornleigh Hall, to see if he sensed there the same aura of corruption she felt, but it seemed a vague beginning to any thorough investigation of the circumstances that had brought the body to the copse on the hill. She said as much to Crowther when she proposed the visit, and was comforted to hear he thought it the right thing to do.

'In my work, Mrs Westerman,' he had said, 'we must often explore in a general fashion at first, till we have specifics with which to grapple. You have suspicions that are still out of reach of language. We must look about us with those sensations in mind, and see if we can put a little meat on the bones of our argument. As to the visit itself, perhaps the local gentry will at this point simply assume you are proud of drawing me out of my seclusion and are parading me about like a leopard on a chain.'

Harriet could not imagine comparing the spare and dry Crowther with a leopard, but the image made her laugh, and that gave her some courage.

It was a long time since the families had done more than exchange compliments via their servants. Rachel felt it her duty to join them, and while Harriet was glad of it for appearance's sake, she felt almost cruel sharing with Crowther what she had gleaned from the little sewing woman in the morning as they drove in the carriage towards the main gates of Thornleigh Hall. As she spoke, she glanced at the pale profile of her sister from time to time, but Rachel seemed determined only to examine the passing countryside and pretend, for the moment at least, not to hear them.

'Mrs Mortimer was quite enlightening in the end about the key personages in the Hall. The last steward of Thornleigh was known as a hard, but practical man. Not popular with the tenants, but a favourite of his master. Then, a little over two years ago, Claver Wicksteed appeared, out of the clear skies, it seemed, and Hugh announced his intention to make him steward. The former steward was bundled out of his place with enough to buy himself a little shop and left within a week, the hisses of the tenants ringing in his ears.'

Crowther turned towards her, one hand holding onto the edge of his seat as the carriage bounced a little on the dry roads.

'Is Wicksteed better liked?'

'No, not at all, and Mrs Mortimer suggested to me that his influence on his master seems . . . unhealthy.'

Crowther looked at her with a lift of his eyebrows. The timing of Wicksteed's arrival and Hugh's change in behaviour was not lost on them.

'She was not more specific? He takes on no more than the usual duties of a steward?' he asked.

Harriet shrugged. Crowther had always thought the gesture a little vulgar in women, but he was learning to allow Mrs Westerman any number of liberties.

'No, though of course in an estate of this size those are considerable enough. He manages the rents and repairs and no one sees Hugh on estate business any more. There was a period where he took a more active role in the management of the estate, but that time seems to have passed. Everything goes to Wicksteed and through Wicksteed – and Mr Thornleigh appears not to give a damn.'

'Strange he should not choose to lose himself in London then.'

Harriet nodded. 'I was surprised he did not leave again. I do not know – he seems restless, but has not visited the capital since Wicksteed arrived. Mrs Mortimer gave me the impression that Wicksteed has the upper hand in the relationship. I suspect that goes against her feelings of the proper order of things. The only people in the village who would speak well of Wicksteed are those young girls with whom he has had nothing to do.'

Crowther looked at her enquiringly.

'No, I mean no scandal. He has never been seen to court any local girl. Only that his looks have won him friends, but his manner of doing business is inclined to be vicious. He knows the benefits that bargaining for such an estate brings, and squeezes his advantage. I believe he takes pleasure in it.'

Crowther looked thoughtful. 'So Wicksteed and Mr Thornleigh had known each other before, we assume?'

'Yes. He told us, soon after Wicksteed arrived, that they had served together in the early days of the American Rebellion, though I never heard his name mentioned when Hugh spoke to us of his experiences previous to that, and I thought we could name every man in his regiment within a month of his coming home.'

Rachel turned from the window and looked at Crowther.

'I think the Americans are quite right to claim independence, don't you, Mr Crowther? Why should they not govern themselves? I think it a great shame my brother James has to serve in such a war.'

Her sister looked annoyed, and drew herself straight.

'My husband does his duty, Rachel.'

The younger woman put a hand out and patted her sister's knee as a mother might encourage a child.

'Of course, Harry. And I am very proud of him, and he does very well with prize money for the ships he takes. I do not like his orders, though.'

Both women radiated a calm certainty which Crowther found entertaining. They might express it in different ways, but they shared strong will as a characteristic, he noted. He wondered what their father had been like.

'You are a defender of liberty, Miss Trench.'

Crowther was rewarded with a smile.

'Yes. But if you have more unpleasant things to say about the Thornleigh family, say them now, Harry, for we are already in the park.'

Thornleigh Hall was first built by the second Earl some two hundred years before, but extensive improvements had been made over the generations to create an elegant and imposing building. Its wide, white-stoned frontage was full of high regular windows which reflected the open green parkland on which it stood. The west and east wings swept back at the same height as the frontage, suggesting a superfluity of apartments. It was designed to impress rather than welcome, and that it did. From the open lawns to the ornamental pools that framed the entrance, from the great doorway that could have swallowed their carriage whole to the innumerable chimney stacks that spoke of a city rather than the home of a single family, from the carved arms above the door to the intricate flourishes of stone below each window, it signalled wealth and power so assured it need never concern itself with anything so small as a single being crossing its threshold.

They sent their compliments to Lady Thornleigh from the carriage, and were invited to step in as quickly as could be hoped. Walking into the entrance hall, the sisters and the maid who was guiding them automatically paused for a moment to let Crowther absorb the grandeur of the place. Huge oils hung up the main stairway that reared in front of them and curled its back over their heads to reach the state rooms on the first floor. The pictures were mostly Biblical scenes of battle and sacrifice, mythical beasts being slain by heroes of almost satirical bodily perfection, accompanied by an array of worthies of the house, all displayed in full-length portraits and surrounded by their own personal signifiers of wealth, civilisation and dominion.

From the foot of the stairs Crowther could look up into the vault of the roof where a domed skylight allowed in sufficient light for him to admire the remarkable frescoes that spun out over the ceiling. Heaven, Hell and the family of Thornleigh crowded round the Christ Child as He sat in His mother's arms delivering judgement over creation from His position in the heart of Thornleigh Hall. No doubt the owners thought it the place He would have chosen from whence to judge.

When Harriet noticed where his attention was directed, she murmured, 'The ceiling was painted soon after the current Earl succeeded his father. That is the current Lord Thornleigh, by the Archangel Michael.'

Crowther looked to where she indicated. A handsome, long-faced man in ermine was shown ignoring the angel and his flaming sword just above him. While piously lifting his hands to the Christ Child, Lord Thornleigh was also glancing backwards towards the torments of the damned, if not with pleasure, then at least with complacency. The impression it made on Crowther was unpleasant.

At that moment, the maid obviously felt they had paused long enough.

'This way, madam.' As they followed her up the stairs, Crowther idly counted the liveried footmen standing to attention among the more valuable artworks they passed, but grew bored after reaching five and quickened his pace to keep up with the ladies.

The drawing room into which they were shown was an assault on the eye such that Crowther was afraid it might permanently damage his sight. The room was gold – exclusively, overpoweringly. The wallpaper was of golden *fleur de lys* embossed in velvet on a paler background, the curtains were looped and spun with heavy golden brocade, each chairback, carved into a profusion of cherubs, clouds and cornucopia, was gold; the portraits on the walls were lapped with heavy golden frames; the mantelpiece over the empty grate was studded with gold trinkets, with, in its centre a clock perhaps two feet high where robust golden shepherds and shepherdesses on golden hills prepared to ring the quarters on golden bells with little golden hammers.

The woman in the room stood among all this splendour like a single lily on a gem-encrusted altar. She was about Harriet's age and a little taller. When they entered, she was leaning among the curtains by one of the long windows that gave out over the front of the house. She turned as the maid announced them and looked at them for a long moment without speaking. Now this, Crowther thought to himself, is beauty.

Lady Thornleigh was dark-haired, with wide eyes and a full mouth, and the outline of her body, showing under the tight formal lacings of her gown, suggested a form to be worshipped. She was the model every artist would want for the Magdalene. A sensuality flowed from her that overpowered even the stench of gold.

Crowther felt his mouth become a little dry, and wondered if Lady Thornleigh always greeted her visitors standing, and began each visit with this moment of silence so they could admire and adjust to her presence among them.

'What an age you've been coming upstairs, Mrs Westerman. I am sure I saw you step out of your carriage ten minutes ago.'

Harriet moved forward into the room. 'We could not help pausing to let Mr Crowther see the paintings, my lady.'

'Ugh!' Lady Thornleigh gave a shudder. 'Horrid things, all that blood one has to see going downstairs every day. I wished for them to be taken down, but my son, Hugh, will have none of it. He calls it our heritage. Some heritage – I would prefer something rather more cheerful. I take my coffee in the upper salon now so I can avoid seeing them before breakfast.' She turned to look at Crowther. Her fine eyes ran him over and he felt as naked and helpless as a punished child.

'Lady Thornleigh, may I present Mr Gabriel Crowther?' Harriet said. 'He has been living in the Laraby House in the village.'

Crowther bowed, and Lady Thornleigh offered him a slight curtsy. Her movements were perfectly graceful, yet made with the minimum of effort. Crowther remembered her former profession was as a dancer. He wished he could have seen her perform.

'Yes, I recognise you. We sent our compliments when you arrived in the village.'

'I have been a slave to my studies, Lady Thornleigh.'

She looked at him again for a long moment, her smile mocking. The word 'slave' seemed to please her. She broke the moment with a sweep of her skirts.

'Well, let us sit down then. Miss Trench, always a pleasure, I'm sure.'

When Lady Thornleigh bothered with the ordinary civilities, she did so with such ill-disguised boredom, Crowther almost laughed. As they sat she leaned back her beautiful head and shouted for her footman at the same volume as a street-seller advertises her mackerel.

'Duncan!' The gold door opened again and a footman leaned in his elaborately powdered and wigged head.

'Tea.' The head nodded and withdrew. Lady Thornleigh stared at them again for a moment. 'Mr Crowther, do you like my drawing room? The Earl had it done for me by way of compliment when we married. He said it suited me. I took it as a great kindness before, but now I wonder if he was being funny.'

She yawned a little behind her hand. All Crowther could think of was a cat. The nature of the smile that hung on her red lips made him hope he was never the bird she chose for sport. He bowed a little. Harriet settled her skirts.

'I hope Lord Thornleigh continues comfortably, my lady?'

My lady leaned back her head to admire the golden ceiling as she replied, 'Oh, just the same. It is so dull – one marries a man for his wits then he loses them.' She looked at each of them in turn with a slow blink. 'He was entertaining company before I married him, you know. He always had the cleverest things to say about his friends and neighbours. What a shame he never met the ladies of Caveley Park before he fell ill.' Lady Thornleigh let this thought sit in the air a moment, then shifted her gaze towards Crowther. 'We were in London at first, you know. He used to promenade with me in the London parks, and all the dowager Duchesses would try to run away. He could make them be civil, of course. Everyone was frightened of him then. Now people just pity him.'

No one could think of a response to this. If Lady Thornleigh found the silence uncomfortable, she did not show it. She turned her focus to Rachel.

'Miss Trench, I must thank you for that preparation you sent us. It smells disgusting, you will admit, but the nurse tells me it has eased the inflammations Lord Thornleigh is prone to suffer on his skin.'

'During my father's last illness, it gave him some relief,' Rachel said softly.

Harriet looked at her sister in surprise. Lady Thornleigh noticed it and tilted her head to one side, her eyes wide.

'Did you not know your sister has turned apothecary, Mrs Westerman? You will hear soon enough how half of Hartswood is in love with her skin salves.' She turned back to Rachel and raised her hand to wag a finger at her. 'Though you should charge a full shilling, dearie − it is a mistake to sell it for only sixpence. People value things according to what they have paid for them. Charge them the shilling and they will tell everyone it is a wonder, for who wants to look a fool spending money on nonsense?'

After this moment of relative animation, Lady Thornleigh sat back in her chair again, watching Harriet's continuing surprise with real pleasure. She looked away again to examine the middle distance of the golden air.

'It is remarkable how little some people know about what is going on in their own house.' A hand lifted to her face and she bit her full lower lip a second, pulling on one dark ringlet. 'And it is not even a very big house.'

Crowther coughed.

The rituals of serving tea followed. Crowther noticed Harriet seemed a little at a loss in the presence of the Earl's wife. Her introduction of the subject of the body in the woods seemed almost clumsy.

'Is it not strange, Lady Thornleigh, that Viscount Hardew's ring was found on the corpse?'

Lady Thornleigh yawned. Even her hands were exceptionally well made, Crowther thought as she lifted one to her mouth before replying. It was always a matter of proportion; the length of the fingerbones compared with those webbing together to make the palm, the ratio of fat and muscle, and of course, the quality and properties of the skin.

'No doubt he found it in London, recognised the arms and was coming to the house to see if he could gain a reward from Hugh,' she said with a shrug. 'It is what *I* would have done.'

Harriet frowned briefly, then struggled on.

'How strange, also, to have had no news of Viscount Hardew for so long, and now the ring. He left the house before we came to Caveley, I believe. I do not think I have ever heard the detail of the case.'

'Have you not? Well, I always thought you above such a romance. I suppose we can pass the time telling the story again. It is almost funny when one considers it.'

Lady Thornleigh paused to reach for one of the dainty cakes provided with her tea, and nibbled at it with her small white teeth. It did not please her, so she replaced it with a little pout of disgust and picked up another from the plate to try instead. It was obviously an improvement as she kept it between her neat white fingers as she continued.

'Alexander fell in love with one of the family with which he was lodging. Some family in Chiswick with a funny name. Ah yes, Ariston-Grey. Sounds a trifle French to me. Musicians. A widowed father and his whelp. Alexander was mad for music, I am told. The old man died still fiddling away for his family's entertainment, though I'm sure my husband paid him enough for keeping Alexander all those years, so he can have had no need to spin out tunes to entertain.'

'Perhaps he did it for the love of the music, Lady Thornleigh,' Rachel suggested.

'If you say so, Miss Trench.' Lady Thornleigh looked at her a little amazed. 'I only ever had to do with music for my profession. No butcher slaughters animals for his own entertainment at the end of a day. Why should a fiddler play?' Rachel had no answer, so Lady Thornleigh continued. 'The funny thing is, the lady turned out to be so terribly virtuous he could not have her without marrying her. My husband was fearfully angry. Thought Alexander a ridiculous fool and said if he couldn't get a girl like that to be friendly without marriage, he was certainly not fit to run the estate, as he would be robbed at every turn. Alexander was a terribly upright sort, by all accounts, so before you could spit he was off out of the house and ready to marry the girl on the little scrap of money the fiddler left, and they've neither of them been heard of since.'

She ate a little more of the cake. 'I say funny because of course Lord Thornleigh was thought to be a little daring to marry me, but I think it was Alexander's priggishness and whining about the virtues of his intended that brought about the breach, more than the rather unequal nature of the match.'

She wiped the crumbs from her mouth and smiled her catlike smile. 'We have so much money that the Thornleigh men could all marry paupers for five generations and it would still be all thoroughbred horses and ices in July.' Her dark eyes drifted over Rachel's face. 'That is, if they really wished to do so.'

The rest of the visit was nothing but awkward banalities, and an attempt to discuss the weather which made Lady Thornleigh yawn so widely Crowther was afraid she was in danger of dislocating her elegant jaw. Her remarks had been unpleasant enough that he expected Rachel and Harriet to be very angry when they left, but they were oddly forgiving. He was surprised by their generosity.

'No one would receive her in town, even when Lord Thornleigh was well, for all her talk of scaring Duchesses,' Harriet said as the coach set off again.

Crowther remarked, 'But why did she not make more friends when her husband became ill? I would have thought she still had an acquaintance wide enough after a year of marriage that would be eager to spend his money.'

Rachel turned towards them from the window and smoothed her skirts.

'She has very little money of her own, as a matter of fact. And she must be resident wherever Lord Thornleigh is, to receive anything at all. The articles of the marriage contract were very strict. When Lord Thornleigh dies she will be guardian of their little boy and have charge of his money, though not much is settled on him direct. He gets everything at the discretion of the new Earl – Alexander, if he can be found. Hugh as well has only a little of his own. In her position, I think I would bundle up that horrible clock in a blanket and make a run for London, but she is probably too lazy.'

Miss Trench realised that both Crowther and Harriet were looking at her open-mouthed.

'Mr Thornleigh told me,' she said, with an air of slight defiance. 'And Harry, I did tell you I was making skin salves from Mama's old recipes. You just weren't listening.' She pouted a little. 'You would have noticed when you did the accounts for the next quarter, for I have made four pounds, as it happens.'

Harriet was amazed.

'You have surprised your sister into silence, Miss Trench. An achievement, I think.'

Rachel met Crowther's eye and smiled happily. He blinked his hooded eyes at her. 'Now, if you are interested in inflammations of the skin, I have some books I can lend to you. Not usually reading I would recommend to females, but if you find it interesting . . .'

Rachel looked very pleased. Crowther glanced out of the window for a moment, trying to avoid the cheerfulness in her smile defrosting his own bones too far into softness. He was just in time to see a figure standing under the great portico at the Hall. It was a man, slim, but as far as he could tell from this distance, well-formed. It was not Hugh Thornleigh, nor did he have the look of a servant about him. His hair was dark. The man watched their carriage retreat without moving. There was a stillness in his posture that Crowther found oddly disquieting.

II.3

'MAKE WAY THERE for the lady, please. Oi, Joe, move yerself and get a chair for Mrs Westerman, will you? I said, move yer arse, for the love of God! Pardon me, Mrs Westerman.'

The body had been moved from Caveley's stables to those of the inn during the course of the morning. The fifteen jurors, gathered up by the Constable from the customers of the Bear and Crown the previous evening, had had an opportunity to tut over it and look narrowly into the dead man's eyes, and now the jurors, Coroner, witnesses and the curious lookers-on were squeezing into the low, rough room in the back of the Bear and Crown.

Michaels, the landlord, was always insisting he was on the point of presenting a series of musical concerts and private dances there, but Harriet suspected he found it too convenient for the storage of salted pork and potato sacks during the winter to do anything of the sort. However, the polite fiction that renowned musicians were about to take the day's journey from London to entertain them was maintained throughout the neighbourhood, as there was a general agreement that even the rumour enhanced the reputation of the area.

Michaels was a huge man who had started his life on the London streets, and through his love of horses, luck and a good head for business had found himself in his forties a man of property and owner of a flourishing business. No one knew his first name, or even if he had one; his children, his friends and even his wife never used any other form of address to him. He was to be found every morning among the hubbub of his household – to his own offspring were often added cousins and nephews who were thought to be in need of his generosity and rough love – reading the newspapers and drinking his small beer. It was said that he was often appealed to, to arbitrate disputes in the village, and had been consistently found to be fair, and almost unnaturally incorruptible. Some of the villagers were worried that the Squire would not approve of this circumventing of his own authority as local Justice, but Harriet had long believed that Bridges and Michaels had an understanding of their own.

She was glad of his assistance now as Michaels pushed his way through the crowd and set a chair for her near to the table round which the jury were gathered. A fair proportion of the local inhabitants were there, though the county gentry, it seemed, had thought the affair below them, or had not yet heard of it, Harriet thought, looking around her and thinking that the village shops must mostly be closed this afternoon through want of their usual staff, owners and customers. Crowther followed in her wake and took up a position behind her. There were a few murmurs in the crowd as he was recognised, but if he was expecting any hostility he was wrong to do so. A man he thought he might know as the father of his maid grumbled something at him, and he found he was being presented with a chair of his own, and a not unfriendly nod.

He looked about him. On the opposite side of the room – it was arranged a little like a church with the jurors playing the bride, the corner the groom, and the observers seated or standing the length of the space like family and friends – he noticed Hugh. He was as usual looking somewhat dishevelled and uncomfortable. Crowther noticed he had so placed himself that most of the room would be hidden from him by the blindness in his right eye. On his left, leaning back a little in his chair, was the same lithe figure Crowther had spotted on the steps of Thornleigh Hall. His colouring was very dark and his features marked. He looked a little overdrawn, Crowther thought, to be regarded by most women as truly handsome. His cheekbones were a little too high, his chin rather too pronounced. Probably in his early thirties, so of an age with Mr Thornleigh, though a great deal better preserved. He reminded him of the slightly satirical drawings of great male actors he had seen in the *Illustrated News*. Even for a man as controlled in his movements as Crowther, this figure next to Hugh appeared strangely still. Yet his thin lips were moving; he was speaking to his master, and by the bend of his neck, Crowther could see Hugh was listening.

Crowther gave his companion a look of enquiry. She caught his eye and nodded swiftly. So this was Claver Wicksteed. There was a gloss to him, as if he had been polished. Crowther wondered if his pupils were white in a fawn iris, as if constructed out of thin mother-of-pearl veneer and maplewood. The man was prettily made, like a flashy piece of furniture for my lady's chamber, but Crowther doubted the craftsmanship. Hugh's face was set in a deep frown and he stared at the dusty floor to the side of his crossed ankles.

Crowther looked behind him and caught the cautious smile and nod of the Squire, who was conversing with a couple of middle-aged men Crowther assumed to be farmers. Turning his eyes to the front again, he saw Joshua Cartwright standing unhappily by the window. He spoke to no one, and continuously picked at the lint on his sleeve till Crowther was afraid his cuffs would be bald by the end of the session.

The Coroner looked about him, then stood and shushed the crowd.

The appeal for quiet was picked up and carried to the rear doors, where it was reinforced with a growl from Michaels. The air was still: the Coroner looked pleased with the effect.

Evidence was called, and questions asked. Harriet spoke of finding the body on her morning walk, her inspiration to fetch Crowther as well as the Squire, and sending to Hugh – and of Hugh's resolution that the body was not that of her brother. That gentleman had shifted in his chair a full quarter-turn to look at her as she spoke. His expression was still sullen.

Harriet's short narrative was received respectfully. The foreman of the jury thanked her on behalf of them all for her actions and courtesy in coming to speak with them. Crowther watched her as she spoke and noted an uncharacteristic shrinking in her demeanour, a tendency to look up at the Coroner and foreman from under her long eyelashes, hiding the green flash of her eyes, a mute appeal to the gentlemen to treat her kindly. They responded happily and there was an air of manly solicitude almost palpable in the air when she took her seat again. Only Hugh and Wicksteed did not, it seemed, take a proprietorial delight in looking at her.

As she sat down, Harriet shot Crowther a look of apology. He found he was impressed by the performance and could see the advantages and cover a little feminine reticence in such a company might give her, but he fancied she hated being anything other than what she naturally was, and pitied her that it was necessary. He wondered if women would ever be able to be themselves if they fell into such tricks, but having never known the dangers to which a frank woman might expose herself, he was disinclined to judge. His ruminations were broken by the sound of the Coroner calling his name.

Crowther was also listened to with respect, though he failed to win any affection from the room. He spoke of the wound, the likely time of the death and his investigations to try the soundness of the body's lower limbs. He had to be stopped from time to time to convert his naturally Latinate, scholarly language into something more easily digestible to the jury, and when he reported Hugh's remark that Alexander had had a bad leg due to a youthful injury, he was a little surprised to hear corroborating shouts from some of the men in the room of, 'True, true!' and, 'He did indeed, since he was seven!' and, 'His horse tripped in the warren on Blackamore Hill!' and, in a deep bass from somewhere near the door, 'Landed on him!' It was as if the village had agreed to be a chorus to the court, and Crowther had an uncomfortable sense of fellow feeling with the players at Drury Lane.

It seemed from the tone of questions and responses that the general opinion in the room was that of Lady Thornleigh: that this stranger had come among them looking for a reward for finding the ring, and had been destroyed by some business that had followed him from town. Therefore it was not surprising that when the Coroner called Joshua Cartwright forward, he did so with the air of a magician summoning a particularly large and impressive rabbit from under his shirt.

Joshua did have something of a rabbity air when he spoke, and had to be encouraged by the crowd to speak up from time to time. He agreed that the body was that of a man he knew, Carter Brook, whom he had asked on Hugh's behalf to try and discover any trace of his elder brother, Viscount Hardew.

The room was amazed, and the whispering rose and fell like a passing shower of rain. Some questions were asked as to Brook's family and situation, and Joshua shared with the jury, with the room at large at least, that to the best of his knowledge Brook had no family. He then engaged, as if by way of apology for bringing such a character into the neighbourhood, to write to Brook's landlady and let her know of what had passed, and inform her that she was free to dispose of the dead man's belongings and rent the room again. The Coroner agreed this was sensible, and offered Cartwright the opportunity to copy down his conclusions at the end of the day's business, and include any passages he thought fitting in the correspondence.

The chorus expressed satisfaction in a series of grunts and nods which spread from the observers to the jury and back again, reinforced like the ripples present on a small pond. More and more people were looking, and looking for longer, at the back of Hugh's head, however, and there was a general sigh of relief when he kicked back his chair and stood up. He addressed himself purely to the Coroner, but Crowther could tell by the flushed profile he presented that he was deeply aware of all the other eyes in the room.

'I wanted to know where my brother was, and assure him, whatever his situation, that I would be glad to know him again.' The room grumbled in an accepting sort of way. 'Good, good,' said the bass from the doorway. 'There's our good Captain,' said another. The Coroner looked seriously at the watchers and they quietened down. Crowther kept his eyes on Hugh, seeing a flick of pain cross his face at hearing his military title spoken aloud.

'Carter Brook wrote to me, saying he had information to give and that it was convenient for him to deliver it in person. I asked him to bring some proof of my brother, as I have been disappointed by false trails in the past.'

Whatever Hugh's misdemeanours, it seemed the village were still disposed to approve of him, as again the anonymous voices in the crowd chorused, 'True, true,' and, 'Cruel thing, cruel thing to lose a brother.' One thin voice lost among the jackets to the rear piped up. 'But a bloody careless thing to lose a son.' Hugh flushed a deeper red, though still did not turn, and Michaels swung his massive head towards the last speaker.

'I've told you before to keep your mouth shut when you aren't drinking, Baker.' There was a general laugh. 'And mind your damn language, there's a lady present.'

General agreement.

The Coroner waited, dignity personified, till the room was attentive again and motioned for Hugh to continue.

'I could not meet Brook at the time arranged, as Young Thorpe wanted to see me, and we talked for a while about the changes he is planning to introduce on the land he rents from me.' The crowd groaned and laughed, and Crowther noticed a young man shrinking into the side wall as if he wished to become a thing immaterial and pass through it, blushing and looking at his feet.

Harriet leaned over to Crowther and whispered, 'He's a bright boy, and his head is full of how to make improvements to the soil. But he has no idea when his conversation becomes tiresome. I think some of his ideas have increased my income by ten pounds a year, but I avoid him unless I am feeling particularly patient.'

Hugh waited for the noise to subside.

'So I was the best part of an hour late to meet with Brook.'

'You got off lightly!' came a voice from the back, and Young Thorpe looked very hard done by.

The Coroner turned to the crowd. 'May I remind you, gentlemen, we are discussing a murder?'

There was some shuffling of feet and a little solemnity returned to the room. The Coroner addressed Hugh again. 'I would like to know, sir, why you did not invite this man to wait on you at your house.'

Hugh looked a little embarrassed, and Crowther noticed Wicksteed's unblinking stare fixed on his back.

'I was afraid the information he might have would be delicate. That it might require some careful handling.' Hugh cleared his throat. 'Much as I trust my household, I did not wish to draw attention to my search, nor to what I might learn before I had had time to consider the implications.' It was interesting that there were no murmurs of approval or doubt in the room at this point, just a steady quiet that suggested judgement could go either way.

'And when you reached the place where you were due to meet . . . ?'

'There was no one there. I waited as long as I could, smoked a cigar, then went home. Next thing I knew, I was brought word a body had been found.'

The Coroner and jury all looked very grave. Hugh glanced about him as if planning to sit down. The Coroner held up his hand.

'Just one more thing, sir. Was the ring Brook brought with him very valuable?'

Hugh looked a little surprised. 'I can't say, sir. It is gold and heavy enough, I suppose. I have it here.' He felt in his pocket and tossed it across to the foreman of the jury. That man plucked it out of the air and he and his fellows bent over and peered at it with great intensity.

'What do you say, Wilton?' shouted Michaels from the middle of the room. 'Your uncle owns the silversmith in Pulborough, doesn't he?'

It seemed accepted by the crowd that this relation was enough to make Wilton, a tiny man with very greasy hair, an expert, so the ring was passed back to him and everyone waited in silence for him to pronounce.

'Two pound at least,' Wilton said with absolute authority. 'Even with the coat of arms scraped off.'

Everyone nodded very wisely, and the ring was passed back to the Coroner, who handed it back to Hugh with elaborate courtesy.

There was no room for the jury to retire as such, but they huddled in the furthest corner of the room for a while, and everyone agreed to appear not to look at them until they had done. Backs were turned and the crowd tried to talk as loudly as possible amongst themselves. A small boy, one of Michaels's offspring, Crowther reckoned, squeezed through the crowd with a glass of lemonade for Mrs Westerman. She gave him a huge smile which made him blush. As the crowd shifted round them, Harriet found the chance to put her hand out and touch Young Thorpe on the sleeve. He turned to her still looking guilty and rather shamed.

110

'Thorpe, I have been telling Mr Crowther here how your ideas must have made the estate ten pounds last year.'

The young man flushed with pleasure, and his back straightened.

'Thank you for that, Mrs Westerman. I'm sorry I delayed Mr Thornleigh, but *Wicksteed*' (he spat the name out) 'told me it would be a good moment to catch him. I know I can run on, but the thing I wanted to make clear to Mr Hugh was . . .' he was about to embark on what Crowther feared might be a very long explanation, when Harriet put her fingers to her lips.

'I think the jury has decided now, Thorpe. Look – the Coroner and foreman are in conversation.'

The young man nodded and smiled again before moving away, and Harriet turned in her chair to face the front again. Crowther leaned towards her.

'I thought you said no one takes estate business to Mr Thornleigh?'

'I did,' she agreed, 'but Young Thorpe can be persistent.'

Crowther looked at her, wondering how to describe the expression on her face. He settled on 'smug', then paid attention as the Coroner began to speak.

'My thanks to everyone who has spoken, and our thanks to the jury as well. We believe that this man was killed by someone planning to steal the ring, probably following Brook from London and taking advantage of his heading off somewhere secluded. We think Mr Hugh Thornleigh disturbed him, so he ran away before he could get it. The jury wish to say to Mr Thornleigh that they are very sorry he did not get to hear any news from Brook about his brother.'

There was a low rumble of agreement in the room; the jury looked a little conscious.

'I have our conclusions here, and if we are all agreed I shall write them up and you can sign them, gentlemen. I won't trouble to read the oath again: you all heard that well enough the first time, did you not?'

The jury variously nodded and waved the oath away. The Coroner looked about to see he had the attention of the room, then held out a document before him, bringing his arms in and pushing them away till he had the focus quite right, then read:

'"We, the jury, find as follows, that a person unknown, not having God before their eyes, but being seduced and moved by the instigation of the devil, in the woodland of Caveley Park and on the night of the first of June in the year of Our Lord 1780, delivered to Carter Brook, a stranger to this parish, a violent and fatal blow to the neck with a sharp instrument who then and there instantly died, and the said jurors upon their oath aforesaid further say, that the said person unknown, after he had committed the said felony and murder in the manner aforesaid, did fly away into the night against the peace of our said Lord the King, his crown and his dignity".'

The jury all nodded very solemnly and there was a satisfied sigh of agreement round the room. 'Good words,' said the bass by the door. 'Almost as good as church,' said another. The Coroner looked a little pink and putting down the paper, smiled up from his chair towards the tower of Michaels at the back of the crowd.

'Thirsty work, Michaels. Is the bar open?'

'Always got a drink for the King's servants, friend. And that stands for the jury men too. The rest of you are buying your own.'

The room began to empty very quickly.

II.4

THERE WAS A good crowd round the open grave. News of Alexander's death and burial had travelled from one side of the city to the other, judging by the variety of faces in the crowd. Even in such days of riot and discord, neighbour spoke to neighbour and the words flew up and out into the breeze, till it seemed one inhaled the latest news with the air itself. Alexander Adams had made good friends during his years in London, and had kept them. Almost every player from the Drury Lane Theatre had attended. Graves watched them huddle together a pace or two away, as if their long association cramped under the stage of that theatre had made it natural to them to bunch together even when the walls around them were removed.

Composers who had relied on Alexander to engrave and print their works had come too. Mr Paxton came over and tried to speak to Susan, but the words had died in his throat, and all he could do was put a hand, briefly, on her shoulder before quickly turning away and marching off among the tombstones with his polished cane glimmering in the sun.

It was a hot and surly day. The signs of riot from the previous night were all around them, and though the streets were quiet enough there was a tension in the air, an uneasy temper to the streets. A man slept across the gutter as they arrived at the churchyard, and had to be stepped around by the bearers. He wore a surplice tied around his hat, and he cradled in his drunken sleep a torn fur fragment as if it were his only love and care. The Constable of the parish, old and dirty, and careful of avoiding any attention from those who might demand his help defending their property from the mob, slunk along in their midst. He kept up a murmuring chant under his breath, 'Poor Mr Adams, poor Mr Adams. What times we live in,' until Graves, afraid that he would prove a strain to Susan, frowned him into embarrassment and silence.

Susan still said nothing, but Graves hoped she was returning a little to herself. He had offered her his hand as they met the body at the door of the shop without thinking, and without thinking she had taken it. Jonathan held her other hand, and he would not move unless he could feel Miss Chase close to him, so, unwieldy and awkward through the narrow streets, the foursome had walked behind the coffin as principal mourners.

Any questions about the death were answered by the common intelligence of the crowd, and Graves felt each pair of eyes tracing the wound on his face when they thought they might not be noticed. He wondered if he would scar. The wound was not deep, and Miss Chase was careful to make sure he kept it clean, though he often wondered if the water of London was of much aid to cleanliness.

The priest was waiting for them by the grave. The sun was even now at its high point, and he was suffering visibly in the heat. He puffed his cheeks, and sweat poured under his wig through the canyons of his red face, but he smiled at Susan, and bent his elderly knees to address Jonathan and whisper to them both a little about how the ceremony would unfold, and tell them their papa was comfortable in heaven before taking his place at the graveside and clearing his throat.

Before he began to speak, however, two carriages bearing variously the arms of the Earl of Cumberland and Viscount Carnathly drew up at the gates. The crowd noticed and murmured. Susan did not look up. Both peers were enthusiasts of music, and Alexander had corresponded with both, Graves knew, and regularly sent them samples of new work. It was a handsome compliment to send their carriages to stand sentinel at the gates.

Graves saw Susan eventually turn to look at them without emotion. Jonathan stared wide-eyed at the horses. They were handsome beasts. Graves hoped they would remain long enough to let the little boy get closer, and talk to the coachmen. He would give anything to put other images in that gentle, forming mind, than those he had been witness to the previous day. Graves felt he was observing all from a great distance and height. The gathered men and women solemnly shuffling through the funeral service, and the way Susan's hand contracted round his own as the first shovelful of earth skittered onto the lid of the coffin. He noticed an acquaintance, a Grub Street hack who wrote up news for the *Daily Advertiser* lurking at the back of the crowd. He looked as hungry and tired as Graves felt himself, and he could not condemn him as he quietly questioned one of Alexander's neighbours. The news-sheets must be fed, the curiosity of the nation satisfied. He looked up and caught Graves's eye with a look of enquiry, but Graves shook his head and with a nod the man retreated again.

The priest reached his 'Amens' and the crowd began to drift away from the graveside and leave the sexton to fill the hole behind them. Graves made no move himself, content to let Susan watch. He realised Miss Chase's thoughts were following a similar pattern to his own, however, regarding Jonathan. As soon as the crowd began to shift she led him quietly towards the horses. Graves watched as the coachmen greeted him. The little boy was lifted up onto the box and allowed to hold the reins, then taken down again to pat the noses of the leading pair of the Earl of Cumberland. Graves looked down at Susan, and saw she was watching her brother also. Her eyes and cheeks were wet with tears, and he could not help pulling her gently to his side. She wept a while longer into his coat, then took a great, shuddering sigh and opened her lips.

'Mr Graves?'

'Yes, Susan?'

'There is a box in the shop. Papa told me to look for it and keep it with me. I'm afraid I forgot it for a while.' Her voice was so dry and whispering, Graves could hardly hear her. 'May we go and fetch it? I remember where it is hidden. Papa said.'

'Of course, Susan.'

They walked through the last of the mourners, each of whom muttered their condolences and lifted their hats to the little girl, till they reached Miss Chase, and as Graves told her of their mission, Susan went across to her brother. The adults watched the children negotiate – Jonathan looked around him with wide eyes, alarmed at any separation, then seemed to grow calm under his sister's caresses and whispers. They saw her pause as if waiting for an answer, and watched Jonathan nod slowly. She then turned and came back to them, and with a composure that almost broke their hearts said, 'I am ready, Mr Graves. May we go?'

He bowed and offered her his arm.

II.5

MRS WESTERMAN, CROWTHER and Rachel were the only mourners at the burial of Carter Brook. When they arrived in the churchyard the sexton and his men were already shuffling the coffin into the open ground. As they crossed from the path to the church door to the graveside, there was a brief conversation between the men, and the youngest, only a boy really, put down his spade and ran swiftly to the vestry. Crowther smiled thinly as the boy returned a moment later with the vicar on his heels, adjusting his collar and trying to look as if he had meant to be there all along.

Crowther glanced at Miss Trench. It was at her insistence they were there at all. The strange sinuous current that spread news between the households, between the sexton's boy and the butcher's, which then found its way into Caveley Park with the beef shanks, meant that Rachel knew that the burial would take place that evening before Harriet and Crowther had even thought of it. When they had returned from the inquest, they found their late dinner already laid out and Rachel determined they should be quick about it as they would have to turn back into the village within the hour. Harriet had protested.

'Rachel, we must have some peace! And some time to talk about what has passed.' She looked up wide-eyed at her sister from the little sofa where she had dropped. 'Surely that is the best service we can render to Mr Brook — that we discover why he died and at whose hand. You don't think it was an unlucky thief, do you?'

Her sister's slim frame shone with all the moral conviction that eighteen years, and only eighteen years, can give.

'No. I wish I could, but no. But you can consider later, or tomorrow, Harriet. You too, Mr Crowther. This poor man will only be buried once, and I think someone should bear witness to that. Would you like to be put in the ground all alone and unmourned?'

'I doubt very much I'd care at that point.' Harriet saw she had lost the argument and abandoned her attempt at reasonable sweetness. She folded her arms and buried her chin in her chest. 'And how are we fit to mourn him, anyway? I only met the man when he was cold.'

Rachel clenched her hands, and looked in danger of stamping her foot.

'Harry, it is the right thing to do, and you know it. You are bearing witness to his death — very well, then bear witness to his funeral. Whatever sort of a man he was, he was one of God's creatures and deserves this courtesy from the rest of us.'

Harriet did not move — except, Crowther noted, to wrinkle her nose when God was mentioned. Rachel narrowed her eyes.

'If you do not come, I shall ask Mr Crowther to take me alone. Really, Harry, if you are going to be thinking about death all evening, you may as well do it in the peace of a churchyard.'

That made her sister laugh at least, and so it was agreed. Before their supper had time to settle in their stomachs they set off for the village again, this time on foot as Harriet felt the carriage would carry, along with themselves, altogether too much noticeable pomp for such a quiet visit.

Seeing the priest tumble out to the graveside, Harriet was glad her sister had bullied her, and it *was* a good place to think about death. She had not been surprised by the verdict of the Coroner, although she wondered how many of the villagers truly believed it. It had been a very convenient conclusion: plausible enough if one could swallow the notion of robbers pursuing each other in leisurely fashion over a day's ride for the sake of a ring. For a moment she considered the option of believing it herself. She could then put on the self-satisfied smile of a country matron, play with the baby and go about seeing only what was in front of her, like her sister. She frowned quickly, knowing the characterisation was untrue and unfair, and angry with herself for thinking it. The priest caught the expression and looked momentarily confused, checking his prayer book to be sure the fiery Mrs Westerman had not found him out in some mistake. Reassured, he read on.

Harriet looked across at her sister. She was not self-satisfied in the least, and knew more than Harriet about the pressures and secrets of life in the country. The trouble with Rachel was, she was actually good. It gave her a patience and moral certainty her sister sometimes envied, and sometimes found almost unbearable. When they had finished their prayers, Rachel gave her hand to the priest with a smile that made him look comically proud. Harriet and Crowther made their bows and the little party moved away back onto the road to Caveley, each travelling in their own thoughts to various destinations.

They had not gone far when they saw the figure of a man ahead of them. The evening was still bright enough to see, before they had approached much further, that it was Hugh Thornleigh. Crowther felt more than saw the slight falter in Rachel's steps, and from the corner of his eye observed her chin lift in determination. What torture it must be, he thought, to live always in the presence of disappointed love. He wondered why Harriet had not taken her sister away. Perhaps it was Rachel's own decision to face her demons daily. It would not be Crowther's recommendation for an easy mind, no matter what the habits of industry and religion did to ease her.

Hugh became conscious of their presence and turned. They exchanged bows.

'I came to see Brook buried,' he told them. 'Thought someone should, and Cartwright wouldn't. Not very happy to be associated with such types as it is. Then I saw you, and thought I wouldn't bother. It was good of you to go. Like you. Well. Good evening.'

There was no doubt in anyone's mind that these words were meant for Rachel, but all maintained the polite pretence that the remarks were general. Harriet cleared her throat as if to begin speaking, though she had no idea at that moment what could be said, when she was saved by a shout from the rising slope behind them on the edge of the park of Thornleigh Hall. A boy was running down the slope towards them, his rough jacket flying out behind him and his feet slipping over the long grass.

'Mr Thornleigh, Mr Thornleigh, come quick, sir!'

'What is it?'

The boy tumbled to a halt beside them. He was very pale.

'Nurse Bray! In the witch's cottage.'

He turned and ran back the way he had come. Crowther looked at Harriet. She was already picking up her skirts to set off after the boy. She said tersely, 'It's an old keeper's cottage on the edge of the wood.'

She began to head up the slope, Crowther, Rachel and Hugh all following. Behind the trees at the top of the rise Crowther got his first sight of the broken-up little house. It was indeed suitable for witches, if your imagination were that way inclined. Its walls and ceiling were punctured and cloaked by trees, and its remaining stonework covered in ivy. The wide door was ajar, hanging with horrible determination by the last of its hinges. The party by a common consent came to a halt in the lee of the wall. The little boy pointed in through the doorway, the whiteness of his skin making the dirt on his face stand out. He looked like a sentimental allegory of the pastoral and picturesque. They stepped forward, Hugh leading the way, their eyes struggling to make sense of the patterns of light and dark in the interior. Rachel suddenly screamed and turned into Harriet's arms. The latter held her, looking past her sister's buried head into the depths with wide eyes. The two men paused as if caught by the withdrawing motion of a great wave.

A woman's body was hanging from one of the low beams that ran over their heads. Her face was dark, her tongue forced out between her teeth. Her feet brushed the air only inches above the stone floor, and with a creak of wood and hemp her body still turned slightly in the vague breeze of the evening. The motion brought her face to face with them. Harriet knew that face, distorted as it was. Nurse Bray, one of the staff at Thornleigh who had arrived like a gift from God soon after the illness of Lord Thornleigh; she had cared for him ever since. Harriet turned away a little, keeping Rachel shielded. She squeezed her eyes shut, very hard, and waited for her heartbeat to slow.

'We must get her down. Is that barrel still sound?' Crowther's voice.

There was a hollow hammer of a gentleman's boot on wood as the barrel was kicked and tried, then a scrape of wood on stone as someone dragged it across the floor.

'Mr Thornleigh, do you carry a knife?'

There was a pause, the snap of an opening blade, then a horrid sawing of rope. Harriet remembered the sounds of the sick room during battle; under the curses and groans and explosions it seemed one could always hear the rasp of the surgeon's saw on bone. There was a snap as the rope gave, a grunt of effort from Hugh as he took the weight, and a sigh as he placed the body on the ground.

'She is dead?' Hugh's voice now.

'Oh, yes.' Crowther's dry response.

Harriet opened her eyes. Crowther was kneeling beside the body, Hugh standing to one side.

'Damn!'

Hugh's curse echoed in the empty ruin, and like the report of a gun it disturbed the crows roosting in the woods around them. They flew up from their nests with angry shouting echoes. Rachel flinched, then pulled herself free from her sister's arm. Keeping her eyes carefully averted from where the body lay, she walked straightbacked to the doorway. Harriet turned to watch her speaking to the boy.

'What's your name?'

'Jack.'

'We must stay outside, Jack.' She put out her hand and the lad fitted his dirty fingers into her black glove and allowed himself to be led out into the fading light.

Harriet leaned her back against the roughly rendered wall and observed Crowther while she calmed herself. He was running his eyes over the body as if he were reading a text. He lifted his hand to move the folds of cloak and rope at the nurse's neck, and then looked up at Harriet. She understood his meaning.

'Mr Thornleigh, perhaps you will be so good as to go and fetch your people? This body at any rate is most decidedly your business.'

Hugh shot her an angry look and strode out of the door. As soon as Harriet heard his steps fading outside she moved across the open space and crouched down opposite Crowther. He looked at her.

'Making him angry certainly made him leave faster. But I'm afraid he'll walk much more quickly now.'

She smiled up at him briefly in return, then gestured towards the doorway just beyond which Rachel and the boy were waiting, and lifted a finger to her lips. Crowther nodded.

He looked back to the body, and lifted the nurse's right wrist with a sudden frown. It was deeply bruised where the radial artery was buried under the soft flesh on the underside of the wrist, and spotted with blood under the skin at the sides where the bones of the arm were tied onto the delicate bones of the hand. The body moved easily; she had not been dead longer than a couple of hours. Harriet had removed her gloves and tucked them into her gown, and having seen what he had noticed, took up the nurse's left hand. Here the bruising was most brutal across the top of the wrist. She lifted it to her eyes, and ran a fingertip over the impressions. She teased something up onto her fingernail then presented it to Crowther. He looked. A fibre. She laid the hand gently down again and stretched her own

121

arms out across the body, crossing them, one on top of the other at the wrist.

'Rope,' she mouthed silently.

Crowther felt a coldness swim through his stomach despite the warmth of the evening. He looked closely again at the nurse's right hand, flexing the dead fingers as an idle man might play with his beloved's hand on a drawing-room sofa. One fingernail was broken, and three were clogged with skin, and a little blood. He looked up to check Harriet was observing, and understood what she saw. Her jaw was set, and her body was all attention. Crowther laid down the hand, and as if of one mind they looked up to the horribly distorted face.

'I shall cut away the rope at the neck,' Crowther said very quietly, and did so, revealing the horrid purple where it had pressed against her throat till she was choked.

He felt with his long fingers for the vertebrae at the back of the neck. They had not broken. She had died from lack of air. It was not a gentle death. Crowther remembered his occasional duties for his professors waiting under the gallows, hoping to claim the body for dissection with the aid of a number of bribes and the assistance of a few men hired to hold back the mob. He had observed both quick and slow deaths from hanging. If the fall did not break the unfortunate's neck, sometimes their friends would rush under the scaffold and cling onto their legs, pulling down with all their weight, so the final agonies would come as quickly as could be managed. He had seen mothers dragging down their sons' feet in that way, killing them quickly being the last service they could render to their children. It was the noise that was most unpleasant; the struggle of air gargling uselessly in the closed bowl of the throat, the swish of the legs kicking out like a puppet show, the dance in the air. He wondered if anyone had held the nurse's legs to shorten her agony.

Harriet, very tenderly, began to feel the back of the nurse's head. She remembered doing the same for a midshipman of her husband in their last cruise together. The surgeon had just removed the boy's leg below the knee, but it was the splinter that Harriet found embedded in the back of the skull, and hidden under his thick black hair, that had done for him. Even as the memory bubbled and fell back in her mind she felt a change of texture in the nurse's scalp, a mass on the back of the skull. She brought up her hand, dirty with blood not yet fully dry, and showed it to Crowther. He too felt the place on the scalp, then ran his hand lightly over the rest of the body, but could find nothing of significance.

He stood and examined the beam above them, the curl of rope over it now looking innocent enough. Harriet stood next to him, trying to clean her hand with her handkerchief. It was too delicate an object for the task. Crowther heard her mild curse, and handed her his own without comment. She worked the stuff off her palm and put her gloves back on, before handing the handkerchief back with a sorry shake of her head. When she spoke, the lowness of her voice made him realise she was still very conscious of the potential listeners outside.

'I did not notice where the barrel was when we came in.'

He wondered if he should still be surprised that their thoughts tended to travel down the same path in these circumstances.

'I was trying to recall. Over there.' He indicated the left-hand wall. 'And it was on its side, so it could have rolled there when Nurse Bray kicked it away.'

She looked at him with an eyebrow raised.

'No, Mrs Westerman, I have not gone mad. This woman was murdered. But I am thinking how a jury might twist it into suicide.'

'Harry?' It was Rachel just beyond the doorway, trying to find her sister in the gloom without having to see the body. Crowther saw Harriet glance down at her glove quickly and pull it further over her wrist before she responded.

'Yes, Rachel?'

'There is something out here. Someone has set a fire and it is still warm. There seems to be something in it . . .'

Before Rachel had a chance to complete the sentence Harriet and Crowther were sweeping by her. She pointed a little way into the wood past the boy Jack, and just off the path that ran in front of the ruined cottage. There was a fresh pile of ash on the bare earth of the floor, containing several charred fragments of wood kindling and the suspicious pale ash of burned paper. Crowther lowered his palm. It was the faintest memory of heat, but it was there. Harriet gently poked at the ash with a thin twig.

'I can't see anything written,' she said.

Crowther poked Hugh's knife deeper into the ash, and found at its tip a slightly larger scrap that had survived the flames. Both sides were written on; it seemed to be the bottom corner of a sheet of paper.

'Letters. I am sure of it.' He pointed to another scrap where the word *Hall* could just be read. Harriet did not respond. She was looking down at his hands with an expression of horror. His glance followed hers. The knife he held was darkly stained. He started.

'Hugh's?' she hissed.

He nodded. Rachel called them.

'Have you found something, Harriet?'

Mrs Westerman stood very quickly, blocking Crowther's slow examination of the knife from the view of her sister.

'Letters. But all burned up.'

Jack looked up from the small section of forest floor he had been studying.

'Nurse Bray was always very pleased to get letters,' he said.

Harriet felt excitement rise in her throat. She stepped over very carefully to the boy, and knelt beside him.

'Who was it wrote her letters, Jack?'

The boy looked a little overawed, and glanced up at Rachel. She smiled down at him, and that seemed to make him braver.

'London. She was very private about them though. Others thought she was a bit stuck up, 'specially after a letter had come. We used to say she wouldn't see fit to know us for a day or two after a letter came, and she never said what was in them. Rest of the time she was all right, though. Used to buy sugar treats sometimes on her day off, and shared them about easily enough.' The boy's lip trembled suddenly. 'I won't have to look after His Lordship now, will I? Now she's dead? I don't like him.'

Rachel crouched and put an arm round his painfully thin shoulders. 'Why don't you like him, Jack?'

The boy looked into her face round-eyed. 'He makes horrid noises, miss. Like this.'

He moaned suddenly, letting his mouth drop open and his head fall forward and rock from side to side. Harriet recoiled slightly.

They were spared having to answer by the sound of footsteps on the path. Hugh came towards them flanked by two of his outside servants. One carried a horse blanket over his shoulder. Harriet stood up and turned to look at Crowther. He was still standing by the fire with Hugh's knife in his hand.

Hugh pointed his men into the cottage and approached them. Crowther spoke to him.

'You hunt, Mr Thornleigh? Much sport recently?'

His voice was very cold. 'I do. And yes, the sport has been good.'

Crowther held the knife out towards him. Thornleigh stepped forward to take it, and as he gripped hold of the handle, he saw the blade and sucked in his breath.

'What have you been doing with it? I never leave my knife dirty!'

'Perhaps,' Crowther said with dry precision, 'your mind was on other matters. I have done nothing with the knife other than cut the rope that held Nurse Bray. It is blood on the blade. But I think it likely the blood is a day or two old.'

Hugh turned very white. It made the angry blur of his scar all the more violently red.

'Some rabbit or hare, probably. I must have forgotten to wipe it.'

Crowther met his eyes. 'Some innocent creature, I am sure.'

Hugh balled his fists, and Crowther felt himself relaxing his muscles to dodge or take a blow, but Hugh controlled himself.

'I shall take care of Nurse Bray now. I would thank you to leave my lands.'

Crowther bowed very low. Harriet carefully took her sister's arm. She could feel it trembling under her own, and turned over her shoulder to look at her neighbour.

'Your father's lands, I think, Mr Thornleigh. Do you not only hold them in trust in hopes of your brother's return?'

Hugh bowed without speaking, and with Crowther following the two sisters began to walk away with dignified calm. Harriet could feel Thornleigh's angry gaze on them as they went.

'Harry, does this mean you think that Hugh . . .' Her sister's voice was a deep whisper. Harriet squeezed Rachel's arm close to her body and shushed her.

II.6

THEY TURNED INTO Holland Street and the road narrowed. Their footsteps slowed, and Graves was not sure whose reluctance held them back. The streets were very quiet for a Saturday; hawkers were few and called out their wares almost softly. It did not seem healthy or right, but if that was the atmosphere of the street, or the heavy dark Graves carried with him, he could not say. There were enough people looking from their windows, or standing at the doorways, however, for their approach to be noticed.

Apprentices and servants from the houses near Alexander's own appeared in the doorways as they passed. The cook from the wig maker came up to them, and pressed a napkin of gingerbread into Susan's hand, 'for little Master Adams'. Susan looked at her blank faced and took the package with a little nod. She had grown up fearing this woman, huge and apparently always covered in flour, ever since she had been caught trying on one of the legal wigs the shop made and sentencing the other children in the street to terrible punishments. She said thank you, and the cook turned away to wipe her eyes on her apron.

They managed only a few steps more before Susan was stopped by a hesitant female hand on her shoulder. The thin, birdlike face of Mrs Service was bending towards her. The bones of her neck stuck out, and her wrists were no thicker than Susan's. She was a widow, starving in genteel poverty in a single room opposite the shop. People took her little bits of sewing from time to time, though it was known she was not particularly skilful, and the work was given more out of charity than any other cause. Susan thought Mrs Service knew this, and it made her sorry for her. She would always have her window open when Susan was practising. Sometimes she could see her leaning out of the window a little, straining to hear over the sounds of the street. Susan would try and play more loudly, impossible of course, but in her heart she sent the music across to her audience.

Looking a little flustered, Mrs Service held out a small cameo brooch of fruits and flowers in front of her, and said in a rush, 'I wanted to give you this at the service, but there were so many people.' Her tired eyes looked to Graves, and Susan, then to the ground again. 'Your father once admired it. It would give me great pleasure to know you had it, and might wear it from time to time. I've liked hearing you play so much.' Her voice cracked a little.

Susan took the brooch. 'It's very pretty.'

Mrs Service began to cry, and turned away from them.

Jane was waiting for them at the door to the shop, and held her arms out. Susan gave a little sob and broke free from Mr Graves to run to her and bury herself in her apron. Graves stepped hurriedly after her, then looked into the room as discreetly as he could. Jane caught where he was looking and nodded. The floorboards were scrubbed white. Susan straightened herself, squeezed Jane's hand in her own, then turned into the shop ahead of them.

'What's going to happen, Mr Graves?' the young maid asked.

Graves looked at the dust and muck on his shoes and shrugged. 'I have no idea. I hope there may be a will. Are you owed?'

Jane waved him away. 'I was paid two days ago, sir. Mr Adams was always most punctual.'

Jane was still a young woman, hardly out of her teens, but there was an air of sense and goodwill about her that made Graves feel a little hopeful. She was a thin girl, but straight and wiry.

'Can you keep an eye on the shop and house a while?' he asked. 'Till we settle what should be done?'

Jane stood considering, and having decided, dusted her hands on her apron and looked him in the eye.

'I've been wondering if you might ask that, and what answer I should give you, so here it is. I'd be happy to. But do you think I might have my mother along with me? I don't like to be here on my own, nor do I want to leave her alone at the moment.' She touched her hand to her head to suggest the blue cockades the rioters of the previous day had been wearing when they burned the Catholic Chapel in Duke Street and Golden Square. 'She is willing,' Jane added. 'She is visiting a friend in Soho Square till I send her word.'

'Perhaps we should ask Susan.'

But when they entered the shop, Susan was nowhere to be seen. A sudden spasm of alarm caught Graves in the throat and he shouted her name perhaps a little more loudly than was necessary. She sprang up from behind the counter.

'I'm here.' She saw the relief on his face and looked a little conscious. 'Will you help me? It's heavy.'

Graves made his way over to join her. She had shifted a bundle of scores to uncover a black wooden box large enough to take a manuscript sheet without folding. It was deep too and Graves felt himself grunt with effort as he brought it out onto the counter-top. He steadied it and told Susan what Jane had suggested.

'Only if that's agreable to you, miss,' the girl added quickly. 'If you think it's for the best.'

Susan bit her lip and nodded quickly. The comb Miss Chase had put in her hair to hold it in place, wobbled a little.

'Yes, please. That's very nice of your mother to come.'

Her lip began to shake, and Jane stepped round the counter to her side.

'Oh, miss! Look at your hair. You've been pulling your ringlets again, and you know your father likes you looking neat.'

She put her hand up to smooth Susan's curls back into place and the tenderness of the gesture overwhelmed the little girl. She began to sob in earnest and, thinking it best to leave them a while, Graves went out into the parlour.

The remains of the dinner, so horribly stopped, had been cleared away, and the space was as tidy and cheerful as normal. Graves paused, as if by a sheer effort of will he could run time backwards, then Alexander would walk in and ask him to dine with the family. They would talk, and Alexander would mock him gently for his mute admiration of Miss Chase, and Graves would ask for all the news of the shop. Then they would look at some new score that had come into Alexander's hands and the evening would melt away.

Graves sighed heavily, and looked around the room without a clear thought in his head, then seeing Alexander's writing desk open in the corner, walked over to it, vaguely wondering if he might find there evidence of a will, or some inspiration as to how to take on the responsibilities with which his friend had left him.

Everything about the desk was neat and orderly. The sight depressed him, thinking of the tattered and scattered papers around his own little table. The lamp set above the desk was carefully trimmed, and the desk contained a convenient series of pigeonholes where bills and receipts could be kept, and correspondence sorted. The little box where Alexander had kept his ring was still there, still, Graves noted as he flicked it open with a fingernail, empty.

Graves sat down sadly and picked at the edge of the blotter, sure that whatever tasks were being given him, he was incapable of shouldering them. There was a sheet of paper under the blotter. He pulled it free and saw the first words of a letter begun on the day of the concert. It had the name and address of the shop at its top, and the date of 31 May 1780 in the firm and confident hand he knew to be that of his friend. It began:

My Dear Hugh,

You know, I think, only too well the reasons that caused my separation from the Hall, but an odd loss on my part, and the knowledge that my children are now growing, motherless and uncertain of their future, has caused me to

Here Alexander had broken off. Graves felt his heart constrict. He remembered the conversation with Alexander that night, his strange hints to his daughter, and the new resolve he had taken to live the life he had chosen, rather than make any attempt at reconciliation with his family. Graves bit his lip. If he had advised differently, the letter might have been completed. He should have questioned his friend more closely before he had given his advice. His answer had perhaps been too full of his own pride. He, after all, had left his own home, and perhaps he had encouraged Alexander to stay away from his to bolster his own decision. He remembered the weight and size of the black box in the shop, thought of its careful concealment away from Alexander's neatly arranged business affairs in this more public room. Perhaps there were answers there, and some help for him.

He stood up swiftly, but in turning towards the door in the shop his eye was caught by a movement in the window into the back yard. His heart froze. *That face.* That yellow leering face that had flashed in front of his mind's eye every other moment since he saw his friend dying on the floorboards in front of him. It was there, looking in at him through the window. He rocked backwards a step. The two men stared at each other a moment through the glass, each held by the other's eyes, then Graves let out a roar of rage and charged to the door from the kitchen into the courtyard. The yellow man had turned and run through the side passage back into Tichfield Street.

'Murderer! Killer! There! There!' Graves screamed after him and threw himself forward in pursuit.

The street came alive as if, as the man dashed past, he transmitted an energy that awoke the people. More cries in the street, the houses themselves seemed to bend forward. More men in pursuit, a woman shrank to the wall with a scream as the yellow man tore past her and spun into Little Angel; he stumbled in the muck, but was up and running again before Graves could do more than brush the edge of his dirty coat. He had been wrong to turn this way. Now Londoners looking cautiously about them for the scenes of last night's riots could see the approach of the chase, and hear the shouts of 'Murder!' as the desperate men charged towards them. The yellow man grabbed a basket from a narrow-waisted street-hawker and threw it back at his pursuers. Her burden of burned pies rolled on the ground, and though it was enough to trip one man, the rest kept coming with Graves at their head, his lungs bursting. The hawker screamed and spat at the yellow man, but was shoved aside in the instant and he ran on. Not far though, not far. He turned sharply into Chapel Street, scattering people and their goods, but a fat coachman, hearing the cry following him, launched himself against him from his right flank, and the yellow man fell into the dirt and refuse of the street with all the coachman's bulk pressing him to the ground. The crowd descended, held his arms away from him, and someone pulled his knife from his

131

pocket. He struggled, and no one man could have held him, but with twenty grasping him and pressing forward, he was lost. Graves came to a stop before him, and without pausing to fill his lungs, threw a punch that landed under the yellow man's chin and let the crowd take his weight as he slumped insensible among them.

'Smartly done,' Graves heard from the crowd. A broad-shouldered man stepped forward and put a hand on his shoulder as Graves raised his fist again. 'But don't kill him, or we'll have to take you in too. Who is he?'

'He killed Alexander Adams,' Graves panted.

The crowd murmured and exclaimed. The broad man nodded soberly. 'What magistrate is closest?'

'Addington! Addington!' the crowd shouted.

A barrow was produced with a young man to push it, and the yellow man was rolled onto it with a bit of rope round his wrist and another round his ankles. His head lolled like a guy's ready for the fire, and the crowd began to process to the magistrate's house to demand satisfaction of the law.

Graves's brain was clogged and weary as he made his way back to the street door of the Chases' home. He had sent messages back to Susan and Miss Chase through the evening, telling them first that the man had been taken, then later that with little ceremony, on his evidence, and to the delight of the crowd that accompanied him, the yellow man had been sent to Newgate to await trial at the Old Bailey sometime in the next week.

Once he had come round and realised his position was hopeless, the yellow man had become surly. He refused to speak other than to curse and call down every revenge imaginable on Graves and the children, but would give neither his name, nor any reason for his attack on Alexander. The crowd had jeered him, the magistrate, looking exhausted and fretful, merely nodded at Graves's evidence and sent the yellow man away under guard within half an hour of reaching his house in Covent Garden.

The crowd that had travelled with Graves were disposed to make a hero of him, and it was with difficulty he had managed to free himself from them and their congratulations. He could have drunk himself to death on their credit, but was haunted by his thoughts of Susan and Miss Chase waiting for him with the black box between them. Still, as he walked past Seven Dials he was aware that his fame had spread. His neighbours approached to pat him on his back, or nod, or smile at him significantly. His legs ached after running down the yellow man, and his knuckles were bruised. He did not think to pause at his lodgings again, merely passing them by on his way to Sutton Street to rejoin the Chase family. As a shadow stirred next to him, he was ready to smile and wave off congratulations again.

'A conquering hero, Mr Graves, you are!'

Graves felt his heart sink. He knew the voice; this was not going to be a pleasant meeting. The shadow unfurled itself from the wall. A tall wizened-looking man with green teeth smiled at him like the crocodile Graves had seen exhibited at Vauxhall the previous year.

'Mr Molloy. Good evening.'

'Isn't it though? Only one thing could make it more pleasant . . .' He paused and pulled Graves back into the shadows for a moment as a group of men wearing blue cockades in their hats, their faces dirty with soot, barrelled past them. He released Graves's arm and continued as if nothing had occurred '. . . and that is my money.'

'I have none.'

'Then you shouldn't have bought yourself that pretty coat, or new shoes. The tailor has sold me your bill, and I'll be paid, or you'll be in the Marshalsea by Monday night.'

The smile never shifted from his face as he spoke. Graves lifted his arms.

'For God's sake, have pity! My friend has been murdered, his children put into my care! I cannot get the money for some days.'

'Yes, I've been hearing all about your adventures, son. Talk of the parish – most commendable. I esteem you for it, and am sorry for your loss, but pity does not make a man wealthy, you know. And I have a fancy to be a wealthy man. Now Adams had a nice little concern in that shop, didn't he?'

Graves pulled himself very straight. 'You think I should steal from his children? What sort of creature are you?'

Molloy laughed till he had to pause for breath and spit on the ground.

'Creature am I, indeed? Well, at least the coat I walk about in I have paid for.' Graves blushed. 'Twenty shillings is how the debt stands. I would not wish to embarrass you by asking for it from Mr Chase while you are under his roof, keeping an eye on your little charges.'

Graves felt himself go pale. 'How twenty shillings? I could not have owed more than half that.'

'You writerly types will never understand the function of interest, will you now?' Molloy shook his head sadly at what passed for an educated man these days. 'Now, perhaps you might get a little reward, or ask for one if you are too busy running about the streets to practise your trade, that is your concern. Just make sure I have the money in my fist by Monday dinnertime, and I shall tip my hat to you all friendly-like. Any later than that and you'll be locked up in the prison before you can spit.'

Graves felt his shoulders sag.

'I shall make it easy for you, Graves. I shan't stir far from Sutton Street over the next day or two. That way you'll know how to find me.'

Molloy put a hand to his hat brim and seemed to disappear into the shadows again without a sound. Graves sagged for a moment then, straightening his back, he walked on towards the home of Mr Chase.

18 April 1775, Boston, Massachusetts Bay, America

IT WAS UNFORTUNATE, and of course, Captain Devaille was known to be a fool, and no one in the regiment could understand why he had not transferred out when they had been sent to America, but he would not have spoken as he did if he had known Hugh was within earshot. Thornleigh had paused in the doorway to the officers' mess to knock some of the dirt of Boston off his boots, so Hawkshaw was a few moments ahead of him, greeting his fellow officers and calling for news and claret in the same breath.

Captain Devaille heard his voice and without turning round called out: 'Hawkshaw! You're thick with Thornleigh, aren't you? How does he take the news that the Earl of Sussex has married his whore? What a mother to come home to!'

There was a horrible silence, and Devaille turned suddenly in his chair and cursed as he saw Hugh's broad shoulders form a shadow in the doorway. He stood, stock still and white. His hands clenched.

'Thornleigh. M-my apologies,' Devaille spluttered. 'I . . . My father wrote me, just came in an hour ago.'

Hugh took a step forward, his face and manner murderous. Hawkshaw moved in front of him, facing Devaille.

'We've been riding out. Not checked for letters yet. No doubt there is some mistake.'

Devaille looked in danger of being sick; he could not meet Hugh's black eyes, still fixed on him over Hawkshaw's shoulder.

'No doubt, Hawkshaw. Of course.'

'Some other Earl of Sussex, presumably,' drawled another voice.

Hawkshaw glanced angrily in the direction it came from. An older Lieutenant, Gregson, who looked in his well-cut coat as if he had mistook the mess for a Duchess's drawing room, smiled sweetly at him. Hawkshaw turned to Hugh.

'Come on, Thornleigh. Leave with me now. Let us see what news from England we have.'

But Hugh took another half-step forward, apparently unhearing. Devaille's chair scraped on the stone floor as he retreated in front of him.

'Damn it, Hugh,' Hawkshaw sighed. 'Time enough to kill and be killed tomorrow.'

'Oh, tomorrow will be like stealing butter from the nursery table,' sang the voice of Gregson again. 'We are to have a brisk walk through the countryside, blow up some powder the rebels have scraped together, and then trot home again.'

Hawkshaw turned on him. 'You are mighty open about our Army's plans, sir.'

Gregson held up his hand, as if gently fending off Hawkshaw's annoyance. 'We are among friends, are we not?'

Before Hawkshaw could reply, Hugh turned and walked out of the door, leaving it to clatter to behind him. Hawkshaw rubbed his face and collapsed into a chair. Food and wine were put in front of him.

'Thanks, Hawkshaw,' Devaille said under his breath.

'You're a fucking idiot, Devaille,' he replied without much heat. 'And if you fight as carelessly as you talk, you won't bother me much longer.'

He began to eat.

As the afternoon slipped towards evening, the atmosphere in the camp became more charged with the promise of action.

Devaille's comments were confirmed, first by another officer whose letters from home contained the same gossip, and then in a paragraph in a month-old copy of the *Gentleman's Magazine* which was being handed round the mess. It was passed to Hawkshaw open at the significant page, and with a tap of a thumb on the middle paragraph.

It seems that no one, not even one of the highest personages in our land, is immune from the terrible passions and persuasions of great beauty. The holder of one of England's oldest and most stainless Earldoms Lord T— of T— Hall in Sussex, has gone against the wishes of all his friends and lately married Miss Jemima B—, also known under her professional name of 'The Glorious Jemima', when she graces the public in Covent Garden with her performances of dances from around the world. The lady in question is known to be the friend of several other members of the aristocracy, if not of their wives. Much as it pains us, we cannot forbear but to point out that Viscount H—, son and heir of Lord T—, was cast out of his family for honourably loving and desiring to marry a humble but beautiful young lady of spotless character some ten years ago, and has made his way in obscurity ever since.

Hawkshaw threw down the paper and went outside, walking without great purpose till he found himself at the edge of the camp. The light began to leach out of the sky in front of him. He thought about the action of the coming day. He could feel the unnatural calm he always experienced before and during action begin to circulate in his veins. He smiled at it, as if greeting an old friend. He heard a footstep beside him; it was Gregson, probably seeking some peace himself. He approached with a nod and offered Hawkshaw a cigar from a leather case he carried in his breast pocket. Hawkshaw hesitated a second, and then took it, thanking him stiffly before lighting it and drawing in the thick grey smoke to roll around his mouth.

'Have you seen Thornleigh since he heard?' The man asked.

Hawkshaw shook his head.

'I decided I'd leave him to his own thoughts. He did get letters from home. Presumably there is something from the Earl. But you know Thornleigh. He won't want to discuss his family with any of us.'

They heard a branch crack behind them.

'Who goes there?' Gregson demanded of the shadows of a small clump of low bushy trees a couple of yards away. 'Come out, and let us see you!'

A thin, middle-aged man stepped into the light. He was carrying firewood under his arm.

'Sorry, sir. I'm Shapin, I help out in the kitchens.'

The man held out his wood in front of him as if he were offering his papers for inspection. He was dressed in the homespun of the country farmers and labourers. His back was a little bent, and a long scar across his neck glittered palely under his otherwise heavy tan. His accent had an American drawl, but you could still hear the old country under it, like a woman's scent clinging to her handkerchief, though the girl herself is long gone.

'What are you doing, skulking about in the shadows, Shapin?'

Shapin looked like he thought this was a rather simple-minded question in the circumstances, and rattled his sticks together.

'Collecting kindling, sir. Then I heard the name Thornleigh, and it brought me up sharp. Is one of the Earl of Sussex's sons serving here? Is it Mr Alexander, or Mr Hugh?' He looked up at them expectantly. The two Captains exchanged glances, and Hawkshaw shrugged.

'The Honourable Hugh Thornleigh is a Captain of the Grenadiers in my regiment.'

Shapin looked pleased. 'That's good to know! I served the family back in England, you see. I knew Mr Hugh when he was just a little boy, before his mother died.' A sudden thought seemed to cross Shapin's mind. He blushed, and gathered his sticks to his breast. 'I must get back. The kitchens will be wanting me.'

He was off again towards camp before the officers could speak to him again. They watched him trot away.

'Do you think he might be a spy, Hawkshaw?'

'Well, if he is, he is a very bad one.'

The gentlemen returned their attention to their cigars, and to discussion of the coming action.

His duties done, Hawkshaw still could not settle, and though he knew he should be resting in preparation of the night march ahead of him, before the hour was out he decided to pay Shapin a visit in the kitchen. He had some vague plan of introducing him to Hugh in an attempt to bring him out of whatever black mood the news of his father's marriage had dropped him into. His visit was not welcome. When he asked after the man, the Quartermaster cursed him.

'So it was you scared Shapin away, was it, Captain?'

'I can't see how I would have made him nervous.'

'Well, someone did.' The man spat onto the soil floor. 'He came in here looking all white and stared about him like his wits were gone, then next thing we know he dropped his kindling and lit out like the devil himself were after him.'

'He claimed some acquaintance with Captain Thornleigh's family in Sussex.'

One of the passing royalists caught this and laughed.

'That'll be what did it. He was transported for stealing from them, came here as an indentured servant a good twenty years ago. Always wondered why he was spending time round our camp anyway. God knows, he's got no reason to love England. Probably thought Captain Thornleigh had come over special to hang him.'

Hawkshaw turned to the man. 'For theft, you say?'

'Yes, that's what I've heard. And I wish you would stop sending your felons over here, too. We already have plenty of people that need hanging, thank you very much.' The man paused and rubbed his chin. 'Mind you, he tried once soon after he arrived to save us the burden of looking after him.' He drew a finger across his throat, and Hawkshaw remembered the scar. 'He proved no better at that than at his thievery. He was patched up and put to work again.'

'He didn't try to get home when the term of his transportation was up?'

'Doubt he had much to go back to. Many of them lose heart, or any idea of going back after ten years.'

Hawkshaw frowned. 'Where do you think he's gone?'

'Probably had a think about his allegiances and has moved over to the rebels. Next time you see him, he'll be waving some grandmother's flint-lock at you.'

Hawkshaw nodded, and wandered out of the building.

PART III

III.1

Sunday, 4 June 1780

C ROWTHER WAS SURPRISED how quickly he warmed to the life
and atmosphere of Caveley Park. Today, the housekeeper smiled
at him when she opened the door, and he was ushered into the salon
to wait for the ladies' return from church. He watched out of the
window as the little boy swooped round the lawns mimicking the
flight of the crows under the eye of his nursemaid, who cradled
the baby of the family in her arms. When Crowther was a boy,
church service every Sunday had been an inescapable duty, until he
learned exactly when to disappear into hiding. It had to be near
enough to the time when the family had to leave to make a thorough
search for him impossible. And this young boy was handed all this
freedom and air as his natural right. He wondered if Stephen would
follow his father to sea. Another few years of play then a life of salt
and bells.

Crowther continued to watch until the boy looked up and, seeing
him, waved. The maid too, her attention caught by Stephen, turned
and raised her hand with a smile. Crowther smiled back, let his hand
flutter up and fall again as the boy flew on. Some unusual emotion
pressed on his chest. He cleared his throat, and turned back into the
room. He had not been waiting long before a flurry at the door, and

141

the shouts of greeting from Stephen announced that Harriet and Rachel had returned.

Mrs Westerman swept into the room, her eyes bright with amusement and her son dancing at her heels. Rachel came in a little more sedately behind her. Crowther stood but was waved back into his chair as Mrs Westerman removed her hat and dropped it on the table, then collapsed onto one of the settees. Rachel picked up the hat, shaking its ribbons straight, before carefully removing her own.

'Crowther! I am glad you are here. We feared for our reputation, but we have become shining moral beacons. Mrs Heathcote!'

That lady put her head into the room. She was smiling broadly.

'You'll be wanting coffee, ma'am?'

'I will. What has made you laugh, madam? Has David been telling you about our leading role in today's sermon? Are you not honoured to be working for such a paragon?'

Mrs Heathcote grinned. 'It is indeed an honour, ma'am.' She turned to Rachel. 'Shall I take those, miss?' and carried away the ladies' bonnets.

Crowther waited and when Harriet looked at him, raised an eyebrow. She burst into laughter and arranged the skirts of her dress, then settled Stephen on her knee and ruffled his hair.

'Oh, it's all too silly. The vicar decided on the Good Samaritan as a text today, and held me, Rachel and yourself as examples for attending – oh, what was the phrase? – "the last lonely rituals in a lost life". I have noted he relies a little too heavily on alliteration for his effects. He should be spoken to.'

Harriet started to pull off her gloves as she spoke. Stephen was allowed to help, and seemed in constant danger of falling off his perch, so vigorous were his efforts tugging on his mother's fingers. Crowther thought briefly of Nurse Bray's blood on her palm.

'Of all the nonsense. He would not have been there himself if we had not arrived, and my sister had to bully us like a she-devil. Rachel is the only one who can think of it and not blush.'

Rachel had tried to look severe during this speech and failed, but at those last words she became a little serious.

'And Mr Thornleigh. *He* meant to come.'

Crowther glanced at Harriet. She wrinkled her nose at him. He was not sure of the implication. Harriet gave her son a fierce hug, set him down on his feet then held him at arm's length and cupped one of her hands around his smooth face.

'Your hair is a mess, young man. Very well – you have seen enough of us for now. Go and get properly dirty until you are called in for your dinner.'

He grinned at her and set off for the lawn again. Rachel turned to Crowther.

'I know about the knife, Mr Crowther. In what way it was stained, I mean. I made Harriet tell me before I would go to bed last night.'

Harriet leaned forward with her elbows on her knees, and put her chin in her hand.

'She was most insistent, I'm afraid, and asked if she could hear us discuss how things stand this morning. I agreed, if you are willing.'

Crowther felt the women's eyes on him, and shifted awkwardly in his chair.

'With the greatest of respect, Miss Trench, Mrs Westerman is a married woman, and of wide experience. Whereas, yourself, there are elements, conjectures we might make that will not be suitable for . . .'

'I am not a child, Mr Crowther!' Rachel said.

The door opened as she spoke and Heathcote came smoothly in with the coffee.

'And miss, you'll sound less like one if you learn to keep your temper, if you don't mind me saying so.' She placed the tray at Harriet's elbow, and turned to Crowther. 'Good girls, the Trench sisters, Mr Crowther. But to hear their tempers fly sometimes, you'd think they had no notion of how to behave in a respectable household. Still, they may mature with age.'

She turned without waiting for a response and sailed out of the room with her head held high. Crowther gazed after her in frank astonishment. The two women looked a little crestfallen for a moment, then seeing Crowther's expression, both laughed. Harriet began to pour the coffee.

'I am mistress of this house, only by Mrs Heathcote's leave, I'm afraid, Crowther. And I fear she may take it all away from me, if she thinks I am behaving badly. She believes we need a mother, as we lost our own when Rachel was just a child, and now she supplies the role.'

Rachel took the full coffee cup from her sister and handed it to Crowther.

'Her husband is just the same. James says he is Captain only as long as Heathcote thinks he is doing a proper job of it. When they are both in the house, we live in terror.'

Crowther smiled and drank some of his coffee, then becoming aware that Rachel was still looking at him with steady attention, he sighed.

'I wish you would not listen to us talk, Miss Trench, because we may, as I've said, have unpleasant things to say, and I do not wish to upset you in any way.' Rachel flushed a little and bit her lip as he went on, 'However, what we imagine is being said is normally worse than what is actually being spoken, so if you have won your sister over, I can have no objections to make.'

Rachel took her own coffee cup and settled herself with evident satisfaction.

'Thank you. Now,' she looked from one to the other, 'explain everything from the beginning.'

The box was laid out in the middle of the table. Susan, Graves and Miss Chase sat round it, regarding its smooth black sides with suspicion.

Jonathan and Mrs Chase, her arms crossed comfortably across her broad stomach, stood to one side. The family had just returned from church and the time they had decided among themselves to examine its secrets had come upon them. Mrs Chase looked at them all, then addressed herself to the little boy at her side.

'Shall we go and help Cook, Jonathan? And then I have a whole box of ribbons that need to be sorted. Shall we leave these folk to their papers?'

The small boy thought seriously for a moment then nodded and allowed himself to be led from the room. The door closed behind them.

'Well, Susan?'

Graves tried to smile at her. She looked up at him.

'Who is that man outside, Mr Graves? You did not seem very pleased to see him.'

'His name is Molloy. I have some business with him, but it is nothing to do with Alexander, Susan, I promise you.'

She nodded and drew the box over to her with an effort, then lifted the lid.

It was mostly papers, but on top of them lay two small packages wrapped in soft leather scraps. Susan lifted the first of them out, and handed it without speaking to Graves. He took it from her and she watched him attentively as he unwrapped it. It was the miniature of Susan's mother that he remembered Alexander showing him once. There was a larger version of the same portrait hanging in the parlour of Alexander's house, there to watch over them, but there was a delicacy in this little portrait missing in the larger version. He handed it back to Susan, and she held it in her palm.

'I think Jonathan and I are rather alone in the world now, are we not?'

Graves felt his throat burn, but nodded slowly.

145

'You and Miss Chase will help us though, won't you, Mr Graves?'

'Always.'

She wiped her eyes with her fingertips and removed the other little bag, again handing it to Graves. He shook it gently and an elegant gold wedding band fell into his hand. Its glittered with a tiny nest of sapphires. He could fancy it felt warm on his hand.

'Your mother's, I think, Susan.'

She took it from him, touching the brilliants with her fingertips, then her shoulders began to shake, and Miss Chase put her hand on the child's arm.

'What is it, Susan? Does it hurt you to see it?'

The girl looked a little wildly from side to side at the adults.

'I don't know what to do with it! Am I to wear it? I think it is too big for my finger. What if it fell off in the street!'

She burrowed her head into the young woman's shoulder and cried so hard, Graves was almost frightened for her. He caught Miss Chase's eye, and opened his mouth hoping to find something of use to say. Miss Chase shook her head very slightly at him, and cradled and shushed the little girl till her sobs lessened a little. With one hand she then felt at her neck, and drew up a simple gold chain that hung under her bodice.

'Susan, my love, I have an idea. I think it would be a fine thing for you to wear your mother's ring. Let's hang it on this old chain of mine.'

Susan looked up, unsure, but hopeful.

'But it is yours,' she said.

Miss Chase looked quite severe.

'It is my gift to you. Look, the clasp is very secure.' Susan operated the little catch and bit her lip. 'Now we may put your ring on it,' she did so, 'and fasten it round your neck.'

Susan let the light chain be placed over her head, and held up the ring so it caught the light.

'There,' said Miss Chase, leaning back. 'You can wear it under your bodice, as I did, so it is always close to your heart, and safe as if it were in the Bank of England.'

Susan smiled consciously and tucked the chain away. Graves watched, his feelings as the admirer of one woman, and protector of the other, tumbling over in his chest like flag-waving acrobats. Susan leaned into Miss Chase's embrace again, and they looked at the box, the great pile of papers it contained making Susan shrink against Miss Chase's arm. Keeping the little girl secure, Miss Chase reached out for the black lid, and closed it over the papers again. Graves stirred a little, as if about to protest. He met command in Miss Chase's eye.

'That is enough for now. We can look at the papers later. They will keep, and I think Susan and I should take a turn round the Square.'

He heard Susan sigh with relief, and kept silent.

III.2

HARRIET TOOK A drink from her coffee cup, tapping her foot impatiently on the carpet. Crowther wondered how she had managed to contain her energy on the relatively small stage of one of His Majesty's ships. Even in the country it seemed that she never had enough room to move. While she gathered her thoughts to speak to her sister he considered. Perhaps it was not the physical space she occupied that bound her, but the delicate pressures of expectation and custom that wove the world around them into such tight ropes and checks. Invisible and made of stuff as slippery and delicate as silk, but strong, and tight, for all that. She sat forward in her chair and began to speak.

'Very well. Hugh, it seems, asked Joshua Cartwright to find someone to look for Alexander, the heir to Thornleigh and its title. This man,

Carter Brook, was engaged, and obviously found something – we know that because of the ring of Alexander's he was carrying – but when he went to meet Hugh in the woods he was attacked and murdered before he could tell Hugh anything.'

'So says Mr Hugh Thornleigh,' murmured Crowther, keeping his eyes on Rachel. She must have prepared herself for this, he thought, since his implication that the man she had once loved might be a liar and murderer drew no reaction.

Instead, she said calmly to her sister, 'Finding, or preventing Alexander from being found, must be at the bottom of this, surely?'

'Yes.' Harriet twisted her head a little to look out of the window as she spoke. 'All the wealth of the estate, and the title depends on Alexander being found, as you know. Though of course if he cannot be traced, or is found to be dead, or is declared to be dead after proper searches have been made, then Hugh inherits everything. For now it is by common consent that he runs the estate.'

Crowther cleared his throat. 'I have wondered why the family have not taken steps to have Viscount Hardew declared dead before now. His absence has been so extended, and nothing seems to have been heard from him.'

Harriet shrugged. 'The current Lord still lives, after a fashion. Perhaps that means the family do not think the case pressing. He has already survived five years in this half-state.'

'You do not think Hugh ambitious to take the title?'

'Hardly! Do you, Crowther?'

'No. From what I have seen of him I think he wishes only to divide his time between the hunt and the bottle. But I could be very wrong. Something grates at him, makes him bitter. It may be the fact he has the responsibility for the wealth of his family, but no power to enjoy it. That may make him wish for Alexander's return, as he says – *or* wish the missing heir to hell.'

Crowther and Harriet's attention had been drawn in the exchange to each other. When Rachel now spoke, calmly and firmly enough, they both turned to her, slightly surprised to find there were three in the conversation.

'Suppose that everything Hugh and Mr Cartwright said in front of the Coroner was true, and Hugh's motives purely looking to the good of his family rather than his own situation within it . . . why did not Hugh instruct his steward, Wicksteed, to try and find out about his brother? He has left everything else of moment about the estate to his care since he arrived.'

'I can only conclude that Hugh wanted to gather, and act on this information in secret, as he hinted at the hearing,' Crowther replied. 'I was surprised, and not a little doubtful when he ascribed that secrecy to a wish to protect the feelings of Lady Thornleigh. Unless he thought she might be harsher in her treatment and attitude to Alexander if he was in straitened or,' he paused, 'disgraceful circumstances of one sort or another. And yet her talk about alarming Duchesses does not suggest she would care much if his position were . . . irregular. And if he is alive, she is quite as dependent on his goodwill as Hugh. If not more so.'

Rachel nodded. Crowther leaned back in his chair with his fingers touching tips in front of his chest and continued, 'From whom did he wish to keep matters secret then? Is Wicksteed more loyal to Hugh, due to their connection in the Army, or has Lady Thornleigh gained influence with him? And what has Hugh to fear from either of them? What did our lady of the needle say, Mrs Westerman?'

Harriet made a face. 'There is some gossip in the Hall that Wicksteed has made himself useful to Lady Thornleigh, and whatever their previous relations, no one in the Hall thinks Wicksteed is a favourite of Hugh's.'

'She must be very lonely in that big house,' Rachel murmured.

'And is,' Crowther leaned forward, 'Lady Thornleigh feared in any way by Hugh?'

149

'He tolerates her presence with a bad grace and thinks nothing about her at all, I think,' Harriet answered. 'At least, that was the feeling I had when we were friendly.' She paused and looked a little conscious. 'But I have often thought there is something mysterious in his relationship with Claver Wicksteed. That man does seem to wield great power in the house, and I have always had the impression that he makes Hugh uneasy. I cannot think why Hugh put a man he seems to dislike so in such a position of power in his household.'

'So Wicksteed – a man, we assume, of relatively obscure origin, and whatever talents or graces he has, there is nothing in his previous life we know of to suggest why he is qualified to be the centre of power in one of the richest houses in the county – and yet he is.' Crowther scratched his chin. 'We must see what we can do to find a little more out about the man. If he has some secret hold over Hugh, it is unlikely he would want to see the rightful heir return to Thornleigh Hall. Wicksteed may well not have that same power over the heir, Alexander, if he is found and tempted back home.'

Harriet stared into her coffee cup as if searching for runes.

'That does make some sort of sense,' she agreed.

'But what is the nature of the power Wicksteed has over Hugh? Does it really exist? Might not Hugh simply think him a good manager, even if he is not personally fond?' Rachel said doubtfully.

Crowther looked at her seriously. 'We must suspect everything, and believe nothing till we have proof of it.'

'That sounds like an immoral philosophy, Mr Crowther.' Rachel smiled at him and he smiled back at her.

Harriet had begun to rap her fingers against the fabric of her sofa again.

'Mrs Mortimer does not know of any hold Wicksteed has over Hugh, and if Belinda Mortimer does not know, I can guarantee you that no one else in the household can understand it either. And I think she has told me everything she knows.'

'I saw her nephew arriving at the stables looking very bright,' Rachel said.

Harriet grinned at her. 'Well, I intend on spending your earnings from the skin salves on employing him, and getting him and James new boots.'

'If Hugh is innocent,' Rachel said with a sigh, 'do you think perhaps Wicksteed might have killed Brook to stop Hugh finding out where Alexander is, Mr Crowther?'

'Perhaps. It sounds to me as if what Wicksteed has, he has fought for. And it is generally acknowledged that when a man has had to strive for position or money, he is loath to give it up.'

Rachel looked sadly into the middle distance and twisted a corner of her dress with her right hand, before saying in a low voice, 'Unlike Alexander, who just walked away from it all.'

Crowther felt the back of his neck prickle and his voice, when he spoke, seemed very far from him.

'What we grow up with in profusion, we are less likely to value, as a rule.'

Each of them stared quietly for a few moments at different parts of the foliage artfully woven into the Commodore's carpets. Harriet stirred first.

'You are full of epigrams today, Crowther. We should gather them all together in a book for the edification of the public.' He gave her a slight bow from his chair. 'We must go and see Mr Thornleigh,' she said, and added to her sister, 'Not you, my love, just Crowther and I.'

'I doubt he will do anything other than damn us to hell, let alone tell us what, if any, hold Wicksteed has over him.'

'Then let him. But if he is innocent, we must try to help him.'

'And the nurse? Why was *she* murdered?' Rachel looked up at them. 'I presume it was not by her own hand that she died.'

'She was murdered,' Crowther agreed heavily. 'I have no doubt on that score.'

Harriet stood up and began to pace the salon between Crowther and her sister. Rachel followed her with her eyes, Crowther put his palms together as if in prayer and continued to stare at the floor and listen to the sisters speak.

'But what possible share could she have had in the business?' Harriet wondered aloud.

'Perhaps she did know the nature of Wicksteed's hold on Hugh.' Rachel replied.

Harriet stopped in her pacing and turned back to her sister. 'Perhaps that was what was contained in those letters − but how could she know what it was, on a much shorter acquaintance with the house, when Mrs Mortimer, who has been there regularly since before Hugh and Alexander were born, does not!'

Crowther felt the air around him shift; a space, ready for a new thought, seemed to open up in the centre of his mind. The shreds of some inspiration hung around him; if only he could knit them together in his brain . . . There was something there, longing to take form.

'When did Lord Thornleigh's nurse arrive at the Hall?' he asked.

Harriet turned to him with a shrug. 'She has been in the area longer than us.' She swung back towards her sister. 'Didn't she arrive, by accident almost, a month or two after Lord Thornleigh became ill?'

Rachel nodded. 'Yes, she happened to be staging down to Brighton to stay with her sister, and heard about Lord Thornleigh on her way. She has had all sorts of experience with these illnesses in the past − acting as a nurse, you know − so she decided to walk over from Pulborough and offer her services. The household was very pleased to receive her.'

The two women looked towards Crowther with curiosity, aware of the tension in his narrow frame. Even as the thoughts bound together like rope in his mind, he was ashamed to realise he was drawing great satisfaction from their attentive eyes, and when he spoke again, it was not without the air of an actor claiming the stage.

'Of course. The mysterious letters from London. The timely arrival, then her murder. I have it!' He looked up from the floor, his eyes suddenly and almost unnaturally blue in his pale face. 'Alexander sent her.'

III.3

HARRIET ATE HER dinner quickly, and Crowther barely ate at all. As soon as the servants left the three to themselves, the revelation that Alexander might have sent Nurse Bray to Thornleigh was picked over again, and the women seemed ready to accept it as fact.

'We have no proof,' said Crowther wearily, and for the third time.

'There must be an inquest tomorrow,' Harriet replied a little crossly. 'Perhaps Nurse Bray had friends at the Hall of whom we know nothing as yet. They may be able to inform us.'

'I hope for their sake, if they exist, they do not know Alexander's address,' Rachel sighed. 'Having it seems to be very dangerous.'

Crowther and Harriet looked at her, suddenly stilled.

'If I were you,' she continued, 'before going to the Hall and demanding that Hugh tell us if he is in the power of his steward, I would see what you can get from Mr Cartwright. He is the only one we know who met Carter Brook when he lived, after all. He was so miserable to be seen to know Brook, perhaps he did not say everything he knew of him.'

Crowther nodded. 'You are quite right, Miss Trench. That is perhaps the best course of action.'

Rachel helped herself to a little more of the fish, and grinned a little pertly at Harriet.

'He will probably not wish to see you. So I would suggest a long walk in the heat to the village and a sudden attack of faintness just outside his shop, Harriet.'

Crowther saw Harriet smile, and commented, 'This country lost a great general when you were born a woman, Miss Trench.'

'Every woman must think like a general from time to time, I think,' she answered with a slight bow. 'And you'll be glad to know the country also lost a great actress when my sister was brought up to be a respectable married woman.'

Harriet mirrored her sister's bow back to her with a slightly twisted smile.

'I'm not sure I am behaving like a respectable married woman at the moment, Rachel.'

Her sister widened her eyes a little. 'Oh Harry, I did not say you were a respectable woman, just that you were brought up to be one!'

Crowther wondered if Mrs Westerman were about to throw her napkin, and suspected Miss Trench was saved only by the door opening and Mrs Heathcote's arrival to clear the dishes.

Miss Trench had not exaggerated her sister's skills. Crowther saw Mrs Westerman prepare herself as they approached the shutters of Cartwright's shop, taking her breaths in a shallow rush, but as her weight fell against him, just where Crowther could still reach the door-knocker, he could not have distinguished between a genuine spell of weakness and those symptoms that Harriet displayed. He only hoped his performance would be equal. He struck an urgent double clap at the door, and as soon as it was opened by a sweetheart-faced maid, the girl who became nervous when left alone, he supposed, he half-led, half-carried Mrs Westerman in before the girl could do any more than open and close her mouth. Crowther pushed at the first door he could see, which led into a modest parlour, and supported Harriet into a chair.

The maid looked at them rather nervously, then said firmly, 'Mr Cartwright sends his apologies but he is much engaged with business today, and unable to receive callers.'

Crowther composed his face into a severe frown and turned round sharply on his heel.

'Dear girl, do you suppose Mrs Westerman or myself are in the habit of making social calls in this manner?' The child lifted her chin. 'Mrs Westerman has been taken ill in the heat, and requires a place to rest. Your master may go to the devil, for all I care.'

Harriet looked up, her face flushed, her breathing still short, her eyes moist with appeal.

'I just need a glass of water, and a chance to recover myself, Hannah. We found Nurse Bray yesterday, you know . . . I began to think of her poor face, and . . .'

Crowther was fascinated to see a large tear run down her cheek. Without thinking, he took her wrist in one hand and his watch in the other and started to take her pulse. Hannah stepped forward with a little sigh, and her shoulders relaxed.

'Of course I'll get you some water. You stay right there, ma'am.' She shot a bitter look at Crowther and turned quickly enough for her skirts to swish. The door rattled on its latch behind her.

Mrs Westerman's pulse was steady and even as any man could wish. Crowther looked up from his watch and caught her eye. She winked at him. They could hear a muttered conversation in the hallway outside, and the door opened to allow the master himself in, bearing the water and leaning his upper body forward as he walked, as if he felt it dangerous to have his own head higher than either of his guests'.

'Dear Mrs Westerman! So sorry you are unwell.'

He offered the glass. Harriet took it with a trembling hand.

'Mr Cartwright, so sorry to disturb you!' Her eyelashes fluttered, and he tutted away her apologies. 'You know Mr Crowther, I presume. Mr Crowther, this is Mr Cartwright.'

Crowther drew himself up very straight and looked down his nose. 'Ah, yes! The glove man.'

Cartwright gave a slightly sick smile. 'That's right, sir. As I have had occasion to remark to you before, the name is above the door. But do take a seat.' He took a step back and opened the door into

155

the hallway again. 'Hannah! Fetch in some of that lemonade, if you will.'

Harriet raised a hand. 'We trouble you too much, sir.'

'Not at all, not at all, Mrs Westerman!'

Crowther settled himself with a convincingly bored sigh and there was a moment of silence as the two men watched Mrs Westerman take a sip of her water, and then, as if the effort of holding it were almost too much, place the glass on the table beside her. She then said rather more brightly: 'So it was you who found the unfortunate Brook for Mr Thornleigh, Mr Cartwright. And how did that come about?'

The little man stiffened and looked confused. Hannah re-entered with lemonade and three empty glasses. Harriet seemed to fall back into her chair a little, and took hers with a weak, 'Thank you,' but as soon as Hannah was out of the room again her condition seemed to improve, and she looked at Mr Cartwright with steady, friendly attention. He glanced from one to the other and his skin acquired a slight sheen. He reminded Crowther of a cornered amphibian.

'There is a coffee shop I visit during my buying trips to London. I knew Brook very slightly from there. I may, in my dealings with Captain Thornleigh, have mentioned some of the types I had met in London.' He seemed to feel the importance of at least appearing to become a little more comfortable and leaned back in his chair, crossing his legs. Crowther noticed for the first time that his pantaloons were a most remarkable shade of yellow.

'Sometimes, for the amusement of my friends, I am in the habit of composing little character sketches of some of those I come across in the great city. I always hope to have something new for Captain Thornleigh when I see him.'

Harriet smiled broadly at him. 'It is such a thing to have the talent to amuse!' Cartwright raised his hand as if to brush away this praise, colouring faintly. 'So he knew that you might be able to find help for him?'

'I suppose so, though I stressed I could not answer for Brook's character, and advised Captain Thornleigh most strongly that he should make no advances of money without some tokens of proof.'

Crowther put his fingers together and let his gaze travel slowly over Cartwright, until he was sure the man was aware of the scrutiny, and uneasy under it.

'Why do you always refer to Mr Thornleigh by his military title, Mr Cartwright?'

The little man bristled again. 'I had a wife and a son once, Mr Crowther. A daughter too, and though she is off and married now, thank the Lord. Both my wife and son were lost to me in the first years of the American Rebellion. My son was killed in Boston, and my wife took ill and died within a month of the news arriving. Captain Thornleigh knew my boy all his life. Carried him to the camp on his own shoulders, and held his hand while he died.

Crowther thought again of the masks people wore, blended into their skins like cosmetics for the show of the day-to-day. How much more interesting people were when grief or consideration cleaned their grease-paint away.

'First thing Captain Thornleigh did when he got back was come and see me here, before he even went to his own home to change his coat. He came here to tell me Tom died like a man – something that would make any father proud.'

'That was very good of him, Joshua,' Harriet said quietly.

The man sniffed a little and nodded.

'He keeps me in mind too, even after all these years. He brought me a bottle of something from the Hall this morning with his apologies for involving me in this business. He can have a sharp tongue and rough manner at times, but he is a good soul still. And if he asked me any favour in the world, I'd do it. Not much one can do to thank a man for being there when your boy dies, and seeing he doesn't die alone. Our Tom wouldn't have been so scared, not with Captain

Thornleigh there. So if he asks me to find him someone who'll be thorough and cunning in his enquiries, I'll walk to the end of the earth to do it.'

Crowther let the ice in his own voice thaw.

'So your son knew Claver Wicksteed as well?' he said.

Mr Cartwright pulled himself together and looked up with a shrug of surprise.

'He did, yes – though there was only one mention of him in Tom's letters. Mr Wicksteed was not a favourite, I think. Tom thought he was a spy. He said the lads mistrusted him as he was always writing things down in his little leather books. He does so still. I've seen him often enough, writing away with his glass beside him in the Bear and Crown. Though he keeps more to the Hall now, than he did at first. Even Captain Thornleigh we see less of these last months.' Cartwright frowned. 'Not that Wicksteed ever bothered himself to say anything to me about Tom. Probably never even realised the connection. Only cares for himself and his position.'

His voice was bitter. Harriet sipped her lemonade.

'It appears Mr Thornleigh trusts you more than his own steward, judging by the request he made of you regarding Brook.'

Mr Cartwright scratched a little under his ear as he considered.

'Oh, I don't know if I could say that, Mrs Westerman. It is most likely Captain Thornleigh just remembered that I had mentioned Brook, or a man like him in conversation.'

Harriet nodded. Crowther tilted his head on one side.

'Did you see Brook on his way to meet Mr Thornleigh?'

Cartwright started.

'You did? Mr Cartwright, do tell us,' Harriet said eagerly.

Mr Cartwright looked about him with great nervousness. 'How can that matter? The Coroner said that it was a thief come from London who killed him. Let it rest.'

'And Nurse Bray?'

'It was a suicide, they are saying. Undoubtedly. She was no doubt depressed by being always in company with Lord Thornleigh, and if she wished to burn her papers before taking such a desperate step, then why should she not?'

'Mr Cartwright, whatever is being said, I tell you sure as I sit here, that that poor lady was murdered,' Harriet informed him. 'And it must be bound up with Brook's death, you see? You're probably right that any meeting you had with Brook just before his death is of no significance, but please do tell us anything you can. I pray I am wrong, but I cannot sleep easy in my bed, or think of my little boy, my sister, or the baby at play with any calmness while I suspect there may be darker dealings taking place. You're a good man and father. You would feel the same, would you not?'

The appeal to Cartwright as parent and protector was a wise one. He looked down at his knees and sighed, then seemed to make up his mind to speak.

'I did see Brook on his way into town, and spoke to him.'

'And did you observe anyone on the road behind him?' Crowther asked.

'No, sir.' Cartwright glanced at them sadly. 'I am afraid I did not.'

Crowther was almost sorry himself. 'And what passed between Brook and yourself?'

'He hailed me at the edge of the village, to thank me for putting some work his way. He seemed very pleased with himself.' Cartwright paused and looked about him guiltily. 'He showed me the ring – said he got it while the family were out visiting neighbours. Which shows he may have boasted about it elsewhere, and to the wrong man, does it not?'

Harriet said very softly, as if she was pulling free a strand of some very delicate fibre, 'Did he tell you how he got the ring?'

Cartwright resumed contemplation of his knee, and coughed a little before replying. 'Said he lifted it from the man's bureau in his parlour – from Alexander.'

Crowther's tongue felt thick and heavy in his mouth. 'And did he tell you where Alexander was?'

Cartwright looked deeply distressed.

'He had it written on a bit of paper,' he mumbled.

Harriet looked up sharply and caught Crowther's eye.

'He waved it about, talking of the money he would get for it,' Cartwright went on. 'Better than a banknote, he said. I've tried so hard to remember. I told Captain Thornleigh I have tried, but nothing comes. Meadow Street, perhaps – I cannot be sure.'

Crowther felt his heart thud heavily in his chest. Harriet wet her lips.

'Anything more, Joshua? Did he say anything more about Alexander?'

'Only that it had been the devil's own work to find him. New name, new situation. He said he thought no other man in London could have done it, and that was as much by luck. Said it was my mention of Alexander being wild for music, he followed that route first. And I'd told him all I knew of Alexander – his looks, and the bad leg and all. It was that and some child he chanced upon which led him to the right place. Thought himself very smart for taking a sketch of the Thornleigh coat of arms with him too.' He looked up at them again. 'It was getting late, so he took himself off. Never seen a man look so pleased with himself.'

'He was on foot?' Crowther asked.

'Yes. Must have staged down to Pulborough.' The little man looked up at them again. 'I didn't know what to say at the hearing. They didn't ask me anything. I told Mr Hugh afterwards, though it felt like a cruelty, and Wicksteed stuck to his side throughout. It didn't seem to add anything but salt to the problem. I wish I could see that paper in my mind more clearly.'

Crowther blinked slowly over his tented fingertips. 'The mind is a mystery, Mr Cartwright. Try not to struggle with it too much. As you go about the work of the day, let the meeting with Brook play in your imagination from time to time. You may well know more than you think.'

Cartwright looked at him hopefully. 'Do you think so, sir?'

'Such things have occurred in the past.'

'It would be such a comfort to help the Captain. I shall do as you say.'

They left him soon afterwards, with all the proper compliments and considerations. Crowther turned back to see the draper standing lost in thought at the street door where he had showed them out. His bulging eyes were fixed on the ground, his lips moving gently as he attempted to recover those lost filaments of memory – the only things, it seemed, that now bound Alexander to Hartswood at all.

III. 4

MRS WESTERMAN WAS lost in thought as they followed the path back to Caveley. Crowther looked about him at the thick and heavy hedgerows, fat with new growth, fists of Queen Anne's Lace and curls of white bindweed. He wondered how his old lands were thriving under a new master. He had never met the man who bought the estate. He knew from his former agent that he was a brewer who, having established a fortune and married his daughter to a Lord, now wanted some slice of convenient county to call his own. The agent had quoted him: 'A true Englishman will never count himself truly happy till he has a bit of land to feed his children from.' Crowther had been glad to be rid of it. It was never supposed to be his, like the title, until the hanging of his elder brother. The ground would recognise a better master and flourish under a wise hand rather than an old name.

He realised they had turned up towards the copse where Brook had been discovered and glanced at his companion, wondering if the direction of her steps was unconscious or the result of some plan on her part. She caught the look and the question without him having to speak it.

'I was wondering if there were anything we could learn from the scene of the first murder. We would not have noticed the ashes of the letters by the witch's cottage if Rachel had not seen the fire.'

Crowther considered a second.

'You think we may at least find Mr Thornleigh's cigar end, if he waited as he said?'

She nodded. 'It would prove nothing, of course. But I might feel more like trusting him if we were to find it.'

They reached the spot and Mrs Westerman went to the little bench in the clearing and took a seat as if waiting for an appointment there. She then bent far forward and turned the dry leaves at her feet over with her gloved hand. He stood to one side watching her. She worked with delicate and precise attention widening the arc of her hand with each sweep, softly biting her lower lip in concentration.

'Ahh!' She straightened, the fat brown squib of a smoked cigar held between thumb and forefinger. He approached and took it from her, and held it up to his long thin nose as she dusted her hands clean.

'Yes, I think so, Mrs Westerman.' He placed it in his palm and poked at it with one fingernail. 'I would say this has not been here long, and that it was a good smoke in its time.'

'So Hugh did sit here awhile.' She looked at the view, with her hand cupping her chin. However, Brook was surprised, so Hugh is unlikely to have sat here waiting for him in full view – if he was the murderer.'

'And the fact that the ring was left on the body would suggest the murderer had no time to search it when the killing was done, so it is unlikely he took his ease, having murdered Brook.'

'Unlikely, but not impossible. Hugh may have forgotten all about the ring, and wished to compose himself before returning to the house.'

'Indeed.'

Crowther took out his handkerchief and wrapped the stub in it, unsure why he did so, only thinking that it seemed disrespectful to her efforts in finding it to throw it back onto the ground. She looked out into the view again. The leaves of the oak on the slope before them stirred in the wind, the dense flowers of green shifting forward and falling back again.

'I would give a great deal to see those notebooks of Wicksteed's,' she said to the air.

'Do you think it likely he will have written down what he knows? No one has told us he is an imbecile.'

Crowther took a seat beside her, but facing away towards where Brook was found. She did not reply for a while. The quiet of the place, its comfort began to reach into his bones. He was as far above it as the clouds. He looked up to where they swelled and towered in the blue and amongst the leaves. She spoke again, as if there had been no gap in the conversation.

'I think he is an intelligent man, and a ruthless one. But I suspect myself: perhaps I still do not wish to call Hugh a murderer. And whoever killed Brook must have been in at the death of that poor woman also. I could not forgive myself if a man whom I had trusted had had a hand in the hanging of a middle-aged woman. I must think of her, and it makes my blood cold. She fought, and no help came.'

Crowther let the picture form in his mind. The older woman . . . was she tricked into going to the cottage of her own free will with the letters in her hand? Perhaps — but by whom? He could not think of anyone but Hugh with whom she could have made such an appointment. It was he who had been searching for Alexander. Surely if she had decided to reveal her supposed secret knowledge of Alexander's whereabouts, she would have gone to him. Whoever she had agreed to meet, she had come in trust and been attacked. She must have realised that whoever she had met had meant her harm, for she had struck out, caught someone.

'Were the Thornleigh family at church this morning?' Crowther asked suddenly.

'Yes. Lady Thornleigh came in on Hugh's arm. She likes to give the populace a chance to admire her from time to time and we do. It is impossible not to.'

'And Wicksteed?' She nodded. 'I take it you would have mentioned to me by now if anyone attending had scratchmarks apparent.'

She did not look at him, but he could hear the dry smile in her voice.

'Yes, I rather think I should have done.'

'If not the face, then it is most likely the arms of the attacker that are scratched.' Crowther pictured a man, waiting for the nurse in the cottage with the rope standing by, removing his coat in preparation for the heavy, physical work of killing another human being. The scene shifted in his head. The woman with her wrists bound, struggling, watching the rope being slung over the beam.

Harriet spoke. 'She must have been gagged.'

No ride to Tyburn with all the crowd hooting and leering could be more terrifying than lying in that cottage on a summer afternoon, wrists tearing at the rope, gagging at the fine linen in one's throat. He looked deep into the wood.

'I know you are not looking for comfort, but remember that blow to the back of her head. She may have been unconscious from that injury when her murderer put the rope around her neck.'

Harriet kicked at the ground beneath her feet.

'Perhaps. The wound was bloody, but the skull was not broken. It is as likely the blow was to stop her struggling while her wrists were tied, and she woke straining against them.'

Crowther could feel the cold earth of the ground against his cheek, the aching head, the desperate pull at the wrists. He could see the gloom, a gentleman's boots stepping in and out of his range of vision as the slow preparations were made. He felt terror run through under his skin as if it had been injected into his bloodstream like mercury, slippery and cold.

'That is as likely, Mrs Westerman.' He squeezed his eyes shut for a moment. 'We should ask the Squire to make a search of Thornleigh Hall. Check everyone in the household for scratches. Do you think he would dare?'

She shifted a little in her seat to look at him, her head to one side.

'Perhaps if the Coroner finds the case to be one of Murder, but I doubt it. Even if he found something suspicious, such scratches could be explained away, and the unpleasantness could be extreme.'

Crowther nodded slowly and got to his feet.

'Then we must find it ourselves – and quickly. In three or four days any wounds Nurse Bray left on her killer will have healed, and the moment be lost.'

Graves felt his heart sink. Having persuaded Susan and Miss Chase back to the table on which the black box lay, and lifted up the first armful of papers it held, he found only faulty copies of old scores. His stomach lurched. He had not realised what faith he had put in the contents of the box. He stood to hide his emotion from the ladies and walked over to the window to stare down into the street – only to find himself looking directly into the upturned face of Molloy. He moved away again sharply.

Miss Chase had taken a handful of papers and was carefully turning them over in front of her, when she said, 'Mr Graves, I think I have found something.'

He took a seat opposite her and she slid a letter over to him. It was written in a simple, careful hand – female, he would guess – and dated some four years in the past. Above the date was written simply *Thornleigh Hall, Sussex*. He looked across at Susan, who blinked widely at him, and began to read aloud:

Dear Mr Adams,

I have been received into the household with much relief. The people here have no experience, I think, in dealing with such an illness as the Earl's. He has lost his powers of speech almost entirely, and they fear the noises he makes. I believe he is just as he ever was behind his eyes though, and am happy to offer the poor gentleman what comfort I can. My lady visits from time to time, and I think it pleases him to look at her. I admire her devotion in remaining in residence. She has asked if he might ever be able to travel, and gave him a bitter look when I said I thought it not advisable. I think the Earl must have missed the look though, for he continued to seem very content. They say that Mr Hugh Thornleigh has decided to return from the wars in America to take charge of the estate in a few months, as soon as he can take passage over.

I should like to thank you again, Mr Adams, for putting me in the way of this position, which I think shall suit me very well, and for your kindness in fitting me out for the journey. I shall continue to write every six months as we agreed, and of course keep quiet about how I happened upon this place. I would of course respect your wishes in these regards without your continued generosity.

Yours most sincerely,
Madeleine Bray

Graves ran a hand across his forehead. 'What can this mean? Who *are* these people? Have you heard of them, Miss Chase? Do you recognise any of the names, Susan?'

The little girl shook her head and looked afraid. Graves was worried he had spoken with more heat than he had intended.

Miss Chase took hold of the little hand and patted it. Then she said slowly, 'Was there not an Earl who married a dancer a few years ago, then fell ill within a year?'

Graves frowned at the table-top in front of him, trying to pull the threads together.

Miss Chase continued: 'Perhaps Alexander had family at the house. He was an educated man. I remember once hearing of a gentleman who was brought up very well in a country house. He was the son of the steward, got a thorough education and was raised to take his father's place. He fell out with the family as a young man though, wanted to go and make his own fortune rather than look after that of another man.'

Mr Graves looked at his fingernails, then curled them into his palms. 'What became of him?' he asked.

'He became rich and bought an estate of his own. That is the way of the world these days, I think. Good men can make their own way, if they keep their courage.' She looked at him with a gentle smile and he felt his heart lift a little.

Susan turned another letter towards Graves, her smooth forehead drawn down into a rather fierce frown.

'This is a funny letter! From the same lady, I think. Will you read it, Mr Graves? I am not sure I understand it.'

He took it from her and cleared his throat.

Thornleigh Hall, Sussex

Dear Mr Adams,

All continues here much as in my last. Mr Hugh Thornleigh and Lady Thornleigh are not very friendly, and it is a shame when a family cannot comfort each other in such times, do you not think, Mr Adams? I have learned however that the eldest son, Alexander, Viscount Hardew, has been missing from this place some years — indeed, I had the opportunity to see a portrait of that gentleman in his youth while cleaning some miniatures with the housekeeper and heard the whole story. I would tell it to you now, sir,

but I suspect you know it already! I do not wish to give you any disquiet,
Mr Adams. Your secret, I swear, will never be won from my lips, nor will
I ever make allusion to it again.

Yours,
Madeleine Bray

Graves stopped reading, and there was a heavy silence in the room. He looked cautiously at the little girl, trying to guess if she had understood.

Susan stared hard at the table-top; she could feel nothing but the gentle weight of the ring around her neck. A lost son? An Alexander? Her father was Alexander and a gentleman, but could he be so grand? She had seen Earls while walking out in the park. They had none of them looked like her papa, and they had none of them seemed comfortable to her. Her mouth was dry. She blinked and looked up into Graves's dark blue eyes.

'Might my papa have been the son of this sick man?'

Graves wet his lips and looked down a little hopelessly at the paper in his hand.

'This Miss Bray seemed to think so! It all seems very strange, Susan. Did your father ever say anything to you, that might have suggested . . .'

Susan shook her head vehemently. 'No. Only when he asked about carriages and dresses the other evening.'

'There must be something else here.' Graves reached into the box again. 'Let us go through the pages one by one.'

They set to work on the box again, each apparent off-cut of score turned over, every bundle shaken to check nothing hid within.

It was Miss Chase who found it – a trio of papers concealed within a bundle of music Graves had previously put aside as mere camouflage.

'Here! Oh here, Mr Graves.'

She spread them out on the table. A marriage certificate and two others registering the births of Susan and Jonathan. The names on the marriage were Elizabeth Ariston-Grey and Alexander Thornleigh. The children were Susan and Jonathan Thornleigh.

They stared at the writing until Graves was sure he would be able to recall the penmanship on his deathbed. He looked at the little girl.

'It seems . . .' His voice cracked and he swallowed as the little girl stared up at him, her eyes wide. 'It seems Alexander always wanted you to have the means to return to the Thornleigh family, if you wished it, Susan. There is no doubt. These are your true names.'

'So I am not Susan Adams at all?'

'You are your father's daughter, and he was too honourable a man to deny you what he chose to deny himself.'

He looked up, feeling Miss Chase's eyes on him. She smiled at him and nodded. Susan's hand suddenly flew up and covered her mouth with a little cry.

'Oh! But we must not say, we must say nothing! I do not think they are good people!' Her eyes filled with tears.

Miss Chase took her hand and held it between her own. 'What is it, Susan? Why are they not good people?'

Susan turned her head from one to the other a little wildly.

'The man, the yellow man, said it was a message from the Hall! That's what he said: "a message from the Hall". That must be this Hall, mustn't it? If we say anything, they may send another man to kill Jonathan and me.'

III.5

MRS WESTERMAN'S THOUGHTS, as they walked down the slope to Caveley, still ran on Wicksteed's journal.

'There must be a way I can get sight of his papers. There is business enough between the estates to justify me visiting the housekeeper, or Wicksteed himself. If I could get into his office and find a way to make him leave me there alone a little while . . .'

Crowther sighed. 'Mrs Westerman, he may not keep his diary in his office, and if it contains anything that might be incriminating, it is probably locked away.'

She looked up at him angrily, then kicked an offending branch clear of the path in front of her with a soft leather boot.

'I shall try, however. I will not slink away from this. I may find nothing, but I know we will learn nothing if we do not make the attempt.' And when Crowther allowed himself a roll of his eyes: 'Do you have any better plan, sir?'

He studied the earth in front of him. 'No.'

'Well then.'

There was a clap of a door slamming in front of them and they looked up to see Rachel hurrying across the grass towards them. They glanced at each other, saw their own worries reflected, and lengthened their stride to join her.

'Mr Crowther, oh Harry! Thank goodness! It is Mr Cartwright!'

Harriet looked confused. 'What do you mean, Rachel? We were there only half an hour ago.'

'Michaels has just ridden up this minute. Cartwright has been taken very ill and the doctor is attending a sickbed in Pulborough. He has come to ask your help, Crowther.'

She was very pale. Crowther did not think to question or protest but, spotting where Michaels waited, mounted at the corner of the house with his own horse beside him, set off swiftly towards him. He climbed into the saddle with a vigour he would have thought impossible days before.

'How bad?'

Michaels handed him the reins. 'Bad.'

The big man dug his heels into the horse's flanks and Crowther set off after him at a gallop, the hooves throwing dust and grass out behind them, their bodies held straight and low. He caught a glimpse of the women stranded on the grass behind him, pale and distant on the great lawn of Caveley.

Harriet turned to her sister and took her arm.

'What do you know?' she asked.

Rachel was flushed, her breathing still shallow.

'Very little. Michaels arrived only a moment ago. Cartwright has violent pains. Michaels met his girl on the street, crying her eyes out because she could not find the doctor, and so he has taken charge of the situation.'

Harriet felt her head crowd with violent fears, felt her own hand tremble on Rachel's arm.

'Let us go in, and send David after Crowther. He may carry messages to and fro for us. And Rachel . . .' her sister looked up at her fearfully . . . 'I do not wish any family of mine to make use of any gifts we receive from the Hall for a little while. Can you find a way to manage that? Discreetly if you can.'

Rachel went very white, but nodded and they turned towards the house.

Michaels led Crowther into the house and straight up the narrow stairway to Cartwright's room. The smell of vomit and bile as the door opened was enough to make Crowther sway on his feet. Both men paused, then Michaels took a chair from the middle of the room and seated himself on it in a corner. He was silent, but had the look of a guard dog about him. Crowther moved towards the bed. It was wet with sweat, and a basin sat beside it, half-filled with a yellowish vomit. Cartwright moaned, and opening his eyes and seeing Crowther, tried to pull himself up.

'Mr Crowther! Are you well? Mrs Westerman . . . ?'

Crowther sat on the bed and took the man's wrist in his hand. The pulse was exhausted, thready and jumping.

'I am quite well, and I left Mrs Westerman in perfect health.'

Cartwright fell back on his pillows and let his eyes flutter shut.

'Thank God. I feared . . .' His body convulsed; he pulled his knees to his chest with a low groan. Crowther removed his coat.

'Mr Michaels – water and all the salt in the house, please. We must do what we can to drive this from him.'

He did not look round, but heard the man stand and leave the room with quick steps. Cartwright tried to open his eyes again, panting.

'I have been poisoned, have I not, Mr Crowther?'

'I fear so.'

'And will it kill me?'

Crowther hesitated, then let himself meet the red glittering eyes of his patient.

'The violence of the attack suggests you have been subject to a heavy dose. But we will purge you, and recovery may be possible.'

Another cry, and Cartwright's knuckles whitened as his hands and jaws clenched. As the spasm passed, his hands loosened again and Crowther saw the tears in his palm where his neat nails had dug at the flesh. The sick man breathed hard a moment, then looked up again.

'It came so sudden. A strange taste . . .'

'Like metal?'

'Yes.' Cartwright looked confused. 'How did you know?'

'Arsenic. Then came a violent headache and the sickness?'

Cartwright nodded again, though this time he kept his eyes shut. His skin was clammy and yellow. Crowther smoothed the man's hair away from his forehead.

'I have some things in my store so we can make you more comfortable.' He did not know if he was heard.

Michaels came up the stair again, with Hannah on his heels.

Crowther realised as he mixed the salt and water together and held it to Cartwright's lips that this was his first ever living patient. He doubted the case would be a credit to him; the dose must have been very large, and other than purging his stomach, there was little he could do but keep vigil. The effect of the salts was almost immediate. Cartwright groaned and twisted in his bed to vomit again into the bowl. It lay in a patch of late-afternoon sunlight on the dark wooden flooring, lapped by the edges of Joshua's bedlinen. They caught a little of the spatter of bile from his mouth. There was some blood. Crowther wondered if the stomach was already bleeding, but perhaps it was only that Joshua had bitten the lining of his mouth while caught in one of the spasms.

Taking the glass, he filled it with clean water and raised his patient a little from the bed with an arm round his shoulders, getting him to drink. Cartwright took greedy draughts of it, and fell back against Crowther's shoulder. Some water dribbled down the side of his face. Crowther removed his handkerchief and gently cleaned it away. The man let him, panting again, the body waiting for the next attack. His eyes opened briefly, the cornea flushed scarlet with blood. It was like coming face to face with hell itself.

'Will it take long, Mr Crowther?' he panted.

'Perhaps a day.'

Cartwright grunted and turned his face away. Crowther stood and noticed Hannah.

'Can you read, girl?' She nodded. 'Then go to my house and bring me the jar from the cabinet in the study marked *Valerian*.'

She looked confused and Crowther sighed impatiently. Michaels opened a drawer under a little table against the dark wall at the back of the room, then pointed to the ink and paper it contained. Crowther thanked him and wrote the word on the paper.

'And here is the key. My servants will show you where the cupboard is. Hurry back.'

She flew out of the room and Crowther watched the door shut behind her without moving. Michaels spoke.

'Do you know what's doing it, Mr Crowther?'

'From the violence of the attack and the metal taste he noticed – arsenic, I should think.'

'Any hope?'

Crowther shook his head.

'When Hannah gets back I'll go down with her and stop up the bottles,' Michaels said.

'Check the food too, if he has eaten in the last hour.'

'Why did he ask after you and Mrs Westerman?'

'We were here a little while ago, to ask if he saw Brook on his way into town,' Crowther replied. 'He gave us lemonade.'

'Which did you no harm.'

'As you see.'

Michaels bit the side of his thumb and turned away a little. 'And *did* he see Brook?'

'Yes. And had Viscount Hardew's address waved in his face. He could not remember it, though.'

Michaels clenched his fists. 'You found that nurse from the Hall?'

'Yes.'

'Murdered too, I'm guessing. Though the village is trying to tell itself suicide.'

'Yes. Murdered.' Crowther did not elaborate, but picked up another chair and set it by his patient's head, He then arranged his limbs as one prepared to wait a long time.

Michaels looked at him sideways. 'What was it you sent for?'

'An opiate. It should lessen his pain at the end.'

Michaels sighed and took his own seat again in the shadows.

Rachel picked up her book and then put it down again, having stared at the same paragraph she had just read twice without understanding it. Harriet continued to walk up and down the room. There was a light knock at the door and Mrs Heathcote came in with a paper folded once. Harriet snatched it from her and opened it, biting her lip.

'Harriet?'

She turned to her sister and put the note in her hand.

'Poisoned. There is nothing to be done.'

Mrs Heathcote started. Then recovered herself.

'I'll send David back again to wait for more news, ma'am – if there's no message, of course.'

Harriet nodded without looking up.

'Do, please. There is no message.'

Crowther was not sure if Michaels had sent for the Squire himself, or if the air had carried the news to him without need of human informer. Whatever way, Bridges had arrived, and having spoken to the maid now took his place in the growing dark alongside Crowther and Michaels. The air in the room was heavy and fetid, and though Crowther had flung up the window there was not enough breeze in the air to carry much relief. Cartwright was becoming delirious, calling on his wife and son, sometimes in tones of desperate loss, at others joyously as if he saw them just in front of him.

Bridges waited till Crowther had cooled his patient's forehead and measured again the struggling pulse before taking his arm and leading him into the hall.

'You think it is poison?' he asked.

'I am sure of it.'

'Is his mind still secure? Can we find from him how this came about? Some accident, perhaps.'

'I have given him a sleeping draught: if you wish to talk to him, do so now, then I may dose him with a more generous hand. His suffering is extreme.'

The Squire sucked his teeth and nodded. 'Very well, very well. From where do you think the poison came?'

'I have not yet examined the bottles or foodstuffs in the kitchen, but I suspect the aqua vitae he received from the hand of Mr Thornleigh. The maid said he took some just after Mrs Westerman and I left here. The symptoms came so hard and sudden I can think of no other cause. The lemonade we drank together was obviously not tainted. You can see that by the fact I stand here and speak to you now.' Crowther's whisper was harsh and violent.

'Indeed.' The Squire replied. 'Unless it was only his glass that was tainted, as you put it.'

'That we can clarify with experiment swiftly enough. Give a sample of the liquor to any dog in the street. If it does not die within the hour you may believe what you like.'

'Very well, very well, Mr Crowther.' The Squire put his hand on Crowther's arm and held it for a moment as a man might steady himself on a moving ship. 'And you maintain the nurse was murdered also.'

'I do. Do you doubt it?'

'It is not a matter of doubt, I simply cannot understand what is happening here. Might it be a series of unrelated, unhappy events? Might that not be the simplest of conclusions?'

'It is unbelievable. These people have been murdered, and not by some lone thief.'

'You point to Mr Hugh Thornleigh.'

'If Alexander is never discovered, or found dead, then he inherits the estate! Who else stands to benefit so?'

The Squire looked at him hard in the gloom. 'And if both brothers are removed? One by stealth and one by the law – who gains there? I would not expect *you* to be so keen to see a man hanged for the murder of one of his family.'

Crowther flushed. 'I am not keen, as you choose to say it, to see any man hanged. But do not ask me to believe this an accident or Nurse Bray a suicide so you can keep Hugh safe!'

'Hugh may be better than what comes after him.'

'Even if he murders?'

'I do not necessarily believe that a murder has been committed.'

'Perhaps you might like to discuss that with the victim.'

Crowther pushed the bedroom door open again. Michaels had taken his place at the bed, and now moved aside to let him approach. He nodded at Crowther in such a way he suspected the conversation outside the door had not gone unheard. Bridges bent over the bed and cleared his throat.

'Now then, Mr Cartwright, I hate to see you in such a state! What has happened here? Some mistake with the household poisons?'

Cartwright opened his eyes and the Squire recoiled slightly. The breath came in rattling gasps.

'Water,' he said.

Crowther filled the glass and pushed past the Squire to give him drink. Cartwright sank back, then sighing, opened his eyes again.

'Perhaps. Yes, perhaps. We were killing mice last Sunday.' He looked up into the Squire's round face with desperate eyes. 'I took water with the liquor Captain Thornleigh brought. Perhaps. Must have been so.'

The Squire rocked back on his heels with a satisfied smile and blinked innocently at Crowther. The latter said nothing, but did not trouble to hide his disdain. Joshua he would not blame. If the draper wished to believe himself a victim of accident, and that belief soothed him, then so be it.

Turning to the table, he added a few drops to the water glass from a brown bottle. A swirl of light purple sunk and spread in the water, and he offered the glass again to his patient. The eyes suddenly opened and locked onto Crowther's face. Cartwright put up his hand and held the glass away from him, his bloody palm fixing round Crowther's

177

wrist with force, pulling him close to his lips. Crowther could smell death on him.

'Tichfield. It was Tichfield Street.'

Crowther felt the blood in his brain stir. He nodded carefully to show he understood; the tension fell away from Cartwright's limbs and his eyes closed. He let himself be fed the water, and with a slow sigh slipped under the waves of his suffering again.

The Squire stepped forward. 'What did he say to you?'

'Nothing but the delirium of his brain.' Crowther did not take his eyes from Joshua's face. 'He will not speak again.'

It was past three in the morning when David returned to Caveley for the last time. The ladies had not gone to bed. Harriet would not give up the watch, and Rachel would not leave her. He came in without removing his cloak and handed over the paper to Harriet, but she could have guessed half of what it contained by the expression on his face. She smiled at him very sadly. He looked pale and uneasy in the candlelight.

'Thank you, David. You have been very good. Rest now.'

He looked for a second as if he wished to say something, then turned away, but paused again at the door.

'Just wished to say, ma'am, Miss Rachel, that Mr Crowther was a gentleman to Cartwright. I hope I get care like that when I go. Though I hope not to die so hard.' He left before they could reply.

The door shut behind him and Rachel got up and took her position behind Harriet's chair, so she could read over her shoulder. The note was short and to the point.

It is over. The dose was massive. I know where Alexander is.

19 April 1775, Boston, Massachusetts Bay, America

THEY SET OUT like boys promised a picnic that morning, but it was a shocked and bloody Army that made its way back to camp the following evening.

Hawkshaw had a tear in his cheek from a farmer's blunderbuss, and he had lost three of his company to the rebels on the retreat from Lexington. He had not seen Hugh since the carnage of Bloody Angles, where the rebels had taken advantage of a sharp turn in the round to ambush and harry his men. He had never felt so exposed. These pretty wooded hills and valleys, their irregular roads and riverways made for pleasant farming country, but it was the devil's own work to fight in. The rebels came up out of nowhere at them as they made their way back into Concorde, some piling right into their midst to send off a shot though it was certain death to do so. The Army could not be sanguine about any meeting with these men in the future, surely. They were ragged and undisciplined, but brave, and knew how to use the land to their advantage.

Hawkshaw pulled off his coat in the relative peace of his quarters and tried to wash out his wound. He took some of the water from his bowl in his mouth and spat it out again, thick with his own blood. He had even seen a woman firing by the side of her husband from one of the farms along the way. Both had been killed, and the house set alight, but it was a chilling scene. If they could make their women fight like that, how great a force would be required to subdue them? More than were here, and more than were likely to come soon, and in the meantime they were in danger of being pinned down in this bloody bay like animals in a pit. The rebels seemed to him like little boys throwing sharp rocks at bears. Not much of a competition in a straight fight perhaps, but if they could not reach out a claw and connect, and the stones were sharp enough, it was plain where any sensible man should lay his bets.

The door behind him opened and he looked up, expecting to see his servant come in with a fresh shirt. It was Hugh. He was worn, and his shoulders slumped, but Hawkshaw could not see any sign of wounds. They looked at each other for a moment with satisfaction, then Hugh held out a long plain bottle towards him.

'Here. Brought this for you. My father sent over a half dozen bottles of brandy so the mess can toast him and his new wife. We'll use it to wash out our wounds.'

Hawkshaw took it from him and lifted it high, letting a long draught into his mouth and swilled it over his gums. It found the wound and made him wince. He could not say anything about the quality of the liquor. All he could taste was his own blood and dirt.

Hugh watched him. 'Can you talk?' he asked.

'Yes. It looks worse than it is. No long speeches from me though. Who did you lose?'

Hugh kicked out at the wall of the little hut hard enough to make the floorboards jump.

'Four good men. Young, Spicely, Ball and Tom Cartwright. Spicely was one of the first killed up at the bridge. The animals scalped him. And Cartwright died hard. He only joined up six months ago, comes from my home, and took one in the guts. He was looking at me in the eye as he died, rattling back on the cart, and all I could think of was how pathetic that little moustache he's been trying to grow looked. He was a baby still. And all the time looking at me like I'm a god who can heal him with a handshake and trying to be brave.'

'It was good you stayed with him.'

'Much good it did him. To hell with it! Four good men! And for what? Throwing half a tonne of shot into a duckpond, and burning a couple of gun carriages.'

Hawkshaw passed him the brandy bottle and Hugh took a long gulp of it before he continued. 'We cannot afford to throw men away like this. Two others wounded, won't be fit for months. I'll

180

have to fill the company again. What about you? Seen your injured yet?'

'Of course. Parkinson looks in a bad way. The others who made it back will live. Thank God Percy made enough noise to be allowed to come up and cover the retreat. There'd be a lot fewer of us here now if he hadn't.'

Hugh sat down heavily on the bed. 'I shall send him some of the brandy.'

Hawkshaw watched him in silence for a moment, then began the work of getting blood and grit out from his fingernails.

'It's true about the marriage, by the way.' Hugh looked at the emptying brandy bottle. 'Of course you know. My father writes to say she will be an ornament to Thornleigh and the London scene.'

Hawkshaw took a seat on his trunk, and reached an arm out for the bottle again without comment.

'My father has made us ridiculous, and thinks it all a very fine joke. I hope he chokes on it.'

'I met an old friend of your family today.'

Hugh looked up with his eyebrows raised.

'A man called Shapin. He heard Gregson mention your name and claimed to know you as a child.'

'I don't recall the name.'

'Seems he was a servant, transported for theft when you were a boy.'

Hugh shrugged and took the bottle back again.

'I am surprised my father didn't arrange to have him swing. He has never been forgiving of other people's sins.'

Hugh held the bottle to his forehead, as if he expected to find some cool and comfort in it.

PART IV

IV.1

Monday, 5 June 1780

SUSAN MUST HAVE slept, but as the light began to crawl between the shutters, and she heard the familiar sounds of a London street beginning to stir like a drunk awakening from bad dreams, it seemed to her she had spent the whole night watching the shadows on the ceiling.

She had asked Graves and Miss Chase if she might be able to tell her brother about his – about *their* – strange change in situation and expectation, and the three of them had decided to say nothing to anyone else, until she had had time to do so. It seemed right to her that she should tell him, but the decision to do so was easier than the telling. She had promised herself it would be after supper, then told herself that Jonathan was tired and needed rest, and now she had lost her own chance of sleep trying to find words that were gentle and right, and would be clearly understood.

She sighed and sat up, then swung her feet to the floor to watch him sleeping in the bed next to hers. His blond hair fell over the pillow, his arms thrown out as if he were racing up some steep slope in his dreams. His skin was as perfect and pale as the first clouds. She reached over and shook his shoulder roughly.

'Jonathan! Jonathan, wake up.'

183

He stirred and opened his eyes. She saw in them the same confusion she felt whenever she woke in this room. Those first few seconds of peace then doubt as the familiar objects of their own room in Tichfield Street above the shop failed to appear, then the squeeze of his eyes, the little gulp in his chest as he remembered where he was, what had happened.

'Jonathan, I have to tell you something.'

He pulled himself up onto his elbows, and rubbed his eyes. 'What is it?'

'Are you awake?'

'Course I'm awake. You just shook me.'

'Our name isn't Adams, it is Thornleigh. You are probably a Viscount, and you'll be an Earl some day.'

Jonathan frowned at his sheets. 'Of where?'

'Sussex.'

He looked across at her. 'Oh. Is that where the picture comes from?'

'What picture?'

'The one on Papa's ring. With the dragon and the bird holding a shield. Perhaps that man knows.'

'It's a phoenix and you're talking silly – what man?'

Jonathan sat up properly and said indignantly, 'I am not talking silly! The man showed me a picture like the one on the ring and asked if I'd seen it. I told him about the ring and he said I was clever. Then he promised he'd come back and give me a waistcoat just like his. I liked it, it was nice. But he hasn't come back.'

'When, Jonathan? What man?'

'Days and days ago. I just told you. He was called Carter. Like horse and Carter. Why?'

'Perhaps he took the ring!' She let her voice drop and plucked at the bedclothes. 'He did not look like . . . the other man?'

Jonathan shook his head. 'No, and he was nice. Why would he take the ring? He had the picture.' They considered this for a moment, then the boy looked at her again with his head on one side. 'If I am a Viscount, does that mean you are a Lady or something?'

Susan swung her feet. 'Probably.'

Jonathan yawned and wriggled back among his sheets, and put his head on the pillow.

'They will make you learn French.'

Susan's eyes widened.

Crowther did not come home till Cartwright's body had been decently laid out, spending the time between his death and the moment the women told him that the body was clean and at rest in the glovemaker's kitchen, drinking red wine with Michaels. The huge man had left the house as soon as Crowther had closed Joshua's eyes with his long white fingers, only to return before many minutes had passed with a bottle of burgundy clasped like a toy in his huge hand, and carrying two glasses which he rubbed briefly on the edge of his shirt and set down on the table without comment.

Crowther took the glass offered him with a nod and drank deep. He wondered if he would be asked to perform an autopsy on the man. He realised he did not wish it. He had seen the effects of arsenic poisoning on the organs of a dog in London, and did not think it would add much to the sum of his knowledge to see what the poison had done to the systems of a man. He felt the wine hit his empty stomach and warm it. Without realising he was doing so, he stretched his limbs and sighed. Michaels was watching him narrowly.

'All the bottles and jars are locked away,' the innkeeper said. 'He had not taken anything to eat before the attack came on since his breakfast. Perhaps, though, you should take away the bottle that was opened from the Hall and lock it up in your medicine cabinet.'

Crowther looked up in surprise. 'You think it unsafe here?'

Michaels shrugged and spread out his thick fingers in front of him. 'I'm not sure, Mr Crowther. There are two bottles. One had been drunk from, the other not. Take the opened one away with you for my peace of mind. I'd rather not say what I think. Hardly know myself.'

Crowther turned back to his wine without commenting further. They remained in silence till the bottle was empty and the sky outside the kitchen window was beginning to thin from a summer dawn to its first full light. The door opened, and a young-looking woman came in with a firm step and a bundle of linens that she took out through the back door. She returned and laid her hand on Michaels's shoulder. He grasped it and held it briefly to his cheek. She bent over to kiss the top of his head, and Crowther felt his heart reach out. He had not seen Michaels's wife before, had not imagined so trim and young a woman, had not imagined they could portray such an allegory of domestic support. She seemed to feel his eyes, and looked up at him.

'Mr Crowther, you and my husband should go home and rest now. Hannah and I will keep vigil.'

He nodded, but when he stood, his feet took him upstairs again to the sick room. There were herbs burning in a little brass dish on one side of the room, and candles had been set on either side of where Joshua lay. Hannah sat in the chair that Crowther had occupied most of the night, and she stood hurriedly when the door creaked open. Crowther waved her back into her seat, and looked at the face of the body on the bed. How strange it was, how dead the dead looked. Joshua could never be mistaken for a man at rest. The body was empty and senseless; whatever had been human had left him. He noticed Hannah wipe her eyes.

'You were fond of your master?'

She nodded, looking a little frightened. 'Yes, sir. And . . .'

Perhaps tiredness was making him gentle, for his voice was softer than usual. 'What, child?'

She sighed and laid her hand on the bed beside her master. 'Squire

Bridges was asking all sorts of things, about the poison for the mice. I'm afraid they'll say it was my fault, sir.' Her hand patted the arm of the corpse like a woman settling a child. 'As if I'd ever hurt him.'

Crowther was silent for a second, looking at her profile in the candlelight.

'I know you did not.' She smiled up at him, quick and grateful. 'And if you have any problem finding another position, you will be welcome in my household.'

'I should like that, sir.' She looked back down at the body beside her. 'But my place is here for now.'

Crowther bowed with no less respect than he would have shown to a Duchess, left the room, and pausing only to receive a bundle from Michaels with a heavy nod, walked out of the front door and back to his own house.

IV.2

SUSAN THOUGHT THAT having told her brother her news she would sleep, but she was more awake than ever. She stepped softly over to the shutter and pulled it open a way, flinching as the brightness of the morning hit her eyes. The room she and Jonathan were sharing was on the upper floor of the house, and she could see across the city strange plumes of smoke exhaling into the sky as if half a dozen giants about London were smoking their first pipes of the day. Something caught her eye and she looked down. The thin man who seemed to be interested in Mr Graves was looking up at her. He caught her eye and swept off his hat with a flourish that made her smile. Then he looked either way along the road and lifted his hand to beckon her. She frowned. He beckoned again. She turned back into the room. Mr Graves did not like this man, she had seen that. In fact, he did not seem comfortable when this man was around. Perhaps if she asked him, he would go away. She did not want Mr Graves to be uncomfortable. She wanted him, she realised, to stay as near to her and Jonathan as it was possible to keep him.

Giving herself a firm little nod, she dressed quickly, padding through the sleeping house and turning the key to the street door as quietly as she could. One of the under-maids was cleaning out the grate in the front parlour, and she turned in surprise to look at her. Susan gave her a tight little smile and slipped out into the street while the maid, hardly older than Susan herself, was still looking about in confusion.

The street was quiet still, but Susan approached Molloy bravely enough.

'You are Miss Adams.'

His face was very lined, but not yellow. She found herself strangely reassured, and almost corrected him, before she remembered the dangers of her new name and replied with a nod.

'And you are Mr Molloy. You make Mr Graves uncomfortable.'

He let out a crack of laughter than made her jump back a step. He put one hand up to reassure her while producing a handkerchief with the other and dabbing his eyes.

'Oh, do I, miss? Do I indeed? Well, it is an uncomfortable thing to owe money, and a more uncomfortable thing still to be held to account for it. Uncomfortable or not, I must be paid today, or I shall see Mr Graves taken up for debt by dinnertime. I have a wife and child to feed.'

'What do you mean, "taken up"?' She frowned up at him.

'Prison, missy,' he said, folding his handkerchief very carefully again and putting it in his waistcoat. 'He must stay there if I cannot have my money.'

Susan put her head on one side. 'Are your wife and child hungry?'

He looked rather surprised. 'No, sunbeam, not yet. But they may come to be for the want of those twenty shillings, some day. The world has a way of spinning awful quick and sudden, you know that.' She nodded slowly, there was truth in that. 'And so we must keep our friends about us, and money is the best friend I know.'

She opened her eyes at him. 'Mr Graves is the best friend my brother and I have. And you want to take him away.'

He stuck out his chin. 'I do not. I just want the money.'

He rubbed the back of his neck and looked past her into the street. Susan continued to examine the end of his chin.

'I don't have any,' she said. He still kept up his casual survey of the street over the top of her head and shrugged. She bit her lip, then breathed in sharply and began to pull on the gold chain about her neck. 'But I do have this ring.'

He looked down quickly enough then. His eyes caught the gold gleam of the ring and the sparkle of the brilliants. His voice became low and lustful.

'That'd do it, girly. That'd do it! We'd be all square if you hand that over.'

'If I give it to you, you'll leave us and not take Mr Graves away?'

He bobbed his head. 'He'll be as safe as safe when I have that in my hand, sunbeam.'

'It was my mother's.' She said it softly.

Molloy glanced up and down the street again. 'Your mother would want you to keep your friends about you, don't you think?'

She thought. She would always have the miniature, and she would rather have Mr Graves than the ring. Susan felt tears behind her eyes. She blinked them away. Strange how these little things could help keep Graves safe. She wished the yellow-faced man had given her a chance to bargain.

'I must keep the chain so Miss Chase does not know it is gone.'

She reached behind her neck to unfasten the clasp. Molloy paused a moment, then shrugged.

'Aye, aye, keep the chain, just the ring, missy.'

He put his hand out, rubbing his thumb and fingertips. There was a sudden clatter, and he looked over her head again with a curse. Susan heard her name called, and turned, her hands still feeling behind her neck, to see Miss Chase striding across to them, her hair all loose and her eyes glittering. She put her hand on Susan's shoulder as she reached them. Molloy straightened, and began to look a little pale.

'Mr Molloy! Explain yourself.'

'Just a bit of business, Miss Chase.' Molloy ran the tip of his tongue over his thin lips. 'No need to concern yourself.'

Susan's heart began to thump heavily in her chest. 'Please, Miss Chase! If I just let him have the ring then he won't take Mr Graves to prison. Please let me. I do not want Mr Graves to go away.'

The last words came almost as a wail. Susan felt Miss Chase's grip on her shoulder tighten. She looked at Molloy.

'Terrify a child two days after she saw her father killed, would you? How dare you call yourself a man?'

Molloy straightened, though he still struggled to look Miss Chase in the eye.

'All very sad, I'm sure, miss. But business is business. You can give me the ring, sunbeam. Miss Chase has nothing to do with it.'

'Oh, is that so?' Miss Chase was quite flushed. Susan put her hands on the clasp again.

'You must let me. Please.'

Miss Chase pulled a little purse from her waistband. 'What is the debt, Molloy? I shall pay it before I let you rob this child.'

He muttered something under his breath Susan was sure she should not hear.

'Twenty shillings. And there is no robbery about it, Miss Chase. You have no right to say so.'

'I wonder what people would say if they heard this story, Molloy.' Miss Chase's eyebrows drew together threateningly.

'You must not pay it!' Susan stamped her foot. 'He wouldn't like it! You know he wouldn't. He'd be ashamed and not come near us. It must be me who pays. He looks after me! We owe him and you do not!'

Miss Chase looked confused. Susan stared up at her with desperate seriousness. Molloy gave a thin smile.

'No matter to me who pays, but I have other business to attend to, so if you don't mind hurrying along, ladies . . .'

Miss Chase glanced up at him with a sneer. 'Oh be quiet, Molloy. You've been hanging round here for days, and I am thinking.'

Molloy dropped his chin. Miss Chase wet her lips.

'Very well, Susan. I shall lend you the twenty shillings –' and as the girl began to protest – 'and I shall take the ring from you as surety. That way, you know the money is yours to spend as you like.'

Molloy did not look up, just traced a half-moon in the dust before him with his boot.

'Looks like you are getting into my business, Miss Chase.'

She looked at him with disgust but did not reply. Susan's heart leaped up happily.

'Yes, please. That would be right. And when I am a lady I can pay you back.' Susan paused. 'And buy you a carriage, if you would like one.'

'Thank you, Susan. But my father has a carriage, and I am happy to share his.' Susan accepted this with a nod.

The business was transacted. Susan took the money from Miss Chase and dropped her ring into the young woman's hand. The latter took it reluctantly, but urged by the determination in Susan's eyes, put it safely away in her purse. Susan then placed the sum owed into Molloy's hand with the bright smile of a girl buying sugar sweets. She turned away again, but Miss Chase kept her hand on her shoulder.

'The note, Molloy.'

He grinned a little ruefully and took a thick wallet from his coat.

It bristled with dirty papers; some had crumpled, and he had tried to smooth them.

'You'd be a caution in business, Miss Chase. Shame you have to stay at home and paint screens all day.'

Again, she said nothing, but watched him steadily as he rifled through his papers, withdrawing one from the centre of the greasy clump with a scowl. He put it into Susan's hand. Miss Chase still watched him.

'And is it noted that the interest has been paid?'

Susan looked blankly at the figures a moment, then turning the page over, said, 'Yes, here it is, Miss Chase.'

'Very well.'

Molloy fitted the money into his wallet and put it back into his coat, tapping it gently where it sat over his heart.

'Joy to do business with you, ladies. Young Graves is a lucky man to have such friends.' Susan looked at him with her head on one side.

'And now you have your friends, too.' He smiled at her curiously. 'The shillings. You said they were your friends.' He gave a sharp bark of laughter.

''Deed I did, sunbeam, 'deed I did!'

He tipped his greasy hat and turned to walk up the street, whistling as he went.

Miss Chase knelt down till she and Susan were looking at each other eye to eye.

'Tell me, sweet, while we are alone. Have you had a moment to say anything to Jonathan?'

Susan's feelings of independence, of power seemed to flood away from her. She looked at Miss Chase very sadly.

'Yes, and he said I would have to learn French!'

Miss Chase laughed, throaty and musical, then standing and hugging the little girl briefly to her side, she led her back into the house.

IV.3

CROWTHER STIRRED AND groaned. The knocking at the front door had been enough to wake him, and now there were voices. He half-listened as he swung from his bed and began to dress, letting the shreds of his too-brief rest scatter about the floorboards of his room. He paused. He could swear he heard a dog yelping. He shook his head and reached for his shirt. The vigil had tired him. His bones felt old.

'Of course he's asleep, girl! He was at Cartwright's bed till after dawn. But I must see him, and you must wake him.'

It was Michaels's voice. Then that yelping again. There was definitely a dog with him. He heard his maid protest once more, though the words were indistinct.

'Oh, just go and get him, for the love of God, Betsy. Or I'll cut off your father's credit at the Bear and tell him why, you see if I don't!'

Another, higher-pitched mumble.

'No, I don't want to be shown into the library, thank you! Who do you think I am? I'll wait in the hall. Now go and wake him before I lose my patience.'

Crowther opened his bedroom door and looked down into the hallway.

'No need, Michaels – you have done the job yourself.' He spoke with a smile in his voice, but catching the other man's eye looking up from the shadowed flags below him, his face became all seriousness. 'What has happened?' He started down the stairs. 'Coffee, please, Betsy. In the study.'

Michaels looked uncomfortably down at the dog by his side, held close on a leather leash. A black whippet bitch, a little grey around the muzzle.

'The dog, though, Mr Crowther.'

193

'It is no matter.'

Crowther pushed open a door on the left of the hall and let Michaels step in front of him. Then he crossed to the shutters and let the summer light in. He turned back. Both Michaels and, it seemed, the dog, were lost in open-mouthed contemplation of the room.

It was a pleasant, generous space, panelled in painted wood. The previous occupants had used it for a dining room, but Crowther did not entertain, and needed the space for his work. He had had shelves built all along the back wall which housed the volumes and preparations he most valued. In the centre of the space was a long, roughly made table, rubbed smooth with much scrubbing, such as one normally finds in the kitchens of better houses. His instruments were laid out upon it. At the far end, under a pair of brass candlesticks sat his writing desk, his neglected notebooks open on top. It was the preparations that held Michaels's eye. They were the products of almost a decade's study and careful collection. Crowther had haunted the auction rooms of London and Europe like other men with money and leisure, but he did not buy Italianate art, or marble fragments of the ancients; he bought body parts, each injected with coloured resins to show the different vessels and forms we carry, floating in sealed heavy jars of alcohol, or those strange freaks of development, opened up like so many strange texts to be absorbed, learned from. Michaels's eyes tracked along the shelves.

'What is that?' He pointed at the delicate tracery of a pair of human lungs. It was a magnificent example of the preparer's art. Each capillary through which air was drawn into the system hung like bare branches on a still day, dazzlingly complex, delicate as lacework.

'The lungs of a young man from Leipzig.'

Michaels's hand rested on his own chest; he felt it rise and fall under his palm.

'It is beautiful,' he said.

Crowther smiled to himself and set a chair by the table in the centre of the room.

'Do sit down.'

The door opened and Betsy came in to set the coffee things between them. Michaels's leg bounced with impatience as she set down the cups. The dog seemed less concerned, and with a wide yawn, curled itself under his chair and rested its nose on its forepaws. Betsy left, still keeping her eyes away from the shelves, and as the door closed, Crowther said one word.

'Well?'

Michaels balled his fist and worked it into the cup of his other hand. 'The kitchen in Cartwright's house is all smashed up.'

Crowther bent forward. 'Good God. Your wife, and Hannah?'

Michaels looked up with a quick smile. 'Both well and more angry than frightened. They did not hear anyone come in, and when the noise started they found they could not leave the bedroom. When things got quiet, my wife climbed out of the window and came to fetch me.' He met Crowther's eye. 'Do you still have the bottle?'

Crowther got up without speaking and crossed to the cabinet in the darkest corner of his room. Drawing a key from his waistcoat he unlocked it and withdrew the bundle that Michaels had handed him the night before. He carried it back and set it down on the table between them, then took up his coffee cup again.

'Good,' Michaels said.

'Who did it?'

Michaels put down Crowther's delicate china with conspicuous care, like a man being careful with his daughter's playhouse things.

'Squire's boys, I reckon.'

Crowther nodded. 'Why?'

'I heard him say it to you outside the door yesterday. He thinks Hugh did it, but he is scared of what will happen if Lady Thornleigh and her son get control of the estate. She's smart. And there is bad blood between them.' Michaels tried to explain. 'I suspect they knew each other in town before she married the Earl, and she reckoned he treated her badly. She looked like she was going to make life difficult for him when she first came out here. Then Lord Thornleigh took ill, and all the power shifted about again.'

Crowther nodded slowly. 'So he thinks it was Hugh, and is aiming to protect him.'

'You'll see enough of it at the inquest this afternoon. The Coroner will be twitching like a rabbit in a snare, not knowing who's going to end up having authority over him.'

'And do you think Hugh was the poisoner?'

'He handed over that bottle, didn't he? I always liked him as a boy, but something went wrong with him in America . . . and even if it wouldn't be pleasant to have that whore collecting our rents and teaching her little boy how to keep us small, I'd rather deal with that than a murderer.' He looked up into Crowther's eyes, the glint of them blue as chipped ice in his dark face. 'And there's such a thing as justice, isn't there, Mr Crowther? You and Mrs Westerman know that. I can see it by the way you are carrying on.'

'We'll do our best. Are you casting your lot in with us then?'

Michaels shifted a little on his chair.

'I reckon I shall. I can always sell the Bear and move away – I've had offers enough in the past. Anyhow. That's why I brought the dog. Let's test the bottle on her and we can see if the Coroner is willing to stare us down then.'

'Very well, but I think we should send for the vicar.'

'For a dog?'

'For another witness to what happens to her.'

'Very well then, Mr Crowther,' Michaels agreed. 'We shall.'

Miss Chase kept her hand on Susan's shoulder as they came back into the house, and sat down with her on the sofa in the front parlour.

Susan looked up into her face, still slightly flushed from the confrontation with Molloy, and saw there confusion, pity and, Susan thought, amusement chasing itself over her pretty features. She shook her head as if hoping the thoughts would settle out a little, then gave a half-laugh. 'Oh Susan, I have no idea what to do. Should I tell Mr Graves of what you have done?'

Susan bit her lip. 'I do not know. I don't want him to worry about Molloy, but it would make him awkward, don't you think, to know that we have paid his debt.'

Miss Chase nodded seriously, studying her hands clasped in front of her and letting Susan think out her thoughts.

'Maybe he will think Molloy has had a change of heart, for our sakes, and gone away for a while,' the girl suggested.

Miss Chase brushed a strand of Susan's hair behind her ear.

'Wise child,' she said. 'It is likely. He thinks, I believe, only of you and Jonathan at the moment.'

Susan's eyes lifted briefly. 'And of you.'

Miss Chase looked conscious and down at the floor again. Then, after a pause: 'Susan. I think it very important that you know, whatever happens, Graves and I will not leave you. We will stand your friends.'

Susan felt her throat close. 'Papa did not mean to leave us either.'

Miss Chase opened up her arms and gathered the girl to her. Susan cried on to her soft shoulder, feeling the young woman's hair falling across her neck, the stroke of her hand across her back. Susan thought of her father, looking up at her with a smile; heard his sharp laugh and felt her bruised heart stutter and complain as if it had just begun to beat again. She wept, but her tears tasted different.

Harriet woke early despite her vigil of the night before. The household was quiet. She left her room and turned up the stairs that led to the nursery in the topmost part of the house, and gently opened the door to the children's room. Stephen had been fighting battles alongside his father in his dream. The sheets were caught up about him, his nightshirt twisted and damp across his thin chest. She knelt down beside the bed and smoothed the hair away from his cheek; he murmured and turned without waking.

She would never cease to be astonished by the beauty of this child she had borne. His skin was as pale as the first warm milk of the day, perfectly smooth. She let the back of her hand rest on his cheek a moment; the pleasure of it was a sort of ideal pain.

The door opened softly and the wetnurse came in with the baby. The women smiled at each other as the nurse settled on the easy chair near the unlit fire where the baby's face would not catch the sun. The child began to feed eagerly, and Harriet felt a dull pull in her own breast, as if of a memory. She knew that women of her class were feeding their own children more and more, and when Stephen was born, rootless and afloat on her husband's own patch of England, she had had no choice but to sustain him herself. Her little girl, Anne, though she had handed over to another woman within hours of her birth, bound her own chest and continued with the business of the estate.

As she watched, Harriet hoped that the decision had not been affected by the sex of the child. She had wanted a daughter, her husband had wanted a girl too, and Harriet looked forward to greeting a child much more herself than Stephen could ever be – but when the midwife had put the child into her arms, she had felt with that first terrifying rush of love a sort of hopelessness. And what can you be? she had thought, examining the neat little nails, the dark fuzz of hair, so different from Stephen. Married. Happily or unhappily, you have only one decision to make in your life and your whole life hangs on it. The weight of the thought had left her breathless, and the midwife lifted the baby from her, thinking her still exhausted by her labours. She had heard the child being handed to the wetnurse as she pretended to sleep, looking out over her gardens from her bedroom window, though of course, like everything she wore or ate, the horse she rode or the pen she used to write up the accounts, it all belonged to her husband. She lived on suffrance, like every prettily dressed lady in the world.

She moved over to stand behind the nurse to watch the little girl feed. Her movement distracted the baby, who whined and refused the breast. Harriet shrunk back a little.

'Hush, little one.' The nurse smiled down softly, then said to her mistress, 'Will you hold her for a moment, ma'am?'

Harriet shook her head. 'Anne is like her mother. Hates to be disturbed at breakfast,' then she leaned down to fit her finger into the tiny balled hand. The child's eyes opened suddenly and they looked long at each other, and in a mist Harriet saw all her possible futures laid out in front of her. Then the child wriggled and opened her pink mouth with a soft mew. The nurse shifted her on her knee.

'She's flourishing, ma'am.'

'Good, good. Thank you for your care of her.' Harriet stood up straight again. Then left the room without looking back, letting the door close soundlessly behind her.

IV.4

IT WAS ONLY an hour later that Harriet stepped firmly into Wicksteed's private study with a nod to the maid, and sat herself in the low armchair by his window without waiting for an invitation. The estate manager looked up at her with surprise from the desk at which he was writing, then stood and bowed swiftly.

Harriet waved her hand to usher him back to his chair and began to pull off her gloves. He watched her without speaking, as if observing some wild but harmless creature. A monkey behind glass, a bird in a cage. She had meant to study him, but found herself subject. There is a certain sort of man who knows how to look intensely at a woman and make her feel exposed. She wondered if even Jemima, Lady Thornleigh, might find something fresh in a gaze of such violent focus, marvelling and amazed, unblinking. It held one. She swallowed before she began to speak.

'Forgive me coming in like this, Wicksteed, so early in the day.' He began to murmur some compliment; she cut across him. 'But I wanted to check with you the figure over the sale of the pretty roan we purchased from the estate for my sister in March.' She peeped at him through her lashes, with a sigh. 'I fear I must have copied the wrong figure into my accounts. The column won't add up correctly now, no matter how many times I try, and that was the one sum where I thought I might have made the error. I had it as twelve guineas, but twenty-one seems a more likely figure for such a pretty mount – and if that was the error, then all my sums will come out right!'

She beamed up at him hopefully. His expression did not change. 'I am happy to check, Mrs Westerman. The books for March are in the main office, though I think you are right and twenty-one guineas was the figure.'

Harriet leaned forwards confidentially. 'Oh, would you, Mr Wicksteed? It would be such a kindness. The Commodore hates coming home to find the accounts in anything but a pristine order, you know.'

Wicksteed stood slowly and looked around the room. 'I may be a few moments . . .'

'Oh, I am most happy to wait!' Harriet leaned back in her chair. 'And I have another favour to ask. Your housekeeper has a receipt for jugged hare I think quite wonderful, and I promised Mrs Heathcote I should try and find the secret of it. Might you ask her to jot it down for me?'

Wicksteed frowned and Harriet thought she might have over-played herself. He looked at her again and suddenly smiled. She had seen him do so rarely and it almost shocked her. His teeth were very white. She felt like a child who has done something charming in its innocent stupidity. He turned and stepped smartly from the room.

Harriet let her smile drop as soon as the catch fell, and began to stand. The door opened again, and she managed to twist her body as if she had been doing no more than make herself comfortable. Wicksteed was still smiling.

'Perhaps I can offer you some refreshment, while you wait.'

'Oh no, I am perfectly comfortable, thank you,' Harriet reassured him.

He bowed and closed the door. She counted to ten as slowly as she could, then stood and moved swiftly to the writing desk where she had found him. There was a heap of offcuts of paper on the table, but her first thought was for the fabled diary. She searched briefly through the neat pigeon-holes on the desk, looking hopefully for his brown books, his journal books. The little desk had two drawers; the first opened easily enough and contained nothing but spare quills and papers; the lower had a little brass lock and would not yield to pressure. She cursed under her breath and wondered if any of her household might confess a colourful enough past to encompass lock-picking, and whether they might teach her. She should have considered that.

There was a noise outside, and she paused, counting the heavy beats of her heart till a footstep had passed in the hall, then turned her attention again to the pile of papers on the blotter. They were drafts or partial drafts of a letter, and she shuffled them between her hands for a few moments, frowning. Wicksteed had a very precise hand, she found herself thinking it a little too florid, too practised for a gentleman . . . then the fragments of phrases began to coalesce in her mind.

'Oh really?' she murmured. 'That is what we are about, is it not?'

Another step. She dropped the papers and turned to the window, so that when Wicksteed pushed the door open again, a little suddenly, she could affect to turn away from the view. He paused in the doorway. Harriet looked at him expectantly.

'Here is the receipt from our cook.' He held it out to her and she folded it neatly and slipped it into her glove. 'And you were correct. The price was indeed twenty-one guineas.'

She clapped her hands together. 'You are so kind! That is perfect!'

His eyes tracked across the room to the papers on the desk. Harriet saw, a little tightness growing in her throat, that she had pulled the locked drawer a little proud of the surrounding timbers as she tugged on it. Wicksteed met her eyes and she felt her smile start to falter from within.

'I hope you have all the information you need now, Mrs Westerman, for your calculations.'

His dry voice seemed to press on each of her vertebrae in turn.

'I have enough for now, I think, Mr Wicksteed.' Her own voice was perhaps a shade too light. 'Thank you for your assistance.' She made as if to go, but he did not move away from the door, lifting and dropping the catch, watching it closely.

'Can I trouble you for a little news?' he said. 'I hear Joshua Cartwright was taken ill last evening, and Mr Crowther was attending to him. Have you heard anything further?' Harriet's mouth went dry. He looked up at her. His eyes were shadowed and black.

'He died early this morning,' she said in a low voice. 'In terrible pain.'

Wicksteed looked away from her to his rather meagre view.

'Poor gentleman!'

He did not move, and continued to deliberately lift and drop the latch as if fascinated by its redundant clatter. Harriet waited for him to speak again, willing herself to keep still as the latch clacked again and again. When she thought another strike would cast her into hysterics, he suddenly stopped and spoke, and she could swear she heard some hiss in his voice.

'It seems none of us, however well established, can be sure to avoid terrible accident and great reversal, does it not?' He smiled a dead smile and then, with sudden energy, pulled the door wide enough for her to pass. 'But I am keeping you from your books.'

Harriet found she had not the voice to reply, and passed him with a slight bow. She had to go so close she could smell his breath, a sweetness, overlaid with lavender. She hurried out of the house, and set off rather fast towards her own estate, her cheeks flushed and her heart dancing against her ribs.

Mr Graves was still too much concerned with what to do next for the children to note the air of collusion and triumph in the faces of Susan and Miss Chase over breakfast. The black box had yielded up some other treasures as he sat with it the previous night, and he was keen to know what the advice of the Chase family would be.

'I have found the will, Mr Chase,' he said, putting that document into the buttery fingers of his host.

Mr Chase nodded a little cautiously and, having drawn a pair of spectacles from his waistcoat, began to read.

'You are named as the guardian of the children then, Mr Graves.'

Susan gave a little yelp of pleasure and Jonathan clapped his hands. Mr Chase looked narrowly at Graves over the top of his spectacles as he grinned back at the children. 'It is a heavy responsibility to place on one so young. I hope you will not take offence when I say I think it wrong of Alexander to place such a burden on you.'

The children's faces fell, but Graves put his hands out to them between the bread rolls and coffee pots.

'I am sure he never thought it would be necessary to pass on their care. I am honoured he thought so well of me.'

Mr Chase continued to frown. 'Yes, yes. That is all very fine and noble, sir, and I know you are a good man. But are you indeed a fit guardian for such young people? You are hardly established in the world yourself.'

Graves instinctively looked out into the street where Molloy had been standing the last day. His place was empty. He turned back to Chase, his face serious.

'You are right, of course, sir. But I am in a position to take over the shop, if necessary, in a way those with greater concerns,' he dropped his eyes, 'might not be able to do.'

'Though that might be moot, given what we have discovered about Alexander's family.'

'As you say.'

'But I told you what that man said!' Susan looked at them both, wide-eyed. 'We must not let him know where we are. The people at the Hall sent him to kill us.'

Mr Chase looked very dark. 'If that is so, Susan, they will be punished. But, you are right, my dear, do not be alarmed, we must be discreet.' He looked at Graves again. 'What do you propose, Graves? You and the children have a home here as long as you require it.'

'You are all kindness, sir.' Graves paused and then declared, 'I propose to write to the local magistrate, if I can find out who he is.' And when Susan shook her head violently, 'No, don't worry, Susan, we can ask for any responses to be sent to the White Horse coffee shop. There is no need for us to tell them where we are.' Susan's shoulders dropped again. 'Then we can see where we are at.'

'Very well, Mr Graves. That seems sensible, but I would be glad to talk to you more on these subjects.' Mr Chase placed his napkin on the tablecloth. 'Perhaps you will walk out with me today. I wish to see what the situation is in the town and would be glad of your company. My daughter and wife will look to the children in our absence.' He turned to his daughter. 'Indulge an old man, my dear. Do not go beyond our street. Mr Graves and I will know more when we return, but I think the streets are still too rough for ladies today.'

IV.5

THE VICAR LOOKED deeply uncomfortable. 'Surely the Squire ...' he began.

Michaels's voice in reply was almost a growl. 'Squire's got work enough. Your word is as good as anyone's in the parish, is it not?'

The vicar decided not to answer directly.

They made an odd little group in the back yard of Crowther's house. Hannah, rather pale, but steady on her feet; Michaels like an oak walking, with his unsuspecting dog at his feet; the vicar, red in the face already; and Crowther with the bundle under his arm.

'Right then,' Michaels announced. 'First off, Hannah, I want you to have a look at the bottle there and say if it is the one Joshua drank out of last afternoon, and if it looks as it did when we sealed it after he was taken ill.'

She stepped forward smartly enough as Crowther unwrapped his bundle and showed her the bottle. She bent forward and ran her finger over the seal.

'Just as it was, sir.' She looked up at the vicar. 'See, the wax we put around the stopper is just as it was last night. That's the colour of our kitchen candles. Look! There's a bit where I let the wax fall crooked, because my hands were shaking a little.'

The vicar caught Michaels's eye and hurriedly leaned forward to peer more closely where she indicated. He looked about him and shuffled his feet.

'Yes, I see, I see.'

The door to the house opened with a clatter and they saw Mrs Westerman step into the yard. She paused for a second to look at them, before saying, 'Good morning, Crowther. Gentlemen, Hannah. Your maid tells me you are about to kill a dog.'

The gentlemen bowed, and Hannah gave a friendly bob. Crowther replied rather wearily, 'Indeed we are, Mrs Westerman. At least, I fear so. Do you wish to observe?'

'If I may.'

Michaels turned to Hannah. 'No need for you to stay now, if you don't wish it, girl.'

Hannah glanced quickly at Crowther. 'I am not afraid to see it,' she said, 'but the kitchen at home is still in an awful mess.'

Crowther blinked at her. 'I don't doubt your stomach. Best go to your work though.'

She smiled in return, and at Harriet as she passed.

'I shan't delay you by asking about Joshua's kitchen,' Harriet said, 'but if you are going to get that poor dog to drink liquor, had you not better pour it onto some meat of some sort?'

The men looked at each other in surprise and nodded. Harriet sighed and turned back into the kitchen, emerging a few moments later with a piece of beef shank on a cracked plate, that Crowther rather suspected had been designed for his own dinner. The dog caught the scent and whined. Harriet passed him the dish, and she saw the face of his own servant appear, then disappear rapidly at the back window.

'Mrs Westerman, you are the handmaiden of science.'

She did not deign to reply, but took a seat on the edge of the raised herb beds. Crowther broke the seal and poured a glassful or so of the liquid over the meat and into the bowl. The dog whined again, and Michaels reached down automatically to stroke her head and pull her soft black ears. Crowther hesitated. Michaels caught his movement and looked up at him with a sad smile.

'Needs must, Mr Crowther. Perhaps I shall put a sign over her grave saying "handmaiden of science" too.'

The dog looked up at her master and licked his hand. Crowther set down the dish, and Michaels pulled free the string around the little bitch's neck. She ran to the plate and paused briefly to sniff it, and then got down to eating with an appetite. They stood around and watched her. The dog dragged the last scraps from the bowl, sitting down to enjoy them in a splayed crouch on the flagstones, looking up every now and then as if afraid the strange figures standing around her might try to snatch it away. More minutes passed, and the dog wagged her tail and looked as if she planned to sleep.

Harriet wondered vaguely if she should ask Betsy to bring out tea. She plucked a sage leaf from the bush beside her and cracked it between her fingertips, holding it to her nose for the scent. There was a sharp whine and she looked at the dog. Her ears were back tightly on her head and she slunk to her master's boot. Crowther picked up the dish by its extreme edge and took it to the pump, washing and filling it with water before putting it in front of the dog again. She sunk her muzzle into it, lapping greedily, then whined and shivered again, then with a retch began to vomit. Crowther touched the vicar's sleeve. He started a little.

'Note the yellow bile. Typical of arsenic, and just as Joshua.'

The vicar nodded, his eyes wide. Michaels got down onto his knees and rubbed the dog's flanks, as she looked up at him. Harriet felt the back of her eyelids twitch. Crowther cleared his throat.

'It will not take long.'

The dog howled and scrabbled her legs, the nails scraping along the stone. Michaels kept his hand on her.

'Easy there, my dear. Easy there.'

The dog tried to lick his hand again, then gave a sudden yelp. Harriet set her jaw. The animal continued to whine and whimper and wriggle under Michaels's heavy paw. Crowther folded his long limbs to crouch alongside him, looking into the dog's pupils.

'Careful it does not bite you, Michaels.'

He looked at his watch again. Michaels kept his eyes on the dog.

'No, she'll not do that. No matter what.'

The dog jerked and yelped again, looking out past them all at the sky visible over the wall of the courtyard, retched again, then with almost a sigh, the cage of her ribs shuddered and was still. Crowther snapped his watch shut, making the vicar jump.

'Half an hour from when she began to eat.'

The vicar, who was very white, simply nodded.

'And you'll testify to what you have seen this afternoon at the inquest?'

'This afternoon, why . . . yes, of course.'

Michaels still knelt by his dead dog, stroking her ears. Harriet watched them.

'Poor little bitch,' she said, and let the last of the crumbled sage fall from between her fingertips.

IV.6

GRAVES WAS AMAZED by the pace at which Mr Chase could walk. Even with the heat of the day boiling up, and the crowds shoving each other horribly near the churning wheels of carriage and cart along High Holborn, he strode forward, and the people of London, recognising a strong will and a firm hand, parted for him. Graves bobbed along in his wake, occasionally shouldered by those who had stepped aside for the older man, and missing his step on the wreckage and rubbish knocked about on the pavements. He wondered if he were being subject to a demonstration; an illustration of his own small powers in contrast to the solidity of his host. He was torn between resenting it, and recognising the justice. He had been quick to calm the children in the morning, but his first sensation on seeing his name as guardian in Alexander's will had been one of fear. He would let no man call him a coward, but this was a burden that terrified him.

Mr Chase came to a sudden stop, and caught up in his own thoughts as he was, Graves almost barrelled into the back of him. Mr Chase paused and put his nose into the air.

'This way, Mr Graves. I should like this over with you away from the house, and I think my coffee house is the place to be.'

Graves put his hand to his pocket. He had four shillings, though they were owing to Molloy, but it would be enough to give him the appearance of a gentleman in a public place. They were not far from the coffee shop, which turned out to be a pleasant enough little house whose high bay windows were already full of customers at their pipes and papers, the long-handled coffee pots set among them like the hookahs in the Arab houses by the wharf. Mr Chase greeted half a dozen men as they entered, but found a table that would admit no more than himself and Graves in a more secluded corner, and ordered drink and pipes from a young serving girl who greeted him by name.

Graves looked about him. Each of the coffee shops that had become so much part of the fabric of London in the last years had developed its own character and its own clientèle within a few months of its existence. Where Graves usually went in Fleet Street to comfort himself in disappointment, or to celebrate any victory real or imagined, the drinkers looked pinched and bitter, or loudly traded barbs and satires. One could not take two steps before a friend or casual acquaintance placed an inkstained palm on one's sleeve to whisper gossip or complain of their outrageous treatment at the hand of a printer, or to claim they had been insulted in the ill-read and ill-rhymed verses of another. Some men scratched at their badly fitting wigs and screwed up their eyes against the smoke to try and find floating free above them the right word, the right ringing phrase to seal a paragraph, make their friends jealous and their enemies fall like so many wooden soldiers. Others boasted at broad tables of their latest commissions and future successes, apparently oblivious to the fact that none of their companions was willing to look them in the eye.

Graves always felt a twinge of sympathy when he saw the boasters, knowing, as sure as he knew himself, that their desks were dusty and the pages empty. No man who has seriously begun a work speaks of it with such pride and pleasure. Only the idea is that delightful. It was the quiet men with an air of abstraction, deep lines in their foreheads and the impression of being continually almost in tears in whom Graves believed as writers, after his faith in the boasters and versifiers continually searching for a patron or cursing their enemies had failed.

Mr Chase's preferred coffee house was altogether more comfortable. The men were as well-dressed as Mr Chase himself, and mostly as broad. There were no pretensions to high fashion – the waistcoats of the gentlemen were not heavily embroidered or strung about with fobs and seals, but the cut of the cloth was universally good, and the quality fine. Graves thought of his mother's two tabbies, sleek, happy animals, licking their paws in front of the fire when they had enjoyed a successful hunt. Business must be in general good, despite the disturbances in town. Graves could fancy he heard an underlying purr among the talk and clatter of cups; the sound of men who even as they drank and drew on their pipes were making more money than their families and other dependants could spend.

Graves looked across at his companion. 'Do you think the rioters are done, Mr Chase?'

Mr Chase looked up, as if surprised to find he was not alone.

'Eh, my boy? Oh, perhaps. We shall know in a few hours.' He pulled at his earlobe and his eyes clouded a little. 'That is Mr Landers standing by the door. He is a Catholic with a neat little warehouse in Smithfields, and he looks a trifle wan. And there is Granger, a rival of his, in the other corner: he would set the mob on him without a second thought if he believed we would not suspect and shun him for it in future. We must wait and observe. The brewers will be nervous. Gordon's lot have decided that brewing is a Catholic trade, and of course a distillery is the crowd's favourite place to pillage and burn.'

Graves frowned and looked around the room again, noticing under the creamy prosperity he had observed at first, signs of abstraction and concern. The low murmur of talk seemed to change key in his inner ear and he felt a tension, overlaid by good manners and reticence, breathe through the air.

Mr Chase sighed. 'But I wish to speak of something else, my boy, touching on these children.'

Graves drew himself straight. He had formed a plan of his own since dawn, deciding to take over Alexander's business in Tichfield Street, and manage it for the sake of the children. Whatever their new prospects, he felt he could provide them with a safe home for some little time there. He prepared to explain himself, but Mr Chase prevented him, lifting his hand.

'I had hoped that there would be something else in that black box of Alexander's,' he said, 'something that would spare me the necessity of speaking to you myself. But I fear there was nothing, or I would see it in your face.'

Graves blushed, which drew a smile from his companion.

'Yes, I think I can read you well enough, young man. But do not let that shame you. It is good to be open in your countenance: it speaks well of your soul.' He drew at his pipe. 'I have known Alexander since his first days in town. It was I that lent him the money to establish himself.' Graves tried to interject. 'It was a loan only, and paid off in good time. The shop is unencumbered.' He paused again and put one fat hand down on the table-top, lifting and dropping his fingers one by one as if observing the functioning of some new mechanical toy. 'I'd give anything not to tell you what I am about to. It was a slip of Alexander's, and – well, there it is. I cannot know it and not tell you. And I cannot *un*know it now, no matter what I would like.'

Graves drank from his coffee and waited. He had never seen Mr Chase look so uncomfortable. He kept pulling his waistcoat straight over his generous belly till Graves worried about the strain on his well-stitched buttonholes.

'Alexander did not only desert his family over love of his wife.' Graves stayed very still. Mr Chase glanced up at him, then back to his waistcoat, turning one bone button back and forth between his thumb and forefinger. 'He suspected his father of something. A crime – a bad one. Something that disgusted him, at any rate. His mother died, you know, when he was just a scrap of a lad.'

Mr Chase abandoned the button and began to draw furiously on his pipe, as if he wished to disappear behind its cloud. His eyes darted back to Graves's brown eyes and away again.

'Can you tell me no more?' Graves looked hard at him.

Mr Chase hunched his shoulders and looked fixedly over Graves's shoulder.

'No. He was drunk when he told me that much. There was mention of a locket. Some tin locket.'

'Alexander was *drunk*?'

'He had his slips, like any man – though I never saw him touch a drop of anything stronger than punch after the children were born. It was hard for him, starting out though, and for Elizabeth. Not a life he was used to. But whatever pride he had, he set it down and set to. The first plates he made, he made a hash of, lost some pounds on it and it hit him hard that night. But I went to see him the following day and he was back at his work. He grew to love it in the end.'

Graves let himself fall back slightly against the dark wood of his little bench.

'I see. But can you really tell me nothing more than this?'

'It may be nothing. Or nonsense.'

'If you thought it all nonsense,' Graves said, 'I don't think you would have told me.'

Mr Chase gave a reluctant smile. 'Maybe. I think I am just adding my warning to Susan's, to deal carefully with the Hall. Alexander had good reasons for staying clear, and we must be circumspect and watch over the children.'

Graves had just opened his mouth to ask something further when the door swung open. A lad in a dirty greatcoat three growths too large for him, his face streaked with soot and sweat, held it wide and yelled into the room. The blue cockade in his hat hung forward like a drunken devil urging him on.

'The mob are up and working! Look to your business, gentlemen! Down with popery!'

Several men stood. Mr Landers crossed himself and shouldered his way out of the door. There was a general bustle as bills and coats were gathered. Mr Chase looked grim.

'Come on, lad. Let us see what is afoot.'

IV.7

THE BACK ROOM of the Bear and Crown was crowded again, and although the populace of Hartswood had brought in the smells and tastes of high summer on their clothes and skin, the mood was dark. The room buzzed with low threat and fear. News passed from mouth to mouth, whispered, urgent; men and women bent their heads together and pulled apart, paler. Harriet found herself looking swiftly about the place as she entered like an animal looking for escape routes and hiding places.

The Coroner was not yet in his chair, but sat in the furthest corner of the room. Towering over him, his hand on his elbow, his heavy face a little flushed, was the Squire. The Coroner looked up at him, and Harriet was reminded of a pet rabbit she had had as a girl, who, if anyone other than her mistress approached the cage, would cringe back, her ears flat, eyes wide, nose twitching. A fox had got her in the end. The jury shuffled in the opposite corner like a threatened flock, pulling themselves inward, looking at their boots.

Crowther set down chairs and Rachel and Harriet took their places beside him. The presence of the vicar had prevented any sort of conversation between them. Harriet had murmured something to him of her visit to Wicksteed and received nothing more than a nod. Her own speaking looks of enquiry met with no better – simply a frown and a wave of the hand. Rachel had hold of the young lad, Jack, who had found Nurse Bray's body, and was trying to talk to him, but Harriet could tell that her sister's thoughts were wandering. The boy had to tell her twice what his favourite duties were in the Thornleigh household. He had arrived walking by Hugh, or rather a little behind him, but when he noticed Rachel in the crowd he had made straight for her and taken her hand. Thornleigh had merely greeted them and turned away.

The Squire released the Coroner and swung his eyes across the room. He offered a stiff nod to the party from Caveley Park, and seemed almost on the point of approaching them when the vicar slid softly to his side. The Squire bent his head to listen, then shot a look of alarm across at them and to where Hannah stood by Michaels's massive bulk and his slim wife at the back of the room. Without taking his eyes off the conversation Crowther leaned over slightly to Mrs Westerman and spoke to her, barely opening his lips.

'The Squire fears we are in danger of hanging Mr Thornleigh, and would rather we did not.' He saw Harriet stiffen slightly. 'He may challenge what we have to say, Mrs Westerman. Are you sure you should be here?'

Harriet looked about her. The faces of her neighbours were uncertain and strained. There was no one in the room who did not know about Joshua, and none, she suspected, that did not know of the experiment with Michaels's dog. The inquest might just have the name of Madeleine Bray on the docket at the moment, but the room was alive with a doubly murderous fear.

'We will stay. But where is Alexander?'

Crowther blinked slowly. 'I have the name of the street in London, but Mrs Westerman, I must tell you, the Squire knows something of me that you do not . . .'

She turned and looked at him sharply, but before he could continue, the Coroner took his place and cleared his throat.

'We are gathered here to enquire into the death of Miss Madeleine Bray who, it seems, hanged herself in the old cottage on the edge of the Thornleigh woods this Saturday just past . . .'

There was a general drawing in of breath, and a groan from the back of the room.

'Murdered, man! Hung 'ersel', indeed.'

Harriet glanced at Michaels, who had moved up alongside them and was staring with steady attention at the Coroner. Another voice growled from the window, 'And Joshua murdered too only yesterday – or are we calling *that* an accident?'

The crowd murmured agreement. The Coroner's eyes flicked round the room, and he licked his lips. The Squire raised his voice.

'There is evidence that that death too was accidental,' he said, and the crowd grumbled, 'but I must have quiet, please. Gentlemen – and ladies,' he added with a nod towards Harriet and Rachel, then shuffling his papers he continued with a sniff, 'Sorry to see you here again, Mrs Westerman.'

Harriet flushed a little, but remained looking straight ahead of her. The Coroner cleared his throat again, his eyes spun about in his head, and Harriet imagined what he would look like if she pulled off his wig and stamped on it. The image gave her a grim satisfaction, though she was careful not to smile.

'But we are here to discuss only the death of Nurse Bray, if you please,' the Coroner continued primly. 'Now the jury have viewed the body in the chapel at Thornleigh Hall.' Crowther turned pointedly in his chair to look at where the Squire was standing, as immobile as Michaels on the other wall. He met his eye steadily. The Coroner hurried on: 'And we saw there no evidence of anything suspicious.'

Crowther stood up. 'Nonsense!'

The crowd began to whisper. The Coroner fluttered his hands in the air.

'Mr Crowther, please be seated! This is a court of law.'

Crowther remained on his feet. He was carrying a cane, and knocked its end against the stone flags so the sound echoed round the room like a gunshot.

'What of her wrists?' he said sharply. 'What of the rope burns on her wrists? Did that strike none of you as strange? The injury to her scalp?'

The noise in the room swelled into a roar.

'Hear him!'

Crowther addressed the jury. 'Was there a surgeon there when you looked at the body?' The Coroner waved his hands at the crowd, many of whom were now standing and looming forward. Harriet saw one of the farmers she knew cross himself.

'There was no time to bring in another surgeon, Mr Crowther, and we considered you perhaps, a little, ahem, close to the events.'

'Damn shame!' cried someone.

'Sneaking business if you ask me,' snarled another voice.

Harriet noted that Michaels made no movement to calm the crowd on this occasion.

'Tell us of these marks! Who killed her?' another voice demanded.

One of the jurors shuffled forward a step and said into the crowd, 'We didn't see her wrists – she had long sleeves on. And her hair was all tidy enough.'

'It wasn't when we saw it,' Crowther said loudly. 'I suggest you go and look again, if this inquest is not to be a complete farce.'

The juryman looked around at his fellows, and seeing them nod, asked a little shyly: 'Perhaps you could come and show us, Mr Crowther?'

But before he could reply, the keening voice of the Coroner cut across them.

'Enough, Edward Hedges! Your role as a juryman does not include addressing the audience gathered here.'

More mutters and low curses from the crowd. Mr Hedges turned to the Coroner with a look of outraged innocence.

'I only said—'

'Enough, I say! Mr Crowther, will you please sit down. The court does not recognise you.'

'Then bugger the court!' came a shout from the middle of the crowd. There was a laugh, and even Harriet smiled. She put out her hand and took Rachel's, holding it firmly in her lap. The Squire took a step forward; he was very red in the face.

'Mr Crowther! By what rights do you lecture us on our business?'

Michaels drew himself straight. Crowther turned to the Squire, and looked at him down his long nose.

'I am trained in anatomy and natural philosophy. I may be of recent residence in this village, but I am and remain a concerned subject of the King. Any knowledge I can offer the jury is freely given. It does not seem that they have been given much assistance in their examinations.'

The crowd cheered him. The Squire looked at him for a long moment and waited till they grew quiet again; his face looked almost black, the colouring on his fleshy cheeks was so high.

'And are those qualifications you hold in the name of Crowther, or your real name?'

Harriet looked up at him suddenly before she could control herself. Rachel's hand trembled under her own. Crowther felt the skin on his neck grow cold. It was inevitable; he had known it must come to this. He was exposed, but he wondered if the Squire was quite the tactician he had thought. He had played his trump early. Even as he waited in those long, silent moments for the words to come to him, he wondered what the Squire feared so much that he would lay down his one good card so early.

Crowther looked about him. Michaels regarded him steadily, the various faces, young and old of the village, observed him with cautious attention.

When he was a very young child his brother would make him perform little plays with him for his father's household. His brother had loved it, loved and hungered for the attention of those ranks of faces in front of him. He himself had always wished to shrink, would hurry through his words in an attempt to retreat to the safety of the wings, shouting out his text in a rush. His brother would put a hand on his sleeve as they rehearsed and counsel him, 'Go quietly, brother. Make them lean forward to hear you. Command their attention, don't bludgeon them with your speeches.' Crowther wondered if his teaching would serve him now. He let his eyes travel slowly across the crowd then looked down at his cane. Then he spoke.

'You force me to recall what I would choose to forget. But I shall answer you, here, and give my history. We shall let these people judge if I am fit to comment.' The crowd seemed to whisper and sigh. 'I was born the second son of the Baron of Keswick.' He paused, and a baritone in the back of the room spoke distinctly.

'A Northerner. Well, any man might wish to hide that.'

The man was shushed, though a quiet smile seemed to travel through the room like a breeze. It caught on Crowther's thin lips and lifted them a little. Only the Squire seemed immune, his thick frame tense and held solid. Harriet looked across to where Hugh and Wicksteed were sitting. Hugh was looking at his shoes, but Wicksteed had turned and was watching with an expression of polite amusement. The smile left Crowther's face and he looked down at the dusty grey flags at his feet as he continued.

'My father was murdered almost twenty years ago, and my brother hanged for the crime.'

He remembered Harriet's performance at the last inquest, her fluttering modesty that had called up all the protective instincts of the village. He kept his eyes low and his voice soft. He could feel the crowd straining forward towards him. You were right, brother, he thought.

'I did not wish the title, so renounced it and have since devoted my time to study throughout the intervening years. I have hidden from the past in my books and in the society of the most learned of men. I have come to know many mysteries of the human body, which is a miracle we each carry with us every day. If I can add but a little to our knowledge of ourselves I will die a happy man.' He could feel the warmth of sympathy in the room. How people love a good tragedy, he thought. Pity and fear ebbed round him, warm waters in which to drown. 'Crowther is a name from my mother's family. I have every right to it. Legal *and* moral.' He lifted his eyes, and let his voice take on its usual dry edge. 'But whatever my name or your . . .' he paused . . . 'insinuations, tell me what they have to do with the fact that Nurse Bray was tied around the wrists and hit over the skull before she was hanged.'

He let his voice grow in volume and pitch; it lifted the crowd to an outraged howl of agreement. The attention of the room, hostile and indigant, turned to the Squire. He was still too angry to feel the mood of the room, and sneered.

'Perhaps your experiences have clouded your mind, Mr Crowther. Given such a pitiable past, you could be forgiven for seeing murder everywhere.'

Crowther felt a spasm of tiredness and irritation. Damn these people. He wanted only to leave here and be among strangers again. The crowd looked at him, wavering. Harriet put down her sister's hand and stood.

219

'And mine, Mr Bridges? What experiences have clouded *my* mind? I saw the same marks as Mr Crowther described.' She felt herself blush. 'And, sir, I think it a shabby thing to force a man to admit his tragedies in public. If Mr Crowther wished to keep his past confidential,' she paused, 'well, he has the same right to his privacy as any freeborn Englishman!'

The noise in the room broke and swelled in approval. Even the Squire could feel the push of it against his sides, and began to look about him, realising too late perhaps that he had misplayed the business.

Michaels leaned back comfortably against the wall with a small smile.

'Go and look at the nurse again!' Harriet saw out of the corner of her eye Hannah cup her hands to her mouth.

'Justice! In the name of the King!' shouted others.

The Coroner waved his hand despairingly, trying to make himself heard over the noise.

'Please, please! If we could just take our seats.' He turned towards where Hugh Thornleigh was sitting. 'Mr Thornleigh, you were there when the body was found, I believe: did you see these marks?' The crowd became suddenly quiet again. It seemed as if every individual in the room had inhaled and now waited for him to speak. Thornleigh did not stand, and seemed to address his words to his boots.

'Yes, I cut her down. Can't say if they are ropemarks. But I saw marks there, true enough.'

The crowd groaned and shouted. The Squire turned white and span on his heel, storming out of the room. The shouts grew again, and a low hissing began to circulate under it around the room. Wicksteed put a hand over his mouth as a man might, trying to hide a laugh. The Coroner trembled, his voice shivering and high.

'This is unacceptable! I cannot run the court in this way! The sitting is suspended. I will return in one week's time.'

'Don't bother, lickspittle,' said the voice at the back.

The Coroner gathered his papers and scuttled out of the room in the wake of the Squire, leaving his jury open-mouthed and directionless behind him. Rachel felt a hand tug gently at her sleeve, and looked into little Jack's white face.

'Am I not to testify? Mr Thornleigh said I was to testify.'

Rachel heard the crowd rock and exclaim around them.

'No, Jack. Not today, I think.'

IV.8

'WELL, THAT WAS exciting,' Rachel said dryly as the room began to empty. Harriet patted her hand, then turned to look a little nervously at Crowther. Now that the passion had left him he looked very grey and older than she had seen him before. His head was bent forward a little, his hands clasped on top of his cane. It was an elegant piece of work, the wood black and heavy, its head, half-covered by Crowther's thin fingers, a ball of worked silver.

'I have not seen you use a cane before.'

He did not look at her.

'I am at a delicate age, Mrs Westerman. One night's loss of rest can make me an old man.'

'You are not so very old.'

There was a flash of a smile in her voice; he looked up at her and she was sorry to see his face looking dry and bitter.

'Indeed, madam? I am so glad you think so.'

The tone was hostile enough to make her blush and look away, but before more could be said, Michaels strode back into the room and spoke.

'His hand has been forced. He's just arrested Hugh for the murder of Joshua Cartwright.'

Rachel put her hand to her face and Harriet stood quickly.

'Here? Now?'

Michaels nodded. 'The Squire said he has taken evidence from the vicar and Hannah, though it's been done informally as yet, and has told him he is to remain at home. Probably in the hopes he'll put a bullet in his brain and spare us the trial. He may do as well, if I know Thornleigh. Innocent or not.'

Crowther still had not altered his posture but spoke. 'Perhaps that would be as well.'

Harriet felt the blood rise in her throat, and she turned on him sharply.

'Really? Perhaps the Squire was right and your secret past . . .' she put enough emphasis on 'secret' to make him wince, 'has made you a lover of neat endings. I am surprised your researches have led you where they have, if you value neatness above truth.' She felt suddenly the cruelty in her own words and put her hand to her eyes. 'This is not right. We must think further, and quickly. Please, let us go somewhere we can talk freely.'

She saw he was become a little grey around the lips, and a panic that she had torn down in an instant whatever trust and companionship that existed between them pricked at her skin, making it hot and angry. She felt tears rise behind her eyes. 'Oh, how can you just sit there?'

He did not look at her; only the tight, thin lips moved.

'You seem capable of talking freely enough here, Mrs Westerman.'

She bit her lip and her words deserted her. Instead, she looked at him for a long moment, then turned with a groan that could have been frustration or grief and got up to leave the room, the need for movement too urgent to resist. Rachel stood to follow her, then hesitated and took a breath.

'Mr Crowther. I do not think Mr Thornleigh is responsible for any of these deaths. You yourself have suggested other scenarios . . .'

Crowther met her eyes, his own heavily lidded, a slight sneer on his lips. 'Perhaps my solitude has made my imagination fantastical.'

She continued to look at him. 'Please help us.'

He returned his gaze to the silver mass of fruit and vines that formed the head of his cane, wondering what gods had prompted him to bring it with him this afternoon. It was the one thing he still possessed that had belonged to his father. Rachel too waited a moment, staring at his sharp profile, then realising she would get no answer either, turned and followed her sister, her pace more respectable, her shoulders drooping. Michaels spread his hands in front of him and picked at something lodged under the nail of his right thumb.

'Terrible creatures, ain't they, Mr Crowther – other people . . .'

Crowther stood and left with a steady stride. Outside, men and women paused in their various conversations to look at him. He walked on.

Graves was surprised to find how close they were to Leicester Fields. He was uncertain if Mr Chase wished to be accompanied any further, since he had set off at his usual punishing pace, but Graves still had his half-story of Alexander turning in his mind, and hoped to learn more, whatever Mr Chase had said about his further ignorance.

They turned into the open space of the fields and found themselves immediately pressed against the wall of one of the houses bordering it by a rush of men wild-eyed and hallooing, driving in front of them a startled cow into Charing Cross Road. Someone had tied a blue cockade to the animal's head, another flicked about on the end of the poor creature's tail. She had, it seemed, been made a temporary mascot. The pinched faces of the men who slapped her sides and urged her on split with glee, their eyes were glittering and small. The cow gave a startled low and tottered on as one man whipped her across the rump.

'Nooo pooopery!' the man cried and his companions hugged themselves with joy and took up the shout, pushing the poor beast past them. Graves thought of the imps in hell on the frescoes of his

father's church. Some had been painted over, their tortures too salty
for the growing nicety of the church, but he had been fascinated as
a child by those that remained, their little dark bodies and wide grins
as they tortured the waxen, naked bodies of the fallen. He thought
he saw them again now, in the smoke-stained faces of these raggedly
dressed warriors of Protestantism, in their wild delight in public
violence and desecration. He was, for a moment, childishly afraid.
Then he heard Mr Chase gasp.

'Oh, good Lord!' Graves turned to see where his companion was
pointing. 'That is Lord Saville's house.'

Graves had walked this way often enough in the past to know what
he should in rights be seeing, an elegant white stone front, with a
clean step and polished fixings, but some dark hand had passed over
it, and everything that had once appeared solid, comfortable, a symbol
of wealth and civility, was on fire. Flames licked out of the top
windows, touching their orange tongues to the roof slates, and sucking
down the guttering; the second floor belched smoke through burning
drapery, and below them, where the flames were still slipping and
curling, Graves could see shadows moving; every minute one would
come forward, smouldering and laughing, to throw plunder down
on the street below. The watching crowds cheered and danced, their
soot-streaked faces shining and joyful, mouths open, wild. Graves
caught his breath and murmured: '"The seas are bright, with splendour
not their own, and shine with Trojan light."'

Mr Chase turned to him, a little confused. 'What, Graves?'

'Virgil. Mr Cowper's translation.'

Mr Chase coughed a little, and turned back to watch the flames.

The fire was too hot even for the bravest of the plunderers now.
As they watched, the last of them scrambled out of a parlour window,
his coat-tails alight and a large gilt mirror tucked under his arm. A
dozen men stamped out the flames for him as he stumbled into the
crowd, laughing like a child, then clapped the man across his narrow

back as if he had saved a soul from the fire. Between the bodies of men gathered around it, Graves could see the pile of plunder on the road. It was like seeing the guts of a carcass spilled out on the back yard of the butcher's shop. He could see carved gilt chairs upended and a leg snapped and splintered, books, open and torn, fluttering helplessly, great tapestries flung down and now being wrestled into improvised cloaks and blankets by the crowd. This was all it took, then. A day or two, a fool with a petition, and there was nothing safe or sacred in London. Mr Chase's thoughts must have been moving in the same direction as his own.

'We walk a narrow path, Mr Graves.'

The young man did not reply, but let his eyes close slowly and breathed in the smoke, trying to feel its texture on his tongue so that if he needed to write about it, he could bring it back. Even at this distance he could feel the heat from the broken, burning house warming his face. He opened his eyes suddenly and looked hard into Mr Chase's face.

'Mr Chase – the locket, I have been thinking on it. Did it belong to Alexander's mother?'

Mr Chase turned back to the fire, to the gibbering crackling crowd below it.

'To a young girl. That's all I know.'

There was a short loud cheer from the other end of the street. Graves and Mr Chase, like the looters, turned to see a company of soldiers, muskets over their shoulders, progressing across the open space of Leicester Fields. There were only twenty of them, but the order and determination of their march made them seem somehow much more considerable.

'A young girl?'

Mr Chase continued to watch the soldiers.

'That was all he said. "I think it was the young girl's".'

The soldiers' red coats stood out against the green, their white chasers glimmered and the dark wood of their muskets looked businesslike. They were followed by a rag/tag of men carrying buckets. Graves thought them too late to do anything to save the house, but it seemed the hopelessness of the case would not be enough to stop them trying. The crowd seemed to shrink, the less bold, or the less drunk, slipping back into its folds, lowering their heads. The company officer called a halt ten yards from them.

'Drop what you are carrying, and leave this place. I order you in the name of the King!'

It was enough, it seemed. The mob, so ungovernable before, began to thin. It was sulky; an overfed child slinking away. The men with the buckets ran forward. Graves wondered if any of them were attached to Lord Saville's family. One at least had tears running down his face. Why were they willing to make the effort, he asked himself. Perhaps to give themselves the comfort in future days of saying they had tried. The officer watched them make for the fire, and in that moment a stone flew, hard and fast from the centre of the retreating crowd, and struck one of the soldiers above the eye. The man's forehead sprang with a flow of blood at once, and he swung his musket from his shoulder into the firing position. His officer stepped forward.

'Put up your arms, Wilson. You'll fire on my order or not at all.'

Wilson froze for a moment, then put up his musket again and wiped the blood out of his eye, his stare fixed all the time on the retreating crowd.

'Bloody/backed fuckers!' someone screamed from the mob as they turned out onto the road. The soldiers did not move, but watched till the last of them scurried out of the Square, one thin man glancing again and again over his shoulders, and trying, it seemed, to dive through the legs of his companions to the relative safety of a guarded position, further away from the polished stocks of the guns.

Graves looked at Mr Chase. 'They are called bloody/backs for the colour of their uniforms, I suppose?'

Mr Chase nodded. 'That, and the Army likes its discipline, I understand. Every man in that company will have whip scars across his back among the war-wounds, I'd reckon.'

Mr Chase continued to watch the flames, and the attempt of the bucket-carrying men to douse them. The older fellow that Graves had noticed had come to a halt, and watched the burning like a child whose favourite toy has been destroyed by some act of adult carelessness.

'I was wondering why Alexander put the children into your care, rather than my own,' Mr Chase said quietly, without looking at Graves. 'Perhaps, for all that he had left his great family, and whatever horrors drove him from them, he still wished his children to be raised by a gentleman.'

Graves looked at him, frowning in surprise. '*You* are a gentleman, sir.'

Chase did not smile. 'No, lad. I am become a little like one, but we both know it goes deeper than that. However many great houses I walk into, they can still scent the workshop and warehouse on me. Oh England! I was born as those fellows there were,' he waved a hand towards the rank and file of the soldiers, 'and every Englishman knows it, soon as I open my mouth, or make a bow. I wonder if Alexander even knew that that was floating in his mind when he wrote down your name. You have something I do not, though I could buy you and a dozen like you with the change in my pocketbook.' Graves looked at his feet, and Mr Chase turned to him with a half-smile. 'Not your fault, boy. I mean nothing against you.' He twisted his hand round the railing beside him, as if preparing to pull it free. 'I have bred a daughter fit for a gentleman, though. That is my comfort.'

Graves coloured a little.

'You have, sir,' he said. 'You have.'

IV.9

THE DAY DROPPED its head towards evening. Caveley Park was quiet. Harriet and Rachel sat in the long salon saying nothing, but neither pretended to be occupied with anything more than their own thoughts. Harriet had gone upstairs for an hour when they had arrived home, and when they sat to eat Rachel thought she had been crying. They had made a poor attempt at dinner. The silence settled unhappily across the furnishings like dust. Time dripped slowly away, measured in quarters by the long-case clock in the hall. The chimes began to strike on Harriet's nerves, their little brass hammers finding the knotted cords in her spine, and making them ring. There was a soft knock at the door and Heathcote came in with a note for Rachel.

'From the Hall, miss,' she said, without meeting her eyes, and withdrew. Harriet looked across at her sister with heavy eyes as the younger woman opened the note and read it, then folded the single sheet again and held it out towards Harriet as she spoke.

'I'm sorry, Harry. But I could not do otherwise. When you went up to rest I sent a note over to Mr Thornleigh, simply to say I thought him innocent of the charge and trusted the truth would come out in time if he had patience.'

Harriet looked at her sister's tranquil face. It was typical of Rachel to do such a thing, an act of kindness and generosity the man did not deserve. She hoped that someone who did merit that tender consideration would eventually appear. The girl should be loved for it, protected from it.

'Of course, my love,' she said. 'No one could blame you for that.'

Rachel's fingers still held the sheet. Harriet waited until her sister was ready to release the paper into her care. Harriet felt her forehead throb as she opened out the sheet. She had felt as weak as a child since they had returned home. She wept very rarely, and when she did it seemed to leave her empty and adrift. She read Hugh's awkward scrawl. There was not much to decipher.

Thank you, Miss Trench. Patience has not served me well in the past, but neither has action improved my lot. I am grateful you do not think me capable of such crimes. Hugh had added his compliments to them both and his name. Harriet turned the paper over in her hands as if she hoped some secret message might appear scribbled in the corner of the sheet.

'I wonder what he means? If one had the mind, one could read this as a full confession, Rachel.'

Her sister looked up at her with a slight frown.

'I thought when he says "action", he meant sending Brook to search for Alexander. That did seem to be the start of all this horror.'

Harriet nodded, and winced a little, her headache still insistent and angry. It had been punishing her all evening, and she always told everyone she was never ill. She would be more sympathetic with ladies who fancied themselves sick and nervous in future.

'Rachel, we have not spoken of Mr Hugh Thornleigh for a long time.'

Rachel smiled a trifle bitterly. 'Indeed? It seems to me we have spoken of little else for the last few days.'

'You know what I have in mind.'

Rachel did not look up, but covered her sister's hand with her own.

'It is passing, Harry. I was very unhappy for a while, you know that. I am a little unhappy from time to time even now, but it is more like a memory of sadness, than sadness itself. Does that make sense?'

Harriet nodded. 'I am so sorry, Rachel.'

'Don't be, Harry.' Rachel looked at her with great tenderness. 'It was through no fault of yours, and though I believe Hugh is innocent, I would not wish to be his wife now, nor have I wished it for many months. I promise you that. I am not the wife he needs, nor is he the man to make me happy. Still, there were moments . . . when he used to talk about his campaigns with such enthusiasm, or his plans for the estate, there was a rightness about it. I miss thinking of the future with such happiness and excitement, Harry, that is all.'

Harriet closed her hand around her sister's, and bowed her head.

There was another knock and Mrs Heathcote opened the door again, with rather more of a flourish this time. The women looked up at her in surprise.

'Mr Crowther for you, ma'am – and a Mr Clode.'

They had not mentioned Crowther on the way home, though for her part Harriet had thought of little else, and she blamed her headache on him and his murderous family. It was not right of him to blame her for knowing. Lying on her bed upstairs she had concocted some half-plan of visiting him in the morning and demanding what he had learned from Cartwright of Alexander's whereabouts, but no righteous indignation she could muster was able to smother the misery of his apparent defection and her own ill-tempered words. She stood cautiously as he was announced. If he gave them his usual dry smile, she would cross to him and give him her hand with all the joy in the world, but she doubted his demons were to be put aside so swiftly. Though if not, why had he come?

Crowther still looked dark and tired as he entered, and his bow to them was at best perfunctory. Harriet held herself back with a sting of regret, making her back straight, and her smile of welcome swift and cautious. He was followed into the room by a far younger man, dark-haired and slim. He was dressed well, the fashions suited him, and he carried about him an air of earnest seriousness. She smiled more gently at him, thinking perhaps she recognised him now, a face from the back of the crowd during the inquest. Crowther waved his hand over his shoulder, without looking at any of them directly.

'Mrs Westerman, Miss Trench. May I present Daniel Clode?'

Rachel too was on her feet. They both curtsied, and Mr Clode bowed. He seemed a little ill at ease, and could not lose his slightly worried smile. A gentleman, Harriet decided, though not an idle one.

Crowther continued: 'Mr Clode is a solicitor from Pulborough. He came to visit me this evening after the inquest, and having heard him explain his matter a little, I have asked him to lay it all before us both, madam.'

'I am happy to know you, Mr Clode,' Harriet said. 'Do take a seat.'

He did so with a small smile and a nod.

'Thank you, Mrs Westerman.' His voice was a smooth baritone, with a touch of the local burr under it. 'I knew this house a little when I was a boy and my uncle had business with the previous occupants. It seems to be doing very well under its present owners.'

Harriet mumured her thanks, and thought him a very sensible-looking man. He paused, and her gaze drifted to where Crowther sat, brooding over his cane as he had done in the back room of the Crown and Bear. At once she could not endure it, she could not sit under this cloud they had made between them, and before she had made, it seemed to her, any conscious decision, she found herself on her feet again. Mr Clode stood also, looking faintly surprised. Crowther merely glanced at her sulkily.

'Mr Clode, forgive my rudeness, but before we hear what you have to say, I must ask Mr Crowther for a word in private. Rachel, perhaps you could ask Mrs Heathcote for some refreshment for our guests.' She turned to Crowther. 'Mr Crowther, if you please, a moment of your time,' and without waiting to see him stand, she left the room and crossed the hallway into the empty dining room, holding the door until he followed her in. She let it close behind her as he walked into the room and turned to rest her back against it.

The lights had not been lit here. They were in a world of dove-grey shadows. Crowther stood in the middle of the room for a moment or two, till it was clear she was not going to speak, then, hardly looking in her direction, he grunted, 'Well, madam?'

She felt her temper snap within her with the sudden concussion of a dried branch underfoot.

'Don't "well, madam" me, Crowther! How dare you? How dare you hate us for knowing your secret? It is appalling of you. I am sorry at what I said, but I was angry with you. You know we had no hand in making your situation public. We had no knowledge of it. Do you fear our sympathy? You shall get none from me. You have had the luxury of being able to run away from any unpleasantness life can offer you. I can only envy you that.'

He stared at her in astonishment, very white about the mouth.

'Unpleasantness, Mrs Westerman? You dare refer to what passed in my family as unpleasantness?'

She cursed herself for the word, but was carried forward again; the wind had caught her and there was no turning now.

'So you *do* wish for sympathy then. My mistake.' She looked him in the eye and would not be afraid. 'Damn it, Crowther, You are perverse! I'm surprised you haven't run through half a dozen identities by now if this is how you react to anyone knowing anything of your past. Strange how pride can make a man into such a coward!'

He took a step towards her; she felt the door at her back.

'If you were a man,' he said quietly, 'I would kill you for such a remark.'

She felt her hand tremble a little where it was clasped behind her back. She turned her head, so her eyes looked directly into his own.

'Killing me would not make it any more or less true.'

Their faces were only a breath apart. She felt her heart beat, she thought of him where she had found him, among his preparations with his back to the world, thought, clearly, swiftly and for the first time how he removed himself from the stream of the day-to-day, had a sort of calm, how she had pulled him back into the swiftest of currents. Her eyes began to tear again; she blinked them away.

'Oh Crowther, I am so sorry. And so sorry if involving you in all this has caused you any distress.'

Her sympathy was a thousand times harder to bear than her anger. Two decades' worth of grief rushed over him in a flood. He dropped the cane with a rattle and turning from her put his head into his hands. His shoulders shook, and a low groan escaped him. She did not move, but felt her body relax. The shadows in the room made him look like a creature of the lonely dark, and cold, but something uncomfortable and cruel between them seemed to fracture and wash away, like a child's dam in a stream overwhelmed by spring floods.

Then she stooped down on her knees to pick up the cane. The long skirts of her day dress billowed out around her. She did not stand up again at once, but remained where she was, looking up at him. He sighed deeply, and passing his hand across his face, stepped slowly past her to one of the suite of long windows that lit the room, and looked out of it onto Harriet's carriageway. It was open, and the oblivious breeze shifted the drapes a little. They carried with them the heavy memory of the heat of the day across the oak that defended the front of the house, and let it drift into the dining room. The scent was peaceful, calming.

'Forgive me.'

His voice sounded awkward, like a man who has not spoken in many years, and has not yet become used to forming words again. Harriet stood and walked to his side. She said nothing, but having put the cane in his hand, she let her fingers rest on his sleeve and left them there, looking out at the oak. It was a full minute before she spoke.

'The tree is one of the reasons we came to Caveley. My husband said he would worry less about us while at sea if he knew we had such a friend and guardian.'

He did not answer at once, but when he did he sounded a little more like his usual self.

'Do you really need a guardian, Mrs Westerman?'

She smiled. 'I'd like to think not. But everyone needs allies, don't you agree, Mr Crowther?'

'Perhaps.'

She glanced up to see the ghost of one of his weary smiles hovering on his lips. She felt her headache lift a little.

'Do you wish to speak of it at all?'

He knew what she had in mind, and shook his head slowly.

'No, not now. But perhaps at some point in the future. Tonight I wish to hear what Mr Clode has to say.'

They remained together in the gloom a little longer, letting the peace between them deepen till it seemed right, sufficient. He offered her his arm, and they began to move away. 'I am sorry I have not yet told you of Alexander's whereabouts. I have feared at every point being overheard. Carter Brook found him in Tichfield Street.'

Harriet's eyes widened. 'I know it. Near Soho Square.' She smiled and Crowther opened the door for her into the salon. 'Oh Crowther, perhaps we will be able to make sense of this horror in the end.'

IV.10

RACHEL AND MR Clode were on their feet when Crowther and Harriet re-entered the room. Rachel appeared to be giving him a tour of some of the curiosities dotted about the salon and describing where on Harriet's and her husband's travels they had been found. Harriet rather wondered if Rachel did not know their stories better than she did herself. They discovered them with Rachel laughing at her companion's rather bemused expression as he looked at the carvings on a small bone flute. Harriet hoped for all their sakes that the serious young man did not examine it too carefully. It was normally played during the fertility rites of an island in the West Indies. Rachel looked into her eyes, and Harriet smiled at her. Mr Clode bowed to them again, and placed the flute very carefully on the table. There was a certain light in his eye that made Harriet wonder if he had looked at the little instrument rather more closely than she had hoped. She was angry to find herself almost blushing.

'Sorry to keep you waiting, Mr Clode. I trust Rachel has not been boring you with sea stories?'

He smiled. 'We have travelled to the Indies and back, crossed Europe and made a brief visit to Gibraltar, Mrs Westerman. I have never been better entertained.'

Rachel looked pleased.

'You are very kind, sir,' Harriet said with a nod.

'I am fascinated, Mrs Westerman.' He looked at her quite seriously, and Harriet recognised the attractiveness of black hair and blue eyes in him that she had first noticed when she met her husband. 'I have barely been out of the county, and would love to travel. It is a joy to hear your stories, and Miss Trench tells them very well, I think.'

How old was he, she wondered – twenty-five, twenty-six? Before she could stop herself she found she was thinking how handsome he and Rachel looked next to each other.

'I am sure she tells them better than I do, and my husband and I trust her to make us appear appropriately heroic. Now, Mr Clode, I am at your disposal if there is something you wish to tell us.'

He immediately frowned again, and took the few moments it required for them to find their seats to consider.

'I feel perhaps – I hope you will indulge me – I should explain why I have not spoken first to the Squire. I would have done, but of course with Mr Thornleigh's arrest immediately after the inquest was suspended . . . In short I walked around the village for some hours, and as the information I have is not strictly confidential, and having seen you both at the inquest . . . And the Squire did not seem . . .'

He looked uncomfortable, but the decision had been taken during his walk about the village, and it seemed that nothing he now saw caused him to re-evaluate it. Harriet wondered if he had any acquaintance with Michaels.

Crowther turned the cane between his palms and spoke calmly. 'We understand you, Mr Clode. And respect your scruples.'

The young man nodded. 'Thank you. My uncle is the senior partner in our practice in Pulborough. I have been with him two years now, but he is away and I thought perhaps I could seek your guidance, the Squire being . . . unavailable.'

'Thank you for your trust,' Harriet said.

They waited a moment longer. Mr Clode looked at his cuff. Harriet felt her impatience rise again, but held herself steady till the young man continued.

'Lord Thornleigh's nurse, Madeleine Bray, left a will with us for safekeeping.'

Harriet straightened suddenly and looked brightly across at Crowther. He held up his hand as if to ward something away.

'That is as much as I know too, Mrs Westerman. When Mr Clode had told me that much, I asked him to accompany me here.'

Harriet was pleased, though felt herself a little guilty for being so. It did not seem appropriate to be jealous of information, and she still had her own secrets to tell, but nevertheless she was glad that what more Mr Clode had to tell, he would share with them both. Crowther turned his eyes back on the young man.

'Tell on, Mr Clode.'

'Drawing up the will was one of the first duties I took on for my uncle, so I remember Mrs Bray well. When I heard of her death in town, I decided to attend the inquest to see if I could make contact with her legatees. My uncle and I are to act as executors.'

Crowther nodded and examined the fingernails on his right hand. Mr Clode looked a little uncertain. Rachel saw he was looking at Crowther and smiled at him.

'Do not mind Mr Crowther. He always does that when he is

particularly interested in what he thinks one is about to say next.'
Crowther looked at her, one eyebrow raised. 'You do, you know,' she
told him.

Crowther cleared his throat and returned his hand to his cane.
Rachel turned back to the young man.

'Do go on, Mr Clode.'

He nodded to her.

'Mrs Bray had, it seems, few relatives or friends in the world, but
to them she left rather more perhaps than one might have expected.
There is a sum of fifty pounds to be paid to her old friend, a Mrs
Service, in Tichfield Street, London.' Harriet suddenly clasped her
hands together very tightly. Mr Clode waited, but when she did not
speak, continued, 'And a little cameo brooch that she notes was given
to her by Mrs Service's mother, but that she wishes to go to the daughter
of her "benefactor". The daughter is called Susan and, really, this is
the part that struck me a little strange and I thought someone's
attention should be drawn to it, this benefactor, the will says, is also
of Tichfield Street and "goes by the name" of Alexander Adams.'
He did not notice quite the effect his words had had on his audience,
as he was frowning at his cuff again. 'I thought as I wrote it down
for her that it was a strange phrase, and questioned her on it. She
seemed most insistent, and there was real delight in her countenance
as she specified the wording . . .'

He paused and looked up. All three of them were staring at him
as if he had just performed some terrible or miraculous trick in the
neat salon. He felt a little at a loss.

'I hope you don't think I have done wrong in sharing this information
with you.'

Crowther smiled narrowly at the top of his cane. 'So Alexander
is called "Adams" now, is he?'

Mrs Westerman stood, her face was flushed, her eyes bright. 'He
has a child! Crowther!'

237

Miss Trench leaned forward over her knees in apparent deep concentration.

'Shush, Harry,' she said urgently. 'That name . . . I remember this morning . . .' Then with a cry of horror she leaped to her feet and ran to the desk at the far end of the room, plucking the *Daily Advertiser* from it and running back to them.

Crowther rose to meet her and Mr Clode stood in confusion to avoid being the only member of the group sitting down. Harriet caught her sister's elbow.

'Rachel, what is it?'

The younger woman began turning the pages of the paper in her hands, then thrust it into her sister's hand.

'There – oh Harry – there!'

She took a step back, and would have stumbled if Mr Clode had not steadied her elbow, and guided her to her seat. She looked up at him gratefully.

Harriet scanned the page and put her hand to her mouth. Crowther tapped the bottom of his cane on the carpet.

'Mrs Westerman, for the love of God, do not keep me in suspense.'

Harriet began to read in an unsteady voice: '"Horrid murder done in Tichfield Street".' Crowther's eyes snapped to her face. She glanced at him, felt her hand tremble and had to steady it before she could read on. '"On this Friday past, among the many disturbances of the crowd was done a most terrible murder in the music shop and printers of Mr Alexander Adams of Tichfield Street". Oh Crowther! They have killed him!'

'Read on, if you would, Mrs Westerman.'

'"A man, his identity at this time still a mystery, came into the shop as Mr Adams and his children were at supper and killed the proprietor with one cruel knife blow to his stomach. It seems that were it not for the accidental arrival of a friend, this devil in human form may have snuffed out too the young lives of Mr Adams's two defenceless and motherless children, Susan Adams, only nine years of age, and her younger brother Jonathan." Oh, the children live then!' She caught Crowther's look and continued to read. "'The murderer lost himself in the crowds, and though Mr Adams lived long enough to comfort his children and confide them to the care of his friend, the efforts of the surgeon were not enough to save his life".'

She looked around, Rachel pale, Mr Clode confused but horrified, Crowther, his hands clasped so tightly round the ball of his cane, his fingers were white.

She almost whispered, 'Who is this friend? He must be warned! There's a little more . . .

"The motive for the killings may most likely be robbery, but what a matter, oh England, when such murder is done in daylight in the home of a respectable man leaving his little son and daughter alone and adrift in this cruel and chaotic world. Mr Adams's funeral was well attended by his many friends, filled with respect for the murdered man's great knowledge of the glorious music available in the city at this time, and his commitment to introduce the finest qualities to the most advanced tastes".'

Harriet dropped the paper to her side. Crowther could almost see her fears and horrors crowding around her in the growing shadows, monsters of imagination and sympathy pulling at her dark red skirts and plucking her hair with long waxy fingers.

Mr Clode looked about him amazed. 'I do not understand. This is the man who was Nurse Bray's benefactor?'

Rachel turned to him, her face calm, but a little emptied; there was a hollow ring in her voice that made Daniel feel as if he were lost in the night and cold.

'We believe that Alexander Adams was by birth Alexander Thornleigh. Heir to Thornleigh Hall and Viscount Hardew.'

It was Mr Clode's turn to look pale. Harriet spoke to the air around her.

'*And* he had children.'

Crowther stooped a little over his cane. 'They may not be legitimate.'

Harriet shook her head. 'If Alexander gave up his family for the love of their mother, I cannot think but he married her and they are legitimate.'

Mr Clode stood again, with sudden urgency.

'They are in danger,' he said. No one replied. He appealed to Crowther. 'Mr Crowther, are they not? I have not your understanding of this business, but I can see there is some desperate hand at work here, and it has stretched its influence to London. Any child can see that. We must warn them, warn their friends, as Mrs Westerman said – take them to some place of safety till the danger is past.'

Crowther did not look up from the top of his cane. He could feel the young rush of blood, the quivering energy in the man across the space between them. One corner of his mouth twisted into a wary smile.

'Yes. I think you have grasped the fundamentals of the situation, Mr Clode.'

Daniel glanced down briefly at Rachel, who was staring off intently into a corner of the room, then back to the figures of Harriet and Crowther, each seemingly cut off in their own worlds. He spoke softly.

'Let me go.'

Harriet seemed to wake and turned with a frown. 'No, Mr Clode, I shall.'

'Sorry, Mrs Westerman, but that makes no sense.' The young man stepped forward. 'These children will not be safe until whoever is behind this is brought to justice. You can help that happen more effectively than I. Let me go. I can set off at once and be in London by dawn.'

Harriet hesitated. She thought of her own children asleep upstairs, then gave a quick nod and turned away. The fears and confusions of the evening still had her by the throat.

Clode continued, 'I only wish I knew of some place to take the children if the need arises. The closer they are to Tichfield Street, the greater their danger, yet I do not think their grandfather's house to be a place of safety for them now, if,' he looked at them. 'If I understand the situation correctly.'

Crowther walked over to Harriet's writing table with quick steps. 'You do, sir. And the place of safety I believe *I* can supply.' He pulled out paper and examined Harriet's quills till with a grunt he selected one he believed would suit him. 'I am writing a note for you to take to a Mr John Hunter. He has been a teacher of mine in London, a great man for many reasons and with better sense than most. He has a house out at Earl's Court. He'll take you in if you think it necessary. He's a rough man, and has a queer household.' Crowther shook sand onto the sheet. 'He also knows some individuals who may be of use if you come under threat.' He folded the note and handed it to Daniel. The latter's face wore a slight frown. 'Grave robbers and their like, Mr Clode,' Crowther explained further. 'He is an anatomist, like myself, and a great one, but his needs for material have led him into some strange alliances. You may trust him with your life, however, and those of the children. He'd not betray you if the King and the Archbishop of Canterbury knocked at his door asking for them.'

Harriet shook herself free from her imaginings and also stepped swiftly behind the desk, making Crowther move quickly out of her way in her impatience to open a little drawer in its honey-coloured side. She withdrew a money box and, opening it with a key from her own pocket, pulled out a handful of notes. Mr Clode looked a little offended and tried to wave her away. She all but stamped her foot.

'Oh, take it, Mr Clode! You may have need of it and have expenses you did not envisage when you left your home this morning.'

He hesitated again, but seeing the sense of what she said, took it from her with a bow.

'I am grateful that you trust me, Mrs Westerman.'

The thought seemed to surprise her, and he watched her exchange a glance and shrug with Crowther.

'It seems we do, Mr Clode. Are we wrong to do so?'

He shook his head. 'No. You are not wrong. I can leave from here now. May I write a note to be sent on to Pulborough in the morning? I would rather not leave my parents worrying for me. I shall say business detains me here a few days.'

'Of course,' Harriet said. 'Good. Rachel, go and fetch one of David's riding cloaks for Mr Clode. We shall tell him what we know.'

Without even troubling to take their seats again, Harriet and Crowther told the young man everything they had seen, thought or suspected since the dawn of Friday. The young man said very little and what questions he had were intelligent and to the point. He had the best of it by the time Rachel returned with the cloak, and a little bag of provisions culled from the kitchen, including half a bottle of Harriet's most expensive brandy. Then he was gone.

The door swung to behind him, and Rachel, Harriet and Crowther looked at each other a little dumbfounded. When Mrs Heathcote came in to clear the almost untouched refreshments as brisk as a lieutenant preparing the decks for action, Harriet drew herself up behind her desk.

'Very well,' she said. 'What next?'

17 June 1775, Breed's Hill near Charlestown, Massachusetts Bay

TRY TO IMAGINE a fog. It is as dense as that which crawls from a still river in darkness so you can see only a few feet in either direction, but it is still tinged yellow by a sun you can no longer see, and it is acrid and smoking in your nose and mouth. Gunsmoke. A world of burned powder. The noises around you are like thunder, but muffled; you can no longer tell the difference between the sound of your own and your companions' feet hitting the ground under your boots and the thump of your own blood. Your eyes are streaming, one is swollen shut and tears at you like a rat trapped in your skull. You would pluck it out and throw it from you, but your hands will not part from the musket they hold. The air is alive with hisses and explosions. There are groans and cries, some in the distance, then suddenly almost under your feet. You can feel wet heat and sear on your cheek. Evil little balls of shot rattling past you. You cannot see where they come from, or from how close. Now, you catch a flash of gunpowder in the gloom in front of you. You are almost upon them. The man to your right stumbles, you curse the broken ground and reach down to pull him up again; only when you are bent by the effort, bring his lolling head up to the level of your stooped shoulder, do you see the man is dead, the side of his face broken away. You let him fall. You call out to the men around you and plough forward again, bayonet raised, knowing that it is impossible you will survive, only sure you will take one of these murderous bastards, cowering behind their defensive arrows, with you, determined to bring a little of your hell over their redoubt and into their midst.

You are there. The fence between you and the other man gives under your weight, he has fumbled his reload. He looks up into your face, you tower above him as he crouches over his cartridge case in his homespun shirt, his ill-shaped cap. There is a scrap of old newspaper at his feet, scattered with crumbs. He must have eaten between the last attack and this. He brought something from home. You see it all without looking away from his face. You lift the barrel and drive the foot of steel at the end of your gun into his chest, thrusting as you breathe out, even while he stares at you. Blood bubbles in his mouth, his eyes go slack. The bayonet is buried so far into his chest you have to stand on his breastbone to pull it clear. You turn to find another. This is dancing. The world has slowed, your movements are fluid and there is time and time to take another partner, obey the impulse of movement, pull free and turn to take another, and another – his flashpan fizzing – lets fly almost into your face. You wait for the world to blacken; it does not, the shot failed him. There is a moment when he realises this as you lift you weapon and fall foward. He crumples, you stumble into him, then back onto your feet. Your eye is caught by another man scrambling away; he is too slow. A shot flashes to your right and he is lifted and thrown forward onto the ground, among the grass, his body shivering with shock and despair.

The dreaming ends, the world speeds up again and you are aware of the desperate gasping for breath, your hands on the stock of your gun slippery with other men's blood. Someone is standing beside you. Their eyes are as black and burning as your own.

'We're done here, Thornleigh. They have taken the redoubt. Christ, man! Your face!'

You spit on the ground. There are bodies all around you. Some in the local linen, some in the blood red of your own coat. You turn back towards the beach without replying. There is a groan on your right-hand side. You crouch down, recognise one of your own. Get his arm round your neck, yours round his waist, pull him back towards the beach. By the time you reach the boats, you are carrying a corpse.

The streets were full of men, bloody and broken, dragged in carts towards the hospitals, or staggering behind them. Some nodded as he passed. Thornleigh paused only long enough at the docks to deliver his report before he started to make his way to the hospital he had visited with Hawkshaw only a few weeks before. He wanted to see if any of his company were there, and if so, what could be done for them. Of the thirty men in his command, only four were capable of walking unaided from the fight. He had seen the bodies of ten. Now he came in search of the rest. The windows of the respectable houses in Boston were mostly shuttered. Here and there civilians, old men mostly in wigs and tight-fitting jackets, dithered at the tops of their steps, jaws hanging slack, all amazement and confusion as they watched the slow, bloody parade. When Hugh turned into the wide gates of the old warehouse, he found a butcher's yard.

The forecourt was full of injured men, groaning and bleeding, waiting their turn with the surgeon. Some of the women of the town moved among them, offering water, the fringes of their long skirts reddening. One girl had turned away into a patch of shadow, her handkerchief at her mouth; even in the dark he could see the whiteness round her lips, one hand pressed against the stone wall. When she moved away it left a rust stain of some man's blood behind her. He wondered whose last minutes she had watched over.

He fetched water from the drinking butt and distributed it; the calls for water came from every side. Some asked after his company, others put a black and red hand on his sleeve and tried to stop him long enough to tell their own stories of the slaughter they had seen around them on the hill. Howe's entire staff dead or wounded, half the companies of Grenadiers down to single figures like his own. A victory, but a disastrous one.

If they had grown less sanguine about their powers on the retreat from Lexington, they were as sober as hell now. A marine was curled up next to the wall, sobbing, and trying to stop his tears with a fist in his mouth. Another young woman tried to approach Hugh, make some move towards his wound; she carried a cloth and basin already pink and dirty. Hugh pushed her away, saying nothing, then heard his own name called, and looked up. A young man from Hawkshaw's company lay propped up against the white wall. Thornleigh walked towards him. The lad's face was grey and waxy. Thornleigh let his eye scan down his body. It was a stomach wound. There was nothing the surgeons would do for this one. Without speaking, Thornleigh crouched beside him and drew out a hipflask from under his jacket, still half-full of his father's celebratory brandy. He put it to the man's lips. The latter drank and grimaced as the heat of it reached down his throat.

'Thanks, Captain. Tastes good.'

Thornleigh did not smile. 'Only the best.'

The man laughed; it pulled at his wound and became a cough which spat a thick red from his mouth. Thornleigh gave him the flask again. He drank, and tried apologetically to wipe the opening clean with his sleeve before Thornleigh gently took it back.

'Don't know if you've heard, sir. I'm afraid Captain Hawkshaw is dead.'

Thornleigh felt it in his own gut like a soft blow of the fist. He bowed his head.

'You saw?' he managed to say.

The man nodded. 'Second wave, he was upfront and charging. The skinny bastard he was bearing down on waited till he was almost there and got him right in the forehead. He just dropped.' The man paused again. 'Got nerve, these little shits, some of them at any rate. I did for him a minute later, then . . .' he put his hand on the red mess at his middle . . . 'then his mate did for me.'

Thornleigh nodded his throbbing head. The man looked at him. 'Musket blow up on you, sir?' Thornleigh put his hand to the right side of his face. He felt flesh rather than skin. The touch seemed to wake the wound; it burned across his cheek in a wave, exploding in a spasm of pain under his eye, scrabbling at his vision until it seemed he could see the pattern of it. He steadied himself. Willed it down.

'Yes. Mine was shot from my hand in the first wave. Made do with a dead rebel's till I could get it back. I suppose it did not like me for a master.'

The man smiled. 'A rebel gun, you see?' He laughed at his own joke, repeating it with a shake of his head. 'A rebel gun. Sorry about Hawkshaw, Captain. He was a good sort of bloke.' The grin became a little lopsided. 'So was I.'

Thornleigh put the hipflask back into his hands and stood. The man looked at it.

'You'll never get it back, Captain.'

Thornleigh waved his hand. 'Drink to Hawkshaw.'

'Will do, sir. Good luck to you.'

Thornleigh stood. The light was softening into the evening of another beautiful summer's day. He turned into the building itself. The groans became screams in the shadows, the smell rank and rusty. The surgeon was hard at work with the saw, the ground below him a swill of blood and vomit. Just visible behind them was a wide barrel; over its edge hung a bloody hand, bent at the wrist, oddly perfect. Thornleigh wondered if the rest of the man had survived.

Moving past them into the wide open space of the hospital itself, he followed the route he had taken with Hawkshaw and Wicksteed into the main area. It was as lofty as a church. The howls from where the surgeon did his work were a little deadened by the stone. The men here were mostly quiet, content now, it seemed, to wait quietly until death took them, or their bodies showed themselves willing to recover. He found three of his men, and heard news of two others who had died under the knife. Two he found with their wounds dressed, but telling him, in dubious tones, that the balls that had wounded them had been left intact rather than dug out. Thornleigh was not fit to talk surgical fashions. The straw scattered between the bedrolls was slippery with blood. He fetched water again. Sat and let the others talk, told the story of his own wound, and heard it being repeated between beds. It began to darken, and the pain was making him sick. He needed to think about Hawkshaw and use all the drink he had to wash some of the day away. He could feel the energy that had carried him through the action retreating, leaving him hollow and sounding to the horrors. He was already on his way out of the doors when he felt a presence at his shoulder and turned to see Wicksteed beside him, washed to his elbows in blood.

'Captain Thornleigh!' Wicksteed came a little closer and peered up at his wound. 'You should let the surgeon look at that, Captain Thornleigh, before you go.'

'He has more pressing business.'

He turned to go again, but Wicksteed's fast right hand caught him on the sleeve and detained him.

'Captain Hawkshaw?'

'Dead.'

Wicksteed plucked his hand back.

'Shame. He was a friend to me. Thought he might think of me, when this is all done.'

Thornleigh stared at him with his one eye. Wicksteed looked at the ground a moment then drew himself closer to the larger man's side, like a girl who needs a partner at a country ball. His hand rested on Thornleigh's sleeve again. His fingers were black with gore.

'Let me wash the dirt out of that wound, Captain Thornleigh.'

Thornleigh didn't reply, simply shook the hand from his sleeve and walked on. The need to escape was becoming a pressure behind his eyes. He was five minutes clear of the yard when a young ensign called him from across the street.

'Captain Thornleigh! Request from the Governor. Soon as you're cleared up, could you go to Stone Gaol and see what you can get from the prisoners.'

Hugh frowned. 'What nonsense is this? Pulling information isn't my style. Why do they ask for me?'

The boy looked confused, he'd got his message the wrong way about.

'There's a prisoner says he knows you. Name of Shapin. Asks for you. Governor hopes he might get chatty with you.'

Hugh remembered Hawkshaw's story, nodded wearily and turned again. The Ensign looked nervous, but lifted his voice.

'Sorry, sir, but soon as you can, they said. Don't know how long he'll last.'

Hugh kept walking, the pressure behind his eyes continuing to build.

PART V

V.1

Tuesday, 6 June 1780

'ON WHOSE ORDERS? On whose orders, I say?'
The shouts came from the side of the house, and with only
a look between them Harriet and Crowther turned off the path to
the front of Thornleigh Hall and made their way in that direction.
Their feet made very little noise on the gravel. They turned the corner
to see Wicksteed with his back to them, one arm raised, a crop in
his hand, his other hand fastened round the wrist of a maid about
Rachel's age. One of the doors to the kitchens in the basement was
open; a number of the Thornleigh domestics crowded round it,
watching. She must have fallen as Wicksteed dragged her out and
up the steps. Some of her hair had escaped from under her cap and
she was crying. The hand that was free she held up, ready to ward
off the crop. She spoke in a high shriek as he lifted his arm still
higher.

'I thought it best! He was drunk! You'd gone to bed, Mr Wicksteed!'
Wicksteed pulled her up to her knees.

'Thought it best! A thinker, are you? You think you can lock your
master in his rooms, for the best?'

He twisted her wrist and she squealed again.

'He was drunk, sir! I don't have the key to the gun room, but the

251

key to the salon was in the lock! He had a fire in there! I thought I could open it in the morning, and no one would know! I'm glad I did it!'

Harriet and Crowther could see the spittle from Wicksteed's mouth hitting her in the face. His voice was almost a scream.

'Glad, are you?' He brought the crop down. The girl squirmed but he had her firmly enough. It struck across her cheek with a slapping crack that rebounded off the walls. Harriet recoiled. As Wicksteed raised his hand again, Crowther closed the last few paces between them and lifted his cane so it held Wicksteed's right arm in the air.

'Little trouble with the domestics, Wicksteed?' he drawled.

Wicksteed whipped round, his breathing hard, his face scarlet.

'My own business,' he hissed.

Crowther smiled thinly at him, kept his cane where it was.

'Come now. I think you have made the girl sorry enough, don't you?'

He kept his eyes on Wicksteed's face, but the latter glanced down at the girl at his feet. The blow showed as a dead white line on the unnatural red of her face. The skin had broken by her eye. Wicksteed spat on the ground.

'Release her, please.' Crowther spoke very softly, very slowly. Wicksteed let her wrist go. She began to massage it. 'Run along now, my dear,' Crowther added, without moving.

She seemed to waken, and scuttled off her knees and back towards the kitchen, where she was hauled in through the door by her fellow servants like a shipwreck victim gathered into a lifeboat. Crowther waited a long moment before moving his cane. Then he set it back on the ground and leaned on it. Wicksteed stared at the space in front of him where the girl had been, his chest rising and falling, then without looking again at Crowther or Harriet, he turned on his heel and marched away.

Harriet took a few steps to bring her to Crowther's side.

'You don't need that stick at all, do you, Crowther?'

He watched Wicksteed's retreating figure.

'I needed it yesterday. Today I am just enjoying its company.'

He offered his arm and they turned back towards the front of the house.

'He wants to be a gentleman,' Harriet commented.

'Wicksteed? Horsewhipping women hardly seems the way to go about it.'

She smiled. 'No, I've had no chance to tell you as yet. I visited yesterday, had a look through his desk.'

'I take it you didn't find the notebooks detailing all his crimes?'

She wrinkled her nose. 'No, one of his desk drawers is locked. I did find drafts of a rather unctuous letter to the College of Arms, though. And we have just seen that he is capable of violence against a woman.'

Crowther murmured, 'There are times when we are all capable of that.'

Harriet chose to ignore him and continue her own train of thought. 'I am sure that he has some hold over Hugh.'

'You think he sent the bottle to Cartwright by Hugh's hand, too?' Crowther gave a slightly exasperated sigh.

And when she nodded: 'Why, though, Mrs Westerman? There is no sense in it. If he has this hold over Mr Thornleigh, then his wishing to remove the threat of Alexander's return, or that of his heirs has some logic to it. But if that is his wish, then he would surely not want Hugh to be hanged for his crimes. And why would he want the man to have the freedom to shoot himself? There can be no other interpretation of the scene we have just witnessed. He was angry that his benefactor could not shoot himself while drunk because of the actions of that little maid. That hardly suggests his fortunes depend on Hugh.'

Mrs Westerman did not look dismayed.

'Perhaps his allegiances are elsewhere now, Crowther. If both Hugh and Alexander are removed, then the control of the family wealth falls to Lady Thornleigh. He may think her a better patron.'

The remark made Crowther stop, then with a shrug he moved on. 'There is no proof,' he said. 'Nothing. Speculation and gossip and a bottle of poison is all we have, and they point clearly at Hugh.'

'Isn't the proper scientific method to suggest a hypothesis and then look for the evidence to support it?'

'No, it certainly is not. It is to observe, gather all the information one can, then hypothesise with a great deal of circumspection and care.'

Harriet shrugged. 'I like my method better.'

Crowther did not reply, only gave a speaking sigh as they approached the entrance to the house.

They were not the first visitors of the morning. As they waited under the heavy ornament of the hallway, they saw Squire Bridges pause on the stairway, taking, it seemed, a very friendly farewell from Lady Thornleigh. He bent low over her hand, his eyes looking up into her lovely face with great warmth. She was smiling at him, with her head a little to one side, and with some last word turned from him and made her way out of sight towards the state rooms above. The Squire began to descend the stair, then caught sight of them, and his step faltered a little. The lines on his forehead deepened.

'Crowther. Mrs Westerman. You are making an early call.'

Crowther smiled. 'Not as early as yourself, sir.'

Bridges drew himself up. 'I have business here at the moment, as I am sure you can imagine. Though I do not understand what might be your matter here.'

They regarded each other steadily for a while. Crowther began to wonder how long the match might last when a maid appeared at their side.

'Lady Thornleigh's apologies, but she is unable to receive guests today. She is feeling a little unwell.'

The Squire's face took on an air of great contentment. Crowther turned to him with one eyebrow raised.

'I do hope your visit did not render her bilious, sir.'

He reddened, and was on the point of reply when Hugh, pale and unshaved, entered from one of the lower corridors.

'Mrs Westerman! Crowther! Come in. I will see you, even if my respected stepmother will not.'

The Squire did not look at him, but turned away. As they followed Hugh through the archway into the old meeting hall, Crowther glanced at Harriet's face.

'The Squire was once a great friend to us, Crowther,' she whispered.

'He is a politician.'

'And seems to have joined the party of Lady Thornleigh. I thought they hated each other.'

'He must believe he has evidence that is sure to hang Hugh, and is hoping to make friends with the new power in the house.'

Hugh looked back at them over his shoulder. 'What are you whispering about?'

They were entering the old hall of the house. It had been built some two hundred years before the rest. The modern property had been conjured around it, an elegant frontage on the ancient heart of the place. It was still stone-flagged, the furniture massive and dark. The walls were hung with old arms and portraits so stained with age one could hardly make out the stiff profiles of the first Earls of Sussex that brooded high above them. At the far end of the Hall two halberds bearing the arms of the family on rotting silk were crossed on the wall. The huge empty fireplace could have roasted a whole ox. Probably had, Harriet thought, as the first Earls drank with their dogs and servants and dragged in parcels of game across the flagstones from their hunt, the stag's head loose and sightless slipping and bouncing over the stone, while the dogs leaped and yapped at it.

Hugh approached the wide oak table in the centre of the room. Harriet moved towards him, her dress whispering on the stone floor as she moved.

'We did not know the Squire and Lady Thornleigh were on such good terms.'

Hugh reached for the wine bottle on the great table a little uncertainly.

'They are negotiating over my blood.' His fingers closed round the thin green neck, he lifted it and began to slop the claret into one of the large glasses. It splashed a little over the rim.

'Bridges is in hock to us. It never worried me – I'm told he pays the interest in a regular fashion. A political loan of my father's, I think. I dare say my beautiful mama has been promising it will cause him no trouble if I am hanged and control comes to her, but if he looks too hard in other directions, then he will not find Thornleigh a friendly broker when I am gone. Or dead by my own hand. She will make him suffer – whatever she says to him now.'

The evenness of his tone horrified Harriet.

'Hugh, please! What is happening in this house?'

Thornleigh put down the wine glass, but kept his head turned away. Harriet walked quickly towards him, brushing off as she did the warning hand Crowther had placed on her sleeve.

'Did you murder that man, Carter Brook, kill Nurse Bridges, poison Joshua? I cannot believe it. Will you not save yourself? Mr Thornleigh, your brother . . .'

Hugh spun round and grabbed her by the wrist. His wine glass toppled from the table and smashed on the old stone flags below them. The shattered crystal seemed to chime in the air.

'What do you know of Alexander, Harriet?' He pulled her towards him. His living eye danced over her face. 'Is he alive? Have you found him?'

She stared at him, caught between fear and pity. The pink and yellow scarring across his cheek and eye looked like a mockery of hope. She felt Crowther move a little closer towards them. She could see tears forming in Hugh's eyes. So the damaged one could still grieve, even when it saw nothing. She gently pulled her wrist free of him and stepped back a little way. She could feel bruises beginning to bloom under her cuffs like sprays of foxglove opening darkly under her skin. She shook her head; spoke softly, hesitating.

'He is dead, we think. Murdered some days ago in London. It was reported in the *Advertiser*. Alexander Adams – we think that is the name he was using in town.'

Hugh turned away with a roar of laughter.

'Done! Done! Dead and done.' Harriet stepped further back. 'Then it is over. They have bound me and whipped me. All over! To think what I would have given to hear that name a week ago, what I was prepared to give to Brook – and now you give it to me during a morning call, and it is nothing. Useless! A thousand times worse than useless.'

He rested his head above the cold maw of the great fireplace, and struck his open palm against the old stone. Harriet waited till the echo had retreated back into the impassive walls. When Hugh dropped his arm to his side again, she could see the place where he had brought down his hand spotted in red.

'Who, Mr Thornleigh? Who has done this? Are you in Wicksteed's power? We must get your neck out of this noose, and show the court where the true blame lies.' When he did not move, she entreated him: 'Would you leave this place in the hands of a pack of murderers? Will you always be remembered as a coward, a poisoner, a killer of the weak? You are a soldier!'

Hugh laughed in her face.

'Oh my dear, idiotic Mrs Westerman. You and your kind are babies! Crowther comes from old blood. He knows as well as I – this place has always been in the hands of a pack of murderers! It is a noble tradition. We take our responsibilities most seriously. And what do I care what is said when I am dead? Do you believe it will trouble me in the other place? I will happily swap this hell for another. I did not kill Brook, or poison Cartwright, but perhaps I deserve the noose just the same. Wicksteed has given Bridges my bloody knife, and I will not explain myself further. Let it come! Let them hang me! I shall avoid putting a bullet in my brain to give them all the grand spectacle. Let them see me choke! That's my gift. The crowd loves to see a noble swing, don't they, Crowther?'

Crowther was looking into the fireplace. Harriet thought she saw him give a simple sharp nod. She stepped forward again.

'Hugh! Is it Wicksteed? What hold can he have on you that you will not break free even now?'

He looked at her. His face was wet and red with tears; it made the scars across his cheek glisten like fresh meat. He trembled; she held his gaze, willing him to open his lips. He looked hard into her face, then sighed and turned away. His passions seemed to fall from his shoulders, leaving him diminished, weak.

'I am guilty. Do not make an enemy of Wicksteed, Mrs Westerman. For the sake of your family.'

He let his boot circle in the space of the grate, as if stirring imaginary ashes. Harriet put her hand on his arm, pulling him round to look at her.

'A man murders your friends, has your brother killed, and you go to the noose for him? This is ridiculous, Thornleigh. What possible—'

He clenched his fists.

'Enough! I have my reasons. And it is my fault, Mrs Westerman.' His fists opened out, anger became supplication in a moment. '*I am guilty*. Now get the hell out of this house, and stay away. Alexander gave me that advice once. I tried to follow it and him, but it pulls us back. You may escape it yet. Go. Please. Go.'

They left the room, but not his house. Crowther thought at first Mrs Westerman would be inclined to withdraw. He could feel the eddies of fear and confusion twisting around her. But she did not lead him to the grand entrance of Thornleigh, rather further into the house.

'Are you quite sure about this?' he murmured as soon as he became aware of the direction she was taking.

'Quite sure.' Then she stopped and looked up at him. He noticed the healthy white of her eyes. Wondered how long she had till they reddened with the scars of seeing to resemble his own. 'Should we have told him about the children?'

Crowther sighed. 'I cannot say. I simply cannot say.'

She seemed satisfied and raised her hand at the door of the housekeeper's sitting room. A small middle-aged woman lifted the latch to them. Her eyes were red, and the apron over her day-dress tied carelessly. Harriet smiled at her, and saw a glint of relief in her eye.

'Mrs Dougherty! My companion here is Mr Crowther. A physician.' She could feel Crowther tense beside her as she said the word, but he did not protest. 'We should like to see Lord Thornleigh.' She gave a matter-of-fact sort of smile.

The little woman in front of them looked confused. She rubbed her hands on the linen of her apron and pushed a stray lock of hair back under her cap.

'He is not a freak show, Mrs Westerman. I am not sure my mistress . . .' There was a movement behind them. The maid they had rescued from being beaten in the courtyard put her head in the doorway. Her hair was neat again, the wound from Wicksteed's crop still vivid, but clean.

'I'll take them, Mrs Dougherty.' She paused. 'Mr Wicksteed and Lady Thornleigh are taking a walk in the lavender garden.'

Mrs Dougherty twisted her hands, then shrugged her thin shoulders.

'Very well. Very well.' She then put her head on one side and asked with an unconvincingly casual tone, 'I suppose Mrs Heathcote has not yet had an opportunity to try my jugged hare receipt?'

Harriet graced her with a full-beam smile.

'We are to enjoy it this evening, but she acknowledged you the master as soon as she looked through your notes.'

The little woman's chin lifted triumphantly. 'Indeed. Most fair-minded people would confess I know what I am about.'

That seemed to form their dismissal; they let themselves be led by the maid.

'I am called Patience, ma'am,' she said, before they had gone many steps.

'I am glad to know you,' Harriet told her.

She conducted them to the back stairs, and lifting her long skirts began the ascent to the upper rooms where Lord Thornleigh had been so long confined.

V.2

DANIEL CLODE WAS anxious. Having made good speed through the night, his progress into town was much delayed by the volume of traffic leaving the city. The possibility that he might be too late to prevent some injury to the children pressed him on. The road was crowded with coaches and wagons full of nervous-looking men and weeping women, their possessions bundled around them, children crying and complaining on their laps. The occasional horseman, head down, his animal panting and sweating, flew by out of Town. What horrors, what news needed to reach their masters at such a speed. It seemed as if the populace were fleeing a plague.

He stopped long enough at the last respectable-looking coaching house outside Southwark to hear a little of the riots and to change horses while he crammed his mouth with hard white rolls and weak beer. He would never get used to the chalk in the London bread, or the stink of the water in the basin where he washed his hands. How people could survive in a city where the necessities of life were so treacherous, he would never know. The landlord was too busy with the full road and the panicked commands of his guests to say much, but the serving girl was glad to talk while he ate, keeping herself tucked behind a bend in the wall to hide her idleness from her master. Clode was the sort of man serving girls spent their time over, and smiled at. Not that he had ever been aware of it himself. Mostly, as now, his mind had been more concerned with other matters.

'Half the city is on fire, they say.' She twisted a thin cord of her hair in her fingertips and examined the black ends as if she could read her fortune in them. 'And the other half as like to burn as not.'

Clode nodded, wiped his mouth and reached for the other white roll on the table, his hunger fiercer than his distaste for it.

'They say even the Jews have put up blue banners and writ "we are all good Protestants here" on the shopfronts.' She sniggered. 'Didn't know they could even write English. Just counting they do, isn't it?'

When Clode spoke he sent a spray of plastery crumbs onto the table. 'Lots of people know how to write.'

She shifted her weight onto one hip and lifted an eyebrow. 'Well, I've never had need of it here.'

The move exposed her to the view of her master.

'Sephy! There's other men need serving here!'

She looked over in his direction, her face a pinched figure of boredom and disgust.

'Coming!' Then, dropping her voice lower, 'I shall turn witch and curse the old goat. I know what service *he* wants.'

She turned and sashayed away, looking back over her shoulder to offer a full smile.

Clode stood, and was out of the door again before his coins had stopped ringing on the table-top.

They were beyond the level of the state rooms and climbing still into the more rarely used parts of the house before they spoke again.

'How is the wound?'

The maid paused and turned on the stair.

'It smarts, ma'am, but it will heal. I shall not stay here, though. This Hall is evil in its bones. I feel these things.'

She turned to continue the climb.

'I have sometimes wondered if this place had an evil at its heart,' Harriet said.

Crowther had seen too many evils done by living breathing men blamed on malignant spirits, even on God Himself. He saw it as excuse, an abnegation of responsibility. A weakness. He spoke sharply.

'For myself, Mrs Westerman, I regard such things in the same manner I do the folk tales of sleeping with a pig's bladder under your bed to bring on the birth of a male child, or leaving bread out for the fairies. I believe in what I can touch and see. If I do not understand it, I think that is a fault of my own intelligence, not proof of its otherworldly nature. I answer the questions of science – the rest I leave to priests and mystics.'

He realised he was speaking with impatience, and regretted it. The women, however, seemed too lost in their own thoughts to catch, or be offended, by his tone.

'There *is* evil here,' murmured the maid. 'I can touch it in this house. I can feel it.' Then: 'We are nearly there.'

They climbed another flight into the uppermost rooms of the house, and Crowther found his eyes struggling in the gloom. The wide-open proportions of the lower storeys tightened and shrank here, and he had to fight the inclination to stoop as they stood on the bare floorboards of the upper landing.

'Lord Thornleigh is cared for in the old nursery.'

Crowther felt his skin crawl as they moved through the shadows. 'Is there anything you can tell us about Lord Thornleigh's current condition?' he asked. Patience turned towards him and blinked slowly.

'He can't speak. He can hardly move. He sleeps most times, but sometimes his eyes are open. He is fed food that does not need to be chewed and a cup is held to his lip to allow him to drink.' The maid paused. 'I think he misses Nurse. He seems a lot less calm since she died. None of us likes to share the room long with him.'

Harriet stayed the girl's arm just as she reached for the handle on one of the corridor's tobacco-brown doors.

'Does Lady Thornleigh visit him?'

'Sometimes. Sometimes she visits him alone – at other times she does not bother to send us away. Not Mr Hugh though. He never comes.'

She turned the handle.

After the gloom of the narrow upper corridor, Crowther was not prepared for the plain white walls of the room he now entered. It gathered the available morning light and threw it at him, so he blinked in the doorway. As his eyes adjusted, he picked out the fireplace, a maid shuffling up onto her feet next to it, placing her needlework down beside her, and only then he saw the high-backed chair facing her. It was as massive as a medieval throne. Encircling the back was a thick belt of leather. Another was visible on the arm of the chair. Crowther could see that it held in place a thin arm in a loose linen shirt, ending in a hand so white it was almost translucent, the fingers twitching convulsively every few seconds.

Harriet turned to the girl who had brought them up. 'Thank you, Patience.'

Crowther heard the click of a coin, felt the girl begin to leave. The maid who had stood, protested.

'Tell them only another hour! I shan't stay longer than that.'

Patience closed the door without replying. The maid turned to them both with a frown. She was a squat little thing, red in the face, and her hands looked too rough to be doing fine needlework. Her eyes flicked from Crowther's face to Harriet's and back.

'What happened to her face?' she asked, referring to Patience.

Harriet looked at her a little coldly. 'Some disagreement with Wicksteed.'

The squat maid screwed her own face up like an old handkerchief. 'That little shite.'

'Take your seat,' Crowther instructed her.

She did so with a shrug.

Harriet waited at the door while Crowther walked around the chair till he could let his eyes fall on this Lord Thornleigh, Earl of Sussex, Baron of Pulborough, Companion of the Arms, one of the richest men in society. He was ready for the sight, but he still felt a cold sliver of shock twist into his spine.

The man in the chair was perhaps between sixty-five and seventy years old. His head had been shaved recently, and his scalp was dusted with new growth. The body was thin and wasted, a transparency wrapped around a skeleton. He would have certainly tumbled under his own weight, were he not held to the back of the chair by the thick leather band under his arms, which kept him pinned upright on his throne. Lord Thornleigh was dressed in a shift, and there was a rug over his knees. His arms were bound to the arms of his chair at the wrists. His jaw was slack, his head slumped loosely to one side, a thin sliver of drool hung from his mouth. His eyes were half-shut.

Crowther bowed. 'Lord Thornleigh, I am Gabriel Crowther. I am a . . . physician. May I examine you?'

He pulled his handkerchief from his pocket and wiped the saliva from the man's mouth. As he did so, Lord Thornleigh's eyes flicked up to his face. They were dead and empty, but still of such a startling

264

ice blue Crowther almost leaped back. They reminded him of his own. Then Lord Thornleigh began to yowl softly. It was not unlike the cry of a baby in its formlessness, but it was older and more animal. Crowther thought of a wolf he had shot in Germany in his youth. It had not been a clean death and the despairing broken growl had affected him to the extent that he had never hunted again. He thought of it now looking into the white face in front of him. He glanced up and met Harriet's eye. She looked a little sickened.

Crowther took the thin flesh of the Lord's right hand between his fingers and pinched hard. The hand jerked, and the sick man yowled again.

'Forgive me, my lord. I wished to understand the capacity for sensation in your limbs.' He watched the skin he had pinched drop back into place with the slowness of age, the blood retreat and return under its thin and failing protection. 'Now if I may, I shall release your arms and look at you more closely.'

He bent over to undo the strap at the elbow and took the bird-like weight of the man's arm between his hands. He glanced up again into the Lord's face. The dead blank look of a few moments before had dissipated. The eyes looked conscious and, to Crowther's astonishment, afraid. The Lord's yowling increased in pitch and volume.

'Indeed, my lord, I promise you I shall not hurt you again, and any discomfort will be slight.'

He did not know if he had been heard or understood. Lord Thornleigh was still looking at him, confused and unhappy. Crowther felt a coldness growing from the base of his stomach.

The maid was on her feet again.

'Aww! He's upset. Perhaps he wants his necklace.'

Harriet and Crowther looked at her in surprise. She was opening a box on the mantelpiece by her chair, and turned towards them with a locket hanging from a thin silvery chain in her hand.

'Here it is now, don't fret.'

Crowther felt the convulsion in the thin arm. Lord Thornleigh's head jerked violently from side to side; the yowl increased in pitch and volume as the maid approached, holding the chain open ready to drop it over his head.

'For God's sake!' Crowther slapped it out of her hands so it flew across the room and skittered to a halt under the window. 'Can't you see he does *not* want it?'

As it hit the floor Lord Thornleigh trembled and the yowl dropped to a mewl. The maid stood back, outraged, with her hands on her hips.

'Well! I've never seen the like! Understand him, do you? Well, you can care for him then. My lady said we were to put it round his neck from time to time as a treat. He's excited, that's all. She said it was a gift from all his sweethearts. She brought it in on Sunday before church. Thought it was a sweet gesture after his nurse up and hanged herself.'

Harriet had crossed the room and picked up the necklace. It was a cheap little thing – she had seen pedlars sell such trinkets for a shilling and thought the price exorbitant. She opened it, revealing a curl of blond hair, nothing else. She snapped it shut again.

'His sweethearts have not been especially generous.'

The maid stood tall. 'I expect it has associations, ma'am.'

'Not pleasant ones, judging by my lord's reactions.'

'Nonsense. He was just excited.'

'Did he get excited like that when Nurse Bray was in charge?' Harriet looked at her hard.

The maid's eyes narrowed. 'Nurse Bray wasn't a very exciting woman, if you ask me.'

Crowther was gently pushing up the sleeve of Lord Thornleigh's shift.

'We didn't ask you anything about Nurse Bray. You may—' He

stopped suddenly. Harriet froze and looked at him. He spun round. 'What is this?'

He moved so that Harriet and the maid could see the quivering forearm he held. Harriet's hand flew to her mouth. On the almost fleshless underside of Thornleigh's right arm were a series of deep cuts. Parallel, fresh, struggling to heal, they shone against the blue of his skin.

'How should I know?' the maid blustered. 'He scratches himself sometimes. His hands fly about when they aren't tied down.'

'Nonsense. This is deliberate. These were made with a knife, and not by Lord Thornleigh's own hand.'

'Nothing to do with me, I just watch here and do my sewing.'

'Get out.'

She needed no further excuse, and slammed the door behind her. Harriet came into Thornleigh's vision; he flinched, then as suddenly relaxed. She curtsied to him then looked at the wounds.

'There are seven.'

'Seven wounds. Yes.' Crowther bent over the man before him. 'My lord, can you understand me? Will you blink once if you can?' The ice-blue eyes skittered back and forth over the room. 'Please, my lord. Just try and listen to me. Blink once if you can understand me.' Again the gaze flittered around, glancing across Crowther's face. Harriet could hear steps outside.

'Crowther . . .'

'Please, sir. Just try.' For a moment the eyes locked onto Crowther's own. The lids dropped and rose again. The door burst open. Lady Thornleigh stood on the threshold. It was as if a phoenix had torn off the front of a dovecote.

'Mrs Westerman. What do you mean by this?'

Harriet moved smoothly forward. 'Lady Thornleigh! I do so hope you are feeling better . . .'

Lady Thornleigh held out her hand in front of her as if driving Harriet off.

'Do not play the lady with me! You come here to torture my husband, do you?' She furned towards Crowther. 'Size him up for specimens, perhaps?' Lord Thornleigh began again his low moan of distress. Lady Thornleigh did not look at him as she said, 'Don't worry, my love. I shall bury you in a lead-lined coffin as soon as your time comes.'

'Is it you that has been torturing him, Lady Thornleigh?' Crowther asked conversationally. Rage made the woman even more beautiful than he had seen her before.

'Get out! Get out at once! I cannot wait to see what the county will make of you now, when the story of this little adventure is known. I hope your husband is no longer interested in a parliamentary career.' Harriet merely folded her wrists in front of her and smiled. 'Get out, I said! *Now!*' Lady Thomleigh crossed to the chair and shoved Crowther away, placing her husband's arm on the chair again, and busying herself with the buckle that held his arm in place. 'If you have not left by the time I have fastened this strap,' she continued with a growl, 'I shall have my footmen throw you out bodily on to the highway.'

Harriet and Crowther made their bows and turned to go, leaving Lady Thornleigh to the straps, her husband's voice rising and falling with all the lonely desperation of the last soul in hell.

V.3

HARRIET AND CROWTHER climbed into the woods where Brook had died. They reached the bench and Harriet sat, covering her face. Crowther lowered himself at her side and waited. The crows bleated above them, the breeze turned a few of the leaves over in its palms. Harriet's shoulders stopped shaking, and after a few minutes she pulled out her handkerchief and blew her nose loudly.

'Thank you,' she said.

'Not at all, Mrs Westerman. Are you recovered?'

'No.' She looked intently in front of her, as if trying to fix her own house and home in her mind, to drive out the other. 'What horrors, Crowther. My head is spinning with them. How can a man be in that condition and live?'

Crowther rolled his cane in his hands. Its foot buried itself among the debris of the ground at their feet with a cracking spin.

'He has been well cared for – at least until recently. Alexander sent a good nurse. I doubt many doctors could have kept him alive so long.'

'But his mind . . . ? Did you really believe it might be possible to communicate with him?'

'The body does not always reflect or obey the mind that dwells within it. I think he is conscious of himself and his condition. At moments, anyway.'

Harriet shuddered and leaned forward, putting her chin in her hand.

'What is the significance of the locket, do you think?' she asked. 'From all his sweethearts . . .'

'I told you of the Squire's suspicions regarding the death of the young girl.'

'Indeed. It did look like the sort of bauble a girl of that age might carry. A relatively poor girl too. I cannot imagine that many of the women that Lord Thornleigh used to associate with wear anything but gold.'

'Who was magistrate at that time?'

Harriet turned to him. 'I have no idea. It would have been more than thirty years ago.'

Crowther lifted his cane from the little pit he had dug with its tip and started on a new excavation.

'More likely forty, I think. But if his family were conscientious about keeping his documents . . .'

'Is it likely that such ancient history would have a bearing on what is happening today?'

Crowther raised his eyebrows.

'It would be kinder not to refer to something as "ancient history", Mrs Westerman, when it took place in my own lifetime.' She gave a swift snort of rather wobbly laughter. Pleased, he continued: 'I've been thinking of what Hugh said about the guilt of his family, and about the locket and those wounds. I wonder if he is being held to account for something in his past, and if we cannot press forward, let us go back. Perhaps that death is like the slip knot of a rope. If we pull it free, the rest may unravel of its own accord.'

The house of Sir Stephen Young was showing signs of neglect. The former magistrate had died at a healthy age and of natural causes some twenty years before. His son and heir, they were told, was a little eccentric.

The maid who showed them in did not seem used to visitors and reacted to them as a bishop might, confronted with a talking lion: curious, but at best a little uncertain. They were hurried into a salon which was dusty and unaired, the furniture bulky and chipped, the paint on the panels blistered and paled where the sunlight reached them, and sooty and greasy where it did not. They had not waited long before the door was pushed open again with a bustle and fuss, and a man of about Crowther's age tumbled into the room. He was remarkably short, and made himself shorter still by carrying his head down and his shoulders bunched. His wig, rather yellow, was slightly adrift and his coat oddly stained about the cuffs. His energy was unmistakable though, and his pleasure at having guests seemed to almost overwhelm him. It was a little, Harriet thought to herself, like being greeted by an enthusiastic mole. He squinted up at them through rather smeared glasses, and wrinkled his nose happily, almost as if he sought to identify them by smell rather than sight.

'So happy, so happy! Such great visitors! I hope you will forgive my home. I have no time for it! No eyes for it! It is a mere shell! My work is the heart of it, and I need no salons for that.' He nodded rapidly as he spoke.

'You are very kind to receive us, sir.'

Harriet extended her hand. He snuffled over it.

'I am honoured! When I heard that the great Mr Crowther himself was in my home – such a joy! So good to meet a fellow natural philosopher, an explorer of the universal beauty of God's creation.' He turned to Crowther. 'You know my name from my publications on the beetles of this area, I think, sir? You have found me out for a little further schooling on the subject?'

The violent nodding continued, and Harriet realised why his wig was always likely to be askew. She could not help liking the little man, and hoped only that Crowther would be kind. She could not bear to see her mole crushed underfoot like one of his studies. She need not have feared, however. Crowther seemed in generous mood.

'I have a double purpose in coming here with my friend. I would be honoured to hear more of your work,' Sir Stephen wrinkled his nose again with delight, 'but I wonder if you could also help us with a matter of ancient history.'

Harriet put her hand to her lips to hide a smile, and Sir Stephen blinked rapidly, clasped and unclasped his hands, and flicked his head to one side. The wig did not quite manage to keep pace with the movement, but seemed to stumble after him like a drunken suitor after a lively dancer.

Crowther cleared his throat. 'I believe your father was a magistrate in this area, some forty years ago, and I wondered if you had kept about you any of his papers relating to that time. There is a matter we would be glad to know more of.'

'Oh yes!' More nodding. 'My father was a careful taker of notes. They are all in his library. I mean to send them somewhere sometime.

But anything not related to my work . . . I never find the time to attend to it.'

Crowther bowed. 'I understand, of course.'

Sir Stephen glowed in the glory of the fellow feeling. Crowther seemed to consider a second, and then suggested, 'Perhaps, if you would allow it, Mrs Westerman might have a glance through the papers while we talk a little more about your work.'

The nodding increased to such an intensity, Harriet feared the wig would fly off entirely.

'Of course, of course. I shall have Hester bring you a cup of something, my dear.' He grinned up at her, the smears on his glasses catching the light, then told Crowther in a confidential whisper, 'The fairer sex, I fear, do not always understand the fascinations of the natural sciences.'

Harriet murmured something appropriate and lowered her gaze.

It was some two hours later that Crowther opened the door to the former Sir Stephen's office and found Harriet, her hat and gloves laid aside, coughing through a cloud of dust she had caused to be thrown into the air on placing a volume on the table in front of her a little too emphatically.

'Good hunting, Mrs Westerman?' he enquired after a polite pause.

'Very, Mr Crowther,' she replied with a choke.

Crowther approached the desk and took in the piles of papers balanced on the various chairs surrounding it. He looked at Harriet questioningly.

'Yes, you can move those. I have what I need here.'

He lifted one pile onto the floor and examined the seat. Frowning, he pulled a handkerchief from his pocket and attempted to disperse some of the dirt before he sat down.

'I don't think you will be able to avoid dust here, Crowther. How are the beetles?'

'Numerous. I wonder at the arrogance of humanity that it is assumed we are made in God's image. Judging by the variety and adaptations of Sir Stephen's specimens – their ability to find a hold in any environment – I would not be surprised to discover that our Creator is, in fact, a very large insect.' He grinned. 'Perhaps we should all learn to tread a little more carefully.'

Harriet smiled, though without looking up from her reading.

'I shall be revenged however,' Crowther went on. 'Sir Stephen is to visit me in a week to have a tour of my preparations.'

Harriet looked up at that. 'I don't envy your staff keeping those horrors clean,' she remarked. 'And is Sir Stephen worthy to be shown the discoveries of the great Mr Crowther?'

Crowther placed his hands on top of his cane and rested his chin on them. If he noticed her satirical tone, he refused to rise to it.

'He is not unintelligent, if a little keen to see God in everything – particularly in beetles, though I don't think he would subscribe to my new theology. And my staff are not allowed to go anywhere near my preparations, which are, in their own way, very beautiful.'

'We shall have to differ. I prefer the human body whole, and not injected with resins . . . Damn, I have lost my place with all your chattering! No, here! You are come at a happy moment.'

Crowther stood and stepped carefully around the piles of papers till he could peer over her shoulder. She held a fat, handwritten volume in her hand, and pointed to a passage in it.

'Sir Stephen was right,' she said. 'His father was also a great recorder of his observations, it seems, though he was more interested in men than insects, and I suspect less happy as a result, from what I have read. His notes are plentiful. The volumes for the thirties were behind those for the twenties, rather than alongside, and I now know a lot more about my older neighbour's business than I should, but enough of that. I have found Sir Stephen's journal for the year of Sarah Randle's murder. It was in thirty-nine. He wrote about the death and search, and I have read it.' She looked up at Crowther. 'It was not the Squire who found her. It was our friend here.'

Crowther lifted an eyebrow, and commented, 'The current Sir Stephen cannot have been much more than a boy himself at that time.'

Harriet nodded. 'Only twelve, poor thing. The same age as Sarah. His father spills a lot of ink regretting that it was so, and fearing the shock would affect him badly. Bridges was of the party following, that much is true. Why would he lie to you, do you think?'

'He wished to be at the centre of the story, I imagine. I am flattered he sought to impress me. Is there any description of the body?'

'Yes, but that is not the part I wish to show you.'

'Indulge me, Mrs Westerman.'

She sighed and flicked back through the yellowing pages.

'Here. "Her body was quite cold, and her dress damp with dew . . . One stab wound . . ."'

'One? The Squire spoke of many, of a frenzied attack.'

'More dramatisation on his part, perhaps. One wound through the chest between her fourth and fifth ribs to her left.'

'The heart. She would have died at once if the blade were long and sharp.'

Harriet let her finger slip down the page. 'Here . . . "belly swollen with child . . ." there at least the Squire was accurate. A white scratch on her neck, but it had not bled.' She looked up at him again. 'What is the significance of that?'

'There could be none. But it suggests the injury took place after death.'

'Something taken from round her neck?'

'Something like a locket on a chain, indeed. What colour was her hair?'

'She was dark. He mentions her dark hair against the green of the long grasses. The hair I saw in the locket was blond.'

'And do we know the natural colour of Lord Thornleigh's hair?'

'He is powdered in all the portraits I know of, but Hugh's natural colour is fair, as was Alexander's. Perhaps she was carrying a lock from her lover.'

'The hair of a rich man in a locket she had bought herself . . .' Crowther mused. 'Perhaps that is why the pedlar was caught up in the hue and cry. Some good burgher saw her buying it from him, perhaps. Poor child. Now, Mrs Westerman, what were you so eager to show me?'

She grinned and turned the pages till she found her place again.

'Here. Shortly after the funeral, Lord Thornleigh came to see Sir Stephen. He said he had heard his name mentioned in connection with the murder, and wished Sir Stephen to make it clear there was no truth in the rumour.'

'And Sir Stephen?' Crowther queried.

'Said Lord Thornleigh could make use of the slander laws if he wished. He adds this. "My lord is growing from a wild youth into an unpleasant young man. I pity his tenants, I pity all of us over whom he has power". Then there is this. "I shall warn Bridges not to be so free with his romanticising. I like Thornleigh no better than any of his neighbours do, but one cannot speak evils without proof and escape being damned onself, and Bridges will find, as do we all, that the influence of Thornleigh is deep and dangerous".'

'I grow to like Sir Stephen as I do his son. Will you pass me the diary, Mrs Westerman. My eyes do not perform well in this gloom.'

She handed the book to him, holding the place open rather awkwardly as she did so. There was a rustle as Crowther took the book, and a folded sheet fell from between the pages. Harriet pounced on it like a spaniel, but in a moment her face fell again.

'A letter, but some enquiry and dated years later. An accident.'

'I think Sir Stephen must have got his instinct to catalogue from somewhere. Are you sure it is not relevant?'

She opened the paper again, and began to read. Her eyes widened, she turned the page in search of a signature and sighed again at finding none.

'You are right, Crowther. Which is a rather annoying habit of yours.' Crowther had returned to his chair with the old Justice's journal, and bowed to her gently before he took his seat. She straightened out the sheet with care.

'I shall read it to you: twentieth March 1748. "Dear Sir, I write with a question, though I fear I must ask for your answer to be delivered indirectly, secretly. I know you will take no pleasure in this. Yet I feel – I *fear*, sir – that the question must be asked and the answer given. I hope you shall agree. I have heard of the death some years ago of a young girl, Sarah. My question is this: did she have a locket, a thing of silvered tin, on an old pewter chain? And if so, was it taken from her at the time of her murder? It may seem a strange, meaningless pair of questions to you, sir. But they chill me and have pressed me down through many sleepless nights. If you answer yes to both these questions, then I must tell you that I believe I have seen this locket, and seen it among the possessions of a man of power, position and cruel temper. I may be going mad, and imagining demons at the end of my bed, where there is nothing not built by my own nerves. So I must await your answer. If the locket of which I speak *did* belong to the dead girl, will you wear the fob I enclose on your watch-chain for a few days? I shall certainly see you in that time, and if you give me an answer in this manner I shall write again, and give you the name I dare not form on this paper now, and let you know where the locket may be found".'

Harriet looked up. Crowther was a grey shadow in the gloom, his fingers tented in front of him.

'Yes, I would say that *is* relevant. Is there nothing further? No note from Sir Stephen?'

'Not here. Where would your observers write their thoughts and actions?'

Crowther turned to the last pages of the journal he held on his lap.

'The system holds. Here, on the last pages of the book. My turn to read to you now, madam: "I place this letter alongside my journal for the year of Sarah Randle's murder. I believed, still believe, that it was written by Lady Thornleigh, whose tragic marriage I observed, and whom I could not help. I wore the fob as requested from the moment I received the note, but no further communication arrived. I had been wearing it for two days when Lady Thornleigh suffered her tragic, fatal fall. I have drawn my own conclusions, and leave it to any future reader of these words to do the same. May God have mercy on their souls".'

He closed the pages and shut Sir Stephen's words away from the light once more, then looked across to see Harriet staring blindly out towards the windows, the faint flicker of greenery and sun at the edges of the shutters. The summer afternoon light softened the outline of her face, but he could still see one tear sliding down her pale cheek.

V.4

IT TOOK DANIEL Clode far longer than he had expected to cross London. In the end, he left his horse in a respectable place on the edge of the city, hoping to travel faster on foot. It was already well past noon, and the hope was a vain one. Even before he realised the scale of the chaos that was running across the city in blue waves, he realised he would have trouble finding his way. His geography of the city was hazy at best, and he soon found himself in a tumbling network of streets and buildings and noise that left him startled and nervous. Twice he ended up returning to the same Square when he was sure his direction had been due west. Here, in front and behind him, were things he had only read about. London was a harsher place than he had remembered.

The young man began to wonder if Crowther and Mrs Westerman had chosen him wisely, after all. He had visited the city only once before, a trip organised by his uncle on the graces of one of his better clients when he was a boy. They had travelled through the streets in a carriage. Daniel had hung onto the edge of the rattling vehicle and watched the people swarming past him with wide and curious eyes. He had seen a man, dressed as splendidly as a picturebook, being jostled by a group of ragged-looking boys, their hoots and calls echoing as they waved his own handkerchief at him in farewell. He had seen animals driven through the streets, lifting their tails and fouling the road as gentlemen on high-stepping horses that looked like unicorns in disguise to him whipped them casually out of the way. He had seen the mackerel- and milk-sellers screaming their wares, and against the white stone walls, small groups of men huddled over bottles and dice. He leaned out a little way as they passed, and a woman, her pockmarks not fully concealed by ragged patches and dead white make-up, had reared up under the window and patted his cheek with her bony hand. And laughed at his horror and embarrassment, displaying the stumps of her last black teeth.

Thinking of her again now, he glanced about him and held his bag tight to his chest. She had become in his mind a spirit of London, and he half-turned, expecting to see her on the street in front of him, mocking him. He stood still and the traffic surged round him. At last he put out his hand and stopped a man who looked at least clean, if not friendly. No one looked friendly.

'Tichfield Street?'

The man turned and looked at him suspiciously.

'North of here,' he grunted, then, seeing the confusion on Clode's face, explained further: 'Just go to the end here, then right and follow your nose. It's near Golden Square and if you hit fields, you've gone too far.'

Daniel released him and nodded. The man took a step on, then turned back and scratched his head.

'Mind how you go, sonny. Gordon's lot are pretty hot round there.' As Clode nodded his thanks again, the man sighed and stepped back beside him. 'And for the love of God, don't carry your bag like that. Here – swing it round and to your side under your cloak. Seeing you clinging to it like that, I'm almost tempted to rob you myself.'

He rearranged how it lay, moved back to admire what he had done, then had turned into the surge of the crowd again before Clode could even speak.

'No.'

'Miss, it's very important.'

'No. If you wish to leave a message with me, I shall see it gets to the children, but more than that I shall not do. You can have no business with them that can't wait.'

'I do – I have ridden all night to see them.'

'Then tell it.'

'It is confidential.'

'Then it must wait.'

Jane made to close the door in his face. Daniel held up his hand. 'But I am a lawyer!'

'Well, I'm very happy for you, sir. Goodbye.'

The shop door was slammed. Clode turned and rested his back against it. He did not know what strength had carried him this far. The day was advancing, he could already taste the first notes of evening in the air. He had not slept and the long ride had sewn aches into his muscles like red threads, which pulled whenever he moved. He thought again of Nurse Bray, her wide face and little blue eyes counting off her bequests in the second-best office in his uncle's establishment, his own nervousness in setting pen to paper, watching he made no blot for his uncle to lift his eyebrows at. He remembered the recitation of her modest wealth, her odd phrasing, her pride as she counted the bequests on her pink fingers: the brooch, the surprisingly large bequest for her friend. His tiredeness fell from him, and he spoke aloud to the oblivious air.

'Mrs Service, Tichfield Street.'

He was shown into the modest parlour and took a seat on one of the two armchairs by the empty grate as Mrs Service jiggled tea cups and leaves on her rackety little side-table. Her cheeks were smooth, but each was dotted with red. Clode wished he could tell her she had no need to apologise for the dark little room, or the kitchen girl who had dragged up the hot water from the kitchen with a whistle and wink rather than a curtsy. Mrs Service's dress was worn and patched. Still, everything about her and her room was neat and clean. Clode wondered how many guests she had to entertain and how she spent her evenings in front of that empty fire with nothing but the noise in the street to keep her company.

When it was time to speak, Daniel tried to choose his words carefully. He waited till he had taken and tasted the tea – weak and made with old leaves – and complimented it before he made any mention of the reason for her call.

'I am sorry, ma'am, but I am afraid I have some bad news for you.'

Mrs Service put down her cup with great care and drew herself straight, ready to be brave. Clode's heart pulsed; he could see in every line of her face that Mrs Service had withstood bad news many times, and he silently wished her strength.

'I am afraid a lady I believe to be an old friend of yours, Madeleine Bray, has died.'

He waited for her to begin to cry. Instead her shoulders relaxed and she smiled at him.

'Oh, no! My dear boy! I think you are mistaken. I had a letter from her only this morning.' Doubt suddenly drifted across her face. 'Though I did think the tone of it a little strange. Not like herself.'

He waited, and the fears began to show on her face.

'Perhaps that was . . . oh, oh dear. Really, sir? You are quite sure, the nurse, Madeleine Bray?'

Clode put down his cup. 'Yes, of Thornleigh Hall. I am sorry. It is my understanding she died on Saturday afternoon. My condolences.'

Mrs Service looked down at her lap. One hand tapped on the other on the unfashionable grey-green folds of material of her dress. She did not speak for some time. Clode began to realise she was made of stronger stuff than he had imagined.

'Was it a fever, sir?' she asked quietly. 'They can come on terribly quickly. Perhaps that letter was the first sign.'

He cleared his throat. 'I am sorry, no. I fear I must cause you more distress. She was found hanging in an old cottage on the Thornleigh Estate.' He waited, unsure what he could or should say. He was very aware of those pale eyes watching him closely. 'There is some debate as to whether the death was suicide, or – or something more suspicious.'

The voice of Mrs Service acquired an edge. Daniel realised as she spoke that the old lady was angry.

'My poor Madeleine. She was murdered. She would never have turned her hand against herself.'

'But you said yourself, in the letter, she did not sound herself.'

'Oh, that's quite different.' She got up briskly and pulled at the top drawer of a little chest under the room's one mean window, producing a folded sheet and returning to her seat with it.

'Here is the letter. I shall not bore you with the usual nonsense women of our age write to one another.' She paused suddenly, and her manner lost much of its sudden energy. 'I had already begun my reply to her, Mr Clode. No need to finish that letter now, I suppose. Poor Madeleine.' Then she turned again to the paper in her hands.

'Here is the passage that gave me some cause for concern: "My dear Beatrice" – that is myself, Mr Clode – "I wonder to what extent humble beings such as us should involve ourselves in the matters of our masters. There has been an incident here today, a shocking one, which has caused me much grief, and I shall write to you further of it in a later letter" – oh how the gods laugh at us when we make our plans, Mr Clode – "but it has made me fretful, for I think I have information that may serve some in this household, but I do not know enough of the circumstances to know if I should speak or not. Perhaps I should say nothing, yet something weighs on this house. I have told you before, my dear, I think the Hall for all its comforts an unhappy and corroded place. It has made me suspicious, but I know no great evils of Mr Hugh, so perhaps I should give him a hint. I am sure this reads as nonsense to you, but even writing it, I see your wise kind face, and that gives me the answer I need. I find I have another letter to write this evening, so must close this and leave you in confusion for a day or two. Forgive me, with best love, Madeleine".'

Mrs Service looked up at Clode, and his blue eyes looked steadily back at her.

'Do you know Mr Hugh Thornleigh, sir? I think he is the son of the house where Madeleine was engaged.'

'I have only seen him from a distance, but he is currently under suspicion of Nurse Bray's murder, ma'am.'

She nodded slowly, then said, 'I wonder what the other letter was she had in mind to write . . .'

'Madam, I know nothing can soothe the wound we feel on losing a friend,' Daniel began, and a sad ghost of a smile lifted the corners of her mouth, as if she guessed he was too young to have suffered many such wounds, 'but I drew up Mrs Bray's will for her. She has left you the sum of fifty pounds. If I may take the details of where you would like the money deposited, I can arrange the funds to be sent to you.'

282

Mrs Service opened her eyes very wide.

'Good Lord! Wherever did Madeleine get fifty pounds from?' Daniel smiled at her. 'Well, I am poor, as you see, Mr Clode. Fifty pounds means as much to me as a thousand might to others. She is kind.' She looked down at her lap again, then back at him with a curious tilt to her head. 'She has named you as executor then, I conclude. Well, fifty pounds.' Her eyes dropped again to her clasped hands. 'Thank you, my love. Though I would rather have the company of your letters than all the money in the world.' She was silent a little longer, then said to Clode, 'You may think it wrong of me to ask, but was there any mention of a cameo brooch in her will?'

'Indeed. She asked for it to go to a little girl of her acquaintance. Susan Adams. I believe she lives in this very street.'

Mrs Service started. 'How strange! Yes, Susan Adams lives here. The poor child! Her father was murdered in this very street only a few days ago. What a world we live in, Mr Clode. Strangely enough, I gave her the twin of that cameo brooch. I am glad they will be reunited in her ownership again. You will find her staying with Mr and Mrs Chase under the guardianship of her father's friend, Mr Graves. They are just around the corner in Sutton Street.' She returned to the window, wrote a few words in a notebook and tore out the page, then turned and handed it to him.

'The money can be deposited at this address.' She paused for a second. 'For all those fifty pounds, Mr Clode, Madeleine had few friends, and none of any influence, I think. Will her murderer be found? Was it Mr Hugh Thornleigh?'

Daniel looked at his feet.

'I do not know ma'am,' he confessed. 'But there is a lady at the neighbouring estate, and a gentleman, a natural philosopher of great reputation, I understand, who have already begun to pursue the case, and are trying to discover who was truly to blame, and bring justice to them.'

The old lady nodded slowly and said, 'Thank you for telling me that. I shall rest easier now. I hope you shall write to me and let me know what occurs, if that would not be too much trouble.'

'Of course, ma'am.' Daniel bowed to her. 'You shall have the money in a few weeks.'

So Clode set out again, leaving Mrs Service to contemplate the strange turnings through poverty, death, and wealth along which life dragged her.

V.5

'WHAT NOW, CROWTHER?'

Harriet had been still a long time, her hand resting on the letter in front of her. Crowther lifted his head, and looked at her through half-closed eyes, like a cat summoned by a change in the wind.

'I do not know.'

'Can we force the Squire to examine Hugh and Wicksteed for scratches from Nurse Bray?'

'It is not conclusive. Anyone can get scratched, anyone can say the skin under the nurse's nails comes from another source.'

'But you don't believe it.'

'Of course not. That quantity, that vigour. No, Mrs Bray did damage to her attacker, and he carries those wounds still. On the forearm probably.'

He fell silent, and when he looked up again saw Harriet was watching with narrowed eyes.

'What are you considering, Crowther?'

'Where is Nurse Bray's body?'

'She is in the old ice-house at the Bear and Crown with the village Constable watching the door, and Michaels watching *him* until such time as the inquest is held. What are you planning?'

'Gathering a little further evidence from that good lady.'

'How do you know she was a good lady?' Harriet asked.

'She took good care of her charge. I am extending a professional courtesy.' Crowther then added, 'And I wonder if you might make use of our remaining friend at the Hall.'

'Patience, you mean? The maid attacked by Wicksteed?'

'Yes.'

Harriet looked at the ceiling of Sir Stephen's study, considering. 'She seems not entirely stupid, and is keen to impress a new employer, perhaps. I wonder if she has anything she could tell us about how that bottle made its way from the stores to Cartwright's hands.'

Harriet picked up the anonymous letter again and turned it between her fingers. 'By the time we come to an end of this, our households will have doubled.'

Crowther thought of the intelligent eye of Cartwright's former servant and his promise to her.

'I suspect mine already has.'

'Very well.'

There was a tapping at the door and the young Sir Stephen appeared, searching for their shadows in the gloom and dust.

'Good Lord! How things get themselves into such disorder – and all by themselves! Well? Did you find what you were looking for, Mrs Westerman?'

Harriet stood and smiled. 'Indeed we did, sir. Thank you.' She looked into the wrinkled, glowing face of their host. 'We were searching for any observations your father may have made about the death of Sarah Randle.'

Sir Stephen's face crumpled sadly and he pointed his nose to the ground.

'Poor Sarah. 1739. Summer. Not as warm as this. Sad.'

'Your father mentioned in his notes . . .'

'Yes. Found her. Knew her. Used to play together.' He looked up suddenly and grinned. 'She liked beetles too!' Then his face fell again.

'I remember when Lord Thornleigh came. Shouted at my father. Foul man.' He cocked his head to one side. 'Though I think he saved a footman of his from the noose. Or perhaps he pretended. Failed to hang him. Called it mercy. Juries are funny.'

Harriet bent forward. 'I'm sorry, sir, I don't quite . . .'

Sir Stephen looked up at her. A little of his own white hair had escaped from under the fringe of his wig. It looked as if the wig had been out collecting thistledown.

'Footman of his, good character, but caught stealing in the London house soon after he was moved down there. They transported him for the full fourteen years. Should have been hanged, really.'

Crowther stretched his fingers and looked at them as if noticing them for the first time.

'Do you remember when this was, Sir Stephen?'

'Two months after Lady Thornleigh died, in 1748. She was very beautiful, but rather sad when I knew her.'

His eyes darted up to Harriet's face and he blushed a little, though the usual animation and joy of his character seemed to have vanished as soon as Sarah Randle's name was mentioned, and he had yet to take it up and fit it round his shoulders again.

'Sir Stephen, we should not trouble you any longer,' Harriet said, 'but before we take our leave, and though I have not the learning to fully understand, I would love to see some of the beetles too. Mr Crowther says they are quite remarkable.'

The colour and life sprang back into Sir Stephen's bent form as if a sluice-gate had been opened.

'Would you?! Oh, of course! Some have many pretty colours. I have a niece in London who says she would like a silk dress just the colour of her favourite. Should you like to see it?'

'Very much,' Harriet said, coming round the table and taking his arm. 'And do tell me about your niece.'

Crowther followed, slowly.

Some hours later they were seated in the private parlour of the Bear and Crown. Michaels's massive frame leaned up in a corner and was largely motionless as they narrated what had passed since they last met. He lifted a pewter mug to his lips and drank it off as they finished.

'I know this Patience a little. Don't think much of her or her people myself, mind, but I can get a message to her now. She may not be able to leave the house for some days,' he said in a low growl. 'She had her free afternoon only a week or two ago. But I may be able to contrive something to bring her here this evening. They say the housekeeper is complaining to all and sundry that she is much misunderstood and is becoming lax about discipline, and Wicksteed spends all his time dancing attendance on the lady.' Harriet and Crowther made no comment. 'I can ask about to see if anyone remembers the footman. You have a name?'

'Sir Stephen could not recall,' Harriet said softly.

'As to the other business, Toller is a good man. I can bring him in here for his supper and you can spend some time with the late Mrs Bray without the Squire finding out.'

'What is being said about the Squire?' Crowther asked.

Michaels ran his hand through his black beard, pulling on it a little.

'That he intends to hang Hugh and pin his favours to the lady's mast. *Fool!*'

He said the last word with enough force to make Crowther raise his eyebrow.

Michaels went on: 'He and the lady, and all their sort will wake up one day to find me and Cartwright's daughter have bought up their mortgages and own the silk they wrap themselves in, and they will never think it possible until they find it has happened.'

'That sounds like revolution, Michaels.' Crowther looked faintly amused.

The man swung his great weight round to face him.

'Progress, I call it, Mr Crowther. Progress. Now let's tempt Toller in. My wife will smile at him, and he'll be docile as a kitten for an hour at least.'

Crowther hesitated at the door to the old ice-house, and turned to Harriet with a questioning look. She met his gaze and nodded. He pulled the door open and a rush of cool air spilled over them; it would have been welcome but for the grey high notes of the grave which mixed with it.

Crowther was satisfied. The body had been well placed, and putrefaction was not far advanced. He set down his candle and took flint and strike from his pocket, tapping it till he got flame enough to startle the wick into life. He had to stoop a little under the curve of the wall. It was an intimate space to share with a body three days dead.

Nurse Bray lay on a trestle table in the middle of the round brick building. Harriet remembered the Parthenon in Rome, which she had visited with her husband soon after their marriage. The shape of the country ice-house recalled it to her, however different the dimensions. She could still hear the soft calls of the wood pigeons outside. Michaels had, it seemed, arranged for some of his straw and ice to be brought in to chill the air. She could hear it from time to time crack, delicately echoing, and the slow drip of water fighting to be free of its solid form, and wild again. In this light, and from this distance Nurse Bray did not seem anything other than at peace, though the unnatural stillness, and taste of the air reminded the living woman of the rank dangers and darknesses that so often lie beneath apparent calm. The candle fluttered into life, and the bricks danced with their shadows, looming rather monstrously over the body as Harriet spoke:

'Ay, but to die, and go we know not where;
To lie in cold obstruction and to rot;
This sensible warm motion to become,
A kneaded clod; and the delighted spirit
To bathe in fiery floods, or to reside
In thrilling region of thick-ribbed ice;'

Crowther glanced at her over his shoulder. 'You are a devotee of Shakespeare, Mrs Westerman?'

'I think him the greatest of our poets. Do you not?'

'I know it is fashionable to regard him as such of late. I prefer Pope, myself.'

'That seems appropriate.'

He ignored her, but peered about him, his eyes resting on the blocks of ice hissing under their straw coverings.

'However, I admit your quotation is apt. How came Mrs Bray to lie here? I thought she was to be taken to the Hall.'

'She was,' Harriet agreed, 'but Michaels said that after the inquest he suggested this place to the Coroner, and the Thornleigh party seemed happy to have rid of the charge. Hugh was being arrested at the time, of course, and I believe the Coroner would have agreed to anything put to him at that moment.'

She watched Crowther's thin profile, all its hollows and edges painted by the shadows and the dancing flame on the candle. She could see his thoughts were already elsewhere. He turned to her.

'If I were to attack you, how would you defend yourself?'

'I have a technique my husband taught me that can bring down most men, should the need arise. But I think you are asking me to imagine how Nurse Bray defended herself.'

'I am.'

'Very well. It is under the fingernails of the right hand that she has the skin, if I recall correctly.' She turned to face Crowther. 'Suppose you were holding me, facing towards you, gripping my wrists. I manage to get my right hand free, and swipe with my nails at your arm, in hopes you will free my left. I would imagine my hand would be shaped like this.' She made a rough claw of her right hand. 'The left upper arm would most likely be where I would catch you . . . It is only one scenario of course.' Harriet shrugged.

'But I think it is the most likely,' Crowther said. 'We have seen no one with scratches to the face. If she were to have her hands free to scratch, it seems unlikely she would scratch her attacker's bare back rather than run away. There are no fibres under her nails, so it is unlikely she tore through someone's britches to get to their skin if she had been knocked to the floor.'

Harriet frowned as she replied, 'We are presuming that the blow that knocked her to the floor was enough to render her docile as well. And then her hands were tied.'

Crowther handed the candle to her and removed from his pocket a little rosewood box. He opened it and spat into it, only looking up to see Harriet's surprise as he stirred the resultant mess with his fingertip. He angled the box to show what it contained.

'A contribution to the sciences from the young Michaelses', nursery. It is a watercolour block. We are to do a little finger-painting.'

Harriet nodded, and found she was glad he had chosen the black rather than the scarlet from the paints available.

They moved towards the body. The nurse's skin was beginning to show purple in places. Harriet was careful to hold the candle steady. When Crowther lifted the corpse's right hand, the body sighed with the early stink of corruption, but the light did not waver. He pressed the cold, waxy fingertips into the colour, then setting down the box withdrew a piece of writing paper from his pocket. Harriet saw the little picture of a dancing bear feinting at an outsized diadem printed onto it, a little smudged. He held it up on the nurse's chest. Taking the hand by the wrist, and supporting the palm so the fingers fell into the same, rough claw that Harriet had formed with her own hand, he then dragged it down the length of the sheet. It left four marks, slow trails down the paper, which rustled against the body's grave clothes. Harriet shivered. Crowther looked at his work and gave a nod, then, spitting on his handkerchief began to wipe the pigment away from the dead fingertips.

'I think,' he said, bending over his work, 'that this piece of paper might make it harder for someone to claim the scratches on his arm were the work of an animal.' He paused and looked up at her. 'Though perhaps I should prepare a few others for comparison.'

Harriet watched him in the play of the candlelight, his tone so casual, his hands enfolding those of a dead woman.

'Time enough for that if it proves necessary,' she said. 'Let us give Michaels the nod that Toller can resume his guard duties and see whether he has managed to conjure Patience from the Hall.'

Crowther laid Nurse Bray's arm back along the table, and having blown on it a little, folded his paper.

'What did you think of what Michaels said?' Harriet asked. 'About buying up the Hall before its owner knew what they were about?'

Crowther straightened his coat, replying, 'My old lands are farmed by a former storekeeper who made a fortune in London. That man accumulated as much wealth in twenty years as my family had gathered in hundreds.'

Harriet nodded slowly. 'Do you think there will be revolution here?'

Crowther smiled. 'I doubt it. Every Englishman still has the stink of civil war in his nose. There was forty-five, of course.' He remembered the panic in the London of his boyhood as Prince Charlie came down the country like a comet, the slaughters and reprisals that followed.

'No, I was teasing Michaels when I used the word revolution, but we live now in an age where a man can – indeed, he must – rise by his own talents. That can only be good, I think.'

He held the door open for her and as she paused, startled by the sudden brightness of the day, blew out the candle.

V.6

G RAVES APPROACHED THE street door with wavering confidence. He had only been told that a gentleman wished to see him on confidential business, and preferred to wait in the street, so was expecting to meet the crumpled sneer of Molloy, grown bold and hungry. It was with surprise then that as he stepped out into the street he realised he was being approached by a man of his own age, or perhaps a little older. He was smooth-skinned, blue-eyed, and although he looked exhausted, he also looked healthier, Graves thought, than any London dweller had the right to appear. Only a growing smear of stubble across his chin suggested any urgency in his business, and the flick of his eyes up and down the street as he approached.

'Are you Mr Graves, sir?'

Graves nodded.

'I am Daniel Clode, a solicitor from Sussex.' Graves tried to keep his eye steady, aware that he was being closely watched for a reaction. 'From near Thornleigh Hall.' That did it. Graves looked a little shaken; he glanced back over his shoulder to see if the street door to the Chases' house had been closed behind him, relaxed a little to see that it was. The young solicitor noticed and was relieved.

'Is there somewhere we can talk quietly?' Clode asked him. 'I have been informed correctly, have I not, that you are named guardian of Mr Alexander Adams's two children? I was expecting someone a little older perhaps.'

Graves straightened. The young man in front of him could not have formed a greater contrast with the yellow-faced monster who had killed his friend, but when the devil fails to conquer us with fire and contagion, he can take a more pleasing form. Graves tried to decide what trust to extend.

'I am. Alexander was my best friend.' He looked hard at Clode; the man did seem tired and genuinely concerned. He would have to take his chances, it seemed, but he could not bring a stranger into the house where the children sat at Miss Chase's feet in the parlour until he knew a little more. 'There is a gin shop round the corner here. Rough, but no one cares there for anything but their own business, and I do not like to leave the children for long. Will that suffice?'

Clode nodded shortly and waited while the other man returned to the street door and had some whispered conversation with the servant there. As Graves rejoined him, Clode stopped suddenly and looked into his face.

'Are the children well-guarded?'

The tone of his voice made Graves cold in the pit of his stomach. He swallowed, and looked about the street. Suddenly it seemed to be populated with all the demons and witches from Susan's storybooks.

'Mr Chase and his family are at home.'

Clode put his hand to his face, another wave of tiredness flowing up from the street like a tide, and rubbed the bridge of his nose.

'Good. Come. I shall buy you a glass and explain myself.'

Watching him leaning up against the greasy wall in the gin basement, hearing him talk, Graves began to realise how exhausted Clode actually was. In the gloom his face looked emptied, his cheekbones unnaturally prominent. He was not surprised then to hear that Clode had ridden all night, and fought his way through London in the heat of the day.

'We have only heard a little of the disturbances, being so far back in Sussex,' Daniel explained, 'so I had no idea . . .'

'. . . that London could be brought to its knees so fast.' Graves tossed back the liquor in his glass and felt his throat sting. He hissed in the thick air through his teeth. They spoke low, leaning towards each other in one of several dark corners the gin shop offered. Small clusters of men in dusty coats filled the room with a low mumble and a cloud of tobacco smoke. By the door a woman of middle age crouched against the wall; she began singing some soldier ballad to herself, ignored by the rest of the drinkers. Graves did not bother to look round as he went on, 'The world has turned over in the last week. Pray God it finds its way back to a centre again, before we all lose our footing. Tell me more about Thornleigh Hall.'

Clode lifted his glass and opened his throat. The fire of the gin made him cough, and stung his eyes, but he felt it knit his bones together again, a temporary relief.

'I have told you of our suspicions as to the true name and condition of the children.'

Graves nodded. 'You are correct. I have proof of it, and their legitimate claim.'

'Thank God.' Clode seemed to slump a little further into his corner. 'That should make things easier when the danger is past, but . . .' he leaned forward and placed his hand on his companion's sleeve . . . 'danger there is. We do not know if anyone other than Alexander's murderer knows of the children, and the relief that he is in custody is such I can hardly stand, but Mrs Westerman and Crowther believe that whoever arranged his killing has murdered three times with their own hands in Hartswood. The danger is real. Another man could ride as I have done, make the same enquiries.'

Graves put his own hand over his new friend's where it clutched his coat and tried to speak with more confidence than he felt.

'We can watch over them. We shall, but first I must take you back to Mr Chase's home. You need to rest, and I must find a way to tell the children what you have told me. It seems Susan was right in all her worst suspicions.'

Daniel smiled a little grimly, examining the smears on his dirty glass. 'She sounds a smart girl.'

'And a good one as is her brother. Alexander raised them well.'

At that moment, the door to the outside steps of the gin shop swung open, and Mr Chase's kitchen boy darted in.

'Mr Graves! Quickly, sir! My master's warehouse by the river is on fire and he goes to defend it. You must look to the children.'

Graves swore under his breath and, throwing down his pennies for the liquor, hurled himself out of the door, dragging Clode with him.

The house was all confusion. Graves shoved Clode bodily into Mr Chase's study and instructed him to rest. Between the ride, the day and the gin Daniel managed no more than a mumble of protest before he took to the sofa and drew his cloak over himself.

In the hallway Mr and Mrs Chase argued with their daughter while the carriage rattled to the door and the male servants gathered by it, agonies of hurry and concern on each face.

'Come, Verity! You must come with us! I cannot leave you here!'

Miss Chase seemed the only calm player in the piece, her hands loosely folded in front of her.

'And I cannot leave the children, Papa, and as they cannot – *must not* – go, I'm afraid you must leave me.'

'And if the crowd take it into their heads to come here?'

'You must place me under the protection of Mr Graves and his friend.'

So she at least had noticed Clode's arrival. Graves hoped that Mr Chase would not smell the gin on his breath. Mrs Chase murmured something. Graves caught the word 'reputation' and felt himself wince. Miss Chase replied with a smile in her usual clear tones.

'I shall play guardian to Susan, and she play chaperone to me.'

Her parents exchanged glances, Mr Chase shrugged and having cast a look at Graves that conveyed more than a sermon would from any other man, kissed his daughter's cheek and swept his wife out of the house. The door was slammed and bolted behind them. Graves stepped towards Miss Chase.

'Why has your father been targeted? He is no Catholic.'

She took his arm and began to lead him towards the parlour.

'His neighbour in the docks is, however, and that seems to be enough this evening.'

The parlour door opened and Susan's face peered round anxiously. Her thin shoulders dropped in relief as she saw Miss Chase and Graves approaching her. She stepped forward and pressed her face into his coat. He put his arm around her shoulders and bent forward to kiss the top of her head. She looked up at him.

'Where have you been? Urgh! Your coat smells disgusting! And who is that other man? Is he a friend?'

He smiled down at her. 'He is. But a tired one. I have sent him to rest.' He hesitated. 'He has brought news with him, Susan. Is Jonathan . . . ?'

The young face grew serious. 'He is asleep on the hearth rug like a cat. You can tell us without frightening him. That is what you mean, isn't it?'

He nodded. 'Yes, little woman. It is.'

They walked into the bright of the parlour, and the noise and fury of the crowd seemed to be sealed away as the door fell to behind them.

Graves was frank with the girl, and she heard him out with a quiet gravity, holding onto Miss Chase's hand and apparently studying the sleeping form of her brother, curled on the floor with Miss Chase's shawl over him. She was silent for a moment when he had finished, then, without looking at him she asked, 'What was the name of the man in the wood, the one with Papa's ring? Was it Carter?'

Graves frowned. 'I believe it was, Susan. Carter Brook. But how did you know? Did you ever meet the man?'

She shook her head and the fair ringlets round her ears bobbed and swung like corks in water.

'No, but Jonathan did. The man showed him a picture, the coat-of-arms on Papa's ring, when he was out at play, and Jonathan told him all about the ring, and where it was too, I suppose. Jonathan liked him. Said he was a nice man – that he had a nice waistcoat. He'll talk for ever if he likes someone.' She swallowed. 'If he hadn't have told, then Papa might still be alive, mightn't he? Papa, and those other people.'

Miss Chase bent towards her. 'We cannot know that, my love.'

The little girl was very still and straight. 'No, but I think they would be.' She looked up into Graves's face. He let his eyes travel over her still-forming features, felt his tenderness for her flower. 'Let us never tell him, Mr Graves. It would not be good if he knew.'

Graves could only nod his agreement and all three looked back again towards the form of the Honourable Jonathan Thornleigh, Viscount Hardew, sleeping still with his fingers caught in the tassels of the hearth rug, dreaming of horses.

V.7

PATIENCE WAS WAITING for them in one of the upper private rooms which the Bear and Crown provided for travellers who needed a bed, or for those who wished to take refreshment in privacy for reasons of their own nicety, or protection. She stood when Crowther and Harriet entered and bobbed a curtsy to them. Harriet wondered if she would be able to take this woman into her own household. There was a hardness to her looks and manner that made Harriet mistrust her. Caveley, she feared, would be at her mercy. She stepped forward, however, and took the maid's hand with her usual open manner.

'We meet again, Patience. Thank you for speaking with us.'

Patience smiled a little tightly before retaking her seat. Harriet perched on one of Michaels's mismatched dining chairs, and Crowther took up a position next to the mantelpiece.

'We wanted to ask you about the events of this Saturday just passed,' Harriet began.

'Yes, ma'am. Michaels said.'

'Do you recall what happened when Mr Thornleigh and Wicksteed came back from the inquest into the death of the stranger in the woods?'

Patience shrugged. 'Nothing much. Mr Wicksteed dined alone. Lady Thornleigh had been waiting to dine until my master came home. Then when he did, he said he was not hungry and went into his own apartments to drink and play billiards.' Patience smiled a little. 'Lady Thornleigh was annoyed.'

Harriet cocked her head to one side. 'So Hugh spent the night playing billiards and drinking alone?'

'Mostly, though he has taught me a little,' the maid told her. 'Sometimes he teaches me when I serve him.'

'And he taught you some more on Saturday?'

'Yes, ma'am. He said he would make me an expert. We've been practising a little while now.'

Again the slow smile, and it had such a sensual curve to it Harriet was afraid she might blush; she was aware of the cat-like eyes scanning her face for a reaction.

Crowther shifted his weight against the wall. Patience blinked and turned her head towards him.

'So you were with Mr Thornleigh most of that evening?' he asked.

She lifted her chin towards him. 'Oh, I had other duties to attend to now and then. Like taking Mr Wicksteed his tray. I suppose you would like to know what Mr Wicksteed had with his supper?'

'Would we?'

'Oh yes, I think so. When I took his leavings back to the kitchen he had me fetch back up a bottle of the Aqua Vitae.' She paused to pluck a thread clean of her grey skirt, enjoying the sharpness of their attention. 'Though Lord knows what he did with it, because I never saw the bottle in his room again. Madam Dougherty was all spikes in the morning because she could see there was a bottle missing, but Wicksteed tipped me a shilling not to write it in the book.' She patted her thigh, indicating, Crowther supposed, where her purse lay concealed. 'Of course, later Mr Hugh said he had taken a bottle to old Cartwright, and that sent her quiet again. The old Lady miscounted, like enough. Wouldn't be surprised to know she had her own supply, and has been dipping into that a bit fierce of late.'

Harriet drew in her breath, and leaned forward.

'Patience, think what you have told us. Mr Hugh was drinking and playing billiards all night; Wicksteed had a bottle in his room which seemed to disappear; Cartwright was poisoned by that liquor. You must tell the Squire what you have told us. It could save Mr Hugh from the noose!'

The girl regarded her with great composure.

'Mr Hugh must look to himself. I have my own concerns, and have no mind to talk to the Squire. I have told you, after all.' Her hand drifted across her belly. 'And I have left Thornleigh. I am to go to London. That is why I am here. Michaels's boy met me on the way down from the Hall.' Her face became a little flushed and her eyes brightened. The word 'London' seemed to work on her like a tonic. Crowther looked a little confused.

'You were keen enough to look out for Hugh last night, Patience, when you locked him away from his guns.'

She nodded, and her speaking palm slid back to her thigh and gave it a pat.

'My prospects are much improved today. I am to go into business

299

– my cousin and I have decided to open a little shop. We shall all do quite nicely, I think. But you must let me go now. I am taking a ride to Pulborough to catch the evening stage. George will be wanting to leave by now.'

There was a rattle and shout downstairs. Crowther glanced out of the window to see one of the local farmers' lads on the front of his cart twisting round and looking up towards them, just as the girl had said. Patience bent down to pick up her cloak, and for the first time Crowther noticed the neat little bundle under the chair.

'Be careful,' he said, watching her gather up the little parcel and annoyed, in spite of himself, at the ease and self-satisfaction in her movements. 'From what we hear, Lord Thornleigh's servants do not always prosper in London.'

She stood and pulled her cloak over her shoulders.

'You mean Shapin?' she asked. 'The man that got transported, all those years ago?'

Harriet nodded.

'He was my uncle. He was killed fighting for the rebels in Boston in the end. Mother always said he was a simpleton really, surprised her that he turned thief. She didn't think he had the wit for it.' She gathered her bundle into her arms, holding it over the slight curve of her belly. 'I have wit. But perhaps some day I shall go to America too. They have thrown out all the Kings and Lords there. You will know where to find me in London by applying to Caleb Jackson's tea shop in Southwark.'

Crowther stepped forward.

'One more thing, Patience.' He reached into his pocket and brought out the small shard of embroidery they had found on the thorns in the coppice. 'Do you recognise this?'

She glanced at it. 'I do. Mr Hugh used to have a waistcoat made of such stuff. Mrs Mortimer made it up. He handed it over to Wicksteed

300

in the winter, though. I had to take it in for him. Mr Hugh is naturally broader in his shoulders.'

She lifted the latch to the door, then turned back on her heel.

'I don't think Mr Thornleigh did poison Cartwright, or do for Nurse Bray, but he is probably right when he says that he deserves to hang, you know. Most men do deserve it, I think – don't you, ma'am?'

She smiled at them again, and without waiting for a reply stepped out of the door and away leaving Harriet and Crowther staring after her.

'Good God,' Harriet said after a few moments. They heard a laugh outside and then the cart crunch forward on the road. Patience was away. Harriet imagined her holding onto its rocking sides with her smug smile and wide eyes, for all the world looking as if she had just finished licking cream from her lips. Crowther examined his fingertips.

'What do you think – perhaps four months gone?'

Harriet nodded. 'Hugh's child.'

'So it seems he believes. I think it not unlikely.' A thought seemed to strike Crowther. 'Are you shocked?'

Harriet considered. 'Perhaps I am. How upsetting to find oneself a prude.'

Crowther looked at her. 'I think it is not your prudery, but the fact you do not like the girl that leads you to be shocked. Come. Let us return to Caveley. Your sister will think us lost for ever, and we must decide if we have enough to scare the Squire back into Hugh's camp.'

'I am not sure we will, until Wicksteed's motive and the manner of his hold over Hugh are made clearer. And Patience was right, we still have to struggle with Hugh's conviction that he should hang for some reason. Until we can get under that, we have nothing.'

Rachel had indeed been long anxious for their return. She greeted them rather white-faced, and before the room to the salon door had closed behind them she had put a letter into Harriet's hands.

301

'I have had one. They arrived just after you left. I am sure just such another waits you at home, Crowther.'

She looked in danger of tears, so Crowther took her elbow and guided her to a seat. Harriet meantime had opened the letter and was reading it. High spots of colour appeared in her cheeks. She looked up at her sister.

'Were there any others?'

'Mrs Heathcote received one, and brought it straight to me as I was reading my own. Said she thought we should burn them, and that she would follow us to the ends of the earth.' Rachel smiled faintly. 'I have never see her so indignant.'

'Good.'

Harriet put the sheet in Crowther's hand. It was neatly written, grammatically faultless, twenty lines of pure hate. Harriet was an adulteress, a witch; he an evil heathen who cut souls from men's bodies and ate their flesh. They should leave the area before the populus knew what the letter-writer did and their homes were burned out from under them. *Thou shalt not suffer a witch to live*, it ended. Crowther was not surprised to find there was no signature.

'I agree with Mrs Heathcote,' he said, throwing the sheet onto the side-table. Rachel eyed it nervously as if it still had the power to leap up of its own accord and bite her. 'They should be burned. Do you recognise the writing?'

Harriet sat down and dropped her gloves on top of the letter with studied carelessness.

'Yes. I think it is that of Thornleigh's housekeeper. The Squire has probably been talking to her, or Wicksteed. She needs very little encouragement to be vicious at the best of times, from what I know of her.' She paused and folded her hands on her lap. 'Well, I am glad we have got them.'

'Oh, Harry!'

'No, Rachel, I am. I feel we have been floundering around,

discovering any number of unpleasant things, but getting no nearer to the truth. This . . .' she looked down at the letter, 'seems to show that we are hitting home.'

But Rachel would not be comforted.

'Does it? Or does it mean that the people here are beginning to find us a rather troublesome bunch of neighbours?'

Harriet looked slightly uncomfortable.

'Michaels is with us. Most of the village follow his lead.'

Rachel sighed and stood, walking over to the fireplace and staring down into the empty grate.

'And most of the local gentry follow the Squire.' She turned to look at her sister again. '*We* would have done, Harry, a week ago. If he suggested ill of someone, we would have been guided by it.'

Harriet had no answer to that. Rachel abandoned the fireplace and went to look out of the window where the last light of the summer day struggled to give her a view. 'I just hope Mr Clode has made it to London. If we have put those children out of reach of whatever chases them, I am happy to take the black looks of my neighbours.'

Crowther cleared his throat, then said, 'I believe your sister is right, Miss Trench. We *are* getting close – and as for the letters and our neighbours, I'm afraid the only way out is through the middle of it. We must frighten the truth out of the Hall, find out why the Lord is marked with seven wounds, and who should really be held to account for the deaths amongst us.'

V.8

C LODE WOKE AND rubbed his eyes. In the last sputtering of the candle left for him he could see Mr Chase's clock. Close to midnight. The first confusions of consciousness danced about him, shreds of his dreams and the events of the last days mingling and separating with the shadows in the room. He remembered slowly. He was near the children, he had talked to their young guardian and liked him. He pulled himself up on his elbow and ran one hand round his jaw; it was rough, and he could taste stale gin in his mouth. His shoulder complained as he lifted himself up. He had slept hard, unmoving on Mr Chase's couch. Over his shoulder he could see the last of light had gone, but the house was not at rest. He remembered what had woken him: there had been a clatter at the door.

Graves exchanged a look with Miss Chase and stood. The hammering was too urgent to be ignored. He stepped out into the hall. The kitchenmaid was trembling uncertainly by a display of violets on the hall-stand; such was the knocking the water rippled round them, so they seemed to be quivering in sympathy with the girl's fear. She spotted him over her shoulder and smiled uncertainly.

'Go back to the kitchen and stay there.'

She dashed away, her soft soles scuffing the flags. Graves went to the door.

'Who is it?'

The banging stopped with a shout.

'Graves! That you? It's Molloy! Open up now!'

Graves felt relief and anger run through him. Opening the door, he plucked Molloy in by his collar, using the weight of the man to shut the door again behind him.

'You? Now? God, Molloy – you hammering for money at this time of night? Come to take me to the Marshalsea – on this night? What are you thinking of?'

Molloy was red-faced. The surprised 'o' of his mouth collapsed into a frown as he found his voice.

'We've no more business, you and I. I've come as a friend, so put me down, you idiot.' He pulled himself free of Graves's slackened grip, and looked up at his confused face. 'Yes. Your ladies sorted you out, though that's their business and I'll leave you to ask them of it.'

Graves felt himself colour. Molloy gave him a nasty smile, sniffed and straightened the strip of dirty linen he wore as a cravat.

'Thing is,' he said sullenly, 'Newgate has burned.'

Graves went pale.

'Yes, you do see, don't you. I do come as a friend, though with no glad tidings. Happened a couple of hours ago. The lock tried to keep out the mob, but there were just too many of them. Place is all cinders and everyone who was in there, is out. Not just the blue cockade lot. Everyone.'

Graves put his back to the wall and swore. Molloy smoothed his sleeves.

'Thing is, it gets worse. I was in the White Horse an hour ago, and I heard a man asking about the younglings here. That little girl and her brother. Mean-faced old bugger, makes me look like a fucking cherub. Yellow face.'

Graves put his hand to his face. 'That's him. The man who killed Alexander.'

'Thought it might be, so I put down my glass and dashed over here to tell you, like my arse was on fire. It's no great secret you are here, son. He'll find out before long. He had another bloke with him too, big bastard.'

Molloy stared down at his feet. 'Thought I wouldn't try the heroics,' he muttered. 'Wasn't sure, see? But wanted to get over here and tell you.'

Graves had gone white.

'Thank you. I am in your debt again, it seems.' He looked up a little guiltily. 'And sorry about before.'

Molloy snorted. 'Wouldn't worry about it. I've had worse welcomes in better houses than this, and don't thank me for yourself, I'd still not wipe my shoes on you. But Miss Chase is all right, and the little girl. I have a daughter too.' He cast his eyes over the violets and sniffed again. 'I've got to go and look to my own, but you shouldn't stay here. He knows and he's coming.'

Graves ran his hand through his hair. 'We can put up the shutters, lock the doors.'

Molly shook his head. 'Guess that's what Justice Hyde thought, and they took his house apart in an hour. The yellow fella only has to start it and there will be a hundred ready to help him pull this place down in a minute. Then he can hunt the kids as he pleases. Look, I can recognise a pro when I see him, and he has a mate. You've got no hope here, not when every other bloke in the place is down at the warehouse. You got to run.'

He suddenly straightened. Graves turned to see the doors to the study and parlour had been opened. Clode and Miss Chase stood in the respective doorways. He could tell by their faces they had heard enough. Miss Chase gave a friendly nod to Molloy and he smiled like the Lord Mayor on parade.

'Where can we go?' Graves said.

Clode reached into the pocket of his cloak and withdrew a crumpled letter, held it up in his fist.

'I have a place.'

17 June 1775, Stone Gaol, Boston, Massachusetts

HUGH RESTED AND breathed deeply as he climbed the steps to Stone Gaol. His hearing was still muffled from the shattering fizz and kick of the guns. His wound clawed at him, and every time his vision blurred, he saw again the haze of gunsmoke and the look on the rebel's face he had caught with his bayonet as he scrabbled among the remains of his lunch to reload. The bloom of blood around the man's mouth seemed to grow, blossom, every time the image recurred until, as Hugh closed his eyes now, it seemed a fountain, a wave that had covered them both. He looked at his hand where it rested on the wall, expecting to see it bloody as fresh meat. It was white, passive, obediently holding his weight against the rough surface of the wall. He almost did not recognise it as his own.

'Come to see your friend, Mr Hugh?'

'Wicksteed!' He looked up in mingled horror and surprise. 'How in hell?'

'I heard you had a friend among the wounded rebels, and so hurried down here to see what could be done. Very little, I'm afraid. It is a stomach wound. He won't last the night, poor Shapin.'

'He's no friend of mine.'

'Yet here you are!' Wicksteed shrugged. 'So he must mean something to you. I shall let you talk to him alone. Who knows what he might say to a friend? I will wait for you, though. That wound of yours needs tending.'

Hugh shouldered past him and into the little room, where some dozen men lay sleeping or unconscious on rough straw against the walls. Hugh could see why the rebels had not bothered to carry them with them on their retreat. He would be surprised if any of them made it till morning. There was a movement in the growing gloom. A middle-aged man struggled up onto his forearm.

'Mr Thornleigh? Mr Hugh Thornleigh?'

Hugh stepped forward, and dropped to his knees by the man's bed. 'I am Captain Thornleigh. Are you Shapin?'

The man stared at him hard. 'I am. I used to serve your household in Sussex.'

Thornleigh looked down at him, saw the old scar smile across his neck.

'So how'd you come here then, Shapin?'

The man lay down again and let out a long shuddering breath. He stared at the ceiling.

'Funny you should ask me that, Captain. I have been asking myself the same question every morning for the best part of thirty years. "How did we get here, Shapin?" You see, I still think I'm in the garret of your father's house in London every time I wake up and open my eyes, even now. They said I stole, and they found what was stolen under my bed, and I began to think maybe I had, they told me so often, with such a sorry shaking of their heads.' He turned so that he could look straight into Hugh's eyes. 'But you know, Captain, I think I've finally worked it out. Just since that bloody-backed bastard put a hole in my stomach, it's as if he shot some sense into me. All the pictures came together, and now I can see the whole thing.'

Hugh spat on the straw; the phlegm was mixed with blood. The misfire of the gun had cost him two of his teeth, as well as much of his cheek and the damage to his eye. The man in front of him seemed to be a philosopher, and the constant smell of blood was beginning to itch at him. He thought he could feel it like something alive on his skin, curling down his arms under his sleeves. His head throbbed, a drum that seemed to turn the world darker at every beat; the edges of his vision were hazy, scrabbled with pain and dull red flashes.

'That's all fine, Shapin. Now tell me what you called me here to say.'

The man smiled at him, a smile of great contentment – joy, even. It shone through the dirt and stubble on his face, and the eyes seemed almost childlike.

'Oh yes, sir. Certainly, sir. This is it: your father, Captain, murdered a young girl. Fucked her, got her pregnant, then murdered her. Then, once your mother had pushed out an heir, and an extra son for good measure – that's you, mate, the guarantee – he killed her too. Threw her downstairs right in front of me.'

The words dropped round and distinct like a string of pearls from between Shapin's yellow shredded lips, but could not make themselves understood through the beat of the drum in Hugh's brain. He spoke automatically, flatly.

'You're lying.'

'No. First thing I've got straight in thirty years.' Shapin smiled again as if bestowing a blessing. He licked his lips, savouring the words. 'Lord Thornleigh took a locket from the girl. Had his hair in it, and kept it just to show himself what he had done. Then your mother found it, and he killed her for knowing. It was in her hand when she died. I was there. That's what I remembered out there in the smoke.' He looked as happy as a schoolboy praised for a well done sum. 'I'd seen the girl wear the locket. I heard your mother scream as she fell, and saw Lord Thornleigh watching from above when I picked her up at the foot of the stairs. I saw her blood on her mouth, and the locket in her hand. Yet it was only today, lying there in the field with the grass and sky all above me that I thought of her again, and it all came clear.'

'You're a liar. A thief.'

The joy on the man's face washed away, leaving him spitting and red.

'I'm neither. Your father thought maybe I'd work it all out, and got rid of me before I did. Thirty years in this stinking place, an ocean away from him, then you rock up here, Captain. You. Little Master Hugh.

I was ashamed to see you in my disgrace, at first. But I saw you across the camp and it all came running back. Then I realised, lying in the grass – you're nothing. My blood is better than yours. You are a son of a murderous cunt, your family honour is a joke, your position a fake, you're fucking poison, your bones aren't fit to feed the dogs on . . .'

He continued to talk, his words flinging up from below Hugh, as if he had dug up the devil himself. The drum in Hugh's head seemed to pick up the rhythm of his speech; it was faster, louder. Hugh felt himself back in the haze of smoke, up to his knees in blood, his mother lying over the redoubt in her ballgown, her stomach shot away by a rebel flintlock, a young girl running through the grass towards his father who stood, pistol raised in front of him; there was the rebel he had stuck so hard he had been forced to push him off the end of his bayonet with his boot, only now the rebel had Hawkshaw's face, and he was laughing at him, they were all laughing, toasting his father and his whore, laughing at him as he stumbled towards the young girl through the blood; he felt again the explosion by his face, the whip of hot metal knocking him back to the ground, back into the blood. It swum over him into his mouth and eyes, he floundered to be free, everything was red.

The beat slowed. He blinked, realised he had been kneeling, that his hands were on Shapin's face, one round the back of his head, the other flattened over his nose and mouth. Shapin's hand, which must have been clamped round his wrist, fell back. Hugh pulled his hands away and Shapin's dead eyes stared up at him. Hugh extended his fingers, looked at the back of his hands: they shook. The drumbeat was gone. His brain was suddenly quiet, open.

Getting to his feet, he headed to the door. The fact that Wicksteed flinched as he passed was the only reason he noticed him there. They looked at each other for a moment – Hugh blank-eyed, Wicksteed open-mouthed – then Hugh was gone, his boots striking the steps to echo as he blundered out into the street.

The letter came three weeks later. His father had had a stroke, and his stepmother was pregnant and asked for his help. The letter must have been sent even before his own awkward congratulations had been received. His father's health had lasted for barely three months of married life. His new mother expressed herself reasonably well, and the hand was more genteel than he had feared, knowing her reputation. He read it twice before putting on his uniform in best order and applying to his senior officer for leave. Had he been more himself, he would have noted, perhaps with sadness, the alacrity with which the request was granted, and a space found for him on the next ship to leave for Plymouth.

Standing in the gloom of the camp the evening before his departure, Hugh thought again of Alexander. The notion that his brother might be out in the world, free of Lord Thornleigh and his new wife, free of Shapin and the Hall seemed to drop the smallest measure of comfort into his soul, and for a little while the nightmares whispered rather than roared through his head. The very last conversation they had had was hurried and incomplete, an embrace and whisper as Alexander left the house for the last time. His elder brother had been very white after the conversation with his father, and paused only to hold his brother for a second and say: 'Get out of here, Hugh. Stay away from that man.' Hugh did his best, but his best was not good enough.

Wicksteed found him, as Hugh had felt he must at some point, the afternoon before he was due to sail. The man slipped up to him as he stood watching the ship that would take him home being loaded in the dock.

'Captain Thornleigh?'

Hugh shifted round and blinked at him. The slighter man was holding himself unnaturally still, his hands clasped in front of him.

'Wicksteed.'

'I hear you are to sail tomorrow. I am sorry to hear your father is unwell.'

Hugh said nothing.

'So you may even be Lord Thornleigh? Even now?' Wicksteed could hold his hands still, but his eyes still glittered.

'I have a brother.'

Wicksteed looked out at the ship as he said, 'Not one anyone can lay their hands on, I hear.' Hugh did not reply. 'Lord Thornleigh – there's a title! Lord Thornleigh might be able to do whatever he wants in life, don't you think? But then, perhaps even his son has always been free to do what he likes. Or think he can.'

Hugh felt his stomach tighten as he thought of those final moments with Shapin. He tried not to ask himself what Wicksteed might have seen. His silence seemed to encourage the man into further speech.

'But we must have friends in order to be able to act as we like, you know, Captain. To keep our secrets. To keep the family honour intact. To maintain our influence.'

Hugh reached into his pocket and pulled out a bill he had kept folded there since the Commander had agreed he should leave. He cleared his throat and stood up straight.

'I don't quite understand you, Wicksteed. But I have this for you. In recognition of your services to the regiment.'

He put the note in Wicksteed's hands. The man unfolded it and stared. Hugh waited to be thanked, then watched in surprise as he saw Wicksteed begin to shake. Bright spots of colour stood out in his cheeks.

'Five pounds! How much love do you think that buys, Captain, in these days?' Hugh was shaken enough to step back. Wicksteed followed him, hissing into his face, 'Is my loyalty worth only five pounds to you? With what I know? I know about the girl, I know your father is a murderer, and I know you are the same. Five pounds!'

He twisted the note between his fingers and threw it onto the ground between them. Spittle collected at the corners of his mouth.

'I'm not some fool! I can write. I have written. I can write again. Everything I know I can tell, and then what member of polite society would dare to speak to you? Your family's story could start a revolution anywhere on earth. Will your victims' friends feed you and tend you?'

The last question was shouted into his face and in Hugh's eyes Wicksteed's face suddenly became a canvas on which some demon had painted and repainted the face of everyone he had ever wronged: every man he had ever killed, every woman he had disappointed, every tenant and child of his estate, and Hawkshaw, Shapin, Cartwright's boy. He staggered back, his mouth open.

'Just you wait, Thornleigh. I'll come for you. I'll tear your heart out and eat it in front of you, and then make you thank me for it.'

Wicksteed turned on his heel and walked away. Hugh bent down and picked up the crumpled note, smoothing it flat with trembling fingers before folding it again into his pocket.

PART VI

VI.1

Wednesday, 7 June 1780, Sutton Street, near Soho Square, London

G RAVES TUMBLED BACK in from the street.
'Not a carriage or a chair to be had.' He saw that Clode was on his knees, fastening a cloak round Jonathan's neck. The young man looked up. 'How far away is it?' he asked.

Graves ran a hand through his hair. 'Three, four miles perhaps. It depends if we go through the streets or into the fields.'

Miss Chase was tying a bundle together over her arm, tightening the knot as she spoke.

'Streets. We may be seen, but we'll be better able to hide. Susan, are you ready?'

The little girl was pale, but steady enough on her feet. She nodded.

Miss Chase took her by the shoulders. 'Whatever happens, you must never let go of my hand, do you understand?'

She nodded again.

Graves touched Clode on the elbow and pulled him to one side. 'Are you armed?'

The young man shook his head. 'All I have is a pen-knife.'

'Go into the kitchen and get a couple of good knives. The servants will lock the house after us and take refuge with the neighbours.'

315

Graves put a hand on the other man's shoulder, gripped hard. 'Come on, we have waited too long as it is.'

The little party stumbled out into the dark. The black of the sky was stained orange in places by the various fires. People hurried past them, bundles of shadow and fear, their faces gleaming with sweat where the trembling lights of torches caught them, like passers-by in the tricks of Caravaggio. Graves urged them on. The familiar streets, the uneven way beneath their feet as known to them as their own hands seemed to have been caught and transformed with the powers of nightmare. Jonathan had tripped before they got past their first neighbour's front door; Graves turned to see him being lifted into Clode's arms. He hung around the young man's neck, struggling to find comfort, his hands clasped under Clode's dark hair.

Graves looked about him. There were too many faces – he could not tell friend from fiend in this dark. He ploughed forward, aware of Miss Chase and Susan in step behind him, Clode at the rear, one hand supporting Jonathan, the other tucked ready in his waistcoat. Graves could tell he had his fingers on the handle of a carving knife, for his own hand was folded round its twin.

They turned down through Soho. Every Square seemed alight with hungry flame and drunken laughter. A man staggered backwards almost into his arms; he stank of brandy and soot. Graves shoved him aside.

There was a scream to his right. He spun round to see a young woman, her hair loose and wild, a baby in her arms, screaming up at the roof of a shabby building opposite which flexed and billowed with orange flame.

'Oh God! Where am I to go! Where am I to go?' she screamed as two men, their blue cockades still visible in the glow, poured out of the house. One pushed her hard in the chest, so she sprawled on the pavement.

'Back to Rome, whore!' he said, then turned to laugh with his companion. The woman folded her arms around the baby in her lap and rocked from side to side.

Susan ripped her hand from Miss Chase's grip and ran to the woman's side. She pushed her little purse into her hands.

'Take this! Find somewhere safe.'

The woman looked up and crossed herself, sobbing as she spoke.

'Bless you, miss! But have you a place?'

'Yes, in Earl's Court. But we should all leave here.'

'Susan, for the love of God, get up!' shouted Miss Chase.

The woman nodded. 'I shall,' she vowed. 'I'll never come back here again.'

Miss Chase dragged the girl up. 'Susan, now! Do not let go of me again!'

Susan trotted beside her to where the two men were waiting, watching the crowd.

'She had a baby, Miss Chase!' she panted.

Graves was looking around into the darkness.

'Very well, Susan,' he said. 'Now come on.' He saw Clode start. 'What?'

'Nothing – I don't know. Let's move.'

Crowther pushed open the door to his home a little after midnight, lit the candle he found waiting for him and carried it into the study. His own letter was waiting for him. He read, holding the page by its edge as if he was nervous the poison might leak out over his fingers, then laid it gently down on the table-top. Drawing fresh paper towards him he began to write, recording his observations of each body as he would if studying them for his own interest, or laying them out for his colleagues to ponder over. Then, sharpening his pen once more, he began to write down each thing they knew about the inhabitants and history of Thornleigh Hall, tried to watch his words grow like a spider's web, turn the points of contact between people and events into a mesh, a form. He knew what he believed, that Wicksteed was the centre of it, but all he seemed to do was glower in the middle of it and refuse to be touched by the strands that swung around him. Just the bottle, and the scrap of embroidery, each so explainable, grazed him, but Patience was gone.

Crowther looked up and his eye rested on the dried black hand that stood, fingers pointing casually downward, on the top of his preparation cabinet. It was black with resin, but the veins and arteries which had fed it in life, the muscles that had given it motion, were highlighted in blue and yellow wax. If those muscles contracted, the fist would clench. He stretched his own hands for a moment, then began to read again what he had written. Where did he have to press, what motion make so that the spider would leap up in a fury, dance, and hang himself on his own threads.

The streets were quieter here, and giving way to fields along the King's New Road to Kensington. Daniel had lost feeling in the arm that supported Jonathan's weight; he mechanically followed the shapes in front of him and counted his steps. He thought of Mrs Westerman and Miss Trench at Caveley. He wondered what they would think, seeing him now, carrying the heir to all that wealth and pomp in his arms, covered in soot and dirty from the road. He hoped they would think well of him. He missed a step and landed hard. The jolt shook Jonathan out of the doze he had drifted in for the last half-hour. He stirred against Clode's neck, adjusted his grip. Clode had grown up without younger siblings, so this sensation of a child's arms clasped in such complete trust around his shoulders was new to him. He began to envy men with children of their own. Jonathan mumbled something to him.

'What is it, Jon? I did not hear you.'

'I said have you seen Thornleigh?'

Clode smiled in the darkness. 'I have. I've not been inside, though.'

'Are there horses?'

'Lots.'

The small boy sighed contentedly, then suddenly his body stiffened and he cried out, 'There!'

Clode spun round, pulling the knife free from his waistcoat. He heard Graves running back towards them. Jonathan scrambled down to the ground, but kept at his side under the shelter of Clode's free arm.

'What was it, Jonathan?'

'I saw him, I'm sure! That end of the street where the lamp is.'

The noise of the riots was muffled and distant; when a shutter caught in the breeze and knocked against its frame the noise was like a rifle shot. Graves lifted his hand to his mouth.

'Show yourself if you dare!' he cried.

The lamp continued to swing slightly, but nothing else in the street moved.

Graves leaned towards Clode and whispered, 'Go ahead with the others. I'll wait here to see we are not followed and come after.'

Daniel did not take his eyes from the patch of street in front of him but shook his head.

'No. You know these roads best and besides, we should not split the guard. If we are being followed and he slips past you, I do not like the odds of Miss Chase and I against this man and his friend.'

Graves hesitated. Miss Chase stepped up to them, put her free hand lightly on his arm.

'He is right, Graves. And let us go by the busier routes. This is too isolated a place.'

Her touch acted on Graves like a charm. He nodded. Clode lifted Jonathan into his arms again, and smiled at him.

'You are our lookout, my boy. Keep your eyes open and sing out if you see anything more.'

The boy looked a little white, and tightened his grip, but nodded.

In the distance they heard one of the great bells beginning to peal the hour. Graves put his knife back into his waistcoat and turned towards Knight's Bridge.

'One o'clock. Come then, and let us hurry.'

VI.2

HARRIET HEARD THE clock in the hall mark out one with a brassy chime. It had been foolish to try and sleep; her mind had just chased itself in circles for an hour. She swung her legs to the floor and picked up her dressing-gown with a sigh. Harriet had never known sleeplessness at sea. Whatever her worries or griefs, the motion of the ship had always let her rest. She would still wake now expecting to hear the speaking strain of the timbers around her, the movement of the air.

Crossing the room, she lit the candle on her dressing-table and sat in front of the mirror as the wick caught and the flame steadied, and stared at herself a moment. She looked well in the candlelight. Her friends had told her that a life on the sea would age and blemish her skin, but she had, as yet, hardly any suggestion of lines about the eyes and mouth; she only began to look old when her sister sat by her. Rachel looked almost dewy with youth, as if she were still forming, budding.

Harriet turned the little key in the drawer below the mirror and pulled out the last of her husband's letters. It had arrived almost two months ago, and she could not yet begin to expect another. She smoothed down the pages and smiled at his familiar writing. She let her fingertips rest on the paper, and it seemed to her it was almost like touching his hand. The letter began with frustrations and bargaining to re-equip in Gibraltar, the problems that inevitably followed the victories there. He had found a man on his crew who, although a drinker and inclined to be a fighter too when drunk, had formed an alliance with the daughter of the quartermaster and proved a hard bargainer for the ship. Of the ship herself, the turn of speed the new copper sheathing gave her, he could not say enough. The last lines were a swift farewell. Some of his friends were heading back to the Channel Fleet while he left for the Leeward Isles, and the opportunity to send back mail was not to be missed.

Her husband had ended with words meant only for her, a simple enough declaration of his love, his trust, and commands to kiss the children for him. He always lifted those last lines to his lips, he told her, when the ink was dry, and now she did the same; she could swear the paper smelled of salt and cold winds.

She set it down again with a smile, and looked past her reflection into the black countryside around her. Strange. He loved the sea like a mistress, but she knew his heart was here; that though he had spent only months here since Caveley was his, the place was his home, the core of him. It called to him across oceans. Of course, she was here, and his children, but it was more than that. The stones and soil had sung to him, for him, when they had driven up the carriageway in a borrowed chaise. She had not seen such joy in his face since the day she had agreed to become his wife. She loved her home too, of course, but the affection she felt for the place was only a weak reflection of the fierce love he held for it. He would be able to walk round the house and grounds in his mind with a more exact eye than she; when he slept his mind always took him here.

Her own heart was on the sea still, and she hungered for it. The horrors she had seen there could wake her in the night, but they only bound her more tightly to the ship and the crew. She knew she was still their figurehead, their presiding angel, however many years she was pulled away from them, but she longed to feel those smooth timbers under her hand, hear the whistles and shouts, see the dizzying openness of the water. She remembered the surge in her blood at

321

battle, the politics of harbour and stores, the thick black coffee their steward served them when the bells called out for the day to begin.

An owl called out over the forest, and pictures in her mind of wind and water were swept away by the image of Brook as she had first seen him, the look of faint surprise and disapproval on his face, the obscenity of the wound in his neck. She imagined him alive, standing in the dark, the figure emerging behind him with Hugh's knife in his hand. She played the scene through behind her eyes as she watched the darkness. Thought of Hugh's scarred face emerging from the gloom, then Wicksteed's. Did Wicksteed have the courage to kill a man? What could make him a murderer?

Huddled against the children in the darkness, Verity Chase heard the sound of a sob suppressed and looked down. Susan was crying. She knew the girl did not want it known; she was being as brave as she could for her guardians, for her little brother. Verity pulled her more tightly to her side, letting her fingers press into the girl's shoulder. She hoped to give courage, resolve, but she was not sure she had any left herself to give. Her eyes stung with sleeplessness and fear in the gloom. Ashes from various fires had found their way past her hood to her pale skin and caught on her eyelashes. Her face seemed to have been crying grey, sooty tears. She looked up to where Clode was propped against the side wall of a shuttered coaching inn next to her. Jonathan lay curled on his cloak at the man's feet. Daniel smiled at her – sad, serious. She found herself thinking that, shaved and cleaned, he probably still looked little more than a boy himself. At the moment he looked more like a woodcut of a highwayman. So much the better. There was a footstep and Graves approached.

'We are very close to Hunter's now. It's not ideal. I can see where the house is from the end of the road here – there are lights burning, it's perhaps half a mile. But it's open ground. If Jonathan is right and that man *is* still following, it is the perfect time for him to make his attack.'

Susan whimpered, and as quickly bit her lip. Graves dropped to his heels beside her.

'My love, I'm sorry to scare you. I'm an idiot.'

Susan shook her head quickly. 'No. *I'm* sorry. I do not mean to be frightened.'

Miss Chase squeezed her shoulder again. 'We are all frightened, Susan. That's just good sense.' She looked between the two men. 'What shall we do?'

Graves stood again. 'We'll have to make a run for it. Miss Chase, could you carry Jonathan that far?'

She nodded.

'Very well. As soon as we come into the open, head right. And run. If the gates are locked you will have to climb them. Whatever happens, do not wait in the road.'

'Of course.'

It was hard for Graves, searching out the edges of her face in the darkness, not to declare his love then and there. He swallowed. 'Clode and I will follow and stop anyone passing us. Are we ready?'

Clode was placing Jonathan in Miss Chase's arms. Susan had taken her bundle from her, and tied it round her waist. They nodded.

'Very well then. Let's go.'

VI.3

THEY REACHED THE corner and without a word Miss Chase turned and plunged off into the darkness, one arm supporting Jonathan, her free hand in Susan's. Clode and Graves began walking backwards behind them. The little light of the new moon caught on the tips of the blades they carried. The footsteps began to fade behind them, for one joyful moment the night was suddenly still, and Daniel thought they might have been wrong – that the paranoia conjured by the riots and their own fear might have deluded them, and the boy – that all was well . . . then there was a shout and two dark shapes reared up along the track.

Clode sprang at the man nearest him. In that moment all his tiredness disappeared; he became something other than himself. He felt the man stumble under his weight, then the world spun as the man's fist slammed into his jaw and his head snapped back. He had his hand on the man's shirt, and while the night exploded with pain that seemed to shatter his bones, he would not let go. He struck back with his free hand, using the fist clasped round the handle of his knife to strike at the place in the darkness where he guessed the man's face would be. He connected, and felt the crunch of bone. The man yelled and reared under him, striking him hard in the side. The blow loosened his grip and the knife skittered on the roadside. The man swung Clode onto his back, and sat over his chest. Time began to slow. Clode saw the man reach into his pocket for his own knife. He was about to be killed by a shadow, his mind informed him gently. His blood beat through his hands, he scrabbled to gather the dirt of the road and threw it into the man's face. The shadow winced and reared back slightly. It was enough for Clode to reach his right hand back, to where he felt rather than saw the pale glint of his own blade. He heard the roar of the giant on his belly, saw the man raise himself, the point of his blade held high and angled straight for Clode's heart. His fingers brushed the wooden handle, he reached, every muscle and bone singing poison with the effort, then felt it, held it, and pulled it towards him. As the man fell on him, his eyes went dark for a second. Then he opened them again. His chest was warm, but he felt no pain there. He struggled out from under the man's bulk and staggered to his feet, putting a hand to his chest. He could feel the blood on him, but knew it was not his own. He turned the body at his feet over with his boot. The bulk shifted and sprawled on its back. The eyes were open and empty. His knife was buried deep in the massive chest. He bent down and pulled it free. Then turned, looking for Graves.

Graves saw Clode pull the man to the ground on his left. He jumped right and managed to connect with the thin figure trying to dart past him, and pushed him off-balance. The man fell on his knees, but before Graves could launch himself on top of him, he had scrambled to his feet again and turned to face him. The moon sighed enough light forward for him to see the yellow face under the peak of his hat.

'You again,' the man said.

Graves stood in front of him. 'Indeed.'

The yellow face cracked with laughter. 'If that's how you want to play it, boy.'

He suddenly danced forward. Graves swiped at him with his right hand. The man giggled, and before Graves could even register his movement, he had closed with him, pinning his knife-arm to his side and catching his left wrist with the same hand. The embrace of an impatient lover. Graves felt the bitter warmth of his breath on his face. He pulled, but the grip was vice-like. The man spoke, softly. Like a disappointed father to a child.

'Don't you gentlemen learn anything useful in your education?' Graves struggled, but the man was rigid as iron. 'Thought I'd taught you, with that little shaving nick I gave you.' Graves felt the rancid breath travelling the still-fresh wound on his face. 'Thing is, boy, thumb on the blade. And strike up.'

Graves looked down at the glint of the blade, the man's thumb pressed on the flat of it; he felt the man's body tense for the blow. So he would fail here; it would end here on the road with London burning in front of him. He thought of Susan, biting her lip, and the anger sung through him. With a roar, he twisted his body away, but not fast or far enough. He felt the cold point of it drive through his skin, and the darkness of the night flood in after it. He fell, the yellow man turned and began to lope off up the track. Then Clode was beside him.

'Graves!'

He shook his head, stumbled upright. He could still walk, the wound could not be deep. The yellow man had got past them. He was heading towards the children. Graves gulped in the air. It tasted like iron, but sweet, black, it bound his wound and threw the pain of it away.

'The children. Come on.'

They raced forward into the dark.

Miss Chase heard the noise behind them on the road and Susan tugged on her hand, tried to turn back. Verity only pulled harder at the girl. The lights of the house were very close. She willed her little party over the last few yards till she reached, half fell on the head-high metal gates. She lifted Jonathan up under his armpits.

'Go, Jonathan. Now.'

His hands fitted and clasped and she felt him pull himself out of her hands, saw his body swing lightly over the spears.

'Now you, Susan.'

She knelt down to make a cradle for the little girl's foot with her hands and boosted her up. She heard her tumble on the other side, then began to search for her own footholds in the brick and iron. One foot pushing against the stone, her hand on the bar, the other slipping on the lock, she dragged herself up and felt with her right hand for a higher grip. Her fingers fitted round the muzzle of a stone lion at the top of the gate-post. She swung to the top, then let herself fall on the far side, her skirts billowing around her. She turned to look out into the roadway, peering out through the bars for a sign of what was happening on the road. With a crash, a body fell against the bars from the outside, and she found herself face to panting face with the yellow man of Susan's nightmares. He smiled, and they held each other's gaze a moment. She put out her hands, felt the little boy and girl take them. She managed to open her lips.

'*Run.*'

The three of them turned and scrambled through the long garden of Mr Hunter's house. She could hear the gate rattle where the man climbed up behind them. Lights were beginning to move in the house. They charged forward, then suddenly Susan screamed and the ground seemed to fall away beneath them. Miss Chase felt her leg twist as she landed. The breath was forced out of her body.

The darkness here was absolute, but living. There was a noise. Something was already here, moving, twisting in the dark. She heard a noise. Something like the sea, or the tearing of rags but animal. She put out her arms and gathered the children towards her, shuffling away from the sound, the movement, with her hands over their mouths to stop their noise. There was no need, their thin bodies were rigid with terror. There was a clank of metal, a chain. The strange purring roar. More voices in the distance now, familiar, Clode and Graves. She felt tears in her eyes. They were alive. There was a sudden impact in front of her. A darker shadow among the shadows.

'What ho, pretty ones. What sort of a cave have you found to hide in?'

Her mouth went dry, she struggled to unclamp her throat and shout, 'Graves! Clode! Here! He has us!'

She heard footsteps running above. She pushed the children behind her, into the extreme corner of whatever space they were in. She could hear the yellow man's breathing as he moved towards them in the dark. He began to laugh. Then the other sound came again – like the grumbles of some huge dog. The yellow man turned back towards it.

'What in hell?'

Then he advanced on them again. Miss Chase began to see now.

327

The yellow man in front of them, bearing down, his arm raised, and behind him a strange rippling movement in the shadows. There was a sudden shout, and she saw a figure of a man dart across her view, knocking the yellow man back into the darkness. The strange alien growl behind him became a roar. The shadows were all movement. There was a scream, high-pitched. The rippling shadows squalled and tore; another scream, another figure, a ripping sound.

'Graves?'

'Here! They have him!'

An exclamation of horror. Suddenly a man appeared in the darkness, half-dressed and holding a flaming torch over his head.

'What in God's name?'

The torchlight swam in. Miss Chase clutched at the children. Two huge, cat-like creatures were at the throat of the yellow man, tossing him around like a rag doll. Graves, his trunk bloody and eyes wide with terror, was scrabbling away on his back. She saw Clode, grabbing one of the animals by its neck and throwing it bodily back into the cave, then seizing the yellow man's leg and attempting to pull him free from those teeth. The torch was dropped; the man who bore it leaped forward to help him, kicking the second cat in the throat till it abandoned its grip. Miss Chase scrambled to her feet, picked up the torch and pointed it into the cave.

'Don't look,' she said to the children, then glancing back saw they had already seen, and could not look away.

The yellow man lay sprawled almost at their feet, his neck a ragged mess of torn flesh. Across his chest the broad even stripes of clawmarks had torn his clothes and fringed them in red. Miss Chase looked at their strange rescuers. The cats were chained at the collar it seemed, their muscular bodies spotted with markings like tiny hoofmarks. They paced forwards to the extent of their reach, their speckled mouths red and running, but they could no longer reach any of their guests. Graves slumped against the far wall, his face white and his side bloody and wet. Susan let out a noise between a whimper and a cry and scrambled over to him. He put his arm round her and pulled her close.

'It's all right, Susan. I'll live.'

Clode was on his knees at the yellow man's side, looking as if he had lost his senses in the fight, panting hard, his front covered in blood. Miss Chase had never thought there was so much blood in the world. They all seemed drenched in it. She glanced at her own hands. Saw them scraped and cut by the walls, and floor. The man who had brought the torch stood in the midst of them, looking around with amazement. She looked up at him.

'What are they?'

'They are two male *panthera pardus* of the *felidae* family. Commonly known as leopards. I am John Hunter. This is my home. Now, madam, who the hell are you?'

Clode blinked and looked about him, then reached into his pocket, dropping his bloody knife on the ground in the process, and pulled out the letter he had received in the Caveley parlour. He remained on his knees, but held the paper up towards Hunter, crumpled and dirty, still struggling to find enough breath to speak. Hunter took it from him as Clode managed in a gasp:

'Sir, with the compliments of Gabriel Crowther.'

VI.4

'**B**RING THEM IN then.'

Hunter's voice was muffled behind one of the heavy doors in the back of his house that separated the living areas from those in which he conducted his research, though, in truth, the whole establishment was a monument to his work. Oils of strange animals, meticulously painted, hung around the walls, along with skulls and bones of creatures Susan could not even imagine. Jonathan was transfixed by the skeleton of a snake coiled as if to strike in a glass case by his feet. His sister held tightly onto Miss Chase's hand as the door swung open.

Hunter was a man in late middle-age. His face was rather squashed and red, with a comfortable belly pushing under his waistcoat. Standing next to him, Clode looked very young. He was wearing a fresh shirt, but there were still bloodstains on the skin around his throat. He tried to smile at them, and winced at the pain in his jaw. In front of the men was a huge oak table; on it two forms, bodies under dirty sheets.

'We wanted you to see them before you go to bed,' Clode said. 'For the last time. To show he is really gone.'

Susan nodded and let go of Miss Chase's hand. Hunter turned down the sheet from the yellow face of the body nearest to her, though he kept the throat covered. The children approached and stared at him for a long time. The eyes were open and blank of meaning. The candlelight pooled over the cracked jaundiced skin, and made puddles of shadow swing around the cloth over his throat. The lips were slightly parted.

Jonathan looked up at Hunter. 'He is dead?'

'Very.'

'And who is that?' Jonathan pointed across at the other body. Hunter folded back the second sheet to reveal the broad features of Yellow Face's companion.

Miss Chase saw Clode flinch as the corpse was exposed. So that was your work, she thought to herself. Again the children looked. This time Susan spoke.

'He looks a bit like Mr Yelling's son.' She glanced up at Clode, who watched her with friendly concern. 'He was a bit simple. It's not him, though. And I'm glad he's dead. Thank you for killing them.'

She stepped back, and Clode looked a little embarrassed. The little girl addressed Hunter.

'What will happen to them now?'

Hunter glanced at the younger man, who answered for him.

'The bodies will disappear,' Clode said. 'That's why we wanted you to see them now.'

Jonathan yawned and leaned against Miss Chase's slender hip. 'How disappear?' he asked.

Hunter grinned at him. 'I shall cut them up to show my students. Though I may keep the skulls.'

The boy smiled sleepily. 'Good.'

Miss Chase placed her arm around his shoulders. 'I must put these children to bed. We are just going to say goodnight to Mr Graves.'

The gentlemen bowed, and she led the children from the room, turning back to the strange, frog-like man among the candles and corpses.

'Thank you, Mr Hunter,' she said quietly.

'Delighted, Miss Chase.'

Graves was comfortable, pale from his loss of blood, but neatly bound up and lucid. The children ran to him and buried themselves in his arms as soon as the door opened.

'Steady there! Lord, you're as much trouble as the man with the knife!' Miss Chase sat at the end of the bed and watched as they burrowed into him like babies. Jonathan looked at him, his eyes shining.

'Mr Hunter is going to cut them up and keep the skulls.'

'That sounds like a fine plan.'

They talked nonsense to each other for a few minutes, laughing more than would have seemed right to anyone who had not been through the tension of the night, felt it release and wash away from them, till Miss Chase noticed the first wakings of dawn outside, and began to stand, ready to gather them back to bed. The door swung open. Clode appeared, his manner all urgency.

'Good! You are still awake. Look what we found in that man's coat!' He thrust a handful of paper at them. Graves reached out over Susan's head to take it. Miss Chase looked at him expectantly. He opened his eyes wide.

'It's a note: "Here is the address. Do him, and any family you find there." Well, that's fairly clear. And this scrap has the address of Alexander's shop written on it. In a different hand.'

Daniel nodded. 'I think I know whose hand wrote the address. Carter Brook.'

'The first man killed at Thornleigh?'

'That's right. And I bet any money Mrs Westerman and Crowther will be able to tell me who the other writer is. We have it! We'll get the vipers out of your house, sir.' He nodded to Jonathan with a wink. 'So by the time you come to it, it'll be fit for you.' He looked around at the faces. 'For you all, I hope. But I must go. Hunter will give me horses, and I should get this into Mrs Westerman's hands as soon as I may.'

Miss Chase put up her hand. 'But Clode, you've hardly slept for days! You are injured! You must rest.'

He shrugged at her, feeling the tender place of his jaw with his free hand.

'There will be time for that later, Miss Chase. This is the endgame, the last cards. I'll rest when this is done.'

He turned on his heel and headed for the door again. There was a soft patter of feet behind him, and he felt Susan's arms close round him. She stood on tiptoe to kiss his dirty, stubbled cheek.

'Thank you, Mr Clode.'

He blushed and as she freed him, gave her a formal bow. 'My pleasure, Miss Thornleigh.'

He looked up and caught Graves's eye. They nodded to each other and in a moment he was gone. Susan watched the space he had occupied for a long time.

Harriet had managed a few ragged hours of sleep, but it was not long after the early dawn that she found herself walking in her woods. Something drew her back here again and again. It was a pleasant situation, right enough, but she knew it was more to see the patch of earth on which Carter Brook had fallen that she came here. She paused there now, her hand resting on the thorn tree where the scrap of embroidery had been found, and walked through her actions of the last few days. Was there something she should have done differently?

Turning back to the bench, she sat down heavily, dropping her head into her hands with a sigh. Images swum around her tired brain. Nurse Bray, hanging in the old cottage, the foul depth of the wound on Brook's neck, the hissing hatred of the letter that had found its way into her hands last night, the pathetic struggles of Michaels's little bitch in the face of the poison, Wicksteed, his hand raised to whip Hugh's lover. Could the poison be tracked? She would ask Crowther who might have such a thing. Why would Hugh not *say* that the bottle had been put into his hands by his steward? What possible hold did the man have over him?

She heard a movement behind her and leaped up, spinning round to see Wicksteed in the flesh smiling at her.

'Wicksteed!'

'Yes, Mrs Westerman. You are having an early walk?'

His manner was oddly brash. He had become less watchful, more triumphant. The deference was stripped out of it. He looked straight at her, and she could not help feeling that he was amused at the sight of her. She drew herself up very straight and tried to look at him with an air of cold command. A smile twitched the corner of his lips.

'Yes. As you see,' she said coolly.

'I like to have a little look around my lands before the work of the day begins, Mrs Westerman.'

'*Your* lands?' The laugh she tried to give to her voice almost choked her.

'The lands of my betters, I should say, shouldn't I? Though, if Captain Thornleigh hangs, the heir will be the son of a cripple and a whore, and I think my blood is as good as his.'

He took a seat on the bench with studied ease and smiled up at her, blinking. She stood in front of him.

'Will they still employ you, do you think, Wicksteed, if it is known you speak of Lady Thornleigh in that way?'

A sudden tenderness touched his face, and for a second he seemed almost gentle. He drew a snuffbox, extravagantly jewelled, from his waistcoat and offered it to her, but she waved him away with disgust. Shrugging, he took his time balancing the powder on the inside of his wrist and inhaling. He then spun the little box in his palm as he replied. She noticed that when he was relaxed in this way his voice had a pleasant tenor lilt; it made his words all the more violent.

'Oh, my lady knows what she is, Mrs Westerman. She is fearless in the face of truth. But what of you – who are *you*? Some sailor's bitch charging about the countryside turning over one affair or another like one of your pissed-up crew on shore-leave.'

Harriet felt suddenly nauseous. She swallowed. 'How dare you speak to me in that way?'

He smiled. 'What have I to fear from you? You and your knife man have tried your best, and done nothing but put Mr Hugh's head more neatly in the noose and the Squire in my pocket.' He tilted his head to one side and his right hand lifted and danced in the air as if directing the flow of affairs with its lazy parabolas. 'No, sweetheart. You should be afraid, not me. I do not like you, and I do not think you should continue at Caveley.'

Harriet blinked. 'What have *you* to say on the matter?'

'Come now! Haven't I just said? Pay attention, dearie! In a month Hugh will be dead, and I'll be the power in the house. You know it, just as clear as I do. Then my first, my only task, will be to make your life here hell on earth. None of the gentry will speak to you, you will not be able to supply your household from any concern that has trade with Thornleigh. Your reputation, such as it is, will be beyond respectable, and your sister will be despised.' He paused and said kindly, 'This will happen, Mrs Westerman. Be assured.'

She took a step back from him, as the image of a yellow lizard who shot out a pink tongue to trap flies in Barbados came back to her. It was like seeing the beast again, dressed and conversing.

'Don't be so sure of yourself, Wicksteed. There is more to come from this. And those scratches on your arm may well condemn you yet.'

He looked genuinely surprised. 'Scratches?'

He shrugged off his coat in a moment, and rolled up the loose linen sleeves of his shirt to his shoulders, turning his wrists slowly so Harriet could see that, shoulder to hand, the skin was unmarked. Buttery and pale, but unmarked. He saw her surprise and laughed again.

'You mean to scare me, and leave me all the more secure, honey!'

Harriet felt her heart beating fast; his face was pink with pleasure. Without thinking, she lifted her crop, aiming to strike him. He was too quick for her. His flying right hand darted across and caught the end of it on his palm. He closed his hand round it and pulled hard, so she stumbled forward. He was breathing hard and the amusement of a few moments before became anger. She could see it glinting in the chips of white in his pale blue eyes.

'Tell you what, bitch.' Their faces were so close she could feel the heat of his breath. 'You leave. Just you. Leave your husband, your sister, your children, go somewhere else and I'll be the sweetest neighbour to them in the world. You stay, or sell and take them with you, and I'll hunt you through society. Your fortune, your husband's, your sister's . . . It'll be gone. Ruined. Nothing left by the time I've done. But leave, and you can save them from your punishment. Yes. That's even better. I'll take your whole family from you.'

His spittle hit her face. He released the end of the crop, and her mind nothing more than white horror, Harriet turned and plunged back down the slope to Caveley.

VI.5

'**S**HE WILL NOT speak to me!'

Crowther patted Rachel's hand as it lay on his arm. 'What happened?'

The young woman looked at him tearfully. 'She came running in just as I came down to breakfast – crying, I think, and Harriet never cries. Then went straight up to her room. I've knocked and knocked, but she just asks to be left alone.'

Crowther frowned. 'No more letters this morning?'

'Nothing. But she did not seem overly concerned about them last night.'

Crowther shrugged, and rested his cane against one of the salon bookshelves.

'Would you like me to go and speak to her, Miss Trench?'

She nodded, and opened the door for him with alacrity.

Crowther was concerned. If, a week ago, he had been told he would be outside a respectable woman's bedroom door asking for admittance, he would have been too surprised and offended even to laugh. Yet here he was. And he thought he knew Mrs Westerman well enough now to know she would not do this without some reason more than the usual feminine hysterics. He knocked softly and called her name.

'Mrs Westerman. It's Crowther. May I speak with you? Your sister is concerned.'

There was a sigh and rustle in the room. A footstep came to the door from within and hesitated. He heard her voice:

'Are you alone?'

'I am.'

The door opened and Crowther saw Harriet, her eyes bruised with tears and her face very white.

'Come in, Crowther. Something has happened.'

He let her relate the conversation with Wicksteed and without interruption, then sat a long moment before he rang the bell. The speed with which the summons was answered suggested Mrs Heathcote had been hovering outside for some time. He met her at the door.

'Mrs Heathcote, I believe Mrs Westerman could do with her coffee and toast in her rooms.' He made to move away, then paused and turned back. 'And would you tell Miss Trench that her sister is quite well.'

Mrs Heathcote looked gratefully at him. 'Of course. Thank you, sir.'

There was such genuine warmth in her tone Crowther smiled. He then returned to the armchair by the fire opposite Harriet and crossed his legs.

'I don't know what to say to you, Mrs Westerman, and that is a shocking confession for our age. Any man of civilisation should know exactly what to say in any circumstances.'

This drew a reluctant laugh.

'I have never thought of you as particularly civilised, Crowther.' He smiled. Then saw the spasm of pain cross her face again. 'Oh, God! Do you think I might have to leave Caveley?'

He was saved from answering by the arrival of Mrs Heathcote with Harriet's breakfast. She had brought him a cup as well, and poured the coffee with ostentatious care. As soon as she pulled the door closed behind her though, he replied.

'Perhaps.'

'But what would I do? He told me I must leave my family here. I have been made an exile.'

'It is not a happy role – that I know. Though it can be bearable.' He spoke gently and she nodded slowly in reply. Crowther cleared his throat, and his voice became more robust. 'His arms were unmarked, you say?'

'Completely. Perhaps it was Hugh.'

'You don't believe that.'

'No.'

He studied his fingernails then picked up his cup, and sat back in his chair.

'Well, Mrs Westerman. Do not abandon hope as yet. We must try to find out something about the poison, and we do have one advantage over Wicksteed.'

She looked up at him quickly.

'We have the children.'

Miss Chase knocked softly at the door and let herself into the room where Graves was resting. He was attended by John Hunter, who looked up fiercely when she entered, then, recognising her, relaxed his face into a smile.

'How is the patient, Mr Hunter?'

The older man finished counting out Graves's pulse before he replied, and laid the patient's hand, with great gentleness, on the bedcover.

'He is young. If there is no infection in the wound, and I see no sign of it, he will do well enough.' Graves settled himself back on the pillows. He looked a little white, but otherwise much as Miss Chase had expected.

'You don't mean to bleed me then, sir?'

Hunter gave a bark of laughter. 'God, no! Other fella bled you enough, I think. Barbaric practice, I believe. I only bleed ladies of fashion, who fancy themselves a little nervous and want an excuse to faint and look pale. It's no part of medicine. Never seen it do anything but make a weak body weaker.'

Miss Chase smiled at him. 'You're a revolutionary, sir.'

He nodded. 'I am proud to call myself a scientist, Miss Chase – like Gabriel Crowther. We learn with the eyes and ears and minds God gave us. Half the men who call themselves physicians in London learned all they know by reciting the Latin of the ancients, and grinding pretty powders. Never take notes. Never really observe the body at work, and so just get in the way.' He seemed to shake himself. 'There, you have got me on one of my hobby horses, Miss Chase, and I could ride it till dinner if I am not careful.' He looked down at the injured man again. 'I shall leave you to the society of this young lady, sir. But you must rest. And do not let the little boy jump all over you and disturb my dressing on your wound. I shall know if you have done so.'

He bowed and left the room, and Miss Chase took a seat by the bed. Graves lifted himself on his shoulder and turned to her. She could see the shape of his collarbone under his shirt, the pool of it at his neck. She smiled briefly and looked down at her hands, suddenly awkward.

'Mr Hunter is very kind to us.'

Graves laughed. 'I suspect we could not have had a better introduction than hauling in a couple of fresh corpses. Particularly ones he did not have to pay the resurrection men for.'

She smiled. 'I tried to explain a little more. He shushed me and told me he had no interest in stories, and had work to do.'

'I pity the colleagues for whom he has so little respect. I doubt he has any compunction about showing it.'

There was a moment of silence; it swam between them. Miss Chase did not look at him, but felt herself so aware of his presence it was almost painful.

'Miss Chase . . .'

She did not remember his voice as being so low. She had always liked him, of course, but thought him a rather awkward young man. She had noticed that he admired her, and was pleased with the attention, but it had not occurred to her for a moment that she would ever develop stronger feelings for him. Then everything seemed to change, and he with it. She interrupted him.

'I have sent to my parents. I hope to hear from them soon.' Then she grinned and glanced up at him. 'And I think you may have a little difficulty with one of your wards. I suspect Miss Susan Thornleigh has fallen violently in love with Daniel Clode.'

Graves laughed hard, then grimaced as the newly forming skin around his wound protested.

'I think she could do a great deal worse. He's a good man, and handsome too, damn his eyes. She has my whole-hearted permission to like him.'

Miss Chase blushed a little and smiled back at him.

'You're a terrible guardian. She is to be rich. Titled. Connected. You should have a Duke in mind for her at least, not the local solicitor.'

He rolled onto his back and contemplated the canopy of bed-hangings above him.

'The rich all need lawyers. It could save the family a fortune in fees. Though the children have a grandfather still living, do they not?'

'That is what Mr Clode said. And an uncle, though I got the feeling he did not like either of them.'

Graves felt suddenly tired. His wound itched and his eyes felt heavy and hot. He let them close briefly and it seemed to him that the presence of the woman in the room formed a glow behind his lids. Golden and right in the darkness.

'He has gone to help clear out the vipers from Thornleigh Hall, remember. We must trust him and our new friends, this Gabriel Crowther and Mrs Westerman, to make the place fit for the children.'

VI.6

THE LITTLE MOLE-LIKE face peered up at them with snuffling animation.

'Mr Crowther, Mrs Westerman! What a joy! A pleasure! Is there something else in my father's papers you wish to examine?' Sir Stephen opened his arms and gathered them into his hallway. Harriet smiled at him and offered her hand.

'Quite right, sir. And we are sorry to trouble you again.'

'Lord, no trouble at all, Mrs Westerman. I have not been so sociable for years. It is all quite heady.'

He trotted them straight to his father's former office and followed them in. Crowther looked briefly around him, then turned back to his host.

'I also have some professional advice to glean from you, sir.' The little man nodded hard enough to send his wig scrambling over one ear. 'I need to find who the better apothecaries are in the area. It is not convenient to continually send to London for my chemical preparations. What gentlemen are skilled with poisons in the area?'

Sir Stephen's face shone. 'Oh, there is not a great deal of choice, Mr Crowther, but I think you should be satisfied with Augustus Gladwell here in Pulborough. He is the apothecary the whole area turns to. His establishment is only a step from here, and though the bulk of his work is household poisons and cures, I think you'll find he is suited to more complex formulations too, if . . .' he bent forward and dropped his voice to a confidential level '. . . if he is properly instructed. I think he sighs a little when he sees me arrive in his shop, for occasionally I like to experiment with the effects of different additions and proportions in my killing gases and preservatives. But his curiosity becomes engaged and we often have quite a little adventure in getting just the sort of mix we need. He collects curiosities himself, so he should revel in your acquaintance.'

He cocked his head and blinked hard. The movement caught the wig unawares, with the result that for one of the first times since Crowther and Harriet had met Sir Stephen, it now sat almost exactly where it should.

Sir Stephen saw them provided with refreshment and left them to their studies. It was not long before Crowther found Harriet calling him to her side.

'You were right. Old Sir Stephen did not let anything escape his diaries. Here is what he said about Lady Thornleigh's death: "I spoke to My Lord, who freely admits he was with his wife when she fell, then looks me in the eye as if curious to see if I dare ask him anything further. Nothing easier than a fall. We all trip from time to time. I saw My Lady laid out, and believe she appeared now to be peaceful, though perhaps that is just my mind trying to quiet itself, particularly given the unquiet moments I have had waiting for her to accuse her husband of the murder of that young girl a few years ago. The body was largely unmarked, though there was some bruising at the wrist as if she had been held. I asked the Earl, who looked a little distressed and said he had tried to grab her wrist and hold her as she fell, but in vain. Whoever made those marks looked like they had a firm enough grip, but whether he tried to save her, or threw her down himself I cannot tell. The servant, Shapin, who saw the fall, had little of use to say – not that his testimony would have ever been taken against his master's. And of course, Thornleigh was there in the room as we spoke. Shapin thinks she was alive still when he got to her. 'I saw the light go out of her eyes, sir,' he said to me. The Earl did not agree. 'When your neck is broken, the lights go out at once, Shapin.' The latter looked meek enough and said he supposed he could be mistaken. My Lord intends to spend most of his time in London when his wife is buried. I am glad of it. I hope his sons turn out to be better men than their father. They have at least half their mother's blood".'

Crowther smiled. 'Do you see it, Mrs Westerman?'

She put her hand to her forehead. 'I think . . .'

He brought his stick down on the heavily carpeted floor with a sudden thump. A little miasma of dust lifted and fell over his polished shoes.

'We *know*. Tell me!'

She looked up at him with sudden intelligence, saw the colour in his cheeks, the chink of ice in his eyes.

'Lord Thornleigh killed Sarah Randle, kept the locket with his own hair in it as a souvenir. His wife found it, challenged him, and was thrown down the stairs for her trouble and Shapin saw, saw perhaps more than he knew at the time.'

'So he was removed from his friends, framed for a theft and transported to America.'

'Where eventually he met Hugh . . .' Harriet said.

'. . . and Wicksteed. I think that is the man for whose sake Captain Thornleigh is punishing himself. He must have killed Shapin. Wicksteed knew it – and knew why.'

'And has used that knowledge to run the Hall since he got free of the Army.'

Crowther relaxed, and smiled at her.

'I believe that may be it. A pretty set of neighbours you have, Mrs Westerman. Shall we go and visit the local poisoner now?'

Augustus Gladwell was one of the tallest men Mrs Westerman had ever laid eyes on, and so thin he made Crowther seem stout. Crowther peered at him with such interest Harriet was almost uncomfortable. His cheeks were hollow, and his hair sparse and silvered, tied simply at the nape of his neck. The shop was of a good size, though the enormous height of its owner made it seem lower and more boxy than it should. The tools of his trade were all about him. The wall behind his counter was fitted with a set of a hundred small drawers, each labelled in a spidery copperplate. The counter itself, and side tables, were stacked with large jars, curled and glittering in the afternoon sun. Harriet was surprised she had never had cause to come here herself in the four years she had called Caveley her home. She had purchased from here, but only via her servants. The smell reminded her of her own kitchen when Mrs Heathcote was making the preserves for winter. Oil of cloves hung in the air which made the room taste to her like autumn even on a summer's day. The counter also supported a number of sets of balance scales, one which would have done for potatoes, down to the smallest which Harriet was sure could measure the weight of her own breath, so fine and delicate it seemed.

Mr Gladwell smiled at them, and stooped forward.

'You are Mr Gladwell, sir?' Crowther asked. The man nodded slowly. 'I am Gabriel Crowther. I was recommended to visit you by Sir Stephen.'

The man's eyes lit up with genuine affection.

'He is one of my best customers, and one of my most challenging. I believe I have heard your name, sir, and was hoping to make your acquaintance.'

His voice was oddly whispering, like parchment being blotted with sand. Crowther looked around him in great contentment.

'I feel I have found a friend here, sir.' Crowther peered into one of the glass jars where something floated that Harriet had decided for her own peace of mind not to attempt to identify. 'How old is this preparation?'

'Two years.'

'Remarkable.'

'I spent as much time on the sealant to the jar as the liquid itself. But I have heard you have a remarkable collection.'

The two men leaned towards each other over the jar. Harriet cleared her throat, and Crowther straightened reluctantly.

'I hope we will have time to discuss these matters fully, but first, my friend wishes to ask you something.'

Harriet smiled politely and stepped forward. 'I need something to kill my mice,' she said.

Gladwell frowned a little. 'Mrs Westerman, your housekeeper had something appropriate from me for the animals in your long barn only a month ago.'

Harriet blinked and fluttered her hands. 'Oh, but I was told by the Thronleigh household that they have something even better, and I think we should try that.'

The frown deepened, and the traces of welcome seemed to disappear from Gladwell's face, as if blown away by a desert wind.

'They have just the same preparation as your house, madam.'

'But I thought Mr Wicksteed—'

Crowther interrupted her. 'Enough, Mrs Westerman.'

Gladwell looked up at him in surprise. Crowther leaned on his cane and looked at his companion.

'Remarkable as your performance often is, I am sure that we shall get more from Mr Gladwell with a little plain dealing.'

Harriet dropped her smile. 'Really?'

'I am sure of it.'

Harriet shrugged and took a seat next to one of the side-tables. The jar at her elbow contained a mouse with two tails. Its lids were closed, dreamily, and it floated as if in free flight across the skies. She resisted the temptation to tap on the glass and see if it would open its eyes and look at her. Mr Gladwell remained frowning behind his counter, watching Crowther.

'Joshua Cartwright was poisoned on Sunday evening in Hartswood. Arsenic. I suspect it was the steward at Thornleigh who had him killed, and wondered if he had recently bought arsenic from you.'

Mr Gladwell held Crowther's gaze for a long moment. At last he cleared his throat.

'I assume, Mr Crowther, that you—'

'Yes, we tested what was left in the bottle on a dog.' Harriet winced in spite of herself. 'It was certainly arsenic. Did Wicksteed buy any from you?'

Rather than answer at once, Mr Gladwell stepped round from the counter and crossed the room to shut the street door and pull down the blind. He seemed to cross the space in a single step, more unfolding and folding his limbs again than walking.

'Perhaps I can offer you both a little refreshment? If you would be so kind as to step into the parlour.'

Mr Gladwell's private rooms at the rear of the shop were not very different in style or furnishing from those in which he conducted his business, but here the chairs were designed for longer occupation, and the drawers of herbs and tinctures gave way to leather-bound volumes. The oddities in jars, however, became a little more prevalent. Mr Gladwell seemed to have a predilection for the unusual in nature, suggested by the mouse with two tails, and confirmed in his sitting room by a lizard with two heads. This specimen the men discussed at some length until tea was served and they took their seats. Mr Gladwell's cup looked like a child's in his long thin hands, so white they made the glistening china look dull and yellowed.

'Thank you for your frankness, Mr Crowther,' Gladwell began in his sandy voice, after a little beat of silence that suggested they were moving forward to a new topic. 'What I told Mrs Westerman is perfectly true. The preparation Thornleigh Hall take for ridding themselves of unwanted animal life is just as we have supplied to Caveley, and it is based on strychnine – not arsenic. But I had a conversation recently that I think I should share with you.'

Harriet put down her cup, making space to do so on the side-table by edging along a jar out of which a bull's eye stared kindly at her.

'We should be interested to hear,' she said.

The giant smiled slowly.

'I have a number of competitors in the area. Some are good men, some I think are not. One of the latter dropped into my shop only yesterday. He hoped he might commission me to carry some pill of his own devising against gout. He made various claims for it, which I thought extravagant and perhaps I did not hide the fact. He grew a little angry with me.'

He smiled thinly at the memory, and raised his hand as if to brush his colleague's crossness away. Harriet was reminded of her horse flicking its tail at the summer midges.

'His pride was a little hurt, I thought, and he told me not to rely on Thornleigh Hall as a customer in the future, as he himself was now having dealings with them. However, it was not Mr Wicksteed who made the purchase of which he spoke. He told me he had sold one hundred grains of arsenic on Saturday morning, to Lady Thornleigh herself.'

Harriet swallowed suddenly and Crowther set down his cup. After a moment he spoke.

'That is a considerable amount.'

'Indeed. Enough to rid the whole town of its mice. And cats. And dogs. I think my colleague was proud to have made such a large sale. He will always sell more than his clients require, and never suffers them to leave his shop empty-handed. I know several people who have entered his shop quite healthy, and left convinced they were in fact on the point of death as a result of any number of maladies. They think themselves blessed and lucky to have chanced in on him at just the right moment to avoid disaster.'

Crowther smiled at his fingertips. 'That cannot be good for your own business, sir.'

The giant lifted his thin shoulders. 'Most return to me in the end. He does not do many of them lasting damage, but the sale of such a large quantity of arsenic stayed in my mind.'

Crowther flexed his hand. 'As you say, Mr Gladwell, it is indeed a thing to be noted. Did you know Mr Cartwright?'

'In passing, as all of us in trade do in the county. He did not seem a man who deserved to die in such a way. Arsenic sends our bodies to hell long before the soul escapes to join it. And Lady Thornleigh took such a quantity. I hope you do not break bread at her table, for your sakes.'

Harriet took up the cup again. The eye in the jar shook a little as if trying to catch her attention.

'We do not. But I do not like living so near.'

VI.7

'DO YOU WISH to go to the Squire?' Crowther was on the point of handing Mrs Westerman into her carriage in the forecourt of Pulborough's best coaching inn. Harriet turned to him, one foot on the ground, one raised onto the step of the elegant little barouche she used for local journeys, her hand in his.

'But we do not know how Wicksteed heard of the meeting with Brook, and our conclusions about Shapin are guesswork at best. Do you think . . . ?'

But before the thought was completed two young men, their rough shirts flying, barrelled into the lady and gentleman. With sudden shock Harriet found herself thrown to the ground, and felt her ankle twist under her. Her back hit hard against the high wheel of her coach. She heard her coachman roar and leap from his seat, shouting at his boy to hold the frightened animals steady. Crowther's cane crashed to the ground, and rolled from his grip across the cobbles. David grabbed one of the lads, twisting him by the collar. The other spotted Crowther's cane, and as Crowther reached for it, brought down his heel on the slender strength of the wood. It cracked between the pillow-like stones of the yard. Crowther struggled to his feet with a yell, managing to catch his attacker's face with the back of his hand as he rose. The youth's head jerked back and he lifted his fist, then laughed, and spat at his feet. Crowther reached for him again, but the lad was too quick and darted over to his companion, throwing himself between him and Harriet's red-faced coachman to break the grip. They ran from the yard at full tilt with David pursuing as Crowther turned to Harriet and began to help her to her feet. Already the inn's landlady had come hurrying across the cobbles, her apron ballooning around her in a cloud of upset.

'Oh, Good Lord! What on earth?' She put her arm around Harriet's shoulder and helped to raise her.

'I'm quite all right. Just winded, I think.' She tried to put her weight on the hurt ankle and went rather white, then shifted her balance to allow Crowther's arm to take most of her weight.

The landlady seemed on the point of tears. 'I cannot believe it! I've never seen such a thing.'

Harriet tried to smile at her. 'Really, Mrs Saunderton, I am quite well. It is nothing. A couple of foolish young men.'

Crowther looked about him. In the doorway of the inn he saw the familiar form of Wicksteed. He was smiling at them, his arms crossed over his chest. David, the coachman, came running back into the yard. Crowther noticed the little boy at the horses' heads look of relief as he handed over the bridle. That must be Jake Mortimer, the sewing woman's nephew. He could see David had been injured in his struggle with the man. The skin around his eye was already very red.

'Sorry, ma'am. They got away from me in the Square.'

Mrs Saunderton was trying to knock the dust of her yard from the long folds of Harriet's dress; the latter put out a hand to stop her.

'Not at all, David. Thank you. Are you injured?'

'Not worth mentioning, Mrs Westerman.'

The landlady was still trembling with distress. 'I don't think I've laid eyes on either of those lads before. Oh, Mrs Westerman, what you must think of us! Will you not come in for a moment to recover? What a shock!'

Harriet managed a smile. 'Thank you, no. I am sure I am quite well, now I have caught my breath. But how strange . . .'

Her eyes drifted away from the landlady and she too caught sight of Wicksteed. Her face lost all its colour and the voice died in her throat.

Crowther stepped forward. 'I think Mrs Westerman would be better recovering from the shock in her own home.'

Harriet nodded and began to turn towards the carriage again. As she put her foot on the step she almost fell. David swung down from his seat.

'Hold the horses, boy.' He was by her side in a second. 'If you'll allow me, ma'am?'

She blushed and nodded, putting an arm around the young man's shoulders, allowing him to lift her bodily in his arms and place her comfortably in the carriage. He returned unsmiling to his seat. Crowther climbed up to take his place, still aware of Wicksteed grinning at them from his post at the edge of the forecourt. He heard a little cough next to him, and peered over the barouche's side into the yard. Harriet's new stable boy stood below him, holding up the two pieces of his cane. He looked up, very white and nervous. His new coat seemed a little on the large side. Crowther looked down into his round, unformed face, a picture of a life yet to begin, then put out his hands to take the pieces, his thin, papery skin, spotting in places with brown, his bony fingers lifting the remains of his cane from the boy's fresh palms. He nodded.

'Good lad. Thank you.'

The boy smiled and clambered up to ride next to David. Wicksteed stood upright and sauntered over to Harriet's side of the carriage. He hardly sketched a bow, but spoke a few words to her, and with a nod to Crowther moved away again. Mrs Saunderton looked a little confused. Wicksteed gave her a broad grin and she bobbed a curtsy, doubtfully, in his direction. Harriet said clearly, 'Drive on.'

David clicked to the horses. They lifted their hooves and with a jerk and clatter the carriage began to move. Crowther carefully placed the remains of his cane on the seat next to him and leaned forward.

'What did he say?'

'That it is beginning.'

Crowther sat back into the corner of the carriage and crossed his hands in his lap.

VI.8

DAVID CARRIED MRS Westerman from the carriage to the salon, then was hurried into the kitchen to have his own injuries dealt with. Mrs Heathcote returned moments later with hot water in a basin, and strips of linen over her shoulder, to find Miss Trench at her sister's feet trying to remove her shoe. The scene was too feminine for Crowther, and with a nod to his hostess over the shoulders of her nurses, he left his broken cane on the desk, and stepped out of the French windows for a moment to walk among the lavender. His steps eventually took him to the front of the house, and he paused under the oak tree that Commodore Westerman had thought would be a guardian to his family in his absence. The summer breathed through the leaves, making them sigh heavily. Crowther leaned his weight against the trunk.

'We have made a poor job of it, friend,' he said, resting his palm against the bark.

There was a movement by the gate, and he turned to see two horsemen entering the driveway. The first was Michaels on his favourite ride, a beast as massive as himself who had the reputation of a biter. He had his arm out to the other rider, as if holding him in his saddle. As they came a little closer Crowther recognised Clode, the lawyer they had sent down to London. Both men started, then encouraged their horses forward as he emerged from the shade of the tree. Daniel began to dismount as they came abreast of him, and his slim form almost dropped into Crowther's arms. The latter held him by the shoulders.

'The children?'

Clode looked feverish, and worryingly pale under his stubble.

'Well. Safe. Legitimate.'

His relief was such, Crowther flung his arms around the boy and held him for a second. Michaels had dismounted, and as Crowther released him, he put a beefy arm around Clode's shoulders.

'I met him on the road two miles out, hardly able to keep on his mount. Let's get him in, Mr Crowther. I don't think he has slept since he left Hartswood.'

Between them they lifted him into the house and Mrs Heathcote found herself with another invalid just as her first was made comfortable. Crowther shouted the same words that Clode had given him over his shoulder as they carried the man upstairs and heard Harriet's cry of relief follow him upstairs.

As soon as he was laid on the bed, Clode fell into an uneasy drifting sleep. Crowther watched over him. His jaw was badly bruised, and there was more heavy bruising on his shoulder and the pale flesh of his side. Crowther had brandy and water brought up, and ordered a fire lit in the room. So there had been some sort of violence given and received in London. He saw the remains of the bloodstains on the young man's chest, but saw no wound, noted the scrapes on his palms and knuckles, the deep cut in his thumb – a sign that he had held a knife and in some press of action used it, not expertly, but with force.

Michaels sat with him. 'You look as if you are reading a book,' he said quietly.

Crowther looked up, and nodded slightly. 'What we do leaves marks on us. Especially if we are involved in violence. When he wakes, I am sure Mr Clode will be able to tell us of some violent altercation on a roadway somewhere. I think the other man died, and that Clode found safe refuge afterwards. Why he should decide to leave it so soon, his body will not tell me.'

'How could you know any of that?'

'There was enough blood, not of his own, that it could not be washed away quickly. Yet he is wearing a clean shirt.'

'Will he survive? I have no great desire to watch someone else die in your company, Mr Crowther.'

Gabriel smiled. 'Aside from the bruising, I think his symptoms are of shock and exhaustion. He is young. He should mend.' Crowther paused and picked up Clode's wrist again; the pulse fluttered and struggled. 'But something is keeping him from the rest he needs.'

There was a gentle knock at the door, and Harriet limped into the room. He smiled at her and turned back to his patient. As the door fell shut again behind Harriet, Clode groaned and opened his eyes.

'Crowther!'

'Yes, Mr Clode, you have reached us. And you must rest.'

The young man lifted himself on his shoulders, shaking his head. He saw Harriet.

'Oh, Mrs Westerman too. So glad.'

He looked like an engraving in her bed, the white of the sheets and his skin contrasting with the dark of his hair and the hollows visible under the collar of his shirt. She smiled at him.

'Crowther told me the children are well.'

'Yes, and under the best of guardians. We killed the man who murdered their father. Or rather a leopard did.' Harriet wondered if he were delirious and glanced at Crowther, her expression all concern. 'At least I think Hunter said it was a leopard.'

Crowther looked confused for a second, then smiled with understanding.

'Mr Hunter has some exotic pets,' he said to Harriet. She raised her eyebrows, but nodded. Michaels sat forward in his chair. Clode did not seem to notice anything; his hands were feeling round the sheets about him.

'I have a paper, rode since dawn to get it to you. I must have it.'

Crowther turned to the end of the bed where Clode's coat was laid over the back of a chair and passed it to him. He reached forward eagerly and dived his hand into the pocket. He pulled out the two sheets folded and creased. He must have put his fingertips to them to check they were still there every other minute during the ride. Now he passed them over to Crowther, and at once fell back on his elbows.

'They were in the yellow man's pocket. The pocket of the man who killed Alexander, I mean. The children called him the Yellow Man. Susan is very brave.' He let himself fall back into the pillows. Crowther put water and brandy to Clode's lips. 'He escaped when Newgate burned . . . Had to run . . . Got them safe . . .'

Daniel sighed, his eyes fluttered closed and his breathing slowed. Crowther watched him for a second.

'Good. It seems he will allow himself to sleep now.'

He picked up the papers and walked round to where Harriet was sitting and put the papers in her hand. Michaels and Crowther stood behind her chair as she unfolded them. They were all silent a few seconds.

'You still have that piece of paper from Brook's body, I trust?'

She nodded. 'Yes. And I know that this is the hand of Claver Wicksteed.'

'Then I suggest it is certainly time we went to see the Squire.'

354

Harriet looked up at him. 'He dines this afternoon at Thornleigh Hall – Mrs Heathcote heard it.'

Crowther removed the papers from between her fingers, folding them and neatly fitting them into his coat.

'Then I suggest we make a visit there. Will you join us, Mr Michaels?'

The man shrugged his bear-like shoulders and coloured a little.

'Not used to going up to the front gate, so much. But I don't see why I should not come with you.'

VI.9

'WE MUST SEE the Squire.' Crowther spoke quietly, but Thornleigh's senior footman had begun to look uncomfortable.

'He is at table, and we have orders that no one from Caveley – or you, Mr Crowther – are to be admitted to this house.' His orders did not seem to make him happy. He turned towards Michaels and straightened a little. 'You, we would not admit in any circumstances.'

Michaels smiled at him and rested his fists on his waist.

'Foolish of you to let us into your hallway, in that case.'

Out of the corner of her eye Harriet noticed the maid who had first opened the door and fallen back to let them enter, blush and take a step back. The footman's eyes travelled the same way.

'That was an error,' he said stiffly.

Michaels looked entirely at his ease.

'Well, if any of you fancy lads want to try and throw us out, good luck to you, that's all I can say.' He flexed his massive hands.

Crowther sighed.

'We must see the Squire,' he repeated.

They were shown into the Great Hall to await the party who were dining and found Hugh already there, slumped in front of the empty fire with a carafe at his side. He looked up at them, his eyes already rather dull.

'What? More corpses?'

Harriet made her way awkwardly over to the other armchair and let herself down into it. Hugh watched her for a few seconds, then realising she was not going to speak, asked grudgingly, 'What happened to you?'

She looked directly at him.

'Wicksteed paid a couple of lads to knock Crowther and me flying in Pulborough earlier today. I hurt my ankle.' Hugh looked confused. She explained, as one might to a rather simple child: 'He has demanded that I leave Caveley, my husband and my children. He is showing me what to expect if I do not comply.'

Hugh shifted in his chair and murmured something no one could make out. He was not asked to repeat himself.

Crowther looked down at the younger man.

'Did you know your father is being tortured, Captain Thornleigh?'

Hugh's eyes struggled to focus.

'Tortured? What do you mean?'

Crowther stared at him for a moment, then turned away as if the sight disgusted him.

'He has been cut. Someone is making him atone for his sins, we think. And perhaps yours.'

Hugh went rather pale, but before he could produce any reply the grand doors were swung open and the party from the table came into the room. Wicksteed and Lady Thornleigh were arm-in-arm; the Squire bobbing in their wake. Harriet had to admit they made a very handsome couple. They looked, both of them, vigorous and aware of their powers. Their dark colourings complemented one another, and Wicksteed had seemed to acquire a grace and control in his movements, as if that animal power had transmitted itself through the perfect arm that rested over his. Only an unhealthy glitter in their eyes, and the strange dark cloud they dragged with them made them unattractive. Harriet felt her skin creep, and wondered if Squire Bridges were choking in the wrongs that streamed behind them both like smoke.

Lady Thornleigh released Wicksteed's arm and made her way to the long oak trestle table that split the hall in two, resting her hand on the wood. Her dress rustled against it. She smiled at them lazily. Harriet blinked her green eyes, unwillingly drinking in all that beauty glowing under the ancient arms and portraits of the Thornleigh family. The woman looked at each of them in turn before she spoke.

'Well?'

Crowther bowed to her. 'We are here to speak to Squire Bridges, Lady Thornleigh.'

My lady arched one eyebrow and looked at her guest. Bridges took a blustering step or two forward.

'Anything you wish to say, you may say in front of these good people, sir.'

Harriet did not quite manage to stifle a bitter laugh that rose in her throat. Wicksteed looked at her angrily. Crowther nodded to the Squire.

'Very well. I shall give you the story. You were right, Bridges, about the murder of Sarah Randle. It was indeed Lord Thornleigh who killed her for her pregnancy or his own pleasure, and for whatever reason of his own, he took her locket. Some years later, Hugh's mother found it, and was thrown down the stairs for her trouble.'

The Squire was open-mouthed. Hugh shrank back into his armchair as if stung. So Shapin had told him. Wicksteed was very pale. Lady Thornleigh silently drummed her fingers on the table, looking at the floor, and apparently rather bored. Crowther continued.

'Hugh Thornleigh was told as much in America by the former servant of this house, Shapin. And I suspect Claver Wicksteed overheard. What happened to him, by the way, Mr Thornleigh?' Hugh seemed struck dumb and Crowther noticed a tight smile on Wicksteed's face. 'You killed him yourself, didn't you? Is that the murder you are willing to hang for now?'

The Squire lifted his hands. 'I really must protest. How dare——?'

Wicksteed spun round on him. 'Shut up, Bridges.'

The Squire recoiled in shock. Crowther nodded to Harriet. She continued.

'Wicksteed, you blackmailed your way into this house, knowing both its masters were sickening.' Some last vestige of sympathy was present in her face as she said this, looking at Hugh. 'You had Hugh, but when he saw your friendship with Lady Thornleigh developing, he made one last struggle and asked Joshua Cartwright to find someone to track down Alexander Thornleigh. In doing so, he gave you a chance to make your hold here complete. You murdered Brook in my copse, stole the address he had provided for Hugh, and sent a hireling of your own to rid Thornleigh of the only heir not under your control.' She looked up at him. 'When did you find out it was Alexander who had sent Nurse Bray to care for Lord Thornleigh?'

Hugh struggled upright in his chair, and looked about him amazed. Wicksteed did not move. Harriet shrugged.

'She wrote a note to Hugh and you found it, did you not? Just as you found Brook's note to him? I doubt any piece of paper has crossed these halls without you taking a look at it since you arrived. Perhaps she tried to speak to Hugh, and you intervened. In any case you removed her, and for good measure you sent Hugh off with the arsenic to poor Joshua, to make sure that no news of Alexander's whereabouts could be found, and to put his head in the noose for your crimes.' She gave a little laugh. 'And while you are causing all this slaughter you are campaigning with the College of Arms to have your name and heritage recognised! Presumably you wish to marry Lady Thornleigh when she becomes a widow. I am sure if Lord Thornleigh survives to see Hugh hang, he will not live long thereafter. You have already carved a score of the bodies mounted up into his arms. No doubt the final mark will be for his own murder.'

Wicksteed coloured a little at these last words. Then he walked across the room to where Lady Thornleigh still lounged against the trestle, took her hand and pressed it to his lips with great delicacy. She gazed into his eyes, and for a moment every other person in the room felt that strange exclusion in the presence of two people who see only each other. Harriet watched them; there was something perfect about them in that moment and part of her was jealous.

Then Wicksteed straightened, and turned back to them, his voice soft and even.

'You cannot prove anything. And no one will listen to the ravings of a madwoman who has deserted her family, and the brother of a parricide.' He sneered at Harriet. 'You saw my arms during our interesting chat in your woods the other day. Where are the marks of Nurse Bray's hands which you insisted would be there? You are storytellers, that is all.'

Michaels shifted out of the shadows behind Harriet's chair.

'Oh, a fair amount of it can be proved, Claver.'

Wicksteed looked vaguely amused. 'You dare call me by my Christian name?'

'I dare call you a murderous dog, Claver,' the big man told him.

Wicksteed laughed, and swung his hand in Lady Thornleigh's; she smiled up at him warmly.

'I always liked you, Michaels,' Wicksteed said. 'Why don't you come and stand with us? I could make you a rich man. Why cast your lot in with *them*?' He nodded towards Crowther and Harriet. 'They may be civil to you, but they will always expect you to stand while they sit, and never ask why that should be.'

'We shall see, Claver,' Michaels said calmly. 'But for all your smarts – and I'm not saying you aren't a sharp lad – I know something you do not.'

Crowther could see the tension appear in Wicksteed's face; it pulsed just under his jawline. Michaels nodded to Crowther, who waited till he could feel the tension in the room like a beat on a distant drum.

'You have miscalculated. Lady Thornleigh's son is not the only heir. Alexander had two children – a boy and a girl. Both legitimate and recorded under their true names. Both safe and under good supervision in London. Your murderer failed to cut off the line, and is dead himself.'

Hugh leaped to his feet and at once stumbled to his knees in front of Harriet.

'It is true? He had children? They live?'

He looked up at her, his face a pattern of confused joy. She put out her hand and touched his cheek.

'They live, and are well, and have precedence. The Hall will be theirs. And we can prove Wicksteed arranged for the murder of their father. He wrote a letter, and it will hang him.' Her tone was soft, comforting.

Crowther turned to Wicksteed. The latter had dropped Lady Thornleigh's hand and looked at the flagstones in front of him. His hands closed into fists at his sides. There was a laugh, and Harriet twisted to see Lady Thornleigh, her body trembling. She put her hand up to the jewels in her hair and began to tear them out, throwing them to the stone floor of the hall.

'Then they should have this, and this!'

Wicksteed tried to grab hold of her wrists but she tore away from him and spun round the far end of the table. Her lazy humour had evaporated; her body seemed to thrill, lit within with rage.

'Poor old yellow-faced Moore!' she said. 'Who killed him? God, there were enough times he was selling me on the streets when I wished I could have stuck a knife in him, but I was only twelve, and he seemed as indestructible as a god!' She laughed again. 'Now he's dead! Burning in hell, just as I always knew he would! Oh, I shall go down there now and pull his hair for playing us such a trick!'

Wicksteed seemed to startle awake and tried to reach her, his face white and sweating.

'My love! Dear God! Say nothing.'

Lady Thornleigh pulled the diamonds from around her throat and sent them skimming across the floor, where they came to rest at Crowther's feet.

'Take 'em! Clever boy! Justice be done! Get away from me, Claver. It's done and I will speak.'

She looked wild-eyed into Harriet's pale face.

'What? You thought I just sat here and let Claver do my work for me?' Her loose hair curled over her bare shoulders. 'It was old Moore, the bastard was a hundred even then, who sold me to my first old man before I could even bleed – though he made me, and others after. I knew who to turn to when Claver got that note out of Brook's hand. And you think those wounds on Thornleigh are for his sad, pretty wife, and his servant?' Her voice rose. 'What do I care about them? No, they are for the little girls like me, younger even than I was, who he raped in London since I knew him. Almost every week he'd have some poor kid brought to him, always dark, always in a plain grey dress to remind him of his first love – just as I did once. I used to see them being bundled out of the back of my fancy house afterwards, crying and stumbling – and I'd get pearls for my silence. I've worn that locket! Each of us did. Perhaps he even put it round his wife's neck. She was a young one too when he got hold of her, I hear. He knew I'd be waiting to pay him back! But he never suspected I'd have the chance. It amused him to have a whore who hated him as a wife. He never dreamed he'd be cowering under my knife.'

She stared up at Crowther again; she had bitten her lip and the blood welled up in her mouth. Her voice dropped a little.

'Wonderful, isn't it, Crowther, how the flesh gives and opens under a blade?'

Harriet looked at her. 'You helped kill Nurse Bray.'

Lady Thornleigh lifted her hand to the shoulder of her dress and tore the sleeve open at the seam. Across the soft white of her upper arm were four deep scratches, just beginning to heal. Crowther thought of the paper in his pocket. He could tell they were a perfect match even at this distance.

'She came to me! To tell me she thought she might know where Alexander was – though she never mentioned the children, I'll give her that. She said she thought it best to speak to the woman of the house. Lord knows, that has always been Hugh!' Lady Thornleigh groaned and spun around on her heel. 'We burned all her papers! How did you know about the children?'

Harriet's voice was trembling as she replied.

'She made a will. She left a cameo brooch to Alexander's little girl.'

The groan became a laugh again, and my lady tore the jewelled bands from her wrists.

'All of this! All of this lost, for a cheap cameo!'

Wicksteed managed to reach her and seized her. 'Stop! Stop! Jemima, why do you give yourself away? My love! Think of your son! Eustache! Please, my darling – stop.'

She seemed to grow suddenly calm at his touch. She lifted one hand to his face, and with her thumb wiped away the tear from his cheek.

'Oh, Claver. I have buried two children, given away another. What should I care for that runt of Thornleigh's, unless he could do you good?'

Claver let his head drop to her shoulder. She rocked and shushed him, letting the fingers play at the back of his neck where his dark hair touched his collar.

'It's all over, my darling.' Claver dropped his head towards her and kissed her mouth hungrily. She slipped her hand into his waistcoat pocket as they embraced. 'But I can do one last thing for you. I shall not let them hang you.' She smiled very softly. '"Thumb on the blade, boy, and strike up".' He pulled away from her a little, confused. Harriet saw her remove her hand from his pocket, saw a twist in her wrist, an evil flash in the air . . .

'Crowther! She has his knife!'

Wicksteed turned towards Harriet as if unsure what was happening. Before Michaels or Crowther could hurl themselves at the couple, Lady Thornleigh threw her arm back and forward again.

'Jemima?' His tone was one of surprise, then he fell forward on his knees at her feet, his forehead resting on the silk of her skirts. She let her free hand rest briefly on his head, as a woman might pet a child or lapdog, then stepped back, shaking her lovely head slightly. Now she turned and began to run from the room, the knife still in her hand. As she passed her, Harriet reached out from her chair to try and stop her. As her hand closed on the rich fabric of her dress, Harriet fell forward, Lady Thornleigh stumbled, turned and saw Harriet clinging on to her. For a brief moment, Harriet looked into her eyes: they were black and dilated. And then my lady was up again, pulling herself free as a country girl does from a bramble, and had fled the room.

Hugh came to himself and went to lift Harriet back to her feet. She managed to stand. The Squire stood white and shaking, unable to comprehend what had happened in front of him. Michaels lifted Wicksteed under his arms as if he were a toy and placed him almost tenderly on the oak table. Crowther joined him. As Harriet looked to where they stood over Wicksteed, the body on the table groaned and shuddered. Crowther caught her eye and shook his head, though he had taken off his coat and was trying to staunch the flow of blood with it. Servants came at a run from within and were sent for linen and water. As Crowther worked, he could feel the body dying under him. At the last, he chanced to look into Wicksteed's deep black eyes. The man had turned to fix them on the arms of Thornleigh Hall, and he was smiling at them as his last breath rasped and faded.

Harriet was not sure if what she was seeing or hearing was real.

The cries of, 'Fire!' were repeated many times before the sense of it reached her.

Other servants were tumbling into the hall. Michaels strode into the midst of them.

'What? Where?'

The footman who had tried to deny them entry came running down the grand stairway.

'In the state rooms and above. Everything is aflame! Everything! My lady will not come down! She has her son!'

Michaels began to tear up the stairway, Crowther and Hugh on his heels. Harriet dragged herself after them, pausing by the footman as he reached the base of the stairs, hissing with the pain of her ankle.

'Get the people out,' she instructed him. 'We'll go after her.'

Crowther turned to Hugh as they reached the level of the state rooms.

'Thornleigh, your father!'

He nodded and raced ahead of them. Michaels and Crowther paused on the main stair. They heard a laugh, and a cry. Smoke billowed along the corridor in front of them – already the flames raced along the draperies and sucked at the ceiling above their heads. A maid stood in front of them like a guardian to the flames.

'She has locked herself in her room with little Master Eustache! I have not got a key!'

Michaels turned back and raced down the stairs again. Crowther turned to the girl.

'Go – get out.'

The maid paused then screamed as one of the windows cracked behind her and sparks showered across them. Crowther threw his weight against the door, but it would not yield. Harriet reached his side and they heard the high wailing of a child in the room. Crowther looked at her.

'You should not be here.'

Their eyes met, and he did not ask again.

Michaels came stumbling towards them, a bunch of keys in his hand. Crowther tied his cravat across his mouth and nose, and Harriet pulled out her handkerchief and did the same. Michaels tried two keys – neither fitted. He cursed, then throwing the keys to the floor, he hurled his whole weight at the lock. Harriet staggered back, and again Michaels and Crowther threw themselves forward. There was a splintering of wood. Michaels kicked hard and the door gave. Clouds of smoke belched out, making Harriet's lungs burn. She turned her face away, coughing violently.

'Lady Thornleigh. Give us the child!' Crowther called into darkness.

A window cracked, and Harriet could see a figure lying prone on the floor, with a little boy kneeling above her. She limped in, the pain in her leg forgotten, and grabbed up the little boy. He fought her, shouting for his mama, but Harriet would not let him go, and began to drag and carry him from the room and down the stairs. She looked up, and where the staircase climbed she could see fresh flames licking from the upper stories. The Earls of Sussex remained immobile in their portraits all down the stairs, watching as the fire tasted the corners of their canvas. At that moment, the fire bit through the wood of the upper balcony, and the stairs groaned.

'Crowther! Michaels!'

They were behind her, Michaels holding Lady Thornleigh in his arms like a doll.

Crowther looked up the stairs.

'Go!' he shouted. 'I must help Hugh.' Harriet began to protest, but he commanded, '*Now!*' And turned to run up the stairs into the inferno above.

Harriet and Michaels staggered through the hallway and down the steps into the drive and the open air. Fire danced at the windows of every room in the east wing. Michaels laid his burden on the gravel, and Harriet set down the little boy. He threw himself on his mother's body and began to bawl. Lady Thornleigh did not move, and Harriet could see no sign of breath coming from her. There was blood on the woman's chest: she had found another use for her knife. The little boy tried to pull her arm over him. Whatever had held Harriet upright till now gave way, and she collapsed to her knees amongst the cries and lamentations of the household.

Crowther found Hugh on the upper corridor, Lord Thornleigh insensible in his arms. A beam had fallen, flaming between them. Crowther kicked it away, and Hugh hobbled towards him, retching.

'Come on!'

They made it to the level of the state rooms, where the fire now seemed to rage at its fiercest. Hugh looked to Crowther.

'We can only go through! Run!'

They leaped forward. Crowther felt the air burning around him, the heat on his face so fierce he felt it would brand him. He somehow got to the bottom of the stairs and looked back, Hugh was on the half-landing, his father's body in his arms, looking around at his flaming relatives like a child caught in a cathedral.

'Hugh! Move!'

He heard another groan in the timbers above him and looked up. Hugh was halfway towards him now, picking up pace. He heard his own name called and saw Michaels racing back into the house towards him. A crack and he looked up again at the fresco of Lord Thornleigh and his family at Judgement Day. Time seemed to slow. The depiction of Hell on the fresco was now smouldering. The young Lord Thornleigh painted in all his glory looked down on his own dirty and bloodied wreck of a body with his usual look of cool, sensuous disdain. Another groan and crack, and even as he felt Michaels's arms grab his shoulders, Crowther watched in horrid fascination as the fresco gave way over father and son and began to fall, leaving a heaven of dark flames. Then everything went black.

IN CONCLUSION

Friday, 9 June 1780

MRS WESTERMAN AND Crowther stood at the entrance to Caveley Park with Daniel Clode beside them as the carriage drew up. The door opened and two children tumbled out and threw themselves at Daniel. He twirled the girl around in his arms before lifting the little boy into the air in turn. A young lady and gentleman stepped down from the carriage in more sedate manner behind them, followed by a woman somewhat older, thin, her cheeks rather pink. Harriet and Crowther exchanged smiles and went forward in welcome.

Graves made his bows.

'Mrs Westerman, Mr Crowther, may I introduce Miss Chase and her companion, Mrs Service.'

The ladies curtsied, and Clode advanced to shake Mrs Service warmly by the hand. Harriet smiled.

'I am so glad to welcome you here,' she said. 'The Hall will not be ready to receive its new masters for some time, I fear. The east wing is destroyed. Only the core of the ancient building remains. The Great Hall was almost untouched.'

Graves nodded. 'Thank you for letting us come to you. We thought it best Lord Thornleigh and his sister attend the services for their grandfather.'

'I quite agree,' Crowther said.

Miss Chase looked up at Harriet with her cornflower eyes. 'How is their uncle?'

Harriet smiled sadly. 'You might think me fanciful, but I believe he lives only to see Alexander's children.'

Hugh lay in what had been until two days before the ladies' morning room. The window was dominated by the foliage of the great oak. Rachel tended him, and said the sight of the great tree seemed to give him peace. Since he had been pulled from the fire, his father's corpse still in his arms like a loved child, he had been rarely conscious for long and his fever was deepening, but at every moment that he woke he asked for the children.

Harriet spoke to them both briefly before they entered the room. She was glad to see they showed no signs of fear. She knocked lightly at the door and pushed it fully open for them. Hugh turned his head towards them.

'Alexander!' he called.

The little boy went forward.

'My name is Jonathan. And you are my uncle, sir,' he said, then added after a pause, 'I am an Earl.' He went up next to the bed and bent forward to kiss Hugh's burned face.

'I am, you are,' Hugh whispered. Susan came forward and bent to kiss him as her brother had done.

Hugh smiled at her. A cough shook him and he closed his eyes and caught his breath.

'Your father showed me a picture of your mother once. You look just like her.'

Susan shook her head. 'I am not so pretty.'

'I think you are prettier.' He coughed again. 'You know I have a little brother?'

'Yes,' said Susan, 'Eustache.'

'He is another uncle – but younger than us,' Jonathan stated with a certain amount of pride.

Hugh smiled, but his eyes were beginning to glaze.

'You must be kind to him,' he said. Susan nodded, and fitted her hand into his. He returned the gentle pressure of her fingers.

'Of course,' she said. 'We lost our father and mother too. We shall take care of him, and Mr Graves will take care of us.'

'He sounds a good man. Do you like him?'

'Oh very much!'

'I am glad. He has our trust and authority.' Hugh sighed deeply, and his eyelids fluttered. 'My brother said he would find a way to come to me – perhaps he did.' He closed his eyes. 'Forgive me, sweethearts. I am tired now.'

It was only a few hours later while the adults sat in the midsummer sunshine and watched the children in their own deep conversations and games in the middle of the lawn, that Rachel came to find them with Mrs Service at her side. She leaned down and put her arms around her sister's neck. They all looked at her. She straightened and wiped her eyes.

'Just a few moments ago. He is gone.'

She looked at the children gossiping on the lawn. Stephen was already Susan's slave and the last of the old Earl's sons was looking at Jonathan as if at a god.

'Shall we tell the children?'

Graves looked in the same direction.

'Let us give them a moment yet. There is time enough.'

Crowther stood and turned away from the family group. It was only when Harriet found him under the oak some moments later that he realised where his steps had taken him. He looked up as she approached, her arms folded across her middle, her green eyes gazing at the ground in front of her.

'Theirs was a strange and dark sort of love, was it not, Crowther?' He did not reply and she leaned against the great trunk of the tree beside him. 'I had a letter from the Squire this morning,' she went on. 'An invitation for Rachel and myself to dine with him, along with profusions of sympathy and goodwill. I must go, though I fear his food will choke me.'

Crowther turned to her with a glint in his eyes.

'I had a similar letter, but I am too jealous of my reputation for eccentricity to accept it. I shall drink with Michaels or dine here when I am in need of company.'

'And when, sir, are you ever in need of company?'

He bowed. 'I fear the habits of sociability have crept in upon me. Perhaps I will retreat into my lair again when we have done discussing the events of the last few days. I will never be interested, or pretend to be interested, in how you intend to improve the upper meadows, or where some particularly cunning fabric may be purchased for a fraction of its usual cost. When those topics become your choice of conversation, madam, you shall see me no more.'

She laughed, making her red curls shake, and he felt his body lighten at the sound.

'I have no doubt you are keen to return to your knives.'

'My "instruments of darkness", is how your sister referred to them once. That morning as I was looking at her sketches of a cat, as I recall.'

'". . . that tell us truths". Apt. How strange she should be quoting *Macbeth* before we had any suspicion . . .' She looked up into the dense foliage above her. The light danced against her throat. 'Lady Thornleigh had more power, more determined energy in her beautiful little finger than I think I have in my whole being, for all my fuss and bother. I wonder what she might have become, born into another life.'

'You sound as if you admire her,' Crowther said, smiling gently at her.

Harriet considered, still watching the shifting leaves.

'No. Perhaps. I simply realise I never feared her enough. It never occurred to me she would ever be capable of doing what she did. Wicksteed blackmailed, but I wonder if he would ever have murdered without her beside him.'

'I have found it is a mistake to underestimate a beautiful woman.' Crowther paused. 'They can be quite alarming.'

Harriet laughed again at that and stood away from the oak.

'What a flatterer you are become, Crowther.' Then, having taken his arm to lead him back to the party on the lawn, she suddenly stopped. 'We almost failed. It seems walls and a great oak are not such a protection as they might seem, yet I think I would do the same again for all that. Would you, Crowther?'

He looked down at her with his eyebrows raised.

'Most certainly not. If I had had any idea what might come about, I would have kept to my bed and dismissed my maid for not being more firm with you.'

Harriet snorted with laughter. 'Indeed? My next strategy, if the note failed, was to sing sea shanties as loudly as possible, till I drove you up and out.'

Crowther looked horrified, and she smiled.

EPILOGUE

8 June 1778

SOME EIGHTEEN MONTHS after his return from America Hugh realised, riding home late from dining at Caveley Park, that he was something like happy. The confusions since he had returned to Thornleigh were beginning to dissipate. At first he had done little other than exist and drink his way through his father's cellar, but since meeting Commodore Westerman, his wife and most particularly Miss Trench at Caveley soon after, something within him was beginning to grow. He had begun to take a firmer control of the estate, he could see where wrongs were being done, and found that when he began to take action his whole being seemed to lift. The anxiety, the dreams, still came, but with every meeting with Miss Trench, with every night he went to bed not quite drunk, with every morning he took action their horrors lessened and the light crept towards him.

This evening something had happened. He did not know what, but some look, some word from Rachel – he whispered her Christian name like a prayer – had caused the vague, weak hope in his heart to blossom forth. He smiled to himself. All was not lost. His own sins and those of his father could be expurgated by hard work and a true heart. He would build an estate worthy of respect, he would make his stepmother and half-brother comfortable. His seeing eye was bright in the gloom, but his thoughts were so far away, it was not until he was abreast of his gates that he saw the man lounging there in the shadows.

The figure stood and looked up at him. The face was tanned and dirty from the road, and Hugh could see the pack at his feet.

'Captain Thornleigh.'

The world trembled and swam. The smell of gunsmoke rose in Hugh's nostrils. He felt suddenly sick.

'Wicksteed.'

'Glad to see you haven't forgotten me yet, sir.'

Hugh's hand trembled on the reins, causing his horse to step unhappily from side to side. He managed to clear his throat enough to speak again.

'So this is how it begins?'

Claver spat on the dust in front of him and straightened up with a smile.

'After a manner of speaking, sir, I suppose so. Yes. This is how it begins.'

HISTORICAL NOTE

All the situations and leading players in *Instruments of Darkness* are fictional, but two characters did exist and deserve to be acknowledged.

John Hunter (1728–93) was a hugely influential surgeon in Georgian London and did own a sort of private zoo, including at one point leopards; his collection of samples and preparations are still on show in the Hunterian Museum, at the Royal College of Surgeons in Lincoln's Inn Fields, London. For an account of his life I recommend *The Knife Man* by Wendy Moore.

Stephen Paxton (1734–87) was born in Durham but became something of a celebrity cellist in London until his death. His music has long been neglected, but the first ever recording of his Concerto –which Susan hears at her father's concert – is now available through the Cello Classics label on *www.celloclassics.com*, played by Sebastian Comberti.

The Gordon Riots brought chaos to London from 2–7 June 1780. The Army were eventually called out and hundreds of rioters were shot. Some were also executed, though Lord George Gordon himself was found Not Guilty of treason.

I owe a huge debt to a number of great historians of the Georgian age, in particular Amanda Vickery for her book *The Gentleman's Daughter: Women's Lives in Georgian England*, and Roy Porter for *Flesh in the Age of Reason* amongst others. Claire Harman's excellent biography of Fanny Burney was also a great resource and inspiration.

All inaccuracies, anachronisms and downright mistakes are my own.